We stood [barcode] n invisible electric cur[barcode] f sparks of hot desire i[barcode] .... The detective's clean, soapy scent filled my nose, overpowering the cumin, red pepper, and other spices in the air. Donovan looked away and cleared his throat.

"You want to tell me what happened?" he asked in a low voice.

"You want to tell me why you're here?" I countered.

Donovan stared at me. "All right. I asked dispatch to let me know if there were any incidents at the Pork Pit."

"Why? Afraid I might take to killing people in my own place of business? You must not have gotten the memo, but I've retired, detective."

His black eyebrows drew together in surprise. "Retired?"

I nodded. "Retired."

Some emotion flared in his amber eyes. It might have been relief or even hope, but it was gone before I could decipher it. "Well, good for you, I suppose."

Praise for Jennifer Estep and *SPIDER'S BITE*

"*Spider's Bite* is a raw, gritty and compelling walk on the wild side, one that had me hooked from the first page. Jennifer Estep has created a fascinating heroine in the morally ambiguous Gin Blanco—I can't wait to read the next chapter of Gin's story."

—Nalini Singh, *New York Times* bestselling author of *Blaze of Memory*

***Web of Lies* is also available as an eBook**

"Watch out world, here comes Gin Blanco. Funny, smart, and dead sexy."

—Lilith Saintcrow, author of *Redemption Alley*

"I love rooting for the bad guy—especially when she's also the heroine. *Spider's Bite* is a sizzling combination of mystery, magic and murder. Kudos to Jennifer Estep!"

—Jackie Kessler, author of *Hotter Than Hell*

"Jennifer Estep is a dark, lyrical, and fresh voice in urban fantasy. Brimming with high-octane–fueled action, labyrinthine conspiracies, and characters who will steal your heart, *Spider's Bite* is an original, fast-paced, tense, and sexy read. Gin is an assassin to die for."

—Adrian Phoenix, author of *In the Blood*

"A sexy and edgy thriller that keeps you turning the pages. In *Spider's Bite*, Jennifer Estep turns up the heat and suspense with Gin Blanco, an assassin whose wit is as sharp as her silverstone knives. . . . She'll leave no stone unturned and no enemy breathing in her quest for revenge. *Spider's Bite* leaves you dying for more."

—Lisa Shearin, national bestselling author of the Raine Benares fantasy series

KARMA GIRL

"Chick lit meets comics lit in Estep's fresh debut. . . . A zippy prose style helps lift this zany caper far above the usual run of paranormal romances."

—*Publishers Weekly*

"Secret identities and superpowers take on a delightful and humorous twist in Estep's exciting debut. Fun and sexy. . . . Here's hoping for more Bigtime adventures from this impressive talent."

—*Romantic Times*

"*Karma Girl* is hilarious and, an even better trick, real. We all know these people, but who among us can say we'd seize our destiny the way brokenhearted Carmen does? *Karma Girl* kicks ass!"

—MaryJanice Davidson, *New York Times* bestselling author of *Undead and Unwelcome*

"Jennifer Estep's action-packed world of radioactive goo, alliterative aliases, and very hot-looking leather tights is outrageously entertaining. Jennifer Estep's exciting new voice will leap into readers' hearts in a single bound."

—Rachel Gibson, *New York Times* bestselling author of *True Love and Other Disasters*

"A big thumbs-up. *Karma Girl* had me laughing and cheering to the end! Engrossing, sexy, laugh-out-loud fun. I want to be a superhero!"

—Candace Havens, author of *Dragons Prefer Blondes*

"A fresh, hilarious new voice. *Karma Girl* will have you rooting for the good girls."

—Erin McCarthy, *USA Today* bestselling author of *Bled Dry*

HOT MAMA

"Snappy and diverting."

—*Entertainment Weekly*

"Smokin'. . . . Feverishly clever plotting fuels Estep's over-the-top romance."

—*Publishers Weekly*

"It's back to Bigtime, NY, for more sexy, sizzling and off-beat adventures with those zany superheroes. Estep's twist on the world of superheroes is kick-ass fun!"

—*Romantic Times*

ALSO BY JENNIFER ESTEP

Spider's Bite

Web OF LIES

AN ELEMENTAL ASSASSIN BOOK

JENNIFER ESTEP

POCKET BOOKS

New York   London   Toronto   Sydney

Pocket Books
A Division of Simon & Schuster, Inc.
1230 Avenue of the Americas
New York, NY 10020

This book is a work of fiction. Names, characters, places, and incidents either are products of the author's imagination or are used fictitiously. Any resemblance to actual events or locales or persons, living or dead, is entirely coincidental.

First Pocket Books paperback edition June 2010

POCKET and colophon are registered trademarks of Simon & Schuster, Inc.

For information about special discounts for bulk purchases, please contact Simon & Schuster Special Sales at 1-866-506-1949 or business@simonandschuster.com.

The Simon & Schuster Speakers Bureau can bring authors to your live event. For more information or to book an event contact the Simon & Schuster Speakers Bureau at 1-866-248-3049 or visit our website at www.simonspeakers.com.

Cover design and illustration by Tony Mauro

Manufactured in the United States of America

10 9 8 7

ISBN 978-1-4391-4799-3
ISBN 978-1-4391-5544-8 (ebook)

As always, this book is dedicated to my mom and grandma for taking such good care of me.

And to Andre for doing the same.

Thanks for always understanding when I have to disappear to do "book stuff." Your love and support mean more to me than you will ever know.

Acknowledgments

Once again, this book would not have been possible without the help of many, many people.

Thanks to Annelise Robey for her unwavering support, and to Megan McKeever and Lauren McKenna for all their editorial advice and encouragement.

Thanks to Kathy Still, who answered my questions about coal mining and more. Any mistakes are mine, not hers.

And finally, thanks to all the readers out there. Knowing that folks enjoy my books is one of the things that makes it all worthwhile.

Happy reading!

✳ 1 ✳

"Freeze! Nobody move! This is a robbery!"

Wow. Three clichés in a row. Somebody was seriously lacking in the imagination department.

But the shouted threats scared someone, who squeaked out a small scream. I sighed. Screams were always bad for business. Which meant I couldn't ignore the trouble that had just walked into my restaurant—or deal with it the quick, violent way I would have preferred. A silverstone knife through the heart is enough to stop most trouble in its tracks. Permanently.

So I pulled my gray eyes up from the paperback copy of the *Odyssey* that I'd been reading to see what all the fuss was about.

Two twentysomething men stood in the middle of the Pork Pit, looking out of place among the restaurant's blue and pink vinyl booths. The dynamic duo sported black trench coats that covered their thin T-shirts and flapped against their ripped, rock star jeans. Neither one wore a hat or gloves, and the fall chill had painted their ears and fingers a bright cherry red. I wondered how long they'd stood outside, gathering up the courage to come in and yell out their trite demands.

Water dripped off their boots and spread across the faded blue and pink pig tracks that covered the restaurant floor. I eyed the men's footwear. Expensive black leather thick enough to keep out the November cold. No holes, no cracks, no missing bootlaces. These two weren't your typical desperate junkies looking for a quick cash score. No, they had their own money—lots of it, from the looks of their pricey shoes, vintage T-shirts, and designer jeans. These two rich punks were robbing my barbecue restaurant just for the thrill of it.

Worst fucking decision they'd ever made.

"Freeze!" the first guy repeated, as if we all hadn't heard him before.

He was a beefy man with spiky blond hair held up by some sort of shiny hair-care product. Probably a little giant blood in his family tree somewhere, judging from his six-foot-six frame and large hands. Despite his twentysomething years, baby fat still puffed out his face like a warm, oozing marshmallow. The guy's brown eyes flicked around the restaurant, taking in everything from the baked beans bubbling on the stove behind me to the hissing french fryer to the battered, bloody copy of *Where the Red Fern Grows* mounted on the wall beside the cash register.

Then Beefcake turned his attention to the people inside the Pork Pit to make sure we were all following his demands. Not many folks to look at. Monday was usually a slow day, made even more so by the cold bluster of wind and rain outside. The only other people in the restaurant besides me and the would-be robbers were my dwarven cook, Sophia Deveraux, and a couple of customers—two college-age women wearing skinny jeans and tight T-shirts not unlike those the robbers sported.

The women sat shocked and frozen, eyes wide, barbecue beef sandwiches halfway to their lips. Sophia stood next to the stove, her black eyes flat and disinterested as she watched the beans bubble. She grunted once and gave them a stir with a metal spoon. Nothing much ever bothered Sophia.

The first guy raised his hand. A small knife glinted in his red, chapped fingers. A hard, thin smile curved my lips. I liked knives.

"Chill out, Jake," the second guy muttered. "There's no need to scream."

I looked at him. Where his buddy was blond and beefy, robber number two was short and bone-thin. His wispy hair stuck up due to uncontrollable cowlicks instead of an overabundance of product. The locks were a bright red that had probably earned him the nickname Carrot at some point. Carrot shoved his hands into his holey pockets, shifted on his feet, and stared at the floor, clearly wanting to be somewhere other than here. A reluctant sidekick at best. Probably tried to talk his buddy out of this nonsense. He should have tried harder.

"No names, *Lance*. Remember?" Jake snarled and glared at his friend.

Lance's bony body jerked at the sound of his own

name, like someone had zapped him with a cattle prod. His mouth dropped open, but he didn't say anything.

I used one of the day's credit card receipts to mark my place in *The Odyssey*. Then I closed my book, straightened, slid off my stool, and stepped around the long counter that ran along the back wall of the Pork Pit. Time to take out the trash.

The first guy, Jake, saw me move, out of the corner of his eye. But instead of charging at me as I'd expected, the half giant moved to his left and jerked one of the girls up and out of her booth—a petite girl with a pixie haircut. She let out another squeaky scream. Her thick beef sandwich flew from her hand and spattered against one of the storefront windows. The barbecue sauce looked like blood running down the smooth, shiny glass.

"Leave her alone, you bastard!" the other woman shouted.

She jumped to her feet and charged at Jake, who backhanded her. He might only have been a half giant, but there was still enough strength in his blow to lift the woman off her feet and send her careening into a table. She flipped over the top, hit the floor hard, and let out a low groan.

By this point, Sophia Deveraux had become a little more interested in things. The dwarf moved to stand beside me. The silver skulls hanging from the black leather collar around her neck tinkled together like wind chimes. The skulls matched the ones on her black T-shirt.

"You take right," I murmured. "I've got left."

Sophia grunted and moved to the other end of the counter, where the second woman had been thrown.

"Lance!" Jake jerked his head at the injured woman and Sophia. "Watch those bitches!"

Lance wet his lips. Pure, uncomfortable misery filled his pale face, but he stepped around his friend and trotted over to the injured woman, who had pushed herself up to her hands and knees. She shoved her wild tangle of blue-black hair out of her face. Her pale blue eyes burned with immediate hate. A fighter, that one.

But Lance didn't see her venomous look. He was too busy staring at Sophia. Most people did. The dwarf had been Goth before Goth was cool—a hundred years ago or so. In addition to her skull collar and matching T-shirt, Sophia Deveraux sported black jeans and boots. Pink lipstick covered her lips, contrasting with the black glitter shadow on her eyelids and the natural pallor of her face. Today, the color motif extended up to her hair. Pale pink streaks shimmered among her cropped black locks.

But Jake wasn't so dumbstruck. He pulled the first woman even closer, turned her around, held her in front of him, and raised the knife to her throat. Now he had a human shield. Terrific.

But that wasn't the worst part. A bit of red sparked in the depths of his brown eyes, like a match flaring to life. Magic surged like a hot summer wind through the restaurant, pricking my skin with power and making the scars on my palms itch. Flames spewed out from between Jake's clenched fingers, traveling up and settling on the knife. The blade glowed red-orange from the sudden burst of heat.

Well, well, well, Jake the robber was just full of surprises. Because in addition to being a petty thief, Jake the half giant was also an elemental—someone who could control one of the four elements. Fire, in his case.

My smile grew a little harder, a little tighter. Jake wasn't the only one here who was an elemental—or very, very dangerous. I cocked my head, reaching out with my Stone magic. All around me, the battered brick of the Pork Pit murmured with unease, sensing the emotional upheaval that had already taken place inside and my dark intentions now.

"I said *nobody fucking move*."

Jake's earlier scream dropped to a hoarse whisper. His eyes were completely red now, as though someone had set two flickering rubies into his baby-fat face. A rivulet of sweat dripped down his temple, and his head bobbed in time to some music only he could hear. Jake was high on something—alcohol, drugs, blood, his own magic, maybe all of the above. Didn't much matter. He was going to be dead in another minute. Two, tops.

The red glow in Jake's eyes brightened as he reached for his magic again. The flames flashing on the silver blade flared hotter and higher, until they licked at the girl's neck, threatening to burn her. Tears streamed down her heart-shaped face, and her breath came in short, choked sobs, but she didn't move. Smart girl.

My eyes narrowed. It was one thing to try to rob the Pork Pit, my barbecue restaurant, my gin joint. Down-on-their-luck elementals, vampire hookers, and other bums strung out on their own magic and jonesing for more could be excused that stupidity. But nobody—*nobody*—threatened my paying customers. I was going to enjoy taking care of this lowlife. As soon as I got him away from the girl.

So I held up my hands in a placating gesture and kept the cold, calm violence out of my gray eyes as best I could. "I'm the owner. Gin Blanco. I don't want any trouble. Let the girl go, and I'll open the cash register for you. I won't even call the police after you leave."

Mainly because it wouldn't do me any good. The cops in the southern metropolis of Ashland were as crooked as forks of lightning. The esteemed members of the po-po barely bothered to respond to robberies, especially in this borderline Southtown neighborhood, much less do something useful, like catch the perps after the fact.

Jake snorted. "Go ahead. The police can't touch me, bitch. Do you know who my father is?"

In addition to being a Fire elemental, Jake was also a name-dropping prima donna. A wonder he'd survived this long.

"Don't tell them *that*!" Lance hissed.

Jake snorted and turned his red eyes to his buddy. "I'll tell them whatever I want. So shut your sniveling mouth."

"Just let the girl go, and I'll open the cash register," I repeated in a firm voice, hoping my words would penetrate Jake's magic high and sink into his thick skull.

His red eyes narrowed to slits. "You'll open the cash register, or the girl dies—and you along with her."

He jerked the girl back against him, and the flames coating the knife burned even brighter, taking on an orange-yellow hue. The silverstone scars on my palms—the ones shaped like spider runes—itched at the influx of magic. I tensed, afraid he was going to do the girl right here, right now. I could kill him—easily—but probably not before he hurt the girl with his magic. I didn't want that to happen. It wasn't going to happen. Not in my restaurant. Not now, not again.

"Jake, calm down," Lance pleaded with his friend. "No one's making any trouble. It's going just like you said it would. Quick and easy. Let's just get the money and go."

Jake stared at me, the flames dancing in his red eyes matching the movement of the ones on the knife blade. Pure, malicious glee filled his crimson gaze. Even if I hadn't been good at reading people, that emotion alone would have told me that Jake enjoyed using his magic, loved the power it gave him, the feeling of being invincible. And that he wasn't going to be satisfied just stealing my money. No, Jake was going to use his Fire power to kill everyone in the restaurant just because he could, because he wanted to show off his magic and prove he was a real badass. Unless I did something to stop him.

"Jake? The money?" Lance asked again.

After a moment, the fire dimmed in Jake's eyes. He lowered the glowing blade a few inches, giving the girl some much-needed air. "Money. Now."

I opened the register, grabbed all the wrinkled bills inside, and held them out. All Jake had to do was let go of the girl long enough to step forward and grab the cash, and I'd have him. *Come on, you bastard. Come and play with Gin.*

But some sense of self-preservation must have kicked in, because the beefy half giant jerked his head. Lance left his post by the injured woman, tiptoed forward, snatched the money out of my hand, and stepped back. I didn't bother grabbing him and using him as a hostage. Guys like Jake weren't above leaving their friends twisting in the wind—or stuck on the end of my blade.

Jake licked his thick, chapped lips. "How much? How much is there?"

Lance rifled through the green bills. "A little more than two hundred."

"That's it? You're holding out on me, bitch," Jake snarled.

I shrugged. "Monday's a slow day. And not many people like to get out in this kind of cold weather, not even for barbecue."

The Fire elemental glared at me, debating my words and what he could do about them. I smiled back. He didn't know what he'd gotten himself into—or whom he was messing with.

"Let's just go, Jake," Lance pleaded. "Some cops could come along any second."

Jake tightened his grip on his flaming knife. "No. Not until this bitch tells me what she did with the rest of the money. This is the most popular restaurant in the neighborhood. There had to be more than two hundred dollars in that cash register. So where did you hide it, bitch? You wearing a money belt underneath that greasy blue apron?"

I shrugged. "Why don't you come and find out, you pathetic fuck?"

His eyes grew darker, redder, angrier, until I thought the sparking flames flickering inside might actually shoot out of his magic-tinted irises. Jake let out a furious growl. He shoved the girl away and charged at me, the knife held straight out.

My smile widened. Finally. Time to play.

I waited until he got in range, then stepped forward and turned my body into his. I slammed my elbow into his solar plexus and swept his feet out from under him. Jake coughed, stumbled, and did a header onto the floor. His temple clipped the side of one of the tables as he went down, and a resulting bit of blood spattered onto my jeans. The sharp blow was enough to make Jake lose his grip on his Fire magic. The prickling power washing off him vanished, and the flames snuffed out on the knife in his hand. The hot metal hissed and smoked as it came into contact with the cool floor.

I looked to my right. The woman Jake had thrown across the room scrambled to her feet and prepared to launch herself at Lance. But Sophia grabbed the girl's waist and pulled her back. The woman started to struggle, but the Goth dwarf shook her head and stepped forward, putting herself in front of the customer. Lance swallowed once and backed up, ready to turn and run. But Sophia was quicker. The dwarf punched him once in the stomach. Lance went down like an anvil had been dropped on him. He crumpled to the floor and didn't move.

One down, one to go.

I turned my attention back to Jake, who'd rolled over onto his side. Blood dripped down the side of his head where he'd cut himself on the corner of the table. The half giant saw me standing over him, curled halfway up, and slashed at me with his cooling knife. Idiot. He didn't even come close to nicking me. After Jake made another flailing pass with the blade, I crouched down and grabbed his wrist, bending it back so he couldn't move it. I eyed the weapon in his locked hand.

"Fuck," I said. "Get a real knife. You couldn't even peel potatoes with that thing."

Then I plucked the blade from his chapped fingers and snapped his thick wrist.

Jake howled in pain, but the noise didn't bother me. Hadn't in years. I shoved him down onto his back, then straddled him, a knee on either side of his beefy chest, squeezing in and putting pressure on his ribs. Giants, even half giants like Jake, hated it when they had trouble breathing. Most people did.

I adjusted and tightened my grip on the knife, ready to drive it into his heart. A flimsy weapon, but it would do the job. Just about anything would, if you had enough strength and determination to put behind it. I had plenty of both.

A small, choked sob sounded, drawing my attention away from Jake and his high-pitched, keening howls. My gray eyes flicked up. The girl huddled underneath a table a few feet away, her knees pulled up to her chest, her eyes as big as quarters in her face, tears sliding down her flushed cheeks.

A position I'd been in, once upon a time.

A couple of months ago, the girl and her tears wouldn't have bothered me. I would have killed Jake and his friend, washed the blood off my hands, and asked Sophia to get rid of the bodies before I closed up the Pork Pit for the night.

That's what assassins did.

And I was the Spider, one of the very best.

But I'd had an epiphany of sorts two months ago when my mentor had been brutally tortured and murdered inside the Pork Pit—in the very spot Jake and I were in right now. The old man, Fletcher Lane, had wanted me to retire, to take a different path in life, to live in the daylight a little, as he was so fond of saying. I'd followed Fletcher's advice and quit the assassin business after I'd killed Alexis James, the Air elemental who'd murdered him.

"Hmph."

Behind me, Sophia grunted. I looked over my shoulder at the dwarf, who still had hold of the other woman. The girl was unsuccessfully trying to pry the dwarf's stubby fingers off her waist. Good luck with that. Sophia had a grip like death. Once she had you, she didn't let go—ever. My gray eyes locked with Sophia's black ones. Regret flashed in her dark gaze, and she shook her head just the tiniest bit. *No*, she was saying. Not in front of two witnesses.

Sophia was right. Witnesses were bad. I couldn't gut Jake with the two girls watching and get rid of the body afterward. Not in my own restaurant. Not without blowing my cover as Gin Blanco and leaving everything behind. And I wasn't going to do that. Not for a piece of trash like the Fire elemental. But that didn't mean I couldn't let Jake know exactly whom he was dealing with.

I waited until there was a lull in Jake's howls, then tipped his head up with the knife point and gazed into his eyes. They'd lost all hint of their red, fiery magic. Now his brown irises were wide and glossy with panic, fear, pain.

"You ever come to my restaurant and fuck with me or my customers again, and I'll carve you up like a Thanksgiving turkey."

I slashed down with the knife, breaking the skin on his beefy neck. Jake yelped at the sting and clawed at the slight wound with his sausage-thick fingers. I slapped his hand away and nicked him again. The smell of warm, coppery blood filled my nose. Something else that hadn't bothered me in a long, long time.

"Every time you move, I'm going to cut you again. Deeper and deeper. Nod your head if you understand."

Hatred flared in his gaze, taking the edge off the pain and panic, but he nodded.

"Good."

I clipped his temple with the knife hilt. Jake's head snapped to one side and fell onto the floor. Unconscious. Just like his friend Lance.

I stood up, wiped my fingerprints off the knife, and dropped the weapon on the floor. The half giant didn't stir. Then I got to my feet and headed for the girl, still crouched underneath the table.

She shrank back against the legs of a chair at my approach, like she wanted to melt into the metal. Her pulse fluttered like a mad butterfly in her temple. I put my friendliest, most trustworthy, charming, Southern smile on my face and crouched down until I was eye level with her.

"Come on, sweetheart," I said, holding out my hand. "It's over. Those men aren't going to hurt you now."

Her chocolate eyes darted to Jake lying on the floor. Her gaze flicked back to me, and she chewed her lip, her teeth white against her dusky skin.

"I'm not going to hurt you either," I said in a soft voice. "Come on, now. I'm sure your friend wants to see how you are."

"Cassidy!" the other woman called out since Sophia still wasn't letting her go. "Are you all right?"

Her friend's voice penetrated Cassidy's fearful daze. She sighed and nodded her head. The girl reached out, and I grabbed her trembling hand. Cassidy's fingers felt like thin, fragile icicles against the thick scar embedded in my palm. I tugged the girl to her feet. She eyed me with understandable caution, so I kept my movements slow and small, not wanting to startle her.

"I'm fine, Eva," Cassidy said in a low voice. "Just a little shook up is all."

Sophia let go of the other woman, and I stepped back. Eva rushed forward and caught her friend in a tight hug. Cassidy wrapped her arms around the other women, and the two of them rocked back and forth in the middle of the restaurant.

I walked over to Sophia, who was watching the two women with a flat expression on her pale face.

"Friendship. Ain't it a beautiful thing?" I quipped.

"Hmph." Sophia grunted again.

But the corners of the Goth dwarf's lips turned up into a tiny smile.

The two girls hugged a minute longer before Eva pulled a cell phone out of her jeans.

"You call the cops," Eva told her friend. "I need to let Owen know I'm okay. You know how he is. He'll freak when he finds out about this."

Cassidy nodded her head in sympathetic agreement and pulled her own phone out of her jeans. The two women started dialing numbers, instead of asking me, the restaurant owner, to do it for them. Not surprising. If you wanted the cops, you called them yourself. You certainly didn't depend on the kindness of strangers to do it. Not in Ashland.

I frowned. Cops. Just what I needed. Some of Ashland's finest getting an eyeful of me, the former assassin, a Goth dwarf who liked to dispose of dead bodies in her spare time, and the two guys we'd so easily dispatched. Not the kind of attention I wanted to draw to myself, even if I was retired. Nothing I could do about it now, though.

Sophia went back to the stove to check on her baked beans. Eva spoke in a low voice to someone on her phone. Cassidy finished her 911 call and sank into the nearest chair.

The girl stared at Jake on the floor; then her brown eyes flicked to the bloody knife. Her lower lip quivered, her eyes grew glossy, and her hands trembled. Trying to hold back the tears. Something else I'd had to do, once.

I walked over to the counter and picked up a glass cake plate filled with the black forest cookies I'd baked this morning.

"Here." I took the top off and held the plate out to her. "Have a cookie. They've got plenty of sugar and butter and chocolate in them. They'll help with the shakes."

Cassidy gave me a wan smile, took one of the treats, and bit into the concoction. The bittersweet chocolate melted in her mouth, and her eyes brightened with pleasure instead of worry.

Eva finished her call and sat down next to her friend. Her hands didn't tremble as she snapped her phone shut, and she looked at Jake with a thoughtful expression. The only sign anything had happened to Eva was a red welt on her cheek, where her face had smacked into the floor. The girl had a level head on her shoulders and a firm grip on her emotions. But that didn't mean she wouldn't crash later.

I held the plate out to her. "You too."

Eva took a cookie, broke it in two, and stuffed half of it into her mouth. Not shy, either.

I also plucked one of the chocolate treats off the stack. Not because I had shaky nerves, but because they were damn fine cookies. I'd made them myself, and I was just as good a cook as I had been an assassin.

I looked at the two unconscious men on the floor. Lance lay spread-eagled next to one of the booths where Sophia had dropped him. Blood continued to drip from the cuts on Jake's throat and temple, staining the floor a rusty brown.

I grabbed another cookie off the plate and watched him bleed.

* ❋ *2* ❋ *

A couple of uniformed patrol officers showed up twenty minutes later. Late, as usual. If we'd really needed them, our bodies would have been getting cold and sticky on the floor. The cops barreled through the front door and stopped, surprised by the calm scene.

Eva and Cassidy sat in their original booth. Cassidy munched on her fourth cookie and took a swig of the milk I'd given her. Eva leaned one elbow on the tabletop, holding her head up with her hand. With her free hand, she methodically broke apart a cookie and slowly ate it, piece by piece. Looked like the shock had finally caught up with her.

At the stove, Sophia ladled baked beans into glass Mason jars to take home to her older sister, Jo-Jo. I perched on my usual stool behind the cash register, eating my third cookie and reading about Odysseus blinding a cyclops.

The first cop was about my height, five seven or so, a wiry guy with nut-brown skin and a mop of matching curls that escaped the toboggan he'd stuffed them under. Dark freckles dotted his cheeks like walnuts. He had his gun out and held down against his leg.

In contrast, the other officer was around seven feet tall, with a shaved head as big as a cantaloupe and matching, ham-size fists. His skin was so dark it was glossy, like polished jet. So were his eyes. His name was Xavier. I'd seen him working as a bouncer out at Northern Aggression, a trendy nightclub I'd had occasion to visit recently. I hadn't realized he was a member of the police force as well.

Xavier recognized me too and tipped his head in my direction. I returned the gesture.

Xavier didn't have his gun out. Didn't need to. Giants could take a couple bullets in the chest before they went down, and one well-placed punch from his fist would snap just about anyone's neck. Strange that he'd be working as a cop, though. Most of the giants in Ashland hired themselves out as private security. Paid better, even if it was just as dangerous.

"We had a call about a robbery," the first cop spoke. His voice was high and whiny, like a power saw.

"Yeah. Those two guys busted in and tried to rob me. That one," I pointed to Jake, "came into the store and told everybody to freeze. When I started to open the cash register for him, he grabbed one of the girls and held a knife to her throat. He's a Fire elemental. Put flames on his knife and almost burned the girl with it. But luckily, my cook and I were able to subdue them both."

The cops looked at the two men, then at me, then Sophia, and finally the girls.

"Is that how it happened?" the short cop asked.

Eva and Cassidy nodded their heads. Sophia grunted her agreement.

"That's exactly how it happened," I said.

The short cop focused on Lance. "And the other guy there?"

"His buddy. Tried to calm him down. Didn't work."

The cop looked at the two men a moment more, then back at me. "And you did this to them? With what? A baseball bat?"

"No," I replied. "I just handled the first guy, the big one. My cook took care of the other man. Neither one of us had a weapon."

With her great strength, Sophia didn't need a weapon anymore than a giant did. And I didn't think it was necessary to mention the five silverstone knives currently hidden on my body. Or the others placed in strategic locations throughout the restaurant. Or the fact that I could have just formed a jagged icicle with my Ice magic and cut Jake's throat with it. Or even used my other elemental Stone power to collapse the whole restaurant on top of his head.

The short cop let out a low whistle. "Picked the wrong place to rob, didn't they?"

I didn't respond. He could see exactly how wrong they'd been from the blood spatters on the floor.

The two men were starting to come around. Lance rocked back and forth on the floor, holding his stomach, as if that would lessen the ache from where Sophia had punched him. Jake lay on his back and blinked up at the ceiling as though he wasn't really seeing it.

The giant cop, Xavier, reached down, picked up Lance by the scruff of his neck with one hand, and slapped a set of silverstone cuffs on him with the other. "You. Stand still."

Lance was too busy trying not to puke to do something stupid, like run. Xavier got down on one knee and started to repeat the handcuff process on Jake. He stared into his face. Xavier frowned, then looked up at me with his black eyes.

"You know who this is?" he rumbled.

"No. Should I?"

The giant nodded his head. "Yeah, Jake McAllister."

My gray eyes narrowed. "McAllister? As in Jonah McAllister? The lawyer?"

"The one and only," Xavier rumbled. "Jake here is his son. Third time he's been in trouble since Halloween."

The beginnings of a headache throbbed behind my eyes. Jonah McAllister was Ashland's highest priced and most successful lawyer. A charismatic showman who could make the most violent, irredeemable, sociopathic criminal seem like an innocent schoolgirl—and make the jury weep with compassion while he did it. McAllister didn't care whether people were guilty or not, as long as they could pay his astronomical fees.

But even more problematic was the fact Jonah McAllister was also personal counsel to Mab Monroe. Ashland might have all the municipal trappings of any other city. Police and fire departments, a city council, a mayor. But Mab Monroe was the one who really ran the town, in addition to her own lucrative, Mob-like empire. To most folks, Mab was the richest businesswoman in the city, who generously, selflessly, used her wealth to help the less fortunate. But those of us who moved in the shady side of life knew Mab did everything from ordering kidnappings, to bribing government officials, to murdering anyone who got in her way.

Mab had money, but her real power came from the fact she was a Fire elemental, just like Jake McAllister. Being an elemental meant Mab could create, control, and manipulate fire just about any way she wanted to. But Mab Monroe had far more power than Jake McAllister had ever dreamed of. Rumor had it that Mab had more magic, more raw power, than any elemental born in the last five hundred years. Given her stranglehold on the city and queenlike position in the Ashland underworld, it wasn't so much a rumor as a commonly known fact. Anyone who went up against Mab Monroe got dead in a hurry.

Jonah McAllister was more than just Mab's lawyer—he was one of her top lieutenants, along with Elliot Slater, the giant who handled Mab's security and brutally enforced her wishes. McAllister's job was to deal with anyone who challenged Mab through legal means. To bury them in enough paperwork and red tape to drown an elephant so that they either gave up outright or were forced to when they went bankrupt trying to pay their own attorneys.

No, Jonah McAllister wouldn't be pleased about my beating down his son. He, and by extension Mab Monroe, could make problems for me—problems that weren't as easily solvable now that I was just Gin Blanco and not moonlighting as the assassin the Spider anymore.

"You sure you want to press charges?" Xavier asked. "Most people don't, after they find out who his daddy is."

I stared at Jake, who kept blinking up at the ceiling. My gaze slid over to Cassidy, who was busy looking at her shoes. She'd heard Xavier's question, and she knew what the McAllister name meant as well as I did. Cassidy thought I was going to fold, and she didn't want to see me tell the cops to let Jake go.

The image of the hot, hungry flames licking at Cassidy's slender throat flashed before my eyes, along with her tear-streaked face. Reminding me of another place, another time, another girl desperate for me to save her, to convince her everything was going to be okay, even if I knew it wasn't. That it would never be all right again.

The memories of my baby sister, Bria, and the horrible night our mother and older sister, Annabella, had been murdered, swam up in the back of my mind, a dark shark rising to surface. The memory sank its cold, jagged teeth into my heart. Fire, torture, destruction, death. All that and more had happened that one, fateful night seventeen years ago. My hands curled into loose fists, hiding the spider rune scars that had been burned into my palms—scars that were a constant reminder of my lost family.

After a few seconds, I uncurled my palms and flexed my fingers, working the tension out of them.

I focused on Jake McAllister again, remembering the sharp, sly way he'd stared at me. Two hundred dollars or not, he'd been ready to kill me and everyone else in the restaurant for nothing more than a thrill. I'd be damned if I was letting him get away with it—any of it.

"Fuck who his daddy is," I said. "He almost slit that girl's throat. I'm pressing charges."

Xavier shrugged. "Your choice. Just don't expect much to come of it."

He clinked the silverstone handcuffs around Jake's wrists and yanked the Fire elemental up to his feet. The abrupt motion snapped Jake out of his blinking trance, and he looked over his shoulder at the cop, then back at me. It took a few seconds for the reality of the situation to penetrate his thick skull.

"You called the cops? You're going to pay for this, bitch!" Jake screamed.

He surged forward, trying to break free of Xavier and get at me. But Xavier easily restrained him with one hand. Hard to break a giant's grip.

But instead of staying where I was, I stepped around the counter and walked over to Jake. This time, I let him see just how cold and flat and hard my gray eyes really were. "You're the one who's going to pay when Daddy finds out you're knocking over restaurants—or trying to. Piss poor job you did, all the way around."

"Bitch!" he screamed again. "You're gonna die for this! Do you hear me? You're dead!"

Jake lunged forward again, but the giant cop jerked him back by the scruff of his neck—none too gently. Xavier winked at me, and I smiled. I was starting to like Xavier. I'd have to slip him an extra C-note or two the next time I saw him working the door at Northern Aggression.

"Come on, Jake," Xavier rumbled. "Let's get you in the squad car so you can call your old man to come bail you out."

*   *   *

Xavier pushed Jake McAllister and his friend Lance through the front door and into the back of a waiting cruiser. The other cop, the short guy, took statements from Cassidy and Eva. He'd just finished talking with the girls when the front door of the Pork Pit opened and another cop stepped inside. A tall, thirtysomething man with short black hair, bronze skin that hinted at his Hispanic heritage, and eyes the color of smoky whiskey.

Detective Donovan Caine.

The majority of cops in Ashland might be known for their apathy and avarice, but Donovan Caine was a rare exception to the rule. He fought against the rampant corruption, bribes, and payoffs most of the police force took to look the other way and actually tried to catch criminals. And the detective really did believe in all that protect and serve, touchy-feely stuff.

My path had first crossed Caine's several months ago when I'd assassinated Cliff Ingles, his corrupt partner. In addition to forcing money and sexual freebies out of vampire hookers while he was on duty, Ingles had viciously raped and beaten one of the prostitutes' teenage daughters. Even among the scum in Ashland, Cliff Ingles had been a real prince, and I'd done him pro bono. My own sort of public service.

Donovan Caine hadn't known how dirty his partner was and became obsessed with catching Cliff Ingles's killer—me. Of course, the trail had gone cold, since I was nothing if not professional, but that hadn't kept Caine from keeping the case alive and digging for information every few weeks.

Then our paths had crossed again—and in person—two months ago when I'd been framed for the murder of a corporate whistle-blower named Gordon Giles. Some nasty people thought the detective had information that could implicate them in the subsequent scheme and cover-up, and they'd been beating it out of him when I'd shown up and taken them out. After that, Donovan Caine had reluctantly joined forces with me to find the real killer.

During the course of our investigation, we'd had a hot one-night stand—well, more like a hot one-hour stand—a couple months ago, but nothing since. The detective's Boy Scout mentality was a sticking point between us. I found his morals admirable, if impractical, in a city as dirty, violent, and corrupt as Ashland. He found my lack of said morals and zero remorse for all the bloody things I'd done in my former profession disturbing, to say the least.

Still, the attraction between us had been intense, and the hurried sex we'd had in a supply closet had been fantastic. I'd only seen the detective once since then, at my mentor, Fletcher Lane's, funeral. Caine had come to offer his condolences and check up on me. I'd kissed him right there in the cemetery. Afterward, he'd bounded away from me like a scared rabbit.

I hadn't seen or spoken to the detective since then. I thought about him a lot, though. More than I wanted to. And now here he was in my gin joint, in my little corner of the city.

Donovan Caine sensed my gaze and raised his head. Our eyes locked, gold on gray. My chest tightened, and the familiar heat flooded my veins, pooling in my stomach before sinking lower. I eyed the detective's navy coat. The wool fabric draped over his shoulders and hinted at his lean, hard body beneath. I remembered the feel of that hard body. His mouth pressed against mine, our tongues crashing together. Hands clawing at each other's clothes. The crisp, clean scent of him filling my nose. The way he'd murmured my name over and over like a curse—or the answer to a prayer—as he'd thrust into me, quick and hard and deep. Mmm.

The short cop saw me staring at the detective. He walked over, murmured something to Caine, and jerked his head in my direction. Probably pointing me out as the owner and prime witness. Most women, most left-behind lovers, would have stalked forward and demanded to know what Donovan Caine was doing here. Why he hadn't so much as called. Instead, I leaned one elbow against the counter and remained nonchalant, even though my stomach clenched at the sight of him. Patience was one of my virtues. Always had been. The detective would come to me soon enough.

Less than a minute later, Caine finished his quiet conversation with the other cop and walked in my direction. He stopped about a foot away, his golden eyes taking in my grease-stained blue apron, worn jeans, and long-sleeved T-shirt. Two scarlet tomatoes decorated the top of the black cotton.

"Gin."

"Detective."

We stood there staring at each other. An invisible electric current hummed between us, firing off sparks of hot desire in every direction. I breathed in. The detective's clean, soapy scent filled my nose, overpowering the cumin, red pepper, and other spices in the air. Donovan looked away and cleared his throat.

He jerked his head, and I followed him to the far side of the restaurant, out of earshot of everyone else.

"You want to tell me what happened?" he asked in a low voice.

"You want to tell me why you're here?" I countered. "Detectives don't usually come out for Southtown robberies, especially those that are thwarted."

Donovan stared at me. "All right. I asked dispatch to let me know if there were any incidents at the Pork Pit."

"Why? Afraid I might take to killing people in my own place of business? You must not have gotten the memo, but I've retired, detective."

His black eyebrows drew together in surprise. "Retired?"

I nodded. "Retired. Now I spend my days here at the Pork Pit serving up the best barbecue, cole slaw, and blackberry iced tea in Ashland."

Some emotion flared in his amber eyes. It might have been relief or even hope, but it was gone before I could decipher it. "Well, good for you, I suppose."

I shrugged. My quitting the assassin business wasn't good or bad. Fletcher Lane had been after me to retire for months before his murder. After his death, I'd decided to honor the old man's final wish. Nothing more, nothing less. But as my eyes slid down Donovan Caine's body, I couldn't help but wonder if my revelation would be enough to get the detective back into my bed. Certainly couldn't hurt.

Donovan dug a pen and notepad out of his hip pocket. "So tell me about it."

I recapped the events of the last hour. After I finished, Caine stilled, his pen frozen on his notepad, turning over something in his mind. Then he raised his golden eyes to me.

"Why didn't you kill them?" he asked in a soft voice. "We both know you could have."

"Easily," I agreed. "But one of the girls was on the floor next to me."

"And you didn't want her to see you do it?"

I shrugged. "Witnesses are bad, detective. I've told you that before."

He snorted. "And here I thought you were developing a heart."

Disappointment tinged his words. I ignored the longing the sound stirred in me.

"Oh, I've always had a heart, detective," I replied in a breezy tone. "I just don't let it keep me from doing what needs to be done. That would be weak, and I'm not weak. Haven't been in a long time."

"No, weak is one thing you're definitely not." Donovan eyed me. "You may be retired, but you really haven't changed at all, have you, Gin?"

"That depends on your definition of *change*. Am I suddenly going to morph into a soccer mom or a bleeding heart who lets people walk all over her? No, and I don't want to. But I've reevaluated my life, my priorities, and I've decided to change them accordingly. That being said, if somebody pushes me, comes at me like those two clowns did, I'm going to push back—three times as hard.

Being an assassin has been my way of life since I was thirteen, detective. I'm not going to forget what I did for the last seventeen years just because I'm not doing it anymore."

"I see."

This time, the disappointment was as sharp as one of the silverstone knives hidden up my sleeves. Donovan Caine still wanted me, but he wanted his conscience to be clear about it too. I wasn't the only one who needed to change.

Caine cleared his throat. "You know who the blond kid is?"

"Jake McAllister. Jonah McAllister's nearest and dearest. The giant cop told me—then asked if I still wanted to press charges."

Donovan looked at the cop, who could be seen standing on the sidewalk through the storefront windows. "Xavier? He's a good guy. Probably thought he was doing you a favor, letting you know about the kid and his connections. Because Jonah McAllister isn't going to like this. He could cause a lot of trouble for you."

"If he does, I'll handle it the way I always do. Quickly. Efficiently. Permanently."

"The way you always do? I thought you were trying to change."

"I am," I replied. "But white trash is still white trash, detective. Nobody comes into my restaurant, tries to hold up the place, and threatens my customers. I don't care who his daddy is."

We stared at each other. Not for the first time, I longed to draw the detective close, to pull his lips down to mine and see if the sex would be as hot and hard and good as it had been before. We'd certainly have more room to maneuver on one of the tables than we'd had in the supply closet. Mmm.

But I wasn't going to make the first move. I'd done that before. If the detective wanted me, he could let me know. But he didn't.

Instead, Donovan Caine stared at me, his eyes tracing over my features, as if he was memorizing them. As if he was never planning on seeing me again. Maybe he wasn't. The idea made my stomach twist, but I kept my face smooth and expressionless. I hadn't survived this long by wearing my heart on my sleeve. I didn't plan on doing it now. Not even for him.

Finally, Donovan held out his hand. I took it. His fingers felt hard, strong, capable against my own, and the heat from him warmed my whole body. Donovan dropped my hand like it burned him. Maybe it did, to want me so much, the woman who'd killed his partner. I'd heard the detective say once that you didn't fuck your partner's murderer. But he'd done it—twice—and enjoyed it. And he still hated himself for it.

"Take care, Gin."

"You too, detective. You too."

Donovan Caine nodded at me a final time. Then the detective turned on his heel and walked out the door, leaving my gin joint and heart a little emptier and colder than they had been before.

* 3 *

Barely a minute passed before the front door opened once more, making the bell chime. I looked up, wondering if the detective had changed his mind about, well, anything. Everything.

But the man who strode into the Pork Pit wasn't Donovan Caine or another cop. His suit was much too nice for that. The black fabric draped off his shoulders, highlighting a frame that was compact, sturdy, strong. Given his body structure, I would have thought him a dwarf. But at six foot one, he was much too tall for that. He had a thick head of hair that was a glossy blue-black, while his eyes were a light violet. A white, thin scar slashed diagonally across his chin. It offset the crooked tilt of his nose. Those were the only two flaws in his chiseled features, which somehow added even more character to his face, rather than detracting from his good looks.

He cut an impressive figure. Striking, confident, aggressive, forceful. Someone who demanded attention. Someone worth watching. Especially since he looked vaguely familiar to me.

I half-expected a couple of giant guards to follow the man into the Pork Pit. Most of the rich folks in Ashland employed at least a couple, and this guy was definitely wealthy, judging by his swanky suit and confident demeanor. But the man entered alone. His light eyes swept over the interior of the restaurant, pausing at the blood spatters on the floor. After a moment, his gaze moved on and settled on the two girls, who were packing up their books to leave.

"Eva," he said in a voice that rumbled like thunder. "Are you all right?"

Eva zipped up her backpack. "I'm fine, Owen."

The man moved to stand beside her. He walked stiffly but with purpose, like a bulldozer plowing through dandelions. "Tell me what happened."

"I said I was fine," she repeated in an irritated voice, as though they'd had this argument many times before. "I also told you there was no need to come down here. You never listen to me."

"I'm your big brother," he said. "I'm supposed to watch out for you."

Big brother? Yeah, I could see that. Eva had the same coloring as the thirtysomething man. Blue-black hair, pale eyes, milky skin. It made her beautiful. Him too, in a cold sort of way.

"Now, tell me what happened," the man demanded again.

Eva rolled her eyes and launched into a recount of the

attempted robbery. As she talked, the man crossed his arms over his chest. His biceps bulged with the motion, and he started tapping one finger on his opposite elbow. Despite the movements, he was totally focused on his sister, as though she was the most important thing in the world to him. Maybe she was. He stared at the red welt on her cheek, and his hands curled into fists. I got the distinct feeling he would love to have some alone time with Jake McAllister.

When Eva finished her story, her big brother turned his attention to me. For the first time, I felt the full force of his gaze. Sharp, shrewd, calculating. Like looking into my own eyes. He walked forward and held out his hand.

"Owen Grayson."

Well, the hits just kept on coming. First, Jake McAllister decided to grace my restaurant with his presence, and now Owen Grayson had come to collect his sister. I'd heard of him, of course. Grayson was one of the city's wealthiest businessmen. Mining, timber, metal manufacturing. He had his fingers in a lot of money-making pies. With his subdued suit and chiseled features, Grayson didn't have the ostentatious, deadly, in-your-face flash of Mab Monroe, who enjoyed flaunting her status as the city's golden girl. Still, I knew power when I saw it—elemental or otherwise. And Owen Grayson had plenty. Definitely someone worth watching.

"Gin Blanco."

"Gin?" he asked.

"Like the liquor," I quipped.

Owen Grayson's eyes glittered at my wry tone, but I still put my hand in his. Grayson's fingers curled around my skin like thick ropes of kudzu. Hard, sturdy, and almost unbreakable. He might not be a dwarf, but there had to be some of the blood in his veins. Only way to explain that kind of grip. Grayson glanced down at our entwined hands and frowned, as though I'd static-shocked him or something. Maybe I had, because I felt a brief prick on my palm.

The sensation vanished, and I tightened my own grip, just to show him I wasn't easily intimidated. A small smile tugged up Grayson's lips, as though he found my show of strength amusing. I gave him a cool stare. The hostility must have flickered in my gray eyes because Owen Grayson let go first.

Eva Grayson watched the exchange with interest. So did her friend Cassidy. Sophia Deveraux had already retreated to the back of the Pork Pit to start closing up the restaurant for the night.

Owen Grayson stared at me a moment more before turning to his sister. "If nothing else, tonight has proven my point about Southtown. From now on, someone will be with you during school hours."

Eva rolled her eyes again. Looked like something she did a lot when her big brother was around. "No. No more bodyguards. I'm nineteen years old, Owen. I'm in *college*. I can take care of myself."

"Like you did tonight?" he replied.

"Tonight was a freak event, and you know it," she retorted. "I'm not going to let you use it as an excuse. Besides, I was perfectly safe the whole time."

"That bruise on your cheek tells me otherwise."

Owen glowered at his sister, but the hostile gaze slid

off her like water. Looked like something she ignored a lot. Instead, Eva gave him a calm, calculating look.

"You want me to have a bodyguard? Then hire her." The girl stabbed her finger at me. "Because she took out a Fire elemental like it was nothing. And she cooks."

Owen's pale eyes swept over my body. Probably wondering how I'd had the strength, balls, or dumb luck to do that.

I'd taken a lot of dirty jobs in my time, but be a bodyguard to a know-it-all college girl? I might have retired from being an assassin, but I hadn't gone insane. "Sorry. My dance card's already full."

Owen nodded. "Job offer notwithstanding, you saved my sister's life. I owe you. Name your price."

My turn to roll my eyes. "I don't want your money, and I don't need it."

His violet gaze flicked around the restaurant, taking in the faded pig tracks on the floor and the well-worn booths, chairs, and tables. Disbelief filled his features, but he was enough of a Southern gentleman not to call me a liar to my face. Little did he know I was telling the truth. I'd salted away a lot of money—a *lot* of money—from my assassin jobs over the years, and Fletcher had left me an exceptionally healthy bequest in his will. I could hemorrhage C-notes for years, decades even, and it wouldn't hurt a bit.

But instead of offering his money to me again, Owen reached into his suit and drew out a small white card. I took it from him. Along with his name and a cell phone number, a hammer was embossed in silver foil on the card. Grayson's rune. A large, heavy hammer, symbolizing strength, power, hard work.

"If you ever need anything, please, don't hesitate to call, day or night," he said.

My finger traced over the hammer rune, and I memorized the number. Might not be a bad thing having someone like Owen Grayson owe me a favor. Besides, Finnegan Lane, my foster brother and general partner in crime, would kill me if I turned him down. "All right."

We locked gazes. Cool, calculating, and shrewd, on both sides. Grayson tipped his head at me. I did the same, and we had an agreement.

Owen turned to the two women. "Come on, girls. Time to go."

He held the door open for them, and they headed outside. Owen Grayson paused, looking over his shoulder. The businessman stared at me a moment more before stepping out into the dark night.

I locked the front door behind the three of them and turned the sign over to *Closed*. It was barely after seven, but we weren't going to have any more customers tonight. This close to Southtown, people could sniff out violence better than bloodhounds. Besides, I didn't feel like mopping up Jake McAllister's blood just yet.

I went into the back and said my good nights to Sophia. The Goth dwarf grunted, gathered up her glass Mason jars full of baked beans, and headed out the back door to go home to her sister, Jo-Jo. After I made sure the stoves, french fryer, and lights were off, I followed her out into the alley that ran behind the restaurant.

I stood in the ink-black shadows next to one of the Dumpsters, looking, listening, searching. But nothing moved in the cold, quiet night, not even the rats and alley cats searching for garbage. Still, I brushed my fingers against the hard brick of the restaurant, using my elemental magic to listen to the stone.

The brick's slow murmur was one of muted, clogged contentment—just the way the stomachs and arteries of the Pork Pit's customers felt after eating a hot, thick, juicy barbecue sandwich. Over time, emotions, feelings, and actions sink into the earth and especially stone, where they can linger indefinitely until something else, some other action, comes along to add to, change, or overpower them. My elemental Stone magic let me sense these vibrations, analyze, interpret, and even tap into them if I wanted to. But the brief bit of violence that had happened earlier tonight hadn't lasted long enough or been brutal enough for the brick to permanently pick up its vibrations. Good.

Still, I looked and listened a moment more, searching for the telltale shape of a half giant or some sort of fire flickering in the shadows. But Jake McAllister wasn't waiting for me. Daddy was probably bailing him out of jail right now. McAllister would be here sooner or later, though. I'd gotten the better of him, and he knew it. He wouldn't be satisfied until he'd returned the favor. I hoped he tried. Might alleviate some of the boredom that had settled over me these last two months during my retirement. For a few minutes, anyway. Guys like Jake McAllister always thought they were tougher than they actually were.

Satisfied the Fire elemental wasn't going to come gunning for me tonight, I dropped my hand from the cold

brick and headed home. I walked three blocks in the drizzling rain, cut through twice as many alleys, and doubled
back five times before I was positive no one was following
me. Sure, I was a retired assassin, but that didn't mean
there weren't people out there who didn't want me dead.
As the Spider, I'd killed my share of powerful men and
women over the years, and I wasn't taking any chances
with my safety—retirement or not.

Twenty minutes later, I retrieved my car—a sturdy, silver
Benz that I'd recently purchased—from one of the parking
garages near the restaurant and headed for Fletcher's.

Traffic was light on the downtown streets that ringed
the Pork Pit. The bankers, businessmen, and other corporate sharks had long since fled the city's spindly skyscrapers for the comfort of their posh homes in Northtown.
Their secretaries and junior staff lived out in the suburbs
that clustered around the heart of the city, while the jani-
tors, maids, and other menial workers made their homes
on the rough streets of Southtown.

The city of Ashland spread over three states—Tennessee,
Virginia, and North Carolina. The official borders might
have shown it to be one cohesive city, but the area was really divided into two distinct sections—Northtown and
Southtown. A holdover from the Civil War days that had
just never faded away. The sprawling, circular confines
of the downtown area joined the two halves of the city
together, but they bore little resemblance to each other.
The working poor and blue-collar folks populated Southtown, along with vampire hookers, gangbangers, junkies,
and all other manner of rednecks and white trash. Most
of them lived in run-down row houses and public hous-

ing units that resembled fallout shelters. The Pork Pit lay close to the Southtown border.

While Southtown resembled the dregs in the bottom of a coffee cup, Northtown was the whipped meringue on top of a chocolate pie. You had to have money to live in Northtown. Lots of it, to afford one of the plantation-style mansions. Connections and a bloodline that went back a few hundred years didn't hurt either. But for all their polish, the folks in Northtown weren't any better than those in Southtown. They were all dangerous. The only difference was the people in Northtown would serve you tea and cucumber sandwiches before they fucked you over. The Southtown hoods were much more efficient. They'd slit your throat, take your wallet, and be ready to do it again to someone else before you even hit the alley floor.

It took me about twenty minutes to wind my way from the downtown district out into the suburbs that lay northwest of the city. I drove past gated communities with cutesy names like Davis Square and Peachtree Acres and eventually turned onto a rutted, gravel road that wound up one of the ridges that slashed through the city. I rode over the lumps and bumps in the road, used to the teeth-rattling sensation by now. Fletcher Lane had liked his privacy, which was why his house squatted on the side of a cliff so steep a mountain goat couldn't climb up it.

I steered the car through the skeletal remains of the trees that flanked what passed for the driveway. Thirty seconds later, the Benz left the bare, clutching branches behind. I crested a hill, and the house popped into sight.

In addition to leaving me the Pork Pit in his last will and testament, Fletcher Lane had also bequeathed me his house—a three-story clapboard structure that had been built before the Civil War. Various improvements and additions had been made to the house over the years, none of which matched. Gray stone, red clay, brown brick. All that and more could be seen on the house, along with a tin roof, black shutters, and blue eaves. The whole thing reminded me of a pincushion someone had haphazardly stuck a variety of implements into, with no thought for whether they actually belonged together or not.

I parked the Benz and ran my eyes over what I could see of the yard. It stretched out a hundred feet in front of the house before falling away in a series of jagged cliffs. Beyond the dropoff, the surrounding Appalachian Mountains were coal smudges in a night sky covered with a blanket of diamond stars and the gleaming crown of a half moon. Hell of a view, especially at night.

I got out of the car and stooped down behind the Benz, keeping it between myself and the sprawling house. To a casual observer, it probably looked like I was tying my shoe. You would have had to look hard to see the glint of magic in my gray eyes or realize I had my hands pressed against the cold, wet gravel of the driveway.

The sounds of the trees, wind, and small, scurrying animals ran through the stones. Soft, comforting murmurs as familiar to me as a lullaby. No visitors today. I hadn't expected any, but it never hurt to double-check. I'd stayed alive this long, despite all the incredible odds and job hazards of my former profession. I wasn't going to get dead now because I'd made a rookie mistake, like not checking the gravel before I stepped into Fletcher's home.

Once I'd assured myself everything was as it should be,

I grabbed my purse and headed for the house. But before I slid my key into the front door lock, I brushed my fingertips against the stone that framed and composed it. Deep, rich, black granite so hard and solid even a giant would have a tough time pounding through it. Thin veins of silverstone glistened in the granite, adding to its dark beauty. But the magical metal served another purpose besides mere decoration. Silverstone could absorb any kind of elemental magic that came its way—Stone, Air, Fire, or Ice—as well as offshoots of the elements. Instead of being true elementals and being able to tap into one of the big four, as they were called, some folks were gifted in other areas, like metal, water, electricity, or even acid.

Regardless, the silverstone in the door would absorb quite a bit of power should anyone decide to use magic to force their way inside. I'd spent a fortune having the granite installed here and in other strategic places throughout the house, along with silverstone bars on the windows, but it was worth it to make sure I was secure. Helped me sleep easier.

The granite's hum was low and muted, just like the gravel in the driveway. Nobody had been near the door all day. Good. I'd had enough excitement already.

I unlocked the door and stepped inside. Given its unusual construction, the interior of the house resembled a rabbit's warren. Small rooms, short hallways, odd spaces here and there that doubled back and opened up into completely new areas. When I was living here as a kid, I'd had to draw myself a map just to get from my upstairs bedroom to the front door and back again. I threw my keys down into a bowl by the front door, kicked off my boots, and headed toward the back of the house, where the kitchen was.

Fletcher Lane had lived in this house seventy-seven years. He'd been born here, and he probably would have died here, if he hadn't been murdered by an Air elemental. The old man had collected a lot of stuff in his time on this earth. Furniture, plates, tools, odd bits of metal, wood, glass. I hadn't had the heart to clean any of it out yet. The air still smelled faintly of him—like sugar, spice, and vinegar swirled together.

But the kitchen, the kitchen was mine. Always had been, from the moment I'd moved in as a homeless teenager to when I'd taken up residence again several weeks ago after Fletcher's funeral. I stepped inside and flipped on the light.

The kitchen was one of the largest rooms in the house, and a long, skinny island divided it from a small den that contained a television, stacks of books, a sofa, and a couple of recliners. Copper pots and pans hung from a metal rack over the island. A brand new, high-end stove, refrigerator, and freezer flanked half of the back wall, while a series of picture windows took up the other side. Several butcher blocks full of silverstone knives also populated the kitchen. On the island. On the counter. In the spice rack. Behind the microwave. You could never have too many knives lying around if you loved to cook like I did—or were a former assassin.

I poured myself a glass of lemonade, then wrapped my hand around the container and concentrated, reaching for the cool power deep inside myself. In addition to being a Stone elemental, I also had the rare talent of being able to manipulate another element—Ice. My Ice magic was far weaker, though. All I could really do with it was make small shapes, like cubes or chips. The occasional lock pick. A knife, when the need arose. But often it was the little things that saved you. A lesson I'd learned when battling Alexis James a few weeks ago. The Air elemental would have killed me, would have flayed me alive with her magic, if I hadn't formed a jagged icicle with my power and cut her throat with it.

I reached for my cool Ice magic, and a moment later, small, snowflake-shaped Ice crystals spread out from my palm and fingertips. They frosted up the side of the glass, arced over the lip, and ran down into the lemonade. Then I held my hand palm up and reached for my magic again. A cold, silver light flickered there, centered in the spider rune scar embedded in my palm. After a moment, the light coalesced into a couple of Ice cubes, which I dropped into the tart beverage.

I took my lemonade into the den, plopped down in one of the recliners, and put my socked feet up on the scarred coffee table. As always, my eyes flicked to a series of framed drawings propped up on the mantel over the fireplace. Three pencil drawings I'd done for one of my community college classes and another, more recent, one.

The first three drawings depicted a series of runes—the symbols of my dead family. A snowflake, the rune for the Snow family, and my mother, Eira's, symbol, representing icy calm. A curling ivy vine for my older sister, Annabella, representing elegance. A delicate, intricate primrose for my younger sister, Bria, symbolizing beauty.

The fourth rune was shaped like a pig holding a platter of food. An exact rendering of the multicolored neon sign that hung over the entrance to the Pork Pit. Not a rune, not really, but I'd drawn it in honor of Fletcher Lane. The Pork Pit had been my home for the past seventeen years, since the murder of my mother and older sister. It and Fletcher were one and the same to me.

I held my lemonade up in a silent toast to the runes, to the family I'd lost long ago, and to Fletcher, whose death was still a raw, aching wound in my chest.

But the drawings on the mantel weren't the only runes to be found in the house. I had a rune as well. Two of them, actually—embedded in my flesh.

I put down my lemonade, uncurled my palms, and looked at the silverstone scars that decorated my skin. A small circle surrounded by eight thin rays, one on either hand. My rune, representing a spider, the symbol for patience. The rune had once been a medallion, an innocent charm strung on a silverstone chain—until the Fire elemental who'd murdered my family had tortured me by duct-taping the rune in between my hands and making me hold on to the metal while she superheated it. The silverstone had eventually melted into my hands, forever marking me with the rune. Forever branding me as the Spider in more ways than one.

And I wasn't the only one who couldn't forget the past. I leaned forward, picked up a thick folder from the coffee table, and plucked a picture out of the file. A woman stared up at me. A beautiful creature, with blond hair, cornflower blue eyes, and rosy skin. But her eyes were cold and hard, her mouth a tight slash in her face that detracted from her delicate features. A rune hung off a chain around her neck. A primrose. The symbol for beauty.

Bria. My baby sister.

For seventeen years, I'd thought Bria had died that night, along with our mother and older sister. Thought that she'd been crushed to death by the falling stones of our burning house. That I'd caused her death by using my Stone magic to collapse the house in order to try to escape my torturers and save her.

But Fletcher Lane had sent me a final gift from beyond the grave—Bria's photo. Proof that she was still alive somewhere out there in the world. The picture was the only nice thing in the folder. The rest of it dealt with my family's murder. Police reports, autopsy photos, and all the speculation that had followed the brutal, unexpected murder of the Snow family.

"Why did you do it, Fletcher?" I murmured. "Why leave me the information about my family? About their murder? Why the picture of Bria? Where is she? How did you find her? When were you going to tell me about her?"

Silence.

Fletcher had gone where I couldn't question him, and he was never coming back. All I had left was this folder of gruesome information and a single picture of Bria, neither of which had helped me locate my baby sister.

But Bria's photo hadn't been the only surprise in the folder. There had also been a slip of paper with a name on it. *Mab Monroe,* written and underlined twice in Fletcher's tight, controlled handwriting. That was all that had been on the paper. I still didn't know why Fletcher had written her name down and slipped it inside with the rest of the information. Was Mab Monroe the Fire elemental who'd killed my mother and older sister? If so, why? Why had she done it?

Mab Monroe might be powerful, but she'd also made a lot of enemies over the years. Back when I'd still been working as the assassin the Spider, Fletcher had gotten several requests a year from folks wanting her to be eliminated. We'd both agreed it was an impossible job, that Mab had too many people around her, that she was just too strong in her magic to be taken down quietly by a single person. But that hadn't stopped Fletcher from compiling all the information he could on the Fire elemental, her minions, and her organization. It had always seemed to me like Fletcher Lane had some secret interest in wanting Mab Monroe dead. A desire I'd never been able to figure out—unless it had something to do with me and my family's murder.

It was all a great big circle of speculation. I just didn't know the answers to anything, and I'd been driving myself crazy trying to figure them out. Frustrated and disgusted once again, I threw the folder and Bria's picture down on the coffee table and got to my feet.

My sudden movements rattled the framed drawings on the mantel. Fletcher's drawing—the one of the pig sign over the Pork Pit—slid down. I stared at it a moment. Then I sighed.

The old man had compiled the information about my family's murder for a reason. He just hadn't told me what it was before he'd been murdered. It wasn't his fault I wasn't smart enough to figure it out—or find Bria. Something I wasn't quite sure I even wanted to do. It had taken me years to put my family's murder behind me. I didn't know if I wanted to dig up the past again—or how Bria would react when she saw me and learned what I'd been doing all these years.

But nothing was going to be resolved tonight. Not tonight, maybe not ever. Fretting over it wouldn't help me unravel the mysteries Fletcher Lane had left behind. Sighing, I went over and ran my fingers over each one of the four drawings, pushing Fletcher's crooked frame back up into its proper position. Then I turned and headed into the bathroom to wash off the day's grease, grime, and blood.

❈ 4 ❈

"I'm going to kill this person," I said in a cold voice.
"Slowly. Painfully. Really make it hurt. Really make him
feel it."

I slapped the morning edition of the *Ashland Trumpet* down onto the empty space beside the cash register.
There it was, on top of the B section. A story detailing the
attempted robbery at the Pork Pit last night, along with
a file shot of the outside of the restaurant. The headline
read "Owner, cook thwart restaurant robbery" and ran
all the way across the damn page in fifty-four-point type.

I drew in a breath, but the grease and spices that flavored the air from the morning's cooking didn't soothe
me the way they usually did. I stared at the newspaper
again, wondering how I'd been so sloppy as to get the
Pork Pit plastered across the front of it.

Publicity was one thing I didn't need. The very *last*
thing I needed. I hadn't advertised my services when I'd

been a working assassin, and I certainly didn't want to broadcast my whereabouts now that I was retired. Not that anyone had any reason to suspect that Gin Blanco, restaurant owner and part-time college student, was actually the renowned assassin the Spider. But still I worried. Paranoia was good. It had kept me alive this long. No reason to abandon it now.

"Come on, Gin. It's not that bad," a deep, male voice cut into my brooding. "At least he made you out to be the hero instead of the villain. How often does that happen?"

I glared at Finnegan Lane, who sat on a stool across from me drinking a cup of chicory coffee. Finnegan looked every bit like the smooth-talking, money-swindling investment banker he was. A fitted gray suit draped over his solid frame, along with a matching wool coat. His starched, tailored sage shirt brightened his eyes, which were the slick green of a soda pop bottle. His walnut-colored hair curled over the collar of his coat. His thick locks had a sexy, stylish, rumpled look that had taken Finn at least ten minutes, two mirrors, and several squirts of product to obtain.

In addition to being my money man, Finnegan Lane was also the son of my mentor, Fletcher. Finn was like a brother to me and one of the few people I trusted since the old man's murder. Finn was also my handler now, for lack of a better word. He didn't like my decision to retire, as it robbed him of his lucrative fifteen percent handling fee, but he understood why I'd done it. That I was honoring Fletcher's wishes. Besides, Finn had plenty of other less-than-legal schemes to keep him busy—when he wasn't out fucking anything in a miniskirt or attending some high-society function and rubbing elbows with his clients who were even more devious, crooked, and dangerous than he was.

"Besides," Finn continued in a matter-of-fact voice. "You can't kill the reporter. Nobody wants him dead, ergo, there's no one to pay your rather substantial fee. And working for nothing is just a crime."

Finn took another sip of his coffee. I drew in a breath, letting the rich caffeine fumes fill my lungs. Fletcher had drunk the same chicory coffee when he'd been alive, and the familiar roasted smell comforted me better than a warm hug. Finn was right. I couldn't kill the reporter for doing his job. No matter how much trouble he'd just caused me with his story.

"All right, so I won't kill him," I said. "How about you ruin his credit instead? Call in his mortgage or something?"

"Mortgages," Finn scoffed. "Dime a dozen in this city, penny ante, and not worth the trouble."

He drained the rest of his coffee and stared at me. "What about the kid, the would-be robber? Did you know he was Jonah McAllister's son when you broke his wrist and threatened to slit him from groin to gills?"

"It wasn't a threat so much as a promise." I shrugged. "And no. Didn't matter to me who his daddy was then, and it doesn't matter to me now."

Finn swiveled around on his stool and looked at the rest of the restaurant. Just before noon on a Tuesday. Despite the gray clouds and cold, rainy weather outside, I should have had at least twenty customers by now, with more coming in every minute, all eager to get their barbecue fix on, and the phone ringing off the hook with take-out orders. Instead, a lone girl huddled in a booth in the back of the restaurant, out of sight of the storefront windows.

Nobody else sat at the long counter or in the booths. Not a single person stood outside staring in through the windows, and no one had called for take-out. Not even my Tuesday regulars. Hell, nobody besides the girl had come in all morning, not even the mailman. He'd just slid the day's bills through the mail slot and scurried on to the next stop on his route as though this were a house of lepers.

"And you wonder why you don't have any customers," Finn murmured. "Jonah McAllister's put the word out that you are persona non grata. And I'm sure the story in the newspaper didn't help matters, either. Nobody wants to eat someplace where they might not have cleaned up the blood yet."

"What does McAllister think he's going to do?" I asked. "He can't keep people away forever. The food's too good. Even if he could, I still wouldn't starve."

"Thanks to my years of wise monetary advice and stellar investing skills," Finn not so humbly stated.

I rolled my eyes. "Yeah, thanks to your skills. If Jonah McAllister thinks a couple of days of lousy business are going to intimidate me into dropping the charges against his loser kid, then he needs to think some more."

"Jonah McAllister doesn't know who he's dealing with," Finn replied. "If he knew you were the assassin the Spider, he'd probably just borrow a couple of Mab

Monroe's giants to try to kill you before you could testify against him."

"Former assassin," I corrected. "And let Jonah McAllister send some of Mab's goons after me. We both know exactly how that would turn out."

Finn snorted. "Yeah, with their blood on the floor of the restaurant."

I grinned. "C'mon. You have to admit I do good work."

"Deadly work, perhaps. You know how I feel about the word *good*." He shuddered.

Like me, Finnegan Lane was firmly entrenched in the shady side of life, with morals that bent easier than wet grass. Banking regulations, married women, public indecency laws. Finn fucked around with whatever and whomever he could without getting caught. Even when he did, he always found a way to wriggle out of whatever messy love triangle he currently found himself in. Finn was more slippery than grease on a hot skillet. He preferred to tackle problems in a roundabout way, which usually involved pulling his pants up while he ran away from whatever gun-toting husband was hot on his trail.

Me? I went at my problems straight on—and knife point first. Another reason Fletcher Lane had trained me to be the assassin, and not his son, even though Finn was two years older than me.

Finn held up his empty cup and let out a low whistle between his teeth. A moment later, Sophia came through the double doors that led to the back of the restaurant. The dwarf clenched a battered silver coffeepot in her stubby fingers. The one she always kept warm for Finn. Fletcher too, before he'd died. Once again, Sophia wore her usual Goth outfit—black jeans, a black T-shirt, and black boots. Today, dainty silverstone hearts hung from her black leather collar. They clanged and clashed like cymbals as she walked.

"Sophia? Pretty please?" Finn smiled and held out his empty cup.

The Goth dwarf grunted, but the corners of her lips, crimson today, twitched upward into a tiny smile. Finnegan Lane could charm any woman he set his mind to, and he enjoyed practicing his skills on every female within a twenty-foot radius. Young, old, pretty, toothless. Didn't much matter to Finn. He enjoyed playing the part of the old-fashioned, charming, Southern gentleman to whatever audience was handy. Even the gruff, tough Sophia Deveraux wasn't immune to his lady-killer smile. Then again, he'd had thirty-two years to wear her down.

Finn batted his green eyes at Sophia while he sipped his fresh cup of coffee. Sophia gave him another minuscule smile, then moved over to the double sink, where she was draining a colander of elbow macaroni to make some salad. Normally, during the lunch hour rush, there wouldn't be room to move or turn around back here. Waitresses would be stacked three deep behind the counter, waiting on Sophia and me to cook up their latest order. But it was just the two of us today. I'd sent the rest of the staff home with pay, after it had become apparent I wouldn't need them to man the Pork Pit.

"What about Owen Grayson?" Finn asked between sips of steaming coffee. "How are you going to cash in that favor?"

Grayson's visit hadn't made the newspaper article, but

I'd mentioned it to Finn last night when I'd called to tell him about the attempted robbery at the Pork Pit. He'd been more excited about Owen Grayson owing me a favor than the fact Sophia and I had foiled the would-be robbers.

"I'm not," I said. "I would have done the exact same thing to Jake McAllister and his friend if a couple of homeless guys had been eating here instead of Eva Grayson. Saving her from getting dead doesn't change anything for me."

Finn shook his head. "Gin, Gin, Gin. You really need to learn to take advantage of these golden opportunities when they present themselves to you."

"And what golden opportunity would that be?"

He gave me a calculating look. "I've had dealings with Owen Grayson before. He's deeply devoted to his sister. Their parents died young, and he raised her himself. A real family guy that way. I imagine you could ask him for the moon right now, and he'd find a way to deliver it."

"Good thing I don't want the moon then."

"But—" Finn started.

"Forget it," I said. "I'm not asking Owen Grayson for anything. All I want to do is cook Fletcher's barbecue sauce, run the restaurant, keep my head down, and make sure Jake McAllister gets what's coming to him."

"Even with your testimony, and the girls' testimony, it'll never go to trial," Finn pointed out. "Jonah McAllister will make sure his boy won't spend a day in jail, no matter what he has to do to accomplish that feat."

"And what if I called in that favor Owen Grayson owes me?" I asked. "You know, take advantage of this *golden opportunity* I have? Asked him to help me make the charges stick?"

Finn snorted. "Then you'd be wasting your favor, and you know it. Even if you got Owen Grayson to back you up, Jake McAllister still would never see the inside of a jail cell. Because Jonah works for Mab Monroe. Even somebody like Grayson would think twice about crossing Mab, especially since he has his sister to think about. I imagine Owen would like to be around to help her finish growing up and not die a fiery, torture-filled death at the hands of Mab or one of her giant flunkies."

"I know. But it's still a nice thought. The idea of Jake McAllister being somebody's prison yard bitch gives me the warm fuzzies."

Finn snorted. "You are deeply disturbed."

I grinned. "And that's why you love me."

Finn snorted again, then batted his eyes at Sophia to get another refill on his chicory coffee. After the dwarf obliged him, Finn stuck his nose in the financial section of the *Ashland Trumpet*, reading a wire story by some reporter named Carmen Cole. I leaned my elbows on the counter, stared at the newspaper photo of the Pork Pit, and brooded about my unwanted publicity. Maybe the reporter could have a small accident. Something painful, but not immediately lethal—

A shadow fell over me, blocking my light. "Ahem." A small, polite sound.

I looked up. My lone customer of the day, the girl, stood in front of me. My eyes immediately flicked to the dishes on her table, the way they always did. I liked knowing my customers enjoyed their meals, and there was no better proof of that than an empty plate.

But food still covered the girl's dishes. She'd barely

touched her grilled cheese sandwich, steak-cut fries, and triple chocolate milkshake. A shame, really. Because with Sophia's sourdough bread, I made the best grilled cheese in Ashland. And the milkshake? Heaven for your taste buds.

The girl cleared her throat again and held out the ticket I'd written her order down on.

"Was there something wrong with your food?" I asked. "Because it doesn't look like you ate a lot of it."

"Oh, it was fine." She shifted on her feet. "Guess I just wasn't as hungry as I thought I was."

I frowned. Everybody got hungry in the Pork Pit. No true Southerner could resist the combination of spices, grease, and artery-clogging fat in the air. But the girl couldn't be a Yankee. Not with that soft drawl that made her voice ooze like warm strawberry preserves. More than likely, she'd thought there was something wrong with the food, considering no one else had been brave enough to come in and try it today. I'd never met Jonah McAllister, but I already disliked the man.

I rang up her total. "That'll be $7.97."

The girl dug through her wallet and handed me a credit card. I raised an eyebrow.

"Sorry," she mumbled. "I don't have any cash on me."

I glanced at the name on the card. *Violet Fox.* I swiped the card through the machine and passed the girl the paper slip to sign. Her cursive was a loopy, feminine swirl.

I tucked the slip under the corner of the battered cash register and gave her my standard, y'all-please-come-back smile. "Have a nice day."

Then I went back to the newspaper.

But the girl didn't move. She just stood there in front of the register, like she wanted something else but didn't know how to ask for it. I decided to let her squirm for ignoring my grilled cheese sandwich. Ten . . . twenty . . . I ticked off the seconds in my head. Thirty . . . forty—

"Um, this might sound strange, but is there an old man who works here?" she asked. "Maybe in the back or something?"

Fletcher. She was asking about Fletcher. Not unusual. The old man and the Pork Pit had been a downtown Ashland institution for more than fifty years. Fletcher Lane had been gone two months now, and people still came in and asked about him. Where he was. How he was doing. When he was coming back. I stared at the copy of *Where the Red Fern Grows* that adorned the wall beside the cash register. Fletcher had been reading the book when he'd died, and the old man's blood had turned the paperback pages a rusty brown.

"No," I said in a quiet voice. "The old man isn't here anymore."

"Are you sure?" she persisted. "He might . . . he might call himself something. Tin Man, I think."

Tin Man. That got my attention. Enough to make me palm one of the silverstone knives tucked up my sleeve. Every assassin has a moniker, a discreet name they go by to ply their services and perhaps give potential customers a clue as to how they operate or off their victims. Tin Man had been Fletcher's name because he'd never let his heart, his emotions, get in the way of a job. But once he'd taken me under his wing and started training me to be an assassin, the old man had cut back on his own jobs and eventually retired from the business altogether. Nobody had asked for the Tin Man in a long, long time.

Except this girl.

For the first time, I really looked at her. *Girl* probably wasn't the right term for her. With her ample breasts, wide hips, and curved booty, she was a full-grown woman. Still young, though. Eighteen, maybe nineteen. She probably thought she was twenty pounds too heavy, but the extra weight rounded her face and filled out her chest.

Square black glasses gave her a slightly brainy air. Her sandy blond hair was cropped short, and the rain outside had turned it into a mound of frizz. Her dark brown eyes and pecan-colored skin whispered of some Hispanic or maybe even Native American ancestry. The Cherokee still inhabited the mountains around Ashland, just as they had before the Civil War, before the settlers, before, well, everything.

I continued my examination. She wore jeans faded from wear, not design, and a heavy black turtleneck sweater that made her eyes seem darker than they were. Scuffed sneakers, a heavy jacket, some silver hoops in her ears. Nothing on her cost more than fifty bucks. Which didn't inspire confidence about her even being able to afford an assassin like the Tin Man.

The words *Tin Man* had also gotten the others' attention. Finn peered at the girl over the top of the financial section. Sophia looked up from the celery she'd been chopping for her macaroni salad.

"Tin Man?" I asked. "That's a funny name."

The girl, Violet, forced out a smile that wilted under my cold gray gaze. "Yeah, that's what I thought too."

"There's nobody here by that name. No old man, either."

Not anymore.

Out of sight below the counter, my thumb traced over the hilt of the silverstone knife that I'd palmed. Violet Fox might look about as dangerous as a wet kitten, but that didn't mean she wasn't working for someone else. Maybe someone who wanted to hire the mysterious Tin Man. Someone looking for revenge. Or maybe even the cops. Didn't much matter who. If the girl breathed wrong, she was going to die where she stood.

Violet chewed her lower lip. For a moment, I thought she might ask me about Fletcher again. But after a moment, her shoulders drooped in defeat.

"Doesn't matter," she said in a tired voice. "He couldn't have helped me anyway. Sorry to bother you."

She turned to go. I glanced at Finn, who shrugged. He didn't know what to make of it either. Sophia grunted and turned back to her celery.

"He couldn't have helped you with what?" I called out.

Curiosity. Something the old man had instilled in me over the years. Fletcher Lane had always wanted to know everything about everyone, and he'd taught me to be the same way. Now it was the one emotion that always seemed to get the best of me, no matter how hard I tried to squash it.

The girl, Violet, turned to look at me. "Oh, um, well, it's sort of personal—"

That's all she got out before someone started shooting at us.

A bullet smacked into one of the storefront windows.

The sharp, sudden burst of sound caught the girl's attention. Her head snapped toward the front of the restaurant. "What was that—"

That was all Violet got out before I darted around the counter and threw myself on top of her, forcing her to the floor.

"Oof!"

We hit the ground hard. I knocked the wind out of the girl, but I didn't care. Until I figured out what she wanted with the Tin Man, Violet Fox needed to keep breathing.

I didn't have to worry about Finn. Like me, he knew exactly what that particular sound was and had heard it too many times before to ignore it now. Somehow, he'd already wormed under one of the tables, with several chairs further shielding him. Finnegan Lane had an excellent sense of self-preservation.

Sophia stood by the back counter and kept chopping celery. She didn't even look up at the crack of the gunshot. Bullets didn't worry her. Dwarves were even tougher than giants, and Sophia could take a couple bullets in the back. They'd catch her in hard muscles long before they hit anything vital. Elemental magic was just about the only thing that could quickly penetrate a dwarf's thick skin. And even the majority of that would only make her angry, instead of doing any real damage.

Smack!

Smack! Smack!

Three more bullets slammed into the front of the restaurant. I looked up, trying to judge where the shots were coming from, but my angle from the floor was all wrong. I could see the storefront windows, but not who or what lay beyond them.

My eyes flicked to the projectiles. A large caliber, probably a fifty, from the looks of them. And whoever was shooting knew what he was doing. Despite their size, the bullets formed a small, circular cluster about the size of my fist. Kill shots, all of them.

The four metal missiles had cracked and caught in the storefront glass, which kept them from punching through into the Pork Pit itself. Still, the sharp, sudden impacts had ruined the windows. Macabre patterns ran out from the bullets, as though a swarm of spiders were stringing their delicate webs through the thick glass.

I shook one of my sleeves, and a knife slipped into my other hand, the hilt resting on the scar on my palm. I hoped the bastard got tired of shooting through the windows and decided to come inside and finish the job. He'd be in for a nasty surprise. One he wouldn't recover from.

With every breath, I expected more bullets to slam into the windows. Or for the door to be yanked open and someone to storm inside. Jake McAllister, most likely, trying to make good on his threat to come back and kill me.

Instead—silence.

I counted off the seconds in my head. Ten . . . twenty . . . thirty . . . forty-five . . .

The girl shifted, trying to get out from underneath me. Or at least get her face up off the floor. I rolled off her so she could catch her breath, but I kept one hand on her back, holding her in place.

"Be still," I snapped. "He could be waiting for us to get to our feet before he fires another shot."

Violet nodded and lay on the floor, sucking in deep breaths through her open mouth.

After ninety seconds had passed without another gunshot, I rose to my knees and looked outside. The cracked glass distorted my vision, but I didn't see anyone standing directly outside the restaurant, gun in hand. No parked cars idling at the curb. No one running down the sidewalk.

I stood up and examined the bullets. Fifty caliber all the way around, probably from a rifle. Not what I'd expected from somebody like Jake McAllister. He struck me as an Uzi kind of guy. Something showy, something flashy, something to prove what a badass he was.

I also noticed the bullets hadn't hit the glass dead-on. They'd struck at a downward angle, which meant they'd been fired from somewhere higher up. Hmm. I moved off to one side to a section of glass that hadn't been cracked by the bullets and peered outside.

There. Across the street, curtains flapped against an open window on the second floor of an apartment building. Not an unusual sight—in the summer. But it was November. Fifty degrees out, with a steady drizzle of cold rain. Nobody in his right mind would have his window open on a day like this unless he had a good reason. Like trying to kill me.

Made sense. I hadn't heard a car peel away from the curb after the shots had been fired, and I didn't see any new tread marks on the street outside, which meant it hadn't been a drive-by. Jake McAllister had been stationary when he'd put four bullets into the front of my restaurant. My eyes focused on the flapping curtain. Time to see if the cuckoo had left his nest or not.

"Stay here," I told Finn.

"Where are you going?" Finn asked from underneath the table.

I gripped my knives a little tighter. "To find the bastard who just ruined my storefront windows."

Normally, I wouldn't have gone out the front door of the Pork Pit. Not after somebody had just shot up my windows. That was just asking for trouble, for the shooter to put a bullet in my chest when I stepped outside to investigate. But I was angry, and I had my elemental magic. So I reached for my Stone power, pulling it up into my veins, letting the cool magic spread out over my skin. It took less than a second for the magic to harden my fingers, torso, toes, and everything in between, to turn my body into a rock-hard shell. As long as I held onto my magic, kept concentrating on it, even my hair would stop a bullet.

Then I yanked open the door and stepped outside.

I stood by the front door a few seconds, my eyes scanning the block again. Nothing. No runners, no parked cars, no flash of light from a rifle scope in the window across the street.

After another thirty seconds, when no more bullets zipped through the air, the people who'd been on the street when the shooting started slowly raised their heads. One by one, they eased out from behind the parked cars and metal mailboxes that they'd ducked behind, got to their feet, and hurried on about their business.

Since the gunman hadn't taken the easy shot I'd offered him, I marched across the street to the apartment building, an older structure with small, dingy windows and a chipped façade that hadn't been upgraded or renovated since it had been built forty years ago. I pressed my hand against the stone that framed the entrance, listening to the murmur of the cold, wet brick underneath my bare fingers. A mishmash of emotions greeted me. Childish shrieks of glee. Older, adult grumbles. Sharp, worried murmurs. A babble of English and Spanish. It all added up to the noises of a typical apartment building. Nothing unusual so far.

Older buildings often lacked good security features, and this one was no different. There wasn't even a lock on the glass door to keep out the homeless stragglers. The door led to a small hallway with stairs branching off either side, and an elevator lying at the end. I headed up the west stairs, staying to the shadows. The building smelled like bleach mixed with garlic and urine.

I reached the second-floor landing and another empty hallway. The walk across the street and up the stairs had cooled my anger. My skin might be as hard as stone, but all it took was one moment, one waver, one second I let my magic slip to get dead. Fletcher Lane had drilled that into me. Jake McAllister might be a punk, but that didn't mean he couldn't get lucky and kill me. I wasn't going to give him that chance, so I paused to listen and evaluate.

Muted quiet. Most of the building's tenants were out working at their day jobs, trying to come up with enough cash for next month's rent. My fingers tightened around the knives in my hands, and I crept forward. Since he hadn't taken a shot at me when I'd crossed the street, there was a very slim chance Jake McAllister was still in the apartment. But I continued to move cautiously, quietly. Three apartments on this floor faced the street. I tip-toed past the first two doors to the third one—the one I wanted.

I paused in front of the beige-painted door, waiting and listening. More silence. I put my hand on the stone that framed the door, but its murmur was low and muted. Nobody lived here, judging from the lack of emotions and vibrations, which was probably why Jake McAllister had picked this apartment to fire from.

I closed my hand around the knob. The cold metal tickled the spider rune scar on my palm. The knob turned, and the door opened.

I nudged the door inward with my boot, careful to stay to one side of the door frame. It didn't even creak as it swung open. I stayed in the hall and waited, counting off the seconds in my head. Ten . . . twenty . . . thirty . . . Noises from the other apartments farther down the hall leaked out to me. A television blaring out some children's cartoon. Another one tuned to a soap opera. A couple arguing about Ralph drinking too much and getting fired from his latest job.

I stayed outside three minutes. Empty. The apartment was empty. If Jake McAllister had been inside to see or hear the door open, he would have come out to investigate by now. Most people weren't good at waiting. They moved too soon, too quickly, and then they got dead. A minute was enough to unnerve most people. Three, enough to drive all but the most consummate professional assassin crazy with adrenaline. Even I didn't like waiting three minutes for something to happen. But there was a reason Fletcher had dubbed me the Spider— because I could be infinitely patient. Because I had that internal restraint. Because I could wait those long, long three minutes, if it meant getting to my target—or not becoming one myself.

I slipped inside the apartment and closed the door behind me.

It was a small space, divided up into even smaller rooms that reminded me of a rat's maze. Knives in hands, I slipped from one room to the next, checking them all with extreme caution and care.

Empty. The place was totally empty.

No furniture, no appliances, not even a couple of fast-food wrappers crumpled and discarded on the linoleum floor. It didn't even smell of anything except the cold rain gusting in through the open window. Not bleach, not food, nothing. I frowned. Not what I'd expected. Jake McAllister didn't strike me as a patient person—much less the kind to pick up after himself. If the Fire elemental had been up here for any length of time, there should have been some evidence of it. Beer cans, cigarettes, an empty soda bottle, some candy bar wrappers. Instead, there was nothing. I didn't even see any roach traps hidden in the corners.

I dropped my Stone magic and let my skin revert back to its normal texture. Then I moved to the back of the apartment and the open window where the shooter had been when he'd fired into the Pork Pit.

Again, there was nothing. No cups, no wrappers, no evidence anyone had been inside the apartment today or anytime in the recent past. I peered under the window. He'd even policed his brass, picking up the spent shell casings from the bullets he'd fired. Again, not something I would expect from a reckless, twitchy, Fire elemental hothead like Jake McAllister.

Dingy exposed brick outlined the window, and I pressed my hand against it. The uneven stone bit into my palm, and I closed my eyes and reached for my magic again, letting the cool power flow through me, attuning myself to the smallest vibrations embedded in the brick.

Nothing. Just calm. I concentrated, going deeper and deeper into the stone, until it felt like a part of me. A natural extension of myself I could examine and analyze the way I might my own fingernails. I felt more calm and . . . the sense of someone waiting. Not particularly bored, but not excited either. Just waiting . . . for the right moment to come along. An emotion, an action, I knew all too well.

My frown deepened. I opened my eyes, dropped my hand, and stepped away from the brick. I looked at the room again with a more critical eye, putting all the facts together.

There was nothing in the apartment, no trash, no shell casings, no emotions, because Jake McAllister hadn't been here. He wasn't smart enough, wasn't calm enough for this sort of action. This—this was the work of a professional.

An assassin, just like me.

My gray eyes narrowed. So Jake, or more likely Jonah McAllister, had hired a big boy to clean up his son's mess. Now I was really annoyed.

But still . . . I couldn't shake the feeling I was missing something. Something important. Vital. Obvious. My reading, my sense, of the vibrations in the stone was correct. I knew it was. Even from an early age, I'd been able to hear the stone murmuring to me, and my power to understand and interpret it had only sharpened and strengthened over time. And would continue to do so until I died, hopefully at the ripe age of a hundred and fifty or so.

From the vibrations I'd picked up, the shooter had been waiting the better part of an hour. Maybe longer. Sophia came in early, usually by nine, to start baking the day's bread. I usually showed up around ten, and the restaurant officially opened for business at eleven. But the shots hadn't been fired until almost noon.

Why? Why had the assassin waited so long? I'd been

moving through the restaurant all morning. Cooking, cleaning, wiping off the tables and booths, flipping the sign on the front door over to *Open*. He could have taken me out at any time during the morning. So why hadn't he taken a shot before lunchtime? Why then?

I went back over the shooting in my mind. I'd been standing behind the counter when the shots had been fired. A tough shot to make, even for a professional assassin, no matter how good with a gun he was. Maybe he'd wanted an audience when he killed me. Maybe that's why he'd waited. Finn had been in the restaurant, sitting off to my right. The girl had been there too, more or less in front of me—

And I realized what I'd been missing. The shooter, the assassin, hadn't been firing at me.

He'd been aiming at the girl.

But I'd been aiming at the girl.

✹ 6 ✹

The girl, Violet. The shooter had been aiming at her, not at me.

That was the only thing that made sense. The assassin could have shot me anytime I'd been close to the storefront windows. But he hadn't. Instead, he'd sat in this apartment for almost an hour, waiting for her. She'd been sitting in a booth in the back, out of sight of the storefront windows, so he'd had to wait for her to finish her lunch. When she'd paid and started for the front door, that's when he'd taken his shot.

My mind processed the information and moved on to the next question. Why shoot her inside the restaurant? Why not wait for her to step outside onto the street? Why not just do her in some back alley?

The answer came to me. The robbery. The assassin must have seen the story in the newspaper about the botched robbery at the Pork Pit.

Maybe the assassin had realized that if he took out the girl in the restaurant, there was a good chance her death would be connected to Jake McAllister and the robbery last night. No doubt the cops would have had the same first thought as me—that Jake or whomever he might have hired had been aiming at me, not the girl. That I'd been the target. That Jake had wanted to silence me and make all the charges against himself just disappear. Given all that, the police wouldn't be inclined to look too hard in other directions, to consider other theories. Like the fact the girl had been the intended victim all along.

And if laying the blame on Jake McAllister didn't work, well, there was another option. The Pork Pit wasn't officially located in Southtown, but it was only a couple of blocks over, which meant the whole area had its share of crime. Drug deals, shootings, domestic disputes. One or more of those happened every day of the week.

Given the rough neighborhood, the girl's death today might have just been chalked up to random violence in the area, if the cops were feeling particularly lazy. Some sort of drive-by or gang shooting that she'd been unlucky enough to get in the middle of. A ten-year-old kid and his younger sister had gotten caught up in one of those last week, less than a half mile from the restaurant.

Either way, nobody would think it had been a planned hit. The best assassinations were always the ones that looked like something else. A nice, neat, easy plan all the way around.

Maybe the assassin had been following the girl, looking for just such an opportunity. Maybe he'd known she was coming to the Pork Pit today to eat lunch and ask about somebody named the Tin Man. Either way, when she'd gone into the restaurant, he'd decided to make sure that she never came out again. It would have been easy for him to slip into the building unseen, find the empty apartment, and jimmy the lock. All he would have had to do after that was wait for the right moment, the right angle, and then pull the trigger.

I stared at the cracked storefront of the Pork Pit. He would have hit her too—four kill shots clustered in her chest.

If the restaurant didn't have bulletproof windows.

No, this didn't have anything to do with Jake McAllister and me. The girl—it was all about the girl. Somebody wanted her dead.

As I stood there brooding, the front door of the restaurant opened. Violet stepped outside and hurried away.

"Fuck," I snarled and sprinted from the apartment.

The assassin was long gone, so I didn't bother reaching for my Stone magic to harden my skin again. Besides, he wasn't after me anyway. Instead, I ran down the stairs and out of the apartment building. I hung a left and sprinted down the block in the direction the girl had gone.

She must have been power walking because she was already a full block ahead of me. She raised her arm, and a cab slid to a stop at the curb in front of her.

"Hey, you!" I yelled. "Stop!"

The girl paid no attention to me. I was too far away for my voice to carry over the traffic on the street. Even if she had heard my cry, she probably wouldn't have thought it was directed at her. *Hey, you* wasn't the most personal of greetings. So I picked up my pace, running at a full sprint. If the street had been empty, I might have reached her. But every five steps, I had to duck right or left to avoid someone talking on their cell phone.

I reached the end of the block. On the corner across from me, the girl had settled into the cab. I stepped out onto the street, my eyes fixed on the bright yellow vehicle—

Beep! Beep!

And abruptly stepped back as a car horn blared out. A second later, a minivan zoomed by, running the red light. The driver shot me a dirty look.

"Red means stop, you twit!" I screamed.

She didn't see me flip her off. Too busy nattering away on her cell phone to do something safe, like pay attention to pedestrians and traffic signals. And she'd cost me any chance I'd had of catching the girl. Up ahead, the cab had already pulled out into traffic. Five seconds later, it turned right, disappearing from sight.

Gone. The girl was gone.

And I had no idea where she went or more importantly, why someone had tried to kill her.

I stood there a moment, cursing my own stupidity. I should have known the second the girl asked for the Tin Man that something was seriously wrong. That it wasn't just a fluke or an accident or dumb luck. That trouble had just walked into the Pork Pit.

Trouble that had gotten away from me.

"Fuck," I snarled again before turning and heading back to the restaurant.

*   *   *

I tucked my knives up my sleeves and slowly, calmly, quietly strolled the block back to the Pork Pit. No need to draw any more attention to myself today. If I kept this up, somebody might call the police and report a crazy woman. Not too long ago, I'd spent several days in Ashland Asylum on one of my jobs. I had no desire to pay the facility a return visit.

A couple minutes later, I stepped into the Pork Pit. Sophia was adding some red pepper and paprika to her macaroni salad. Finn sat on his usual stool, sipping another cup of chicory coffee and reading the rest of the financial section.

"Problems?" he quipped.

I gave him a sour glare.

"I only ask because a) you're not smiling and covered in someone else's blood, and b) I saw you run out of the building across the street like there were a pack of hungry vampires after you," Finn said. "I take it Jake McAllister managed to allude you?"

I shook my head. "It wasn't McAllister. The shooter wasn't even gunning for me. He was aiming at the girl."

I filled Finn and Sophia in on my theory about the shooter being a pro and my conclusion his target had been the girl, not me.

Finn let out a low whistle. "Someone hired an assassin to take out the girl? She must have really pissed somebody off."

"Mmm-hmm." Behind the counter, Sophia grunted her agreement.

"I don't care who she's pissed off right now," I snapped.

"I just need to find her before the assassin decides to make another run at her."

"Why?" Finn asked. "It's her problem, not yours."

I stared at him. "Because she comes in here asking about the Tin Man, asking about Fletcher, and a minute later, somebody's shooting at her. I want to know why. Why she came here, what her connection to Fletcher is, all of it."

Mainly, I wanted to make sure there was no way her almost or future murder was going to get laid on my doorstep or on Finn or the Deveraux sisters. Covering myself had been one of the first things Fletcher Lane had taught me.

"Now, what happened after I left? Did she say anything, do anything?"

Finn shook his head. "No. She sat there a minute getting her breath back; then she got up and left."

My gray eyes narrowed. "And you didn't try to stop her?"

Finn shrugged. "I figured as long as she wasn't screaming and calling the cops, it was all right. We both thought it was Jake McAllister shooting at you, not somebody else gunning for her."

I bit back another curse. Finn was right. It wasn't his fault. It wasn't anybody's fault. Still, I needed some answers, and the girl was the only one who could give them to me. But she was miles away by now. So how could I track her down? I thought for a second, then went over to the counter.

"Uh-oh," Finn muttered. "I know that look."

"What look?" I asked, lifting up the cash register.

"That look. The one that makes you resemble a hibernating bear someone just poked with a sharp stick. The look that says you're not going to let this go, even though it's not your problem."

I put my hand over my heart and batted my lashes at him. "You know me all too well."

"But how are you going to find her?" Finn asked. "She didn't exactly leave you a personal dossier."

My fingers probed the dark space under the cash register. There it was. I pulled out a scrap of paper from beneath the register. The girl's credit card receipt from lunch. The one with her name on it. *Violet Fox.* Not as good as a dossier, but it was a place to start.

"Oh, I'm not going to find her," I said in a sweet voice.

"Don't say it," he pleaded. "Please don't say it."

I held the piece of paper out to him. "I'm not going to find her because you're going to do it for me."

Finn just sighed and took another sip of his coffee.

7

"Anything yet?"

Finn glared over his shoulder at me. "It's only been a few hours, Gin. Keep your panties on."

I glared back and stuck my tongue out at him.

He grinned. "Don't stick it out unless you plan to use it."

I snorted. "You wish."

"Always."

After I'd told Finn to track down the college girl using her credit card receipt, he'd gone to his office to get his laptop and some other supplies and tell the money men he was taking the rest of the day off. While he'd done that, I'd scheduled an appointment for a glazier to come fix the storefront windows in the morning. Then I'd sent Sophia home, closed down the restaurant, and driven to Fletcher's house. That had taken two hours.

Finn had shown up thirty minutes ago. Now he relaxed on the faded plaid sofa in the den, while I puttered around in the kitchen. Given all the excitement, I hadn't had a chance to eat lunch at the restaurant, and I had a feeling it was going to be a long night. That's why I'd made chicken salad sandwiches on thick, honey-wheat bread, along with a fresh fruit salad.

I put the food on a tray, along with plates, silverware, napkins, and a pitcher of raspberry lemonade. Then I reached for my Ice magic. The cold, silver light flickered on my palm, centered in the spider rune scar, and I dropped several Ice cubes into the two glasses on the tray. I took the whole thing into the den and set it on the coffee table.

I sat cross-legged in one of the recliners and munched on a sandwich. Celery, apples, golden raisins, lemon zest, and a sour cream–mayo dressing flavored the chicken salad, while the crusty bread provided crunch and contrast. I alternated with bites of my strawberry-and-kiwi fruit salad, tossed with lime juice, vanilla, and just a hint of honey.

Finn also helped himself to a sandwich and some fruit, and we ate in silence. Finn's laptop whirred softly as it sorted through billions of bytes of data, looking for info on one Violet Fox.

After he'd wolfed down his first sandwich, Finn reached for another. He jerked his head at the far side of the coffee table, where he'd slid the folder Fletcher Lane had left me—the one that contained the information on my murdered family and Bria, my baby sister, who was still alive. Finn had moved the folder out of the way so he could set his laptop on the ancient table.

"Any luck with that?" Finn asked.

"No."

Shortly after Fletcher's funeral, I'd told Finn about the file and the secrets it held, including my real name—Genevieve Snow. I'd let him sort through the information and draw his own conclusions about everything else. Including what had happened the night my mother, Eira, and older sister, Annabella, had been murdered by a Fire elemental. For a moment, orange flames filled my vision. The image of two burned husks of bodies flashed before my eyes, and the air smelled of charred flesh. I willed the memory away.

"You should let me help you with that," Finn said. "I have contacts you don't."

I shook my head. "No. Not . . . yet. I still don't know how I feel about it."

"About what?"

"About the old man knowing who I really was all these years and not saying anything to me about it. About him collecting all that information about my family."

The spider rune scars on my palms started itching, the way they always did when I thought about my dead, lost family. A small circle with eight thin lines radiating out of it. The symbol for patience. I rubbed first one scar with my fingers, then the other, trying to ease the burning sensation. Didn't work. Never did.

"Fletcher loved ferreting out people's secrets. Compiling information, dossiers on them. It made him a good assassin and an even better handler," I said. "I just never thought he'd do it to *me*."

"You're angry at him."

"Hell, yeah, I'm angry," I snapped. My toes pushed off the floor, and the recliner rocked back. "Fletcher spends years putting that folder together and then leaves it with Jo-Jo Deveraux instead of giving it to me. Why? What's the point?"

I was angry, of course, but more than that, I felt betrayed. Like Fletcher Lane had regarded me as nothing more than a mark to gather intel on. Like I wasn't the daughter he'd claimed me to be. Like he hadn't ever really loved me the way that I'd loved him. Or at least trusted me enough to tell me what he was doing.

And I was angry at myself too, because I'd had no clue what the old man had been up to, that he'd been out gathering information on me and my murdered family. I'd never even dreamed that Fletcher would do such a thing—at least not to *me*. Or maybe I just hadn't wanted to consider the possibility. Either way, all that I had left now were questions and more questions.

"Maybe he was planning to give it to you," Finn said. "Before he died."

Another image flashed before my eyes. Fletcher Lane, lying in a pool of his own blood at the Pork Pit, the skin flayed and ripped from his body. His face and chest and arms and hands a ruined mess of raw flesh and bones. I shook my head, trying to banish the memory. Didn't work. Never did.

"I just don't understand what he expected me to do with the information. Take my revenge on the Fire elemental? It's been years, and I still don't know who she was or why she killed my family. I didn't even *see* the elemental before one of her goons caught and blindfolded me.

Just heard her laughing while she tortured me. For all I know, the bitch could be dead by now."

"She was strong enough to kill your mother and sister, two powerful Ice elementals in their own right, and melt that silverstone spider rune into your palms. I doubt she's dead. People like that don't go quietly," Finn said. "Besides, it was only seventeen years ago. Most elementals live to be well over a hundred."

A cold smile curved my lips. "Can't blame a gal for dreaming, can you?"

I stared at the folder, and my smile flipped into a frown. "I just don't understand *why* Fletcher did it. I was there. I lived through it. Nothing in that file tells me anything I don't already know."

"Except that your sister's alive," Finn said in a soft voice.

Bria. Blond hair. Big, blue eyes. A child's soft, sweet, innocent face. A delicate primrose rune hanging from the chain around her neck. She'd been eight the last time I'd seen her, the night I found her blood in the hiding place where I'd left her. The night I thought she'd died.

"Fat lot of good it does me to know she's alive, since I can't find her. That picture could have been taken anywhere, and Fletcher wasn't kind enough to scribble a location on the back of it." Emotion tightened my throat, and I had to force out my next words. "I don't—I don't even know if I want to find her."

"Why not?" Finn asked. "She's your sister."

"She *was* my sister," I replied in a husky voice. "I have no idea what she's like now. If she remembers me, if she'd even want to see me. Hell, she probably thinks I'm dead, just like I thought she was. Then there's the small fact of what I've been doing with my life. Call me crazy, but I doubt anyone would want an assassin for a big sister."

Finn was silent a moment. Then he raised his head and stared at me with his bright green eyes—eyes that were so similar to Fletcher's it made my heart crack. "You might not have been his biological daughter, but Dad loved you just as much as he did me. You said it yourself. He loved knowing other people's secrets. He probably started digging at first just to see who you really were and whether or not he could trust you."

"And then?"

Finn shrugged. "And then you became his daughter, his protégé, and he loved you. Maybe Dad wanted to find the Fire elemental for you. Maybe he realized Bria hadn't died that night. Maybe he wanted to make up for everything that had been done to you and your family."

I'd wondered those same things myself. Because that's exactly the kind of man Fletcher Lane had been. Live and let live, had been his motto. After all, assassins didn't have a lot of moral high ground to stand on and cast stones and aspersions down at others. But if you fucked with somebody Fletcher Lane cared about, you might as well cut out your own heart with a rusty spoon—before he did it for you. The old man had taught me to be the same way. Loyalty, love, whatever you wanted to call it, it was the only thing as important as survival—and the only thing truly worth dying for. Which is why I'd hunted down Alexis James, the Air elemental bitch who'd killed Fletcher and had Finn tortured, even though I'd almost died in the process.

I rubbed my palm over my forehead. The silverstone metal in my skin felt as hard and cold as my heart. "I don't know what Fletcher wanted me to do. Now I'll never know."

"You'll figure it out," Finn said. "And I'll help you."

Spoken like a true brother, blood or not. I smiled at him. "I know you will—"

Click-click. Click-click.

Finn's laptop spit out a different sort of noise, as though the hard drive had caught and snagged on something. I raised my brows. Finn leaned forward and hit a button. Numbers popped up on his laptop monitor, along with what looked like a driver's license photo. Frizzy blond hair. Dark eyes. Dusky skin. Black glasses.

"Got her," Finn said. "Violet Elizabeth Fox. Credit card records, bank accounts, school transcripts. Read all about her."

I joined him on the sofa and read the information on the screen. Violet Elizabeth Fox, age nineteen, parents deceased. A straight-A student on a full scholarship, getting her business degree at Ashland Community College. A couple hundred bucks' worth of charges on her credit card, a couple thousand in a savings account. A small check deposited every two weeks into her checking account from some business called Country Daze. Probably a part-time job of some sort. Nothing out of the ordinary and nothing to suggest why she'd come into the Pork Pit looking for the Tin Man.

"Violet Fox commutes to school," I said.

"How do you know that?" Finn asked.

I tapped the screen with my fingernail. "Because she's

got an ACC parking permit and assigned slip. And look at her home address."

"Ridgeline Hollow Road?" Finn asked. "That's up in the mountains."

"In the coalfields," I added.

Folks had been carving coal out of the Appalachian Mountains for decades, and rich seams of it ran through the mountains just north of Ashland. Coal mining was dangerous, dirty, hard work, not for the claustrophobic or faint of heart. But it paid well enough for generations of men and women to risk life and limb digging the fossil fuel out of the ground. For some, mining was the only job the members of their family had ever known. For others, the mines were the final resting places of their fathers, mothers, brothers, sisters. Dark, silent tombs no machinery and no light would ever be able to penetrate again.

Click-click. Click-click. The computer sounded once more, and a new screen popped up, overwriting the info we'd been looking at.

"What's that?" I asked.

Finn grinned. "I flagged Violet Fox's credit card, which she just used to make a purchase at the campus bookstore."

"What did she buy?"

Finn stared at the monitor. "Two iced teas, two candy bars, and a copy of *The Hero with a Thousand Faces* by Joseph Campbell."

"Two drinks? Sounds like she has a study date with somebody." I got up off the sofa. "Let's go."

"To the college?" Finn asked. "What if she leaves before we get there?"

I pointed to a clock on the wall. "It's not even four thirty yet. The bookstore is inside the student center, and the building doesn't close until six. Violet will probably stay put until then. "

"You're the expert when it comes to the college," Finn said. "Seeing as how you spend so much of your free time there reading books by dead white guys and getting busy with the young studs in your classes."

"That's right," I said. "And your jealousy is unbecoming. Now, get your lazy ass off the sofa. It's time for you to show me just how fast that Aston Martin of yours can go."

"This is pointless," Finn said. "She's not coming back here tonight."

We'd arrived at the college just after five and had walked through the student center, looking for Violet Fox. I knew the center well, along with the rest of campus, since I'd been auditing classes at Ashland Community College for years. Cake decorating, yoga, charcoal drawing, watercolor painting. I'd taken all those and more, as part of my cover as an eternal college student and cook and waitress at the Pork Pit.

This semester, I'd signed up for a course in classic literature, hence the fact I was currently reading *The Odyssey*. I'd always liked learning new things and saw no reason to stop taking classes just because I wasn't killing people anymore. Besides, you just never knew when a new skill might come in handy. Especially given my past.

And I was thinking of taking several classes next semester, because, truth be told, my retirement was turning out to be rather, well, boring. During the day, I worked at the Pork Pit, of course, just as I always had. But at night, I didn't know quite what to do with myself since I wasn't reviewing files, trailing marks, and plotting the best way to kill someone. I could only watch the Food Network for so many hours a night. Most of the time, I ended up staring blankly at the television, wondering if eight o'clock was too early to go to bed. On the bright side, I was always extremely well rested now.

Finn and I hadn't found Violet Fox during our search of the student center. It had lots of little cubbyholes for students to hide and study in. Or Violet and whomever she'd been with might have decided to study in the library or a computer lab or even someone's dorm room. Too many possibilities and no way to narrow them down. So we'd come to the one place Violet Fox had to show up sooner or later—the parking lot.

"Trust me," I said. "She'll come back and get her car. Nobody in their right mind would leave their wheels here overnight."

"I can't imagine why," Finn muttered and shifted in his seat.

I stared out the window. Ashland Community College was located in the downtown district, a small circle of knowledge hidden among the glass-and-chrome corporate buildings that passed for skyscrapers in the city. Even though the college took up a couple of city blocks, the various halls and buildings were more or less grouped together and connected by a series of grassy quads. But space was at a premium in the downtown area, and the lots that surrounded the college had been developed long ago. All of which meant there was no student parking anywhere on campus. Instead, those who commuted every day had to leave their vehicles in a variety of lots and garages on the outskirts of downtown, then hike or bike their way over to the campus.

The parking lot we were in was the farthest one from the campus quads and located just below the Southtown border. A single light flickered overhead, painting the cars below a ghostly silver. Four-foot-high concrete barriers ringed most of the area, warning the drivers away from various potholes in the cracked asphalt. Spray-painted gang symbol runes, including clenched fists and crude outlines of guns and knives, dirtied the stone surfaces. Crumpled fast-food wrappers, crushed-out cigarette butts, and limp, used condoms littered the ground.

According to the info Finn had compiled, Violet Fox drove an old Honda Accord. The midsize serviceable car sat in the center of the lot, dwarfed on one side by a truck on monster wheels covered in army green paint. A Confederate flag covered part of the truck's back window, along with a gun rack. We sat several rows away, parked next to a Volkswagen Bug with a red hood that didn't match the rest of its white body.

"Any more charges on her credit card?" I asked.

Finn reached into the backseat and hit a button on his laptop. "Not since the last time you asked five minutes ago. How long are we going to wait? It's almost six thirty."

"All the campus buildings except the library close at six," I said. "If she's not at the library cramming, Violet Fox should be on her way here right now. We'll give her a few more minutes. This lot is almost a mile from campus.

It takes a good twenty minutes to get here from the student center, and that's if you're hoofing it fast."

Finn sighed and settled a little deeper into his seat. I rolled down the window. It was still drizzling, and the wet sheen of rain made the night seem colder and gloomier than it really was. Even in the Aston Martin's plush confines, I could hear the vibrations of the concrete barriers and broken asphalt of the parking lot. Sharp, worrisome mutters that spoke of violence, blood, fear. This was a place where people got beaten, robbed, and mugged with alarming regularity, even for Ashland—

A figure passed through a gap in the concrete barriers. A short, curvy woman with a mop of blond hair that had frizzed out to TBH—Tennessee Big Hair—proportions thanks to the drizzle. Violet Fox. She wore a heavy down jacket that didn't do enough to shield her from the rain. Her purse was looped over her chest and shoulder. She stepped underneath the flickering light, and a small metal canister glinted in her right hand. Pepper spray, unless I missed my guess. Smart, sensible precautions. This was a girl who was used to walking through here at night.

But she wasn't alone. Another girl was with her. Blue-black hair, pale eyes, slim figure, designer jeans. I recognized her too.

"That's Eva Grayson," I said.

Finn's green eyes latched onto Eva. He smiled and sat up in his seat. "Really? Owen Grayson never told me what a looker his sister is."

"Then he knows you well enough to know not to do that," I replied.

As I watched, a man about my age followed the girls

into the parking lot. His head swiveled right and left, and he stayed as close to Eva as her own shadow. His bulky windbreaker had ridden up, revealing a Glock tucked into the small of his back. Looked like Owen Grayson had gotten his sister that bodyguard after all.

Violet and Eva stopped in the middle of the lot and exchanged a few words. Violet said something that made Eva laugh. Then Violet waved her hand and started walking toward her aging Honda. Eva waved back. The man grabbed her elbow to escort her out of the parking lot, but Eva gave him a nasty glare and shook him off. The two of them turned, walked back through the gap in the concrete barrier, and disappeared from sight.

Since we'd already disabled the light in the front of the car, I opened the door of the Aston Martin and swung my legs outside.

"Well, she's alone now." Finn reached for his own door handle, but I grabbed his arm.

"Wait," I said in a low voice. "Let's see who else is around."

"You think the shooter is here?" he asked. "We would have seen him by now."

I shrugged. "Maybe. Depends on how good he is. He could have slipped in the other side of the lot. The point is he missed her at the Pork Pit and probably couldn't get to her on campus today. Too many witnesses, too many security guards. This is his last shot at her before she goes home for the night."

"And you think he's going to take it," Finn said.

"I would."

So we watched. Violet Fox was no fool. She approached

her car cautiously. She looked right, then left, in front and behind her. She also stayed in the middle of the lot away from the sides of the parked cars. Making sure no one was sneaking up on her or was waiting underneath one of the vehicles to grab her ankles and pull her down. Smart girl.

But she wasn't quite smart enough. Violet Fox reached into her purse, and her steps slowed as she fumbled for her keys. She didn't immediately find them because she stopped, dropped her head, and peered into her bag.

And that's when I saw a shadow slither out of the bed of the monster truck and head toward her.

"There he is," Finn said, scrambling to open his door. "He was hiding in the truck bed the whole time."

I didn't respond. I was already out of the car, running toward the girl.

❊ 8 ❊

Even as I started running, I saw the shadowy figure creep closer to Violet and take on the form of a short, stocky man. A dwarf. I was two hundred feet away. I wasn't going to make it in time. I was going to be too late.

Again.

I opened my mouth to shout a warning, when something *skitter-skittered* across the pavement. The dwarf must have stepped on a soda can. Violet froze at the noise, one of her hands still in her purse. Then she bolted. Didn't look back, didn't check to see what the noise was. She just ran.

She got maybe twenty steps before the man grabbed her by her frizzy blond hair. Violet shrieked in pain and turned to flail at him, her hands arced into claws. He let her slap at him. Those sorts of blows would mean nothing to a dwarf. Magic and weapons were the only things that got their attention. Violet paused half a second to draw in another breath to scream. That's when the man punched her in the face—hard. I heard the crunch of bone a hundred feet away.

Violet moaned, and the man hit her again. Her head snapped to one side, and she fell to her knees, retching. The dwarf kicked her in the stomach, and the force lifted Violet off the pavement and threw her ten feet. She hit the hood of a rusty pickup and slid to the ground. She didn't move.

The dwarf cracked his knuckles and advanced on her again. He picked her up and splayed her out on the hood of the pickup. The motion snapped Violet out of her daze, and she moaned and looked at her attacker. One of the dwarf's hands dropped to his pants. He wasn't using a gun this time. The dwarf was going to beat Violet to death—after he raped her.

I was fifty feet away and closing fast. I wasn't trying to be quiet, not anymore, but the dwarf was too intent on opening his fly to hear the *swish-swish* of my sneakers on the wet pavement.

But the deep, throaty roar of a vehicle rumbling to life somewhere behind me made him turn. The dwarf spotted me running at him, zipped up his pants, and stepped back. Waiting. Just waiting. Violet lay on the hood, her hands underneath her, trying to find the strength to push herself up, to run away. Blood covered most of what I could see of her face, and the bottom half of her nose was no longer in line with the top part. Her glasses barely clung to her distorted features.

Since the dwarf was focused on me, I slowed my steps to a walk. When I was ten feet away, I stopped, palmed the knife hidden up my left sleeve, and studied the man before me.

Since he was a dwarf, he wasn't quite five feet tall, but his shoulders were wider than a chair. His biceps looked like they'd been carved out of steel and attached to his barrel chest. He wore jeans and a black T-shirt, and a large tattoo showed on his left bicep—a lit stick of dynamite. A rune. One I'd seen somewhere before, although I couldn't quite place it at the moment. Didn't much matter. I could study it in further detail when he was dead.

"This isn't your fight, lady," he spat. "This is between the girl and me. Run along before I do you too."

"Oh, but it is my fight," I replied in a cold voice. I shifted the knife in my left hand, moving it into position. "Why's that?"

"Because you shot up my restaurant today."

The dwarf's blue eyes narrowed. "So what if I did? What are you going to do about it?"

"For starters? This."

I threw my knife at him. The dwarf didn't flinch as the blade caught him in the chest and sank into his right pectoral. Damn. I'd missed his heart by at least an inch. Probably closer to two. I hadn't been retired that long, but I hadn't exactly been training every day either. Looked like some rust had already gathered. *Use it or lose it, Gin.* Since I didn't want to lose anything, since I knew I couldn't afford to, I made a mental note to get in some throwing practice after this was over.

The dwarf stared at the knife in his chest. Then he smiled, pulled out the weapon, and let it clatter to the ground. He rolled his shoulders and cracked his knuckles again. The sound ricocheted like a gunshot off the concrete barriers around us. "I'm going to enjoy making you pay for that, bitch."

"Yeah, yeah," I said, palming the knife hidden up my right sleeve. "Let's dance."

The dwarf charged me. I waited until the last possible moment, then stepped to one side. My left foot lashed out, and I tripped him. But he was expecting it. The dwarf tucked into a ball, hit the ground, and rolled right back up. Bastard was quick. Bendy too.

"Nice."

He smiled. "I take yoga."

I smiled back. "Me too."

He came at me again. And then we got down to business. The dwarf swung his hard fists at me. I ducked his blows, not out of cowardice but practicality. No way I was letting his sledgehammer of a hand connect with my face. I'd had my nose and various other body parts broken plenty of times already. I had no desire to repeat that particular pain tonight.

The dwarf swung again, but his foot slipped on a chunk of broken asphalt and he overextended his arm. I came up inside his defense and stabbed him in the chest with my silverstone knife. The smell of coppery blood filled the night air, overpowering the rain. But he jerked back before I could shove the weapon into his heart. The blade skittered across his ribs and caught on one of them. I grunted, but it was like trying to slice through frozen meat. His chest muscles were just too thick and dense for me to do enough damage to put him down quick.

The dwarf chopped at my knife hand with the edge

of his fist. I let go of the weapon. A sharp blow like that would shatter my wrist into matchstick pieces. He swung at me again. I ducked back and plucked a third knife out of the small of my back.

"Knives? Is that all you got, lady?" he drawled. "You can cut me all night long, and I'll stand right here and take it. All I need is one good punch, and you're mine, bitch."

He was right. We'd barely started, and my heart was already racing. My lungs hadn't started to burn yet, but it was only a matter of time. I just didn't have the stamina he had. Never would. The dwarf wasn't even sweating, and the wounds I'd inflicted on him were nothing more than paper cuts. I had to find a way to end this. Now.

Out of the corner of my eye, I saw a large, dark shape creeping up the parking lot. The shape stopped. Waiting.

I slashed at the dwarf with my knife, forcing him toward a sedan a few feet away. He laughed, backed up, and crooked his index finger at me.

"Come on, bitch," he said. "I'm just getting warmed up."

I smiled at him. "Me too."

I braced my hands on the car hood and pushed off. He wasn't expecting me to change tactics, and he paused, just for a second. All the opening I needed. My feet hit the dwarf in the chest with enough force to make him stumble back. His shoe caught on another break in the pavement, and he fell on his ass.

And that's when Finn ran him over with the truck.

While I'd been fighting the dwarf, Finn had made himself useful. He'd broken into and hot-wired the monster truck that had been parked next to Violet Fox's car.

Then he'd pulled the vehicle up into range, waiting for me to notice.

The dwarf *thump-thumped* under the truck's massive, oversize wheels. But Finn wasn't finished. He put the truck in reverse and backed over the dwarf. He went back and forth over the man three more times before I held my hand up, signaling him to stop. Finn pulled the truck forward. He stayed inside the cab, waiting to see if I needed him again. I picked up my dropped knives and walked across the pavement to the dwarf.

The wheels had flattened out the man's thick, strong, compact body until now it resembled a fleshy, bloody pancake that had been pressed into the asphalt. Greasy black tire tracks covered his torso, and his arms and legs lay by his sides, crushed and useless. But Finn hadn't hit his head, and the dwarf was still alive. His blue eyes burned with pain and hate as he watched me come closer.

"Want to tell me who you're working for before I kill you?" I said.

The dwarf spat blood on my jeans.

"I'll take that as a no."

I leaned down and cut his throat. His eyes bulged, and he gurgled once, twice, three times before his head lolled to the side and the light leaked out of his irises. I gave him a minute to bleed out, then put my fingers against his lacerated neck to make sure. No pulse. As dead as dead could be. I wiped off my bloody hand on my jeans and gestured at Finn.

Finn killed the engine, got out of the truck, and walked back to me. His green eyes flicked to the dwarf's body. "You still had to cut his throat? Tough little bugger, wasn't he?"

"He's a dwarf," I replied. "They usually are. Now, give me your cell phone."

Finn dug into his jacket pocket and handed me a slim, silver phone. I used it to snap a picture of the dwarf's frozen face, along with the tattoo on his bicep, the one that resembled a lit stick of dynamite. It had been flattened by the truck tires, but there was still enough flesh there to get an idea of the original shape of the rune. I handed the phone back to Finn, then stuck my hand into the dwarf's front pockets. No wallet, no money, no ID. Probably in his back pocket, but I wasn't going to peel him up off the pavement to look for them. Messier than I wanted to get tonight.

"Get the car," I told Finn. "We need to take the girl to Jo-Jo's."

Finn nodded and trotted off to retrieve his Aston Martin. I walked over to Violet.

Sometime during my fight with the dwarf, Violet Fox had slid off the hood of the pickup. She sat propped up against the tire. Her fingers were stuck in her purse, as though she was trying to get her cell phone out to call the cops. I crouched down until I was eye level with her.

"You're safe now," I said in a soft voice. "He's not going to hurt you anymore."

Violet Fox's face was a mess. Her nose had been pushed halfway across her face, while her jaw reached out in the other direction. Her skin looked like putty that had been stretched to the breaking point over her distorted features. Blood covered the bottom half of her ruined face like a mask, and thick drops of it slid down her neck, staining her coat. Her glasses had been snapped in two in the middle. The glasses were still hooked around her ears, but the two halves dangled like earrings against her bloody cheeks.

Pain filled her brown eyes, and for a moment, I didn't think she'd heard me. But Violet turned her head and stared at me. She squinted, and recognition flickered in her dull gaze.

"You . . ." she mumbled.

"Don't try to talk, sweetheart," I said. "We're going to get you patched up, and then you can tell us all about why somebody wants you dead and how you know about the Tin Man. Okay?"

Violet Fox didn't answer me. She'd already passed out.

Finn brought the car over, and we stuffed Violet Fox into the backseat. I took her broken glasses off her face and passed them to Finn for safekeeping. Then I used one of my knives to cut a strip off the bottom of my long-sleeved T-shirt. I wound the cotton around the girl's face to catch the blood oozing out of her broken nose. She didn't stir.

"She's going to bleed all over the backseat," Finn muttered. "Do you know how much I paid for this car?"

"Too much," I said. "And don't worry about your precious leather seats. I'm sure Sophia can get the blood out."

"You going to call her to get rid of the dwarf's body?" Finn asked.

"Of course. Don't want to scare the coeds by leaving Pancake where he is and having them drive over him in the morning."

I grabbed Finn's cell phone again and hit 7 on the speed dial. Three rings later, she picked up.

"Hmph?" Sophia Deveraux let out her usual grunt of a greeting. The dwarf didn't like to strain her vocal cords with things like conversation.

"It's Gin. There's something you might find interesting over in one of the parking lots near Ashland Community College."

"Hmm." Her interested grunt.

I waited a moment to see if she'd say anything.

"Number?" Sophia asked, referring to the number of bodies I wanted her to come dispose of.

The Goth dwarf's voice came out in a harsh rasp, like she'd spent the last fifty years chain smoking and knocking back jugs of mountain moonshine. I didn't know why Sophia's voice was the way it was, especially since I'd never seen the dwarf light up or drink anything stronger than iced tea. Another mystery I wasn't sure I wanted to solve. Because I had a feeling that there was something real bad in Sophia's past. Some sort of horrific accident, trauma, or even torture. Those were the only things that I could think of that would so completely ruin her vocal cords.

I also wondered why Jo-Jo had never healed her sister. Maybe she'd wanted to and Sophia wouldn't let her. Maybe it had just been too late by the time Jo-Jo had reached her. Whatever it was, whatever had happened to the Goth dwarf, I knew that it couldn't be good.

"Only one, but you might have a little trouble scraping him up off the ground," I replied. "There was a very large truck involved. Think you can handle it?"

"Hmph." Sophia's grunt was more guttural this time. I'd offended her.

"Well, I have faith in you," I replied in a breezy tone. "Are you at Jo-Jo's?"

"Um-mmm." That was a *yes*.

"Tell her to get ready. Finn and I are bringing over someone who needs her help. Badly. We'll be there in a few minutes."

Sophia hung up without another word. I did the same.

Finn drove out of the parking lot. He took great care to steer his car around the dwarf's smushed body.

"You could just run over him," I said. "He's already dead, and it's not like you haven't done it before."

"Yeah, but I don't want bloody bits of dwarf stuck in my wheels for the next two weeks." Finn sniffed. "This is an Aston Martin, Gin. You don't run over dead bodies in an Aston Martin."

"Tell that to James Bond."

Finn shot me a dirty look as he pulled out onto the street.

It took Finn about twenty minutes to drive over to Jo-Jo's house. Jolene "Jo-Jo" Deveraux was Sophia's big sister—a two-hundred-fifty-seven-year-old dwarf and Air elemental of significant power, wealth, status, and social connections. Given all that, Jo-Jo made her home in a ritzy subdivision by the name of Tara Heights. Within a few miles, we left the downtown grit and grime behind and entered an elegant area of carefully landscaped trees and spacious homes fronted by cobblestone sidewalks and yards big enough for the pros to play football in.

Finn eventually steered the car onto a street marked Magnolia Lane, and a few seconds later, Jo-Jo's house came into view—a three-story, plantation-style home straight out of *Gone With the Wind.* The sprawling, white structure perched at the top of a grassy knoll and featured a series of tall, round columns that supported the rest of the building the way a high-backed chair might prop up an old lady.

Finn parked the car and helped me drag the still-unconscious Violet Fox out of the backseat, up three steps, and onto the porch that wrapped around the spacious home. Thick, ropy tendrils of ivy and kudzu covered a trellis attached to the porch, along with the bare brown thorns of several rose bushes. A lone bulb burned on the porch. Out in the sloping yard, the cold, drizzling rain picked up, making the air smell of metal, dead leaves, and wet earth.

I let Finn take Violet's weight so I could pull open the screen door that fronted a heavier wooden one. Then I picked up the knocker and banged it on the interior door. The knocker was shaped like a thick, puffy cloud—Jo-Jo's personal Air elemental rune.

I'd barely set the cloud rune back against the wood when the door wrenched open, and a woman stuck her head outside. Jo-Jo Deveraux looked like she'd planned on staying in for the evening. A short-sleeved, striped pink housecoat covered her stocky, muscular figure, while her bleached blond-white hair was done up in pink sponge curlers. Some sort of blue mud mask covered her face, and a pedicure pad held her toes out wide. She must have just painted her toenails, because the bright pink polish gleamed like it was still wet.

"About time you got here," the middle-aged dwarf said. "I've been pacing back and forth in front of the door for five minutes now."

"Why? Weren't there any parties or dinners on the society circuit tonight?" I asked, taking in the housecoat and curlers.

"Oh, there was a party or two," Jo-Jo drawled in a voice sweeter than clover honey. "But these old bones ain't as young as they used to be. Rain makes 'em ache. Besides, even I need a night off from the bullshit circuit every once in a while."

"Ahem."

Finn cleared his throat, his way of telling me to get down to business and that he was tired of propping up Violet Fox. Jo-Jo's pale gaze cut to the girl. Except for the pinprick of black at their center, the dwarf's eyes were almost colorless, like two cloudy pieces of quartz.

"Hell's bells and panther trails," Jo-Jo said in a soft tone. "What happened to her?"

"She got on the wrong end of a dwarf's fist—twice," I said, shouldering part of Violet's weight again. "Think you can fix her?"

Jo-Jo studied the girl a moment more, then nodded. "Darling, I can fix anything short of death. But this one ain't going to be pretty."

✳ **9** ✳

Jo-Jo stepped aside so Finn and I could drag the unconscious Violet Fox into the house. The sweet smell of Jo-Jo's Chantilly perfume tickled my nose as we walked through a narrow hallway. A hundred feet later, the skinny corridor opened up into an enormous room that took up the back half of the house.

Padded chairs. Hair dryers. Counters crammed full of hairspray, nail polish, makeup, scissors, rollers, curling irons. A long mirror that ran down one wall. Towering stacks of beauty magazines. Photos of various hairstyles taped up everywhere. All that and more could be found in Jo-Jo's beauty salon, the place where the Air elemental used her magic as a self-proclaimed *drama mama*—someone who catered to the endless vanity of Southern women.

Debutantes, pageant contestants, bored trophy wives. Jo-Jo served them all in a variety of ways. Perms, cuts, dye jobs, waxes, manicures, pedicures. If it had anything at all to do with beauty or making a woman's hair twice as big, tall, and hard as her head, Jo-Jo did it in her salon. And then some. Air elemental magic was also terrific for fixing unwanted frown lines or putting someone's boobs back up to where they'd been ten years ago—temporarily, at least.

Of course, turning back the clock wasn't the only thing Jo-Jo did with her Air magic. The dwarf was also one of the best healers in Ashland. Hell, the whole South. Few people knew about her talents in that particular area, but Fletcher Lane had been one of Jo-Jo's oldest friends, and I'd inherited her, along with Sophia, when I'd taken over his assassin business. One sister to heal me, the other to get rid of the bodies I left behind. A nice arrangement. Despite the sisters' hefty fees.

"Put her in one of the chairs," Jo-Jo directed before going over to the sink to wash her hands.

Finn and I hauled Violet Fox over to one of the swivel, cherry-red salon chairs. Then Finn grabbed a bottle of nail glue off the counter, pulled Violet's broken glasses out of his jacket pocket, and used the bonding solution to put the two pieces back together. I lifted Violet's purse from around her neck, perched on a stool a few feet away, and started going through it. Wallet, keys, breath mints, loose change, eyedrops, a compact. Nothing unusual or exciting.

A soft whine sounded in the corner. I looked over to see Rosco, Jo-Jo's fat, lazy basset hound, curled up in his wicker basket by the door. The old dog eyed the purse in my hands. His tail thumped once with hope.

"Sorry, dog," I said. "Nothing in here for you."

Rosco huffed in indignation, then dropped his brown-and-black head down on top of his tubby stomach and went back to sleep. His favorite pastime, other than eating.

Jo-Jo pulled a chair over to Violet, clicked on a light, and gently unwound my T-shirt strip from her face. The damage looked more garish underneath the white fluorescent glow. The swelling had already set in, and Violet's face had puffed up to twice its normal size. Black and green and purple streaked out from her disjointed nose and sliced across her cheeks—what I could see of them underneath the dried blood.

"Hell's bells," the dwarf muttered again. "You said he only hit her twice?"

"Yeah," Finn said, holding the broken glasses together until the glue dried. "But he made them both count."

Jo-Jo shook her head. "Well, let's hope the poor girl remains unconscious for the next little bit. Because putting her face back the way it's supposed to be is going to be just as painful as what he did to her in the first place. No need to traumatize her more than she's already been tonight."

Jo-Jo examined Violet's face another minute before she went to work. She drew in a deep breath and held her hand in front of the girl's ruined features. Her palm hovered just above Violet's skin. A second later, the dwarf's eyes began to glow an opaque white, as though thick clouds wisped through her bright gaze. A similar buttermilk-colored glow coated her open palm. Jo-Jo brought even more of her power to bear, until I could feel it crackling through the salon like static electricity, just itching to zap me. I scooted my stool back another foot from the dwarf.

Of the four elements, two were opposites, and two were complementary. Fire and Ice didn't go together, but Fire and Air did, just like Stone was the natural companion to Ice. Each element also had various offshoots, like metal for Stone, water for Ice, and electricity for Air, that some folks could tap into. Jo-Jo Deveraux was an Air elemental, which meant her magic was the exact opposite of my cool Stone and Ice power. Being in the presence of someone using so much of an opposing element always made me twitchy and unsettled. Jo-Jo's power just felt wrong to me, as would any Air or Fire elemental's magic. Just like my Stone and Ice power would seem foreign to them.

But the worst part was the spider rune scars on my palms. As Jo-Jo brought even more of her power to bear, the silverstone metal embedded in my skin began to itch and burn. Silverstone was a very rare metal, with the unusual property of being able to absorb and store all kinds of magic. Many elementals wore runes made out of silverstone and used them to contain bits and pieces of their power that they could use when needed. Sort of like magical batteries. My mother, Eira, had used her snowflake rune that way, although it hadn't saved her in the end.

But silverstone not only absorbed the magic—it hungered for it, as though the metal was hollow and eager, aching even, for elemental power to fill it up and make it whole. I could feel the silverstone's desire for more magic, for more power, even though the skin on my palms had long ago grown over the metal that had been melted into my hands. I curled my fingers around Violet's purse, hoping the imitation leather would shield my hands enough to block the burning sensations in my palms. Didn't work. Never did. So I sat there and watched Jo-Jo.

The dwarf slowly passed her palm over Violet Fox's face. Air elementals made great healers because of their ability to tap into and use all the natural gases in the air—including oxygen. Right now, Jo-Jo was using her magic to force oxygen into Violet's body, making it circulate under the skin of her face, using the air molecules to heal what had been so viciously broken.

Again and again, Jo-Jo moved her hand over Violet's face. Every time she did, the girl's nose got a little straighter, her jaw a little squarer. The swelling eased, and the nasty streaks of color faded from Violet's cheeks. Watching Jo-Jo work always reminded me of a book I'd had as a child. One that featured a cartoon character. If you looked at the pages one at a time, the character didn't move. But if you flipped through the sheets fast enough, he'd walk from one side of the paper to the other.

Ten minutes later, Jo-Jo dropped her hand. Her eyes dimmed and lost their milky, magical glow. So did her palm. "There," the dwarf said in a low voice. "It's done."

"He also kicked her once," I said. "In the stomach."

Jo-Jo nodded. "He bruised her kidneys bad, but I fixed that too."

The dwarf got to her feet, wet a washcloth in the sink, and used it to wipe the blood off Violet's face. The girl didn't stir. She hadn't made a sound the whole time Jo-Jo was working on her. Not surprising. Her body had gone through serious trauma. She'd probably sleep for at least an hour, maybe longer. Being magically healed always took a lot out of a person, as the body tried to adjust from being injured to suddenly being well again. And using as much magic as Jo-Jo just had would wipe out all but the strongest elementals.

That was one reason I tried not to rely on my magic too much, tried not to use it for big things. I didn't like being left weak and helpless afterward, even if I had retired from the assassin business.

Jo-Jo finished cleaning up Violet and threw the bloody rag into the trash can. Finn slipped Violet's glued together glasses on her face. Then he leaned back and gave her an appreciative glance.

"She cleaned up good, didn't she?" he said in an admiring tone.

"She's unconscious, Finn. At least have the decency to leer at her when she's awake," I said.

Finn laced his hands behind his head and grinned. "I'll be sure and do just that."

Jo-Jo washed her hands again in the sink. She grabbed another rag to dry them off, then turned to me. "Now," the dwarf drawled. "You want to tell me who this girl is, and why someone was beating her?"

I filled Jo-Jo in on everything that had happened over the last twenty-four hours, starting with Sophia and I foiling Jake McAllister's attempted holdup of the Pork Pit, to Violet Fox coming in and asking for the Tin Man, to the shooting, to Finn and I tracking her down and saving her from the dwarven hit man.

"So that's where Sophia went in such a hurry," Jo-Jo

murmured. "I thought it was strange she wanted to leave before the end."

I raised an eyebrow.

"We were watching a western. *The Good, the Bad, and the Ugly* with Clint Eastwood. Sophia hardly ever leaves before the big showdown at the end," Jo-Jo explained. "Her favorite part is when Lee Van Cleef dies."

Sophia Deveraux, the Goth girl dwarf, was also quite the movie buff. Westerns, action flicks, Mob movies. She loved them all. The more violent they were, the better.

"Anyway," I said, finishing my story. "We left the dwarf's body for Sophia to dispose of and brought the girl here. Once she's awake, I plan on asking her some serious questions about Fletcher and where she heard the name *Tin Man*."

Jo-Jo stared at the girl. A frown made the blue mud mask on her face crack. She hadn't bothered to wipe it off yet. "She looks . . . familiar. What did you say her name was again?"

"Violet Elizabeth Fox." I plucked the girl's driver's license out of her wallet and passed it to Jo-Jo.

The dwarf scanned the laminated card. Her frown deepened, and bits of blue mud flaked off her cheeks and settled on her pink housecoat. "She lives up on Ridgeline Hollow Road."

"Do you know her?" Finn asked.

Jo-Jo shook her head. "No, but I'm pretty sure I know the crotchety old bastard who's her grandfather."

* **10** *

Finn and I looked at each other. "Grandfather?" we asked in unison.

Jo-Jo nodded. "Warren T. Fox, of the Ridgeline Hollow Foxes. The girl looks a fair bit like him in the face. I see it, now that the blood's gone."

"And who is this Warren T. Fox?" I asked.

"He used to be a friend of Fletcher's," the dwarf said. "But they had a falling out a long time ago. Haven't spoken since, to my knowledge."

Jo-Jo stared at Violet, who was still unconscious in the chair. An emotion flickered in the dwarf's pale eyes. Regret. I wondered why. Jo-Jo shook her head. More mud mask flaked off her face.

"C'mon," the dwarf said. "Let's make the poor girl comfortable, and I'll tell you what I know."

*   *   *

Since Jo-Jo was stronger than either Finn or me, she picked up Violet, carried the girl into the downstairs den, and arranged her on an overstuffed sofa. I pulled off Violet's bloody jacket and shoes; then Jo-Jo covered her with a soft, warm quilt. The dwarf trudged into the downstairs bathroom to wash the blue mud off her face. I stepped through the doorway that led into the kitchen.

Most people went straight to Jo-Jo's salon when they came to the house, but my favorite room had always been the kitchen. A long, skinny room with a rectangular butcher's block table set in the middle surrounded by several tall stools. Appliances done in a variety of pastel shades ringed three walls, while the fourth opened up into the den where Violet Fox snoozed. Runelike clouds could be found everywhere, from the placemats on the table to the dish towels piled next to the sink to the fresco that covered the ceiling. When I was younger, I used to lie on the kitchen floor for hours and stare at the painting on the ceiling, pretending the clouds really were moving. One of the few childish fancies I'd allowed myself after the loss of my mother and older sister.

Finn was already in the kitchen, pouring himself a cup of chicory coffee. Jo-Jo had always kept a pot on in case Fletcher dropped by. Now that the old man was gone, Finn drank his share—and then some. I breathed in, enjoying the warm, comforting caffeine fumes that always reminded me of Fletcher Lane. Then I went over to the refrigerator, pulled open the door, and peered inside.

"What are you thinking? Sandwiches?" Finn asked in a hopeful voice.

"No. I'm in the mood for something sweet."

I grabbed the butter out of the fridge, then rummaged through the cabinets. Flour, oats, dried apricots, golden raisins, brown sugar, vanilla. I pulled them out, along with some mixing cups, a baking pan, a spatula, and a bowl. Finn settled himself at the kitchen table and drank his coffee while I worked. By the time Jo-Jo walked back into the kitchen, I was sliding the batter into the oven.

"Whatcha making?" the dwarf asked, pouring herself a cup of coffee.

"Apricot bars," I replied, wiping my hands off on a cloud-covered dish towel. "Which I'm going to turn into a poor man's cobbler. They'll be done in a few minutes, which should give you just enough time to tell us all about Fletcher and Warren T. Fox."

Jo-Jo nodded. She took her coffee to the table and sat down next to Finn. I leaned against the refrigerator so I could keep an eye on the oven. It just wouldn't do to get the apricot bars too brown.

"Fletcher and Warren grew up together in Ridgeline Hollow," Jo-Jo said. "Best friends who were thick as thieves. More like brothers. Always together, from sunup till sundown. Sophia and I knew their parents. Grandparents too."

Finn shook his head. "Dad never mentioned anyone named Warren Fox to me. Never. Especially someone who was his best childhood friend. What happened between them?"

"A girl," Jo-Jo said. "They both fell in love with the same girl. Stella. She was a pretty thing who lived up in the hollow. Stella knew Fletcher and Warren were both in love with her. She'd go out courting with first one, then the other. She liked playing them against each other. Pretty soon, they were fighting over her."

"So who got her in the end?" I asked.

A wry smile curved Jo-Jo's lips. "Neither one of them. She ran off with a boy from the city. But by then, it was too late for Fletcher and Warren to repair their friendship. Fletcher bought a storefront downtown and started the Pork Pit. Warren stayed where he was up in the hills and took over his family's general store."

I looked at Finn. With his walnut hair, green eyes, and smooth smile, Finn was the spitting image of Fletcher at his age—and handsome to a fault. I wondered what Warren T. Fox had looked like in his youth, to give Fletcher Lane a run for his money.

"Warren's store, is it called Country Daze?" Finn took another sip of his chicory coffee. "Because that's where Violet Fox gets her paycheck from every two weeks."

Jo-Jo nodded. "Been in the family for four generations now, counting the girl in there."

My gray eyes flicked to Violet Fox, who continued to sleep on the sofa. "If Warren and Fletcher had a falling out all those years ago, why would Warren's granddaughter come looking for Fletcher now?"

Jo-Jo shrugged. "I don't know. But if the girl or Warren are in trouble like you think they are, asking Fletcher Lane for help would be the very last thing the Warren T. Fox that I know would do. Pride's one of the most important things to him. Which is why he never made up with Fletcher. Stella humiliated them both, and Fletcher reminded Warren too much of that."

I grabbed a cloud-shaped oven mitt, opened the oven door, and took out the apricot bars. The smell of warm fruit, sugar, and melted butter filled the kitchen, along with a blast of heat. A combination I never grew tired of, especially on a cold, gray night like this one. I grabbed another oven mitt, set it on the table, then put the pan on top of it. Finn's fingers crept toward the edge of the container, but I smacked his hand away.

"I'm not done with them yet," I said.

"Come on, Gin," he whined. "I just want a taste."

"And you're just going to have to wait, like the rest of us."

Jo-Jo chuckled, amused by our squabbling. I moved over to the cabinets and got out four bowls, some spoons, and a couple of knives. I also grabbed a gallon of vanilla bean ice cream out of the freezer. After the apricot bars had cooled enough so they wouldn't immediately fall apart, I cut out big chunks of the bars, dumped them in the bowls, and topped them all with two scoops of the ice cream. My own version of a quick homemade cobbler.

Jo-Jo swallowed a mouthful of the confection and sighed. "Heaven, pure, sweet heaven."

Finn didn't agree with her. He was too busy stuffing his face to chime in.

I took a bite. The ice cream was a cool, soft contrast to the warm, heavy richness of the apricot bars, and both melted together in my mouth in a symphony of flavors. Jo-Jo was right. I'd outdone myself again.

We were scraping up the remains of our dessert when

the front door to the house banged open. Heavy, familiar footsteps sounded, and a moment later, Sophia Deveraux entered the kitchen. Her black Goth clothes looked out of place among the pastel appliances, like a storm cloud suddenly passing in front of the sun.

"Want some dessert?" I asked, fixing another bowl of apricot bars and ice cream for her.

"Um-mmm." Sophia grunted *yes* and sat down next to Jo-Jo.

Finn waited until Sophia was halfway through her ice cream before he asked her the inevitable question. "Any trouble picking up the body?"

Sophia's flat, black eyes met his green ones. "Nuh-uh." The Goth dwarf's version of *no*.

I looked at Sophia's clothes, but I couldn't see any blood spatters on her T-shirt, jeans, or boots. Even though the fabric was black, I was good at noticing that sort of thing. But Sophia's clothes were spotless as always. The truth was I didn't know exactly how Sophia Deveraux disposed of the bodies I sent her way. Didn't know if she buried 'em, burned 'em, crushed 'em, or put 'em in cold storage. Hell, I didn't even know where she took the remains in the first place.

But the grumpy Goth dwarf could get rid of evidence like it had never even existed. DNA, hairs, fibers, blood. Not a thing remained after she got through cleaning up a murder scene. I'd often wondered if Sophia had the same Air elemental magic Jo-Jo did, if she used it to help her destroy evidence. In addition to smoothing out wrinkles, Air magic was also good for disintegrating things like flesh or sandblasting blood off a floor. But I'd never seen Sophia do any sort of magic, Air or otherwise, never felt any kind of power crackle off her. Another mystery I'd never been able to puzzle out, along with why Sophia's voice was so broken and raspy. She was only a hundred and thirteen, far too young for her body to be failing her already. Dwarves could easily live to be five hundred or older. Sophia Deveraux wasn't forthcoming with any answers, but still I wondered.

Sophia finished her cobbler, pushed her bowl back, and looked at Jo-Jo. "Movie?"

"I paused it," Jo-Jo said. "Still on the TV in the den, if you want to finish it."

Sophia nodded, got to her feet, and walked into the next room. I grabbed her bowl to rinse it out in the sink. I reached for the faucet to turn on the water—

And someone screamed.

I whirled around, one of my silverstone knives already sliding into my right hand. Another scream rang out, followed by some frantic rustling. Sophia sighed and stepped out of the den. A moment later, Violet Fox lurched into view.

The girl looked no worse for wear, despite her ordeal. The only hint anything violent had even happened was the crusted blood that coated her sweater. And the fact that her black glasses were just a tiny bit off center on her nose. Finn hadn't fixed them perfectly. Or maybe Jo-Jo had straightened the girl's nose more than it had been before. Occasionally, the dwarf would throw in a little rhinoplasty while she was working her healing Air magic. An added bonus, if you asked me.

Violet Fox stared at the four of us, surprised and further startled by our presence. The girl's eyes fell on a knife on the kitchen table. She darted forward, picked it up, turned, and brandished it at us. "Who are you people?"

* 11 *

I slid my silverstone knife back up my sleeve and ran water in the dirty bowl before I turned to face the college girl.

"Sweetheart," I said in a cool voice. "That's a butter knife. You couldn't even file your nails with it. Put it down before I take it away from you."

"Who are you people?" Violet Fox asked in a shaky voice, still clutching the pitiful weapon. She stepped back until her body pressed against the refrigerator. If the door had been open, she probably would have stuffed herself inside, like a box turtle retreating into its shell. "Where am I? What do you want with me?"

I sighed and looked at Finn. He was much better at making nice than I was. He stepped forward, his hands held wide. A charming smile showed off his white teeth to their dazzling perfection.

"You're somewhere safe," Finn said in a calm tone that could have soothed an angry grizzly. "We're not going to hurt you. We saved you from that dwarf in the parking lot at the community college, remember?"

Shadows turned Violet's eyes an even darker brown, and she twitched her nose, trying to see if it was still intact. She remembered, all right. The knowledge bruised her features just like the dwarf's fists had. Jo-Jo might have healed all the physical damage from the attack, but Violet Fox wasn't going to forget the emotional trauma anytime soon. If ever. Something else I was all too familiar with.

Violet Fox didn't look anything like me, of course, but for a moment, staring at her was like seeing myself at thirteen again, just after the Fire elemental had murdered my family. I'd had the same haunted, wounded look that this other girl did right now. I pushed the memory away.

Finn crept a little closer and turned up the wattage on his smile. "We don't mean you any harm. We just want to ask you some questions about your grandfather. His name is Warren, right? Warren T. Fox?"

Doubt flickered in her dark, haunted eyes. "Why do you want to know about my grandfather?"

"Because your grandfather used to be an old friend of my dad's," Finn kept up his calming tone. "His name was Fletcher Lane. You came into the Pork Pit today asking about him, asking about the Tin Man, remember?"

Some of Violet's panic slackened, and she studied Finn with a lot more interest.

"C'mon," Finn said. "If we wanted to hurt you, we would have done it already. We just want to talk. Promise."

It was the same smooth voice he'd used to talk so many women out of their panties. Including me in my younger, more foolish years. *You'll be so much more comfortable if you get out of those wet clothes. Let me help you unzip your dress. Whoops, did I just spill coffee all over your jeans? Guess you'll have to take them off.*

And it worked. Violet Fox never stood a chance against the sheer, overpowering, slightly smarmy charm of Finnegan Lane. She lowered the knife and studied us all again, carefully this time, without fear clouding her gaze. She stared at Finn the longest.

"You look exactly like your dad," she said. "Or at least an old photo my grandfather has of him. Same eyes, same hair, same nice smile."

Finn grinned a little wider. Nothing he loved better than being told how handsome he was.

Violet nodded at Jo-Jo. "And I've seen you once or twice up at the store, haven't I?"

"You sure have, darling. Your grandfather has the best homemade honey in the city. I always stop and get some when I'm up that way," Jo-Jo said. "Now, why don't you put that knife to good use and help yourself to some dessert while we talk?"

After a moment, Violet nodded, stepped forward, and put the knife back down on the table. Finn gently took her arm, gave her another smile, and sat her down on one of the stools. I made her a bowl of apricot bars and ice cream and passed her a spoon. Violet stared at me.

"And you," she murmured. "I talked to you at the restaurant today. And in the parking lot, after, after—"

"After I killed the man who attacked you," I said.

Violet gulped down a mouthful of air. Jo-Jo reached over, patted the girl on the hand, and shot me a pointed look. I sighed. I was a former assassin, not a babysitter. Wasn't my job to sugarcoat what had happened tonight—or skirt around the trouble the girl was in. But I was patient enough to let Violet Fox get through with her psuedocobbler before I started asking her questions. Besides, there were plenty of apricot bars left. Be a shame, really, to let them go to waste.

"Why did you come into the Pork Pit today looking for the Tin Man?" I asked. "Who told you that name?"

Violet fiddled with her spoon, then pushed it and her empty bowl aside. She drew in a breath. She knew it was time to get down to business. "You're going to think it's stupid. Childish."

"Oh, I doubt that," I drawled.

Violet's brows drew together in confusion at my sarcastic tone. Jo-Jo patted her hand again, encouraging her to go on with her story. Violet shook her head and continued.

"When I was a kid, my grandfather used to tell me stories about the Tin Man. He told me the Tin Man helped people who couldn't help themselves. That he ran a barbecue restaurant called the Pork Pit and that all you had to do was go in and ask for him, and he'd make all your problems disappear. I thought it was the most wonderful story, a sort of Southern fairy tale."

Warren Fox might have been estranged from Fletcher, but he'd still thought about his childhood friend, enough to tell his granddaughter about the old man and what he did, in a roundabout way. Although I wouldn't call assassinating folks a real help—

"Oh, yes. Fletcher helped lots of people over the years,"

Jo-Jo said, cutting into my musings. "He was a wonderful man that way."

I stared at the dwarf, then at Sophia, who grunted her agreement. Even Finn nodded his head in a knowing way. Over the years, I'd done a few pro bono jobs. So had Fletcher. But helping people on the sly? As a regular gig? When had the old man done that? And more importantly, why?

"So he's real then?" Violet asked. "The Tin Man?"

"Sure, he's real, darling," Jo-Jo said. "His name was Fletcher Lane. He was Finn's father."

Violet's face fell. "Was?"

Finn nodded. "He died a few months ago. But don't worry about that right now. Tell us the rest of your story."

Violet drew in another breath. "Anyway, I hadn't really thought about the Tin Man in years—until this morning."

"What happened this morning?" Finn gave Violet another encouraging smile.

Violet ducked her head and smiled back, as though she wasn't used to so much male attention. Probably not. Girls with glasses, and all that. "I'm a business major at Ashland Community College. Eva Grayson's my best friend. She was at the Pork Pit last night. All she could talk about today was the robbery and how the woman behind the cash register stopped it."

Sophia snorted.

"Well, I did have some help," I said to appease the Goth dwarf. "So you talked to Eva, and you remembered this story your grandfather had told you about the Tin Man. Okay, I'll buy that. But why do you even need the Tin Man's help in the first place?"

Violet chewed on one of her fingernails. "It's a long story."

"Good thing we've got nothing but time then."

I didn't mention to the girl that she wasn't going anywhere until I'd determined she wasn't a threat to me, Finn, the Deveraux sisters, or the restaurant. Jake McAllister was going to make enough problems for me. I didn't need any more.

Violet nodded. "All right. My grandfather, Warren Fox, owns a store up on Ridgeline Hollow Road called Country Daze. It's an old-timey country store with glass soda pop bottles, barrels full of penny candy, locally made goods, that kind of thing. It's also right next to one of the big coal mines—Dawson Number Three. It started out as an underground mine with a big seam of coal. But the coal ran out a few years ago, so the underground part has been idle since then. Now it's just a strip mine. The owner of the mine, Tobias Dawson, has been after my grandfather to sell the store, land, and mineral rights to him for years so he can expand the mine and search for more coal. But the store and the land have been in our family for generations. Grandfather has always refused, saying he'd rather die than see any more of the mountain destroyed."

Tobias Dawson. I knew that name. Dawson was one of the biggest mine operators in Ashland, a dwarf who'd pulled coal out of the mountains for years himself as a miner before making enough money to start up his own company. He'd had nothing but success ever since. A true miner through and through who was always on the lookout for the next big seam of coal in the mountains. If Tobias Dawson wanted something, he usually got it—

no matter who got dead in the process. Dawson was also deep in bed with Mab Monroe. I remembered seeing his name in the file Fletcher had compiled on the Fire elemental queen.

Hearing Dawson's name also made me recall where I'd seen the symbol that had been tattooed on the bicep of Violet Fox's attacker. Unless I was mistaken, a lit stick of dynamite was Tobias Dawson's rune for his mining company.

Violet continued with her story. "In the past, Dawson was content just to wait. He's a dwarf, after all, just a bit over two hundred. He's bound to outlive Grandfather and me too. But he's not taking no for an answer anymore. He's sent some of his men out to harass us. They've broken the windows in the store, threatened customers, interfered with our deliveries. You name it, they've done all that and more the last two months, trying to drive us out of business. Grandfather's been able to handle Dawson's men so far, but I worry about him. Dawson's more or less told Grandfather that he'll kill us both if Grandfather doesn't sell out to him. Grandfather said no, of course."

I didn't bother asking Violet Fox if they'd gone to the police to complain about Tobias Dawson. The dwarven mine owner had more than enough money to bribe the po-po to look the other way, and he could always use his connection to Mab Monroe to get the cops in her pocket to back off and let him go about his intimidation business. The only person who might listen to the Foxes would be Donovan Caine. Even then, the detective couldn't take on someone like Tobias Dawson by himself. Not and live to tell about it.

"So that's why that dwarf attacked you tonight," I murmured. "You grandfather wasn't budging, so Dawson decided to give him some incentive to sell out—your body."

Violet shook her head. "That wouldn't have worked, either. If anything, Grandfather would have gotten his shotgun and gone over to the mine to have it out with Dawson."

"Where Dawson could justifiably kill him in self-defense in front of any number of witnesses," Finn pointed out. "Either way, Dawson would have gotten what he wanted—you and your grandfather out of the way."

Violet shivered and hugged her arms to her chest.

Nobody said anything for the better part of a minute.

Then Jo-Jo looked at me with her pale, colorless eyes. "Gin?"

Gin. My adopted name. Such a short, simple word. But that single syllable was imbued with a world of meaning. I knew what Jo-Jo was asking. If I was going to help Violet and her grandfather, Warren T. Fox. Because without someone like me on their side, someone just as cold, ruthless, and dangerous as Tobias Dawson, the Foxes weren't long for this earth. If I hadn't gotten curious and intervened tonight, Violet would already be raped, dead, and cold in that parking lot.

I rubbed my head. I didn't need this right now. I was supposed to be retired, not sticking my nose into someone else's problems. Especially not for *free*. Then there was Jake McAllister and his well-connected, lawyer father, Jonah. I had no doubt the younger McAllister would make good on his threat to try and kill me. And finally, there was the folder of information Fletcher Lane had left me—the one about my murdered mother and older sister. The photo of Bria that proved she was still alive, still out there somewhere.

I needed to figure out what to do about all that. How to take care of Jake McAllister without pointing the finger back at myself. What to do about his father. How to find my baby sister, Bria. Decide whether I actually wanted to do that or not. Fletcher had left me all these questions to find the answers to. I didn't need to go gallivanting up into the Appalachian Mountains to help an old geezer and his granddaughter take on someone as dangerous and potentially lethal as Tobias Dawson.

But my decision had already been made. It had been the moment I'd become curious enough to track down Violet Fox and see what kind of trouble she was in, see why she wanted to speak to the Tin Man. Curiosity. Definitely going to get me killed one day. Probably real, real soon.

"Sophia," I said. "I'm going to need you to watch the Pork Pit for a few days. Maybe help me out with some other things too, if the need arises."

The Goth dwarf nodded. A tiny smile softened her hard, pale face. Nothing Sophia liked better than handling the *other things* I sent her way.

"Finn, I need everything you can get on Tobias Dawson, his mining operation, and why he might want the Foxes' land so badly."

Finn nodded.

"Jo-Jo, I'll probably need some healing supplies."

The older dwarf nodded her head as well.

Violet looked back and forth between the four of us. "I don't understand. I thought Finn's father, the Tin Man, was dead? How is any of this going to help me and my grandfather?"

"Because, sweetheart," I said. "I might not be the Tin Man, and I'm definitely no fairy-tale hero, but I'm the closest thing you're going to get."

12

Once my professional help was secured, Violet Fox immediately wanted to go home and make sure her grandfather was okay.

"Forget it," I said. "You're not going home tonight. You need to stay here and rest. You've been through a serious trauma. Despite being magically healed, you still need some downtime to recover."

By this point, purple circles rimmed her dark eyes, and she moved slowly, like every motion was an enormous effort. Violet Fox was about to pass out from sheer exhaustion. I didn't add the fact I wanted Violet to stay right where she was so Jo-Jo and Sophia Deveraux could babysit her. The dwarves would make sure Violet didn't do anything stupid, like tell her grandfather about the attack and have him go tearing off after Tobias Dawson in a rage.

"But what if Dawson sends some men after Grandfather?" Violet asked.

"He won't," I replied. "You said it yourself. Your grand-father and his shotgun can handle Dawson's men. That's why the dwarf came after you instead. He wasn't getting anywhere threatening your grandfather."

"But how do you *know*?" she persisted.

I gave her a flat look. "Because I've had a lot of experi-ence with this sort of thing. Dawson's probably waiting for his cell phone to ring, for his man to check in and tell him that you're dead. When he realizes something went wrong, Dawson will be too busy trying to find his own man and figure out what the hell happened to him to worry about your grandfather. At least for tonight. Trust me. We've got time for you to get some beauty sleep."

Violet opened her mouth to argue with me some more, but I cut her off.

"You can call your grandfather and check in. See how he is, and tell him you'll see him tomorrow. But if you want my help, you're staying here tonight. *Capisce?*"

Violet Fox might be a straight-A business student, but her resistance wilted under my cold stare. "All right," she murmured. "I'll call my grandfather."

"Good," I replied and pushed her bowl back over to her. "Now, eat some more cobbler."

Violet Fox ate some more apricot bars and vanilla ice cream, while the rest of us plotted. Jo-Jo and Sophia agreed to keep an eye on her until Finn and I showed up tomorrow. The two of us would drive Violet back home, meet with Warren T. Fox, and see what we could do to get Tobias Dawson to back off.

Jo-Jo settled Violet in one of her upstairs bedrooms,

while Finn sweet-talked Sophia into going out into the rain and seeing what she could do about the blood Violet had dripped all over the backseat of his precious Aston Martin. Once Jo-Jo finished with Violet, the dwarf took me into the salon, where she gave me a plastic tub. The dwarf's cloud rune decorated the top of the container. I traced my fingernail over the pale blue paint.

In addition to healing with their hands, Air elementals like Jo-Jo could also infuse their magic in various products, like the ointment she'd just handed me. The ointment wouldn't work as well as Jo-Jo healing me herself, but it would keep me from keeling over until I could get to her. Jo-Jo also gave me a couple of smaller containers of the ointment, including one that looked like a makeup compact and another a solid tube that resembled lipstick.

"Thanks," I said. "I have a feeling I'm going to need these, if I'm getting mixed up with Tobias Dawson."

Jo-Jo's white eyes clouded over. "Maybe. Although I don't think the tub will be much help. Not this time."

Her voice was soft and distant, like she was somewhere far away instead of standing in front of me. In addition to her healing powers, Jo-Jo also had a bit of precognition. Most Airs did. They could read vibrations and feelings in the wind just like I could in whatever stone was near me. But where my element whispered to me of the past, theirs often hinted at the future. Another way the two elements opposed each other.

After a moment, Jo-Jo's eyes cleared, and she stared at me. "So, are we ever going to talk about it?"

"Talk about what?" I asked, sliding the compact and lipstick tube into my jeans pocket.

"That folder I gave you. The one Fletcher spent so long working on."

I grimaced. Jo-Jo had been the one who'd given me the folder about my murdered family two months ago soon after Fletcher's funeral. The dwarf had told me to come talk to her about the information when I was ready. Something else I hadn't done yet.

"What's there to talk about?" I shrugged. "For some reason, Fletcher Lane knew who I really was all along, and he never said a word to me about it. Instead, he spent his free time compiling all the info he could on my dead family, like I was another one of his targets. Some hit he was trying to figure out how to do. The old man gives the folder to you, then gets murdered before he can tell me about it—or what the hell he wanted me to do with the information. I don't see what we have to discuss."

Jo-Jo stared at me. "Your sister, for starters."

I snorted. "Oh yes, my baby sister, Bria, who I find out is alive after thinking she was dead for seventeen years."

"I can understand why you feel hurt, why you feel like Fletcher betrayed you. But family is everything, Gin," the dwarf said in a soft voice. "Whether it's the one you're born into or the one you make for yourself. Bria is your blood, your sister, and she's alive. You can't just ignore that."

"Fletcher left me a picture of her, but he didn't tell me how to find her. Where she's at, what she's even like now. Kind of sloppy of him to omit that information, don't you think?" I snapped.

"Fletcher Lane never did anything he didn't mean to," Jo-Jo said. "He left you that picture for a reason. You'll understand why one day."

The tone of her voice made the wheels of my brain grind together—just like my teeth were doing. My gray eyes burned into her light ones. "You know, don't you? You know why he compiled that information."

Jo-Jo tilted her head. "I have some ideas."

"Care to share?" I asked in a sarcastic tone.

The dwarf shook her head. "It's not my place. This is between you and Fletcher."

"He's *dead*."

"Doesn't mean he still can't speak to you," Jo-Jo said. "All you have to do is be willing to listen."

I opened my mouth to tell her to cut out the cryptic talk, that it was a little hard to have a conversation with someone who was buried six feet under. But Finn chose that moment to stroll into the salon. He jangled his car keys in his hand.

"You ready?" Finn asked.

I glanced at him. "Sophia cleaned the blood out of the back of the Aston already? How the hell did she do that?"

"Soap, water, and some dwarven elbow grease," Finn replied. "That woman's a genius. Smells and looks just like it did the day I got it."

There were only so many things you could do with soap and water. I didn't think getting blood out of leather was one of them. I looked at Jo-Jo, who gave me a guileless grin I didn't buy for a minute. I loved the two dwarven sisters, but the longer I was around Jo-Jo and Sophia Deveraux, the more I realized I didn't know anything about them. Not really. Not anything that seemed to matter, like the truth. Just as I hadn't seemed to know the real Fletcher Lane, either.

You ready?" Finn asked again.

I stared at Jo-Jo a moment longer, then turned to him. "Yeah. Let's get out of here."

Finn dropped me off at Fletcher's house, agreed to meet me at the Pork Pit tomorrow, then headed back to his apartment in the city. I checked the gravel in the driveway and the granite around the front door, using my Stone magic to listen for disturbances. But all the stones gave off their usual low, quiet vibrations. No visitors today.

But I always checked. Even in my retirement, I couldn't afford to lower my guard, especially not now with this mess with Jake McAllister going on. Because Jake had been royally pissed when the cops had dragged him away the other night. I had no doubt he was thinking about what he could do to hurt me, to get me to drop the charges against him. After all, he'd been ready to fry me with his Fire elemental magic just for what was in the cash register. Torture and murder wasn't a big leap to make from there. Whether Jake actually made a run at me or not was still up in the air. But I'd be ready either way.

It wasn't that late, but it had been a hell of a day. So I took a shower, threw on a pair of pajamas, and went to bed. I fell asleep almost immediately, and sometime later, the dream began . . .

I stood in the Pork Pit, chopping onions to add to tomorrow's baked beans. Despite the harsh, stinging aroma, my eyes didn't water. I never cried. Not anymore. Not since my family had been murdered. But that didn't mean I couldn't worry. My eyes flicked up to the clock on the wall: 10:05. A minute later than the last time I'd looked. Fear tightened my stomach until it felt as hard as the brick of the restaurant around me.

"He's late," I said in a soft voice.

"Don't be a worrywart, Gin," a teenage voice sneered behind me. "He always comes back."

I stopped my chopping and turned to look at Finnegan Lane. At fifteen, Finn was two years older than me, with a mop of dark brown hair and eyes that reminded me of wet grass. He was tall, with a solid chest that was already filling out. Nothing like my long, gangly, spider-thin arms and legs.

Finn perched on a stool in front of the cash register and sucked up the last dregs of the triple chocolate milkshake I'd made him. Finn didn't like me much, seeing me as competition for his widowed father's time, attention, and affection. I'd hoped my small bribe would at least make him tolerable while we waited for Fletcher. It had worked. Finn had been too busy gulping down the rich, sweet concoction to mock me. For a change.

It had been three months since Fletcher Lane had taken me in, and my life had become as normal as it was ever going to get. During the day, I attended school under the name Gin Blanco, catching up on what I'd missed while I'd been living on the streets and hiding from the Fire elemental who'd murdered my family. After school, I came straight to the Pork Pit to help Fletcher cook and clean and earn my keep. He might be putting a roof over my head, but I was determined to work for it as much as I could. Not a glamorous life by any means, and nothing like the soft, warm comfort I'd had before, but it had a thin illusion of safety. Something I appreciated now more than ever.

Only one thing bothered me—Fletcher's late-night jaunts.

About once a month, he'd disappear. Sometimes for a few hours, other times for a few days. He never said where he went or what he did, and I didn't ask. But I knew blood when I saw it, and Fletcher was often covered with it. Fresh, sticky, wet blood. Spattered all over his clothes, as though he'd just killed someone. Something else I knew about, even at thirteen.

My eyes drifted back to the clock: 10:07. Fletcher had vanished as soon as I'd come in this afternoon, saying he'd be back by seven, more than three hours ago. He'd never been this late before. What would I do if he didn't come back? Where would I go? Back on the streets most likely, begging for food, clothes, and shelter once more. My stomach twisted a little tighter—

The front door of the restaurant jerked open, making the bell chime. My heart lifted. A moment later, a pair of long arms tossed Fletcher Lane inside. He flew through the air, hit a table, flopped off it, and landed hard. Fletcher groaned and coughed. His blood flecked all over the clean floor I'd spent the afternoon mopping.

Another man stepped inside the Pork Pit, closed the door behind him, and turned around. Even above the roaring in my ears, I could still hear the bolt click home. Locking us in.

"Dad!" Finn yelled.

Finn started toward his injured father, but the man stepped in front of Fletcher's prone form and backhanded Finn. The teenager flew across the room. He too hit a table, bounced off, slid to the floor, and was still. I stood behind the counter, eyes wide, not believing this was really happening. Not now. Not again. Please, please, not again.

"You should have taken the job, Lane," the strange man growled.

He was a giant, almost two feet taller than me, with a wide, stout chest that reminded me of an iron park bench turned sideways. His black hair ringed his scalp like an upside-down bowl, while a curly goatee covered his square chin.

"I told you . . . Douglas," Fletcher rasped. "I don't . . . kill . . . kids . . . ever."

"You should have made an exception. Because now you're the one who's going to die."

Douglas slammed his booted foot into Fletcher's side. Fletcher groaned and coughed up more blood. I gasped. The giant's hazel eyes snapped up to me, settling on my nonexistent chest.

"Well, well." He smacked his lips. "Hello, pretty girl. We'll have some fun when I get through over here."

"Leave her alone," Fletcher said. "She's just a kid."

Fletcher tried to get up, but Douglas leaned down and punched him in the face. I heard his jaw crack across the room, and he fell back to the floor with a sharp grunt of pain. Finn still hadn't moved from where he'd fallen. I clamped a hand over my mouth to keep from screaming.

"You know," Douglas said, rolling up his shirtsleeves. "I'm going to enjoy beating you to death, Lane. It's been a while since I've gotten my hands good and bloody."

My stomach lurched, and for a moment, I thought I might vomit. My mother, my older sister, Annabella, my baby sister, Bria. In the last few months, I'd lost everyone I'd ever cared about. I couldn't lose Fletcher too. I just couldn't. He'd been the only person who'd shown me any kindness, any compassion. He was the only one left who cared whether I lived or died.

But what could I do? Douglas wouldn't stop until Fletcher

was dead—or he was. He'd said as much, and Fletcher was in no position to fight back. Not now.

In that moment, I knew what I had to do if I wanted to save Fletcher, if I wanted to save myself and the fragile little bubble of life, of normalcy, of security, that I'd built at the Pork Pit.

My gray eyes skipped down to the knife I still clutched, the one I'd been chopping onions with. A strange calm settled over me, and my fingers tightened around the handle until the stainless steel imprinted itself over the silverstone spider rune scar on my palm.

"Leave him alone," I said and dropped the knife below the counter, out of the giant's line of sight.

Douglas stopped rolling up his sleeves long enough to stare at me. "What did you say, little girl?"

I drew in a breath. "I said leave him alone, you fat, ugly, cow-faced bastard."

Douglas's eyes narrowed. "Well, aren't you a feisty one? A shame you're going to die so young—and so painfully."

The giant stepped over Fletcher and started toward me. Fletcher reached out, trying to stop him, but he was too weak and injured to hold onto the bigger, stronger man. I stayed where I was behind the counter and moved my right arm behind my leg, hiding the knife. Douglas came around the counter and reached for me.

His left hand grabbed my shoulder, yanking me toward him. Something wrenched in my arm, and pain exploded in my body. His right fist was already drawing back to hit me. Somehow, I pushed the pain away, gulped down a breath, lunged forward, and slammed the knife into his chest as hard and deep as I could.

My aim must have been better than I'd thought, because Douglas's hazel eyes bulged in surprise and pain. But he didn't go down. He staggered back. I kept my grip on the knife, and it slid free from his chest. Blood coated my fingers like hot grease, burning my skin. I wanted to drop the weapon. Oh, how I wanted to drop it. I might have, if Douglas hadn't started laughing.

"Stupid bitch," he said. "You think one little stab wound is going to stop me? I'll enjoy making you pay for that."

He came at me again, fist drawn back, but I didn't hesitate. Before he could hit me, I lurched forward and stabbed him again. I felt the blade slide off something in his chest. A rib, maybe, or some other bone. The sensation made me want to retch.

Douglas screamed and his beefy hand tangled in my brown hair, yanking my head back until I thought my neck would break. Out of the corner of my eye, I saw the glitter of yellowish fangs in his mouth. A vampire. He was a giant, and he was vampire. One who wanted to drink my blood to replace his own.

Panic filled me. Before he could sink his teeth into my neck, I wrested the knife out of his massive chest and plunged it into his body again.

And again.

And again.

Over and over I stabbed him, blood and tears and mucus covering me like a second skin. Someone was screaming. Me. Douglas let go of my hair and slid to the floor, but I didn't stop my assault. He kicked out, catching my leg. My knee buckled, and I stumbled back, grabbing the edge of the cash register for support. My shoulder burned with pain, just like my palms had when the Fire elemental who'd murdered my family had tortured me by making me hold onto my own spider rune medallion. The giant vampire flopped on his stomach and crawled around the counter. Some small part of my mind realized that he wasn't fighting me anymore, that he was actually trying to get away from me.

But I still went after him.

I threw myself onto his back and plunged the knife in between his shoulder blades. With my weight behind it, the weapon sank up to the hilt in his flesh. This time, Douglas didn't scream. Something seemed to give in his body, and he stilled. I raised the knife and stabbed him again—

Rough hands settled on my shoulders. I flailed against them, but they were stronger, pinning my arms to my sides. He pulled me close to his chest, and the smell of chicory coffee washed over me, penetrating the coppery stench of fresh blood.

"It's over, Gin," Fletcher said in my ear. "It's over. He's dead. You can quit stabbing him."

Fletcher crooned soft words into my ear, still cradling me in his arms. The knife slipped from my cramping hand and clattered onto the floor—

The sound might have only been in my dream, but its sharp echo woke me. So suddenly, that I was standing in the middle of my bedroom headed for the door before I realized it was only a dream, another one of my ugly memories manifesting itself. For a moment, I felt that hysterical rage burning through me, that gut-deep, primal need to survive no matter what the cost or consequences. The instinct that had dictated so much of my life.

I sighed and rubbed the gritty crud out of the corners

of my eyes. My psych professor at the community college would have said the dreams, the flashes of my past, were my psyche's way of dealing with the trauma. Of healing. Quack. To me, the dreams, the memories, were tiring trials, like Marley's ghost rattling his heavy chains at Scrooge. I'd lived through the events once already. I didn't need the Technicolor replay at night.

And I certainly didn't need to dwell on them now.

So I crawled into bed, snuggled back into the warm spot underneath the flannel sheets, and forced myself to relax. To let my body sink into the mattress. To unclench my jaw, uncurl my fists, and forget about the night I'd so brutally killed a man inside the Pork Pit. One of many.

But despite my best efforts, it was still a long, long time before I drifted off to sleep once more.

13

"This is getting to be an annoying occurrence," I said.

Just before noon the next day, I stood in the storefront of the Pork Pit. Once more, the restaurant was as empty as a church on Saturday night, except for Sophia Deveraux, who was at the back counter mixing white vinegar, sugar, mayonnaise, and black pepper to make the dressing for a batch of coleslaw. The Goth dwarf had lightened up her wardrobe a bit today. Instead of her usual black T-shirt, she wore one that was blood red—and decorated with lacy cutouts of white coffins. The collar around her neck resembled a thick garnet snake, with chunky square rhinestones for scales.

My eyes flicked over the empty booths, the abandoned tables, the deserted stools. Normally, Wednesday was a busy day, with people coming in to get their midweek barbecue fix. But not today. I knew Jonah McAllister was Mab Monroe's number-two guru, that he was a slick, powerful, corrupt lawyer in his own right, but he must have had more influence than I'd realized, if he could convince people to stay away from the Pork Pit two days in a row. I wondered how long the lawyer could keep up the pressure—and what I could do about it. Other than kill the bastard. Which would only cause more problems for me, in the end.

"Did you send everyone home with pay already?" I asked. "Is that why there's nobody here but you?"

"Um-mmm." Sophia's grunt for *yes.*

The Goth dwarf started stirring the dressing into a mound of chopped green and purple cabbage and carrots, even though there wasn't going to be anyone around to eat it. A shame, really.

Finn wasn't due to show up for a few more minutes, so I decided to fix myself a plate of food while I waited. Nobody else was going to be clamoring for barbecue today. A barbecue beef sandwich, baked beans, iced blackberry tea, some coleslaw from the dwarf's metal vat. I took my food and sat at one of the tables in the middle of the restaurant, so I could watch for Finn coming down the street and still talk to Sophia.

I was halfway through my food when the bell over the front door chimed. I looked up, expecting to see Finn. The man wore an impeccable business suit and polished wingtips, but that's where his resemblance to Finnegan Lane ended.

His gunmetal gray hair was parted on the side, with a thick doo-wop that curled up, down, and around his forehead like a scoop of vanilla soft serve. Given the gray hair, I would have put his age at around sixty. But he had the face of a much younger man—smooth, clean-shaven, and curiously free of wrinkles, even around the corners of his brown eyes. My guess? The finest Air elemental facials and skin treatments his hefty retainers could buy. Debutantes and trophy wives weren't the only vain folks in Ashland. He'd left his hair au naturel, though. Probably thought the silver color made him look more distinguished.

Still, for all his youthful vigor, the man radiated aw-shucks charm the way a snake-oil salesman might. Shake his hand, and you'd be wiping the grease off yours for the next ten minutes. And wondering where your wallet went. I recognized him from his many pictures in the newspaper and Fletcher's thick file on Mab Monroe and her flunkies.

Jonah McAllister, Ashland's slickest attorney and personal counsel to Mab herself, had just walked into my restaurant.

And he wasn't alone.

Jake McAllister strutted in through the door behind his old man. Rock-star jeans, vintage T-shirt, heavy boots, a black leather coat that skirted the floor. Another punk getup.

Two giant bodyguards also stepped inside the restaurant, taking up all the available space by the front door. The goons were probably on loan from Mab Monroe, via her other number-two man, enforcer Elliot Slater, who was a giant himself. Even if I'd had a customer today, she wouldn't have been able to get inside with the two behemoths blocking the entrance.

I stared at the giants, with their big, buglike eyes and

black suits that had probably taken a whole field of cotton to construct. No telltale bulges could be seen under their arms. At least I wouldn't have to worry about them shooting me, if things went badly here. They'd enjoy beating me to death more anyway. Giants who worked for Elliot Slater were notorious for that.

And they just might get a chance, the way the hate and magic sparked in Jake McAllister's brown eyes.

Jonah McAllister stood in the middle of the Pork Pit. But instead of looking at me or even Sophia, McAllister's gaze slid over the blue and pink booths, the faded pig tracks on the floor, the clean tabletops, the ancient cash register. His eyes resembled his son's—flat, brown, hard— but without the fiery glint of magic. Jake must have gotten his Fire power from his mother. She died several years ago, from what I remember having read in Fletcher's file.

Jonah McAllister didn't say anything. I might as well not have even been in the same room with the man for all the attention he paid me. His arrogance annoyed me. If that was the game he wanted to play, I was more than happy to participate. I sprinkled some more black pepper on top of my coleslaw, dug my fork into the colorful mound, and took another bite. Sweet and sour. Yeah, that's the way things were going today.

Finally, after two minutes of intense perusal, Jonah McAllister turned his head to me. I got the same treatment he'd given the rest of the restaurant. A slow, thoughtful gaze that weighed, measured, and calculated my worth down to the last rusty penny.

"I assume you're Gin Blanco, the owner of this fine establishment," McAllister said in a rich, deep, sonorous baritone voice that would boom like thunder in the closed confines of a courtroom.

I chewed another bite of coleslaw and tilted my head. "I am. Don't bother introducing yourself. I already know who you are, Mr. McAllister."

Jonah nodded his head back at me and gestured at the chair on the opposite side of the table. "May I be so kind as to take advantage of your hospitality?"

My lips twitched. My, my, my, he was slathering on the charm already, like sweet butter on a hot biscuit. "Sure."

McAllister unbuttoned his suit jacket and sat down. Jake made a move to join us, but his father turned a pair of cold eyes in his son's direction. "In the booth, Jake. Now."

Jake jerked like a dog who'd been whipped so many times all it took to make him cower was the faintest whisper of its owner's voice. But he did as his father asked and slid into a booth by the front window—the same one Eva Grayson and her friend Cassidy had sat in two nights ago.

The two giant guards remained where they were by the front door. Hands loose by their sides, chests puffed out, spines as tall and straight as flagpoles on the Fourth of July. They could have been statues for all the emotion or interest they showed, although their pale, bulging eyes never left me, not even for an instant. Still, sloppy, sloppy of them standing so far away. I could have easily palmed one of my silverstone knives and cut Jonah McAllister's throat before the guards took two steps.

Jonah McAllister turned his full attention to me. A thin smile pulled up his lips, although his face had been so sandblasted by Air elemental magic, no lines appeared anywhere. The curve of his lips did little to disguise the calculating glint in his eyes. Still, he had a presence about him, a commanding sort of air that probably made people promise him their first-born, if only he'd give them a moment of his time. The hard stare made me want to chuckle. McAllister was nothing compared to some of the folks I'd been up against as the Spider.

"Now, Ms. Blanco," he said in a smooth voice. "Let's talk."

"Sure," I replied. "Let's chat."

"Now, I know about your difficulties with my son the other night, but you have to realize that he just wasn't feeling like himself. Were you, Jake?"

Jake McAllister stared at the floor. "No," he muttered and kicked the underside of the booth opposite him.

Jonah nodded his head at the expected answer, no matter how sullen, fake, and reluctant it had been. "As you can see, my son feels terrible about his part in the incident on Monday night. I came here today hoping we could resolve this situation without any further interference by the police or the court system. What do you say?"

For a moment, I just stared at him. The man had a set of silverstone balls, I'd give him that. Jonah McAllister had nerve to spare, coming into my place of business and trying to talk his psychopathic son out of a lengthy jail term. I thought about stringing him along, pretending to be the weak, country bumpkin he so obviously thought I was. Letting him try to manipulate me the same way he did all those juries, all those people who tried to stand up to Mab Monroe. It'd be a hell of a show, if nothing else. But I had other things to do today, other problems to take care of, namely finding out why Tobias Dawson wanted Violet Fox dead. I didn't have the time or more importantly the inclination to go along quietly. Besides, I'd never been good at playing the victim.

"Let's be clear," I replied. "You're asking me to drop the charges against your son, right? Recant my statement to the police, refuse to testify, et cetera, et cetera, et cetera. That's what all the eye contact, oily words, and fake charm are about, yes?"

Jonah McAllister frowned, taken aback by my blunt tone. His eyes narrowed, and I met his gaze with a level one of my own. Something in my gray eyes must have registered with him, because the smile dropped from his face. Time to change tactics.

"All right," Jonah McAllister said. "You want to be compensated for your trouble. I can certainly understand that."

He reached into his suit and pulled out a slim black checkbook and a matching Mont Blanc fountain pen. "How much do you want?"

I laughed.

The chuckles rumbled out of my throat like motorcycle exhaust. Low, thick, black. Once more, McAllister's lips tightened into a thin, hard line, even if the rest of his face couldn't follow suit. The attorney didn't appreciate being laughed at. Too bad. Because he'd just tickled my funny bone with his blatant bribery attempt, whether he'd intended to or not.

"Sorry," I murmured. "I didn't actually expect you to bring your checkbook along, much less whip it out. You certainly have a style about you, Mr. McAllister, trying to bribe me in my own restaurant."

"I'm just trying to get this mess taken care of, Ms. Blanco," McAllister replied in a smooth tone. "It's not the first one I've cleaned up for my son, and I'm sure it won't be the last, no matter how many reformatory schools I've shipped him off to over the years. So why don't you just answer my question, and we can be done with this little charade."

I raised an eyebrow. "And what charade would that be?"

McAllister allowed himself a brief chuckle. Low, thick, black, just like mine had been. "The ludicrous idea you're going to testify against my son in any court of law in Ashland or anywhere else. The absurd notion I'd ever *allow* such a thing to happen."

"It's not a charade, Mr. McAllister," I said. "I fully intend to testify against your son—and there's nothing you can offer me to get me to change my mind. Certainly not money."

Jonah McAllister leaned forward. His brown eyes burned now, though not with Fire elemental magic. Instead, the lawyer put the full force of his charm into his gaze. "Come, come now, Ms. Blanco. There's no need to play the upstanding citizen with me. I've researched you. You're an orphan, aimless, a drifter who lucked into running this restaurant after the owner, the distant cousin who took you in, was murdered a few months ago. Hell, you can't even decide on a major so you can graduate from the community college you take so many classes from."

Good to know the Gin Blanco cover identity I'd worked so hard to build over the years had passed the thorough inspection of someone like Jonah McAllister. But that didn't stop the knife of pain that sliced through me. Because his words were truer than he realized. I had been something of a drifter, aimless, until Fletcher's murder. That brutal event and its aftermath had made me take a hard look at my life—and made me start to change. I was still a work in progress, but I'd be damned if Jonah McAllister was going to threaten anything that was mine.

McAllister took my silence to mean I was considering his proposal and decided to up the ante. "Besides, I'm certain there's something I have you might find of value or interest."

I shook my head. "You don't have anything I want, McAllister. Not a thing. Now why don't you drop the charade of a concerned father just trying to do what's best for his son? We both know little Jakie is an embarrassment all the way around. Did he tell you he was going to kill two girls just for kicks?"

"Shut up, bitch," Jake growled from his booth. "Or I'll fry your ass."

I stared at him. "You don't scare me, Jakie. I would have thought our encounter the other night would have proven that to you, even if you were high on your own Fire elemental magic at the time."

More sparks of hatred flashed to life in Jake's eyes, and the red, magical rage slowly filled his gaze. Jake opened his mouth, but his father held up a manicured hand. It was as free of wrinkles as his ageless face was.

"If you know who I am, Ms. Blanco, then you know who I work for," Jonah said in a smooth voice. Changing tactics again. Bringing out the big guns.

"Mab Monroe," I replied. "Everyone knows that."

"Then you know the connections I have, the power,

the influence. I can make things very difficult for you, if I so choose. You'll find standing up and doing the so-called right thing to be a very trying proposition."

My eyes narrowed, but I didn't respond.

"Have you wondered why you haven't had any customers the past two days?" Jonah said in a soft voice.

"No," I replied. "I figured it was you, telling people to steer clear of the Pork Pit. Just how long do you think you can do that?"

"As long as it takes for you to realize you can't win," he replied. "I'll keep people away every day until you go out of business, if I have to. I have the money, time, resources, and motivation to pull it off. Maybe you should think about that, before you so cavalierly throw away my generous offer. I'm trying to be civil about things. Trust me when I say you wouldn't like the alternative."

The bastard was actually trying to bully me. Trying to squeeze me the way he had so many other people over the years. It might have worked, if I'd still been thirteen, living on the streets, and mourning the loss of my family. It might have worked, if I'd still been Genevieve Snow. But no matter how much I changed, no matter how I tried to be different and leave my past profession behind, part of me would always be the Spider, the assassin as sharp as the silverstone knives she carried. I hadn't been small, weak, or frightened in a long time. And I certainly wasn't now.

"Keep it up as long as you like," I said. "Do whatever you want to keep people away from the Pork Pit. I'll still be here every single day, doors wide open, food hot and ready. I'd rather give my food to the rats in the streets than shut down for one fucking *hour* because of a slime-ball like you. Is that clear enough?"

The charm oozed out of Jonah McAllister's eyes, like syrup slopping over a pancake. "Crystal clear. Too bad, Ms. Blanco. Too bad for you."

"I told you we should have just killed the bitch," Jake snapped. "Come on, Dad. Let me do her, right here, right now. That dwarven bitch behind the counter too."

Cold rage filled me at his words. It was one thing to come into my restaurant, Fletcher's restaurant, and threaten me. I'd expected nothing less from the father-and-son duo. I knew I'd brought it on myself by having Jake McAllister arrested in the first place. But I'd be damned if the Fire elemental punk was going to talk trash about my family—or threaten them in any way. And Sophia Deveraux was family. So were Jo-Jo and Finn.

Fletcher Lane had been murdered five feet from where we were sitting. Been horribly, brutally tortured by a sadistic Air elemental. Nothing like that was ever going to happen to my family again. Not as long as I was still breathing. Especially not in here.

It was time to let Jake McAllister know I wasn't afraid of him and his petty threats—and exactly what I was capable of if push came to shove.

"You weren't man enough to take me out by yourself, Jakie," I snapped. "So what? Now, you're going to get Daddy and his guards to help you? Pathetic."

Evidently, Jake McAllister couldn't take a little criticism because he surged to his feet. Fire flashed in his eyes, and orange-red flames spurted out between his clenched fists. He charged at me.

For a second, I sat there and considered my options, something I probably should have done before I opened my smart mouth and started antagonizing the McAllisters. But somebody needed to wipe that bullying sneer off Jake McAllister's face, and I'd wanted to be the one to do it. I'd succeeded too, because now, hot anger filled Jake's eyes. If I let him put his hands on me, I was going to be in for a painful beat-down. One that might not stop until I was dead, especially with Jonah's giant bodyguards in the restaurant. Only one thing to do now. Fight back and make Jake think twice before he messed with me again. It was the only thing I knew how to do anyway.

Just before Jake hit me, I got to my feet, grabbed my plate off the table, stepped forward, and slammed the whole thing into his face as hard as I could.

Food splattered into Jake's eyes, and the cumin, red pepper, and other spices in the barbecue sauce caused him to scream. He stumbled back, flipped over a chair, and landed on his ass—hard. Jake cursed and tried to claw the mess off his face. He was too busy doing that to hold on to his magic, and the flames dancing on his fists snuffed out.

I turned back to Jonah McAllister and the two giant guards. Waiting.

Out of the corner of my eye, I saw Sophia come out from around the counter. The dwarf held a metal spoon in her hand. With her strength, it might as well have been a baseball bat. Sophia would back me up just like she had the other night. That's what family did.

Jonah McAllister saw her too and realized the odds had slipped to four on two. He looked through the storefront windows. People moved back and forth on the street outside, going out to lunch and back to work. More than one glanced inside the Pork Pit as they passed. A few slowed down long enough to get a good long gawk.

I could see the wheels turning in the lawyer's mind, as he considered the benefits of ordering his giant bodyguards to kill us now versus the possibility of folks witnessing it and more people potentially causing problems for him. His boss, Mab Monroe, might run Ashland, but I imagined she liked her flunkies to take care of their own business without involving her or being implicated in something unseemly themselves.

Jake threw aside a glop of coleslaw and scrambled to his feet. But before the Fire elemental could charge me again, Jonah McAllister shook his head. One of the giants stepped forward and put a restraining hand on Jake's shoulder, holding him in place. His neck almost snapped from the abrupt stop. The skin around his eyes was red and irritated from the spicy food, but it didn't compare to the sparks of hot magic that flickered in his hate-filled gaze.

"C'mon, Dad," Jake said, looking around the giant's arm and pleading with his father. "Let's do the bitch. She's not going to play ball with us."

Jonah McAllister looked at his son, then at me. He got to his feet and buttoned his suit jacket. "What have I told you about ruining people, Jake?"

"That it's more fun to do it slowly," Jake muttered.

Jonah nodded. "That's right. We'll see how Ms. Blanco feels in a few more days when she hasn't gotten any customers, and she has bills to pay. Until then, Ms. Blanco."

So Jonah McAllister had decided to stick to his specialty—squeezing people through somewhat legal means.

"Until then, Mr. McAllister." My eyes cut to Jake. "Just because you've gotten your daddy involved doesn't negate my threat. You come near me or my restaurant again, and I'll break more than just your wrist. You understand me?"

Jake surged against the giant. "You're dead, bitch! Dead! Do you hear me? Dead!"

Jonah gave his son a disgusted look and swept out of the Pork Pit. The giants flanked the still-struggling Jake, picked him up by his arms, and hauled him outside.

His hoarse screams reverberated all the way down the street—and so did his threats. The other night, I'd just insulted Jake by getting the upper hand. Now I'd humiliated him in front of his father. The Fire elemental couldn't allow that to slide. Not if he wanted the old man to at least pretend to respect him.

Daddy's orders or not, Jake McAllister was going to come for me, sooner rather than later, with all his Fire elemental–fueled rage.

And when he did, I'd gut the bastard—once and for all. No matter how many problems it might cause me.

* 14 *

Once Jake McAllister's screams faded away, I glanced over my shoulder at Sophia. "Was it good for you too?"

"Hmph." The dwarf gave me her usual grunt and headed toward the mop and bucket in the far corner.

"Leave the food where it is," I said. "It's my mess. I'll clean it up later. Besides, we're not going to have any more customers today. Go home, Sophia. Get some rest. You've earned it."

Sophia's black eyes met mine. She grunted again and got the mop anyway. I sighed. Brick was more talkative and responsive than the Goth dwarf. So I got on my knees and picked up the broken dish and smashed bits of food. I'd just thrown everything away and washed my hands in the sink when the bell over the front door chimed again. I turned, a silverstone knife already sliding into my hand.

But this time it was just Finn.

His green eyes went to Sophia and the mess she was mopping up. "Did I miss something?"

"Yeah," I replied. "Jake McAllister just dropped by—and he had his daddy with him."

Finn blinked. "Jonah McAllister came to the restaurant? What did he want? What did he say?"

I shrugged. "Drop the charges against his son or else. It went downhill from there. Attempted bribery, threats of violence, the promise of my own murder. The Ashland special."

Finn sighed. "And let me guess; you told the McAllisters exactly what they could do with their threats."

I grinned. "You know me."

Finn shook his head. "Gin, do you really want to start a family feud with the McAllisters? I thought you wanted to enjoy your retirement, live a nice, clean, simple life."

"No, I don't want to start a war with the McAllisters."

Finn raised his eyebrows in disbelief. "C'mon, Gin. Just admit it. You like thumbing your nose at bad guys and showing everyone exactly how strong and capable you are. You always have. That's why you pushed the McAllisters so hard today."

"All right, all right," I muttered. "So maybe my retirement's been a little more boring than I thought it would be. So maybe it felt good to knock Jake's nose out of joint when he made the stupid mistake of trying to rob me. Maybe it felt even better to do the same to his old man. But if I'd let Jake go that night, I'd have a dozen Jake McAllisters in here today, all thinking they could knock over my joint for a quick wad of cash. You know it. Ashland's all about survival of the toughest. It always has been. Word gets out you're weak or an easy mark, and you're finished, no matter what business you're in."

Finn shrugged his agreement.

"Besides, if I give in to the McAllisters now, they'll think they own me, that they actually *frightened* me today. Jake would start coming in here all the time, just to lord it over me. He'd think the restaurant was his own personal little fiefdom, take my money, and terrorize my customers. And I just couldn't stand that. Not in Fletcher's restaurant. Not when he worked so hard for so long to keep from paying protection money to anyone." I sighed. "Besides, it's too late for all that now anyway. I pissed off Jake McAllister again, embarrassed him in front of his father. He's not going to forget that. He's going to kill me—or at least try. He has to, or he'll never have his father's respect again. What little of it there was to start with."

"And then what are you going to do?" Finn asked. "You kill Jake, and Jonah will come down on you like a ton of bricks. Hell, he might even get Mab Monroe involved at that point."

A few weeks ago, someone had set me up to be killed as part of a larger power play against Mab Monroe, to try to wrest control of Ashland away from her. I'd gotten caught in the middle, which meant I was already more involved with the Fire elemental than I'd ever wanted to be.

I thought of that piece of paper in the file Fletcher had compiled about my family's murder, the one with Mab's name on it. Maybe I'd always been involved with the Fire elemental—I just hadn't known it. "I'll deal with Jake McAllister when he makes his move."

Finn opened his mouth again, but I held up my hand to cut him off.

"Enough talk," I said. "We have other people to deal with today, remember? Warren T. Fox. So let's go get Violet and see what Grandpa has to say for himself."

Finn and I left Sophia to clean up the remaining mess and headed over to Jo-Jo's to pick up Violet Fox. Finn had called ahead to say we were on our way, and the two of them waited on the front porch for us. Both sat in rocking chairs that creaked and cracked with every pass back and forth. Jo-Jo had dragged Rosco's basket outside, and the fat, lazy basset hound sat at the dwarf's feet, snoozing in a patch of sunlight that sliced across the porch slats.

Sophia must have lent Violet some of her clothes, because the girl was dressed in a pair of black jeans and a matching T-shirt with an enormous set of red lips on it. Despite Violet's full figure, the clothes sagged off her frame. Sophia Deveraux had quite a bit more muscle on her than Violet did.

Jo-Jo wore one of her many pink flowered dresses and a string of pearls that were each as big as a giant's tooth. Her bleached white-blond hair was arranged into its typical helmet of curls, and perfect makeup covered her face. As usual, the dwarf's feet were bare, despite the November chill in the air. Jo-Jo hated wearing socks. Said they made her feet hurt.

Finn and I stepped up onto the porch. Violet stood up, but Jo-Jo kept rocking in her chair.

"Sleep well?" I asked.

"As well as could be expected, I suppose. But Jo-Jo really made me feel at home." Violet gave her hostess a shy smile.

"Jo-Jo's good at that. We should get going."

"Say hello to Warren for me," Jo-Jo told Violet. "Tell him I'll be up that way for some more honey real soon."

Violet nodded. "Thank you. For everything."

Jo-Jo smiled at her. "No problem. Come on back sometime, and we'll work on your hair, darling."

Violet frowned, and her hand crept up to her frizzy blond locks. "What's wrong with my hair?"

Jo-Jo speared her with a hard look. "Nothing a hot-oil treatment and some good conditioning can't take care of."

Violet's confused frown deepened, but I grabbed her arm and pulled her off the porch before she could think too much about her split ends. Finn followed us, and we walked out to his car. Since we were going to be tooling up into the mountains today, Finn had decided to drive his oh-so-rugged Cadillac Escalade instead of his Aston Martin.

Violet stopped in front of the SUV and looked at us. "What about my car? Did you guys drive it somewhere last night?"

Finn and I exchanged a look. Driving Violet Fox's car to a safer location had been the last thing on my mind.

"We had to leave it in the parking lot," I said. "We were more concerned with getting you patched up than what to do with your car."

Violet's face paled. "You mean—you mean you left it there in that Southtown parking lot? All night?"

Her concern was more than warranted. Leaving a car in that neighborhood was just begging for trouble. By now, the vehicle had probably been stripped of everything but the cigarette lighter. Hell, somebody had probably taken that too. Barracudas couldn't pick a corpse any cleaner than the white trash and gangbangers in Southtown.

"It might be okay," Finn replied in a hopeful tone. "It's just a Honda. Several years old at that. It's not like I left my Aston Martin down there."

He shuddered at the thought. Violet chewed her lower lip.

"You have insurance, don't you?" I asked.

Violet nodded.

"Then you can worry about your car later. Right now we need to go see your grandfather. You still want us to help the two of you, right?"

Violet nodded again. "Of course. Like I said, the Tin Man was my only hope. Now you're my only hope."

Only hope? How very *Star Wars*. I grimaced. But I didn't tell Violet Fox how misplaced her trust in me was, how misguided, how laughable, even. That I only brought death to people, not hope. That I was doing this rare, pro bono good deed out of my own fucking insatiable curiosity more than anything else.

"Come on," I said, opening the door on the SUV. "Let's go."

Finn steered out of Jo-Jo's subdivision and headed north. Following Violet Fox's directions, we left the suburbs behind and drove through the heart of Northtown, where the rich, richer, and richest lived. People didn't have mansions in Northtown—they had estates. If not for the driveways, iron gates, and tasteful brick walls that could be seen from the streets, you might have thought the area was deserted. Because nobody with real wealth, magic, or power was gauche enough to let their home be seen from the road.

We drove on, still heading north. The terrain became rockier, more rugged, as the rolling hills of the lowlands gave way to knobby ridges and pine-covered mountains. Houses began to appear on the side of the road, although they were far less grand than the hidden McMansions that populated the Northtown estates. The road narrowed from four lanes to two and twisted back on itself in a series of switchbacks that would give most folks nausea. Instead of sleek sedans and chrome-covered SUVs, we began to pass dump- and coal trucks on the road.

After about thirty minutes of driving, Violet pointed out the windshield. "That's it, just up ahead at the crossroads."

Finn slowed, turned into a gravel lot, and parked. I peered out the window at the structure before us. The two-story clapboard building might have been a home or perhaps a hunting cabin, once upon a time. Although it was obviously old, the building sported a fresh coat of white paint, with the shutters trimmed in a pale green. Smaller, matching outbuildings squatted next to the main structure, connected to it by short, covered walkways.

Wooden steps led up to a front porch that was even wider than Jo-Jo's. The porch ran the length of all three buildings. Rocking chairs lined either side of the front door, along with barrels topped with checkerboards. The tin sign mounted above the main entrance gleamed like a new nickel in the sun. Country Daze, it read in green paint that matched the shutters. The roofs of all three buildings were also tin, the kind that made a slow, steady rain sound like a classical sonata.

The parking lot—if you wanted to call it that and not just loose gravel—curved around the store like a crescent moon. A stop sign squatted off to the right, and the road came to a T, forcing you to go right or left. One of the road signs pointed the way back to the interstate and declared that this stretch of pavement was part of some scenic, tourist-trap highway. The other sign featured an arrow and the words *Dawson No. 3*. Less than a mile away. Interesting. I might have to go check out the coal mine, after I met the illustrious Warren T. Fox.

We got out of the car. Underneath my boots, the parking lot gravel vibrated with the sounds of traffic and tires continually rolling across it. A low growl that told me the stones had seen a lot of people and cars go by in their time. Nothing sinister, just the everyday facts of life.

A smile brightened Violet Fox's face and softened her eyes, chasing away some of the lingering shadows from last night.

"You really love this place, don't you?" I asked.

She nodded. "My parents died when I was ten. My grandfather took me in and raised me. I've been helping him with the store ever since. It's like my second home, you know?"

Violet Fox and I were more alike than she realized, because I did know. Because I felt the same way about the Pork Pit. That's why I'd reacted so badly, so defensively, when Jonah McAllister had come calling today—because he wasn't just threatening my business, my livelihood, he was threatening my home as well. A piece of my heart.

The last piece of Fletcher Lane that I had since the old man was dead and gone and had left me nothing but riddles to solve.

Violet started to walk ahead to the store, but I grabbed her arm.

"Stay behind me."

"Why?" she asked.

"Just do it, all right?"

Finn stared at me over the hood of the SUV. "You think there's going to be trouble inside, Gin?"

I shrugged. "I don't know. But if this is such a popular place, why aren't there more cars here? It's lunchtime. Folks should be packed in here, getting a sandwich or a cold drink."

Finn's green eyes flicked over the gravel lot. Only one other car was parked in it, an anonymous navy sedan. His eyes drifted out to the road. A steady stream of traffic came and went at the crossroads, but none of the drivers looked at the store, much less pulled into the lot. Finn's face tightened.

"It's been quiet since Dawson started sending his men over to harass us," Violet explained. "People don't like to stop somewhere there might be trouble. Sometimes, we're lucky if we get five customers in eight hours. It's probably just a slow day."

"Come on," I said. "Let's go find out."

I led the way, with Finn behind me and Violet bringing up the rear. As we crossed the parking lot, I palmed one of my silverstone knives. If there was trouble inside, I'd be the first one to see it—and I wanted to be ready to deal with it.

The porch stairs didn't creak under my weight. They were too smooth and well-worn to do that. I walked up them, opened the front door, and stepped inside.

Country Daze was exactly what I'd expected. Scarred, ancient wooden floors. Displays of tourist T-shirts, key chains, and other doodads. An odd assortment of tools and outdoor equipment. Barrels full of rock candy, salt-water taffy, and cellophane-wrapped sugary pralines. A couple of coolers filled with old-fashioned glass soda pop bottles. A few more with sandwiches and other snacks. Tables full of honey, strawberry preserves, and apple butter. A revolving rack of cheap sunglasses. Nicer arrangements of quilts, baskets, and other, more expensive handmade items.

A large counter filled with silver jewelry formed a solid square in the middle of the store. An old man stood behind it, one hand resting on a large shotgun with a scarred wooden stock.

What little there was of his wispy white hair stuck up over his forehead as if it had been shocked upright by my appearance. His eyes were dark and shiny, as though two chocolate caramels had been stuffed in his face. He was about my size, stooped with age from his original, taller height. His skin was a dark, burnished brown, marking him as having some Native American heritage, most likely Cherokee in this neck of the woods. Deep lines grooved his face around his pinched mouth, as if he frowned a lot.

But perhaps most unsettling was the fact he wore a blue work shirt that could have come straight out of Fletcher Lane's closet. His dark eyes held the same fierce determination that Fletcher's had always had, and I could tell by his proud stance that this store was his life, his kingdom, and meant as much to him as the Pork Pit had to Fletcher. The man in front of me didn't look anything like my murdered mentor, but in some ways, he was a mirror image of Fletcher. It unsettled me—and made me feel a softness toward him that he'd done absolutely nothing to earn.

I didn't need Violet to tell me this was her grandfather, Warren T. Fox. A crotchety old coot who'd probably just as soon cuss as look at you. I knew the type. I'd been raised by one.

But Warren T. Fox wasn't alone.

There was another man with him, someone who needed no introduction, either. Someone I already knew all too well.

Detective Donovan Caine.

15

Now I knew whom the sedan outside belonged to. It had *cop car* written all over it. I just didn't realize it belonged to *my* cop.

The two men turned at the sound of my footsteps on the worn floor. Warren T. Fox frowned. Surprise filled Donovan Caine's golden eyes.

"Gin?" the detective asked. "What are you doing here?"

"You know her?" Warren Fox asked. His voice was high, thin, and reedy, like someone whistling through a broken flute.

"Yeah," Caine said in a low voice. "You might say I know her."

Well enough to sleep with me. Well enough to want to do the same again. Despite the fact I'd killed his former partner.

I opened my mouth to respond when Finn and Violet entered the store behind me. The girl walked around me, went straight to her grandfather, leaned across the wooden counter, and hugged his neck tight.

The old man's face softened for a moment, and the sheen of moisture dampened his eyes. Then he scowled and pulled away from the younger woman.

"Where have you been?" he snapped. "I've been worried sick about you."

Violet sighed. "I called you last night, Grandpa, remember? I told you I was staying with Eva."

The old man's brown eyes narrowed. "Yes, you called, and you sounded peculiar. But I wasn't really worried until Eva called here this morning. She said you two were supposed to have breakfast, and you didn't show."

Violet's face pinched up into an oh-shit-I've-just-been-caught look.

"I tried your cell phone to clarify the matter," Warren continued. "No answer."

"The battery died," Violet said in a soft, desperate voice.

I didn't know why she was still trying to stick to her story. The truth was going to come out in the next minute, two tops. I supposed Violet just wanted to spare her grandfather the ugly details about what had been done to her last night. Most people tended to block out things like that. Sometimes I wished I could do the same, instead of dwelling on the past the way I always did.

"I called the college, Eva again, and all your other friends I could remember. Nobody had seen you since last night," Warren replied in a curt tone. "Do you know how worried I was about you? With everything that's been going on? So I called Donovan to report you missing."

I eyed Caine. So that's what the detective was doing

here. And from Warren's use of his first name, it sounded like the two of them knew each other. The detective saw me looking and shrugged his lean shoulders.

Violet cringed again, and Warren opened his mouth to tear into his granddaughter some more for worrying him. But I cut him off.

"Enough. Violet didn't come home last night because someone tried to kill her."

That shut him up. Warren's mouth fell open, and he just stared at me. So did Donovan Caine. Violet shifted on her feet. Finn leaned against one of the coolers. Amusement filled his bright green eyes.

"Now that I have your attention," I said. "Let me tell you exactly what happened last night."

The five of us ended up on the store's wide front porch. I sat on the porch railing and leaned against one of the columns that supported the sloping tin roof. Finn was in a similar position across from me. Donovan Caine slouched on the steps between us, while Warren T. Fox and Violet rocked back and forth in two of the old-fashioned chairs.

"And there you have it," I said, wrapping up my tale. "That's why Violet didn't come home last night. Because she was a little busy getting her face put back together by an Air elemental. Her name's Jo-Jo Deveraux. You might know her."

Warren stared at me, his dark eyes narrowed and thoughtful. His gaze cut to Finn, then back to me. Thinking about something—or rather someone. Fletcher Lane.

"Let me get this straight, Gin," Donovan Caine said. "Violet went to the restaurant looking for some guy who called himself the Tin Man. Then someone shot up the Pork Pit, but you backtracked the shooter and realized he was aiming at Violet. So you used her credit card receipt to hack into her personal information and find her at Ashland Community College.

"Actually, that was me, detective," Finn said. "The only thing Gin knows how to hack into is warm bodies."

I shot him a dirty look. I hadn't exactly told Warren and Violet what I used to do, but I was sure the old coot had guessed. After all, he'd known Fletcher.

Donovan shook his head, ignoring Finn's remark. "You guys go to the college and see a dwarf attack Violet. Gin intervenes, and the two of you cart her off to some healer you know. Did I get it right?"

"More or less," Finn replied. "Although you left out the part where I helped Gin subdue the assailant."

"You and a monster truck," I sniped. "I did all the hard, dirty work, if you'll remember."

Finn grinned at me.

At the sight, Warren Fox made a deep sound in his throat, almost like a choking cough. He stared at Finn. "You're the spitting image of your father when you smile like that."

Some of the cheer drained out of Finn's green eyes. "That's what people tell me. He's dead, you know. Two months now."

Warren rocked back in his chair and nodded. "I know. Saw the obit in the newspaper." The old man stared at Finn a moment longer, then turned to me. "And you're Fletcher's girl, aren't you? The one he took in off the streets all those years ago?"

I frowned. "Yeah, I am. How do you know about that?"

Warren shrugged his stooped shoulders. "Fletcher and I might have had a falling out, but I kept tabs on him."

Nobody said anything. But Donovan Caine looked at me, questions in his golden eyes. Despite our having slept together, the detective didn't know about my time living on the streets—or that my family had been brutally murdered by a Fire elemental when I was thirteen. That I'd been tortured by the sadistic bitch and barely escaped with my life. I wasn't sure I wanted him to know. Pity was the last thing I wanted from the detective—or from anyone else.

Violet reached over, put her young, smooth hand on top of Warren's brown, speckled one, and stopped his rocking. "Gin came here to help us, Grandfather."

"Did she now?" Warren muttered.

Donovan frowned. "Help you with what, Warren?"

The old man resumed his rocking. "It's nothing. Just that bastard Tobias Dawson."

The detective's frown deepened. "Tobias Dawson? The dwarven mine owner?"

"He wants the land the store sits on," Violet explained in a quiet voice. "He's always wanted it, but he's become more and more insistent in the last two months."

"It's nothing," Warren muttered again. "Just his usual threats and bluster. He knows he'll never get the store or the land until I'm spinning in my grave."

"Or until your granddaughter's untimely rape and death puts you there," Finn pointed out. "Whatever Tobias Dawson's done in the past, he's decided to play hardball now—starting with Violet."

The college girl's fingers crept up to her face, and her nose twitched, as if she was reliving the pain she'd suffered last night. She shivered.

Donovan noticed Violet's reaction, and a sad, sick look filled his eyes. As a detective, Donovan had seen his share of victims. He knew how badly Violet had been hurt, how an innocent piece of her had been stripped away that she'd never get back. Anger and helplessness tightened Donovan's rough features. Because he also knew how hard it could be to get justice for victims like Violet. Especially in Ashland.

Warren noticed Violet's shiver as well. His wrinkled face tightened, and rage flashed like black lightning in his eyes. He reached over and patted his granddaughter's hand.

"Don't think about it, honey," Warren said. "Don't you ever think about what happened last night again. Because Tobias Dawson and his men will never lay another hand on you. I promise. No matter what I have to do to stop them." He muttered the last few words.

"You should have told me," Donovan Caine cut in. "I could help you with Dawson. Get him to back off."

Finn snorted his disbelief. The detective glared at him.

"Please," Finn scoffed. "Most of the Ashland po-po couldn't get a puppy to give up a chew toy, much less manage someone like Tobias Dawson. You know he's friends with Mab Monroe, right? You giving Dawson the hard cop stare isn't going to cause him indigestion, much less get him to back off."

"So what do you suggest?" the detective snapped.

"Well," I drawled. "There was a reason I drove up here today."

Donovan turned his golden eyes to me. Disappointment shimmered in his gaze. "To offer your services to Warren, right? To take care of Tobias Dawson in your own special way?"

"Something like that."

Disgust filled the detective's rugged face. "Once an assassin, always an assassin."

Violet let out a soft gasp.

Warren stared at me. "So you do what Fletcher Lane, what the Tin Man did."

"I used to. I'm retired now."

Warren peered at me with his shiny brown eyes. "And what did he call you?"

I met his gaze with a flat stare. "The Spider." The rune scars on my hand itched at the sound of my former assassin moniker. My mouth twisted. "Perhaps you've heard of me."

Warren gave a curt nod of his head. "I have."

Nobody said anything. A bit of wind gusted down off the mountaintop overhead and stirred up dust in the gravel parking lot. The breeze swept on, and the tiny whirlwinds died down.

"I want to thank you for saving my granddaughter's life," Warren said. "But why did you really come here? Why do you want to stick your neck out for two people you don't even know? Why do you want to tangle with somebody like Tobias Dawson? Like your friend said, he's not someone whose bad side you want to get on."

"Yeah," Donovan chimed in. "I thought you'd retired."

I stared at the detective. Our eyes met and held, and the familiar heat warmed the pit of my stomach. Answering warmth sparked in Donovan's eyes, although he tried to smother it with cool indifference.

I held the detective's gaze a moment longer, then turned my attention to Warren T. Fox, who'd stopped his rocking. His wrinkled face was blank and free of emotion, as though he couldn't care less about my answer, but his fingers dug into the arms of his chair. Warren needed me, and he knew it—even if Donovan Caine didn't.

"You're right," I said in a quiet voice. "I don't know you and your granddaughter, don't care about you. Why am I here? Because you once told your granddaughter a story about the Tin Man, about how he helped people with problems. You and Fletcher Lane might not have spoken in decades, but you still cared enough, thought enough about him to tell Violet that story. So I'm here because of Fletcher. Because the two of you were like brothers once upon a time. Because if Fletcher were still alive, he'd be sitting right here, whether you wanted him to or not."

There was more to it than that, of course. Much more. Like the fact that I felt this peculiar kinship with the Foxes. That in a weird way, seeing Violet and Warren together was like looking at a sweeter, more innocent version of Fletcher Lane and myself. What we might have been, if circumstances had been different. Maybe it was crazy, but I wanted the Foxes to stay just the way they were. To keep on loving and fighting. To keep what was left of their innocence, especially Violet.

My mouth twisted again. "Besides, my retirement's been pretty boring. Last night was the most excitement I've had in ages. And I find myself interested in why somebody like Tobias Dawson wants to get his hands on your land so badly he'd be willing to kill for it. I don't care much for bullies like that."

"A curious sort, huh?" Warren asked.

I smiled. "It's a trait I got from Fletcher. So what do you say? Shall I poke around and see what I can come up with? Or should Finn and I get in his car and go back to the Pork Pit? It's your choice, Warren."

The old man stared at me, that thoughtful look in his eyes once again. As though he knew something about me that I didn't even know myself. But Warren didn't get a chance to answer.

On the highway, a black SUV slowed. Instead of passing by like all the other cars and trucks, it pulled into the gravel lot. For a moment, I thought the Foxes were going to get their first customer of the day. Then I saw the white banner on the car door. The one that read *Dawson Mining Company*. The two *i*'s in *Mining* had been changed to resemble a rune—a lit stick of dynamite. The same rune the dwarf who'd attacked Violet had had tattooed on his biceps.

Finn noticed the writing and rune as well and glanced at me. "Trouble," he said in a low voice.

"You think?" I asked, already reaching for one of my knives.

16

The SUV stopped, the doors opened, and several men poured out. One after another, they kept coming, like they were clowns crammed into a circus car and this was their only chance of escape. Five men total: two giants, two shorter, burly guys, and a dwarf. The giants and other men wore work clothes—grimy coveralls, sturdy boots, thick gloves. The dwarf was dressed a little nicer—clean jeans, boots, a black T-shirt, and a tight black blazer that looked like it would do a Hulk rip down the sleeves if he breathed too hard.

The dwarf headed toward the front porch, and the rest of the men fell in step behind him. Finn and I exchanged a quick glance, and he made a motion with his hand. I nodded and slid left into a shadow that pooled on the porch. Finn moved off to the right. Donovan Caine stayed where he was on the porch steps, although the detective got to his feet. Warren and Violet Fox remained seated in their rocking chairs. Violet's face paled, and she crossed her arms over her stomach, like she was trying not to vomit. A scowl deepened the lines around Warren's mouth.

The dwarf stopped at the base of the stairs that led up to the wooden porch. He hitched his thumbs in the belt loops on his jeans and put a foot up on one of the stairs. Black snakeskin boots covered his feet. Orange-red flames spread over the tops, while silverstone tipped the pointed ends. A black ten-gallon hat rested on the dwarf's head, making him seem taller than his five feet, and the lariat tie around his neck featured a piece of turquoise almost as big as my fist. Somebody liked playing cowboy.

The dwarf's hair was a curly, sandy blond mane that fell to his shoulders. His nose was a bulbous piece of flesh that puckered out from his face like a boil, and a wide, fuzzy mustache drooped over his lips. His eyes were a pale, piercing blue in his tan face.

"Warren," the dwarf rumbled.

"Tobias," the old man replied.

The two men looked each other square in the eye the way old enemies do. Squinting, staring hard, neither one willing to back down, look away, or even fucking blink first.

While Tobias Dawson and Warren T. Fox played eye-ball chicken, my gaze flicked to the men standing behind the dwarf. The two shorter guys were human, although they probably had some giant blood mixed in them, from the looks of their powerful muscles and fists. Easy enough to put down with my knives. The giants standing behind them would be a bit more of a challenge—especially considering the fact each of their fists was only a little smaller than my head. I'd have to bob and weave with them, just like I'd done with the dwarven assassin last night. Still, nothing I couldn't handle.

My gray eyes rested on Tobias Dawson once more. He'd be the real problem, the real test. Especially since I felt the faintest bit of power trickling off him, like a piece of sandpaper just brushing against my skin. Magic. The blond, mustached dwarf had some kind of elemental magic.

Being an elemental myself, I could sense when others used their magic, of course. But there were some folks like Dawson who, well, *leaked* magic, for lack of a better word. Even when those elementals weren't actively using their power, magic still trickled out of them, like water from a leaky faucet. *Drip, drip, drip.* The magical runoff was easy to sense. Then there were people like me, whose magic was completely self-contained. No leaks, no drips, no runoff. My magic couldn't be felt at all unless I used it in an overt, forceful manner or someone had a particular knack for sniffing out elemental power.

Dawson's magic felt similar to my own, although I couldn't quite tell if the dwarf was a Stone or Ice. If I had to guess, I'd say Stone. The sensation rippling off him would have seemed smoother, cooler if he'd been an Ice elemental. Either way, I felt it. If things went badly, I'd go for the dwarf first, then his goons. With his magic and inherent dwarven strength and toughness, Tobias Dawson was definitely the greater threat.

My thumb rubbed over the hilt of the silverstone knife I'd already palmed. Even though I hadn't gotten in much practice with my knives lately, the weapon felt cold and comforting in my hand, just like always. An old, familiar friend.

Donovan Caine cleared his throat. Tobias tore his gaze away from Warren and stared at the detective. The dwarf gave Donovan the once-over, dismissed him as unimportant, and turned his attention back to Warren.

"Have you thought any more about my latest offer?" Tobias Dawson asked in a voice that was pure twangy country.

Warren's eyes narrowed. "I'll tell you the same thing I've been saying for two months now. I'm not interested in selling a soda pop to you, much less my store. You coming down here and asking me every other day isn't going to change my mind. No matter how much money you offer me."

Tobias leaned forward and spit. Tobacco juice stained the wooden plank an ugly brown at Warren's feet. "Now that's a damn shame, especially considering the most recent, more-than-generous offer I made you. Why don't you do the smart thing and sell out, old man?"

"Because this store, this land, has been in my family for more than three hundred years," Warren replied in a testy tone. "And I'm not letting someone like you come in and strip-mine it like you have the rest of the mountain."

Tobias sighed. A long, drawn-out see-what-I-have-to-put-up-with sigh that sounded as phony as Jonah McAllister had at the Pork Pit. "Now, you know that it's not exactly strip-mining, Warren. It's called mountaintop removal, and there's nothing illegal about it. We're just getting the coal out of the ground the quickest way we know how."

"And leaving everybody else with your mess," Warren

snapped. "Like I said, I'm not interested in letting you do that to my land. My whole backyard's turned into a damn sinkhole already from you and your mining."

Tobias's face hardened, and his mustache bristled with barely restrained anger. "I'm tired of waiting you out, old man. You can either sell out now, and get a good price for your land. Or—"

"Or what?" Warren snapped, cutting off the dwarf's threat. "You'll send some of your boys over here to make me see the light of day? You've tried that before, and it didn't work. A couple of shotgun blasts in their asses sent your boys running for the hills."

Tobias glared over his shoulder at his men, who all shuffled on their feet and stared at the ground.

I looked at Warren with a little more respect. Violet had told me that Warren had fought off Dawson's goons by himself, but I hadn't realized the old coot had put buckshot in their hides. Brave but stupid of him. Because Warren's shotgun and sheer stubbornness must have been part of the reason why the dwarf had decided to go after Violet instead.

Tobias turned back to face us and spit another mouthful of tobacco juice onto the porch. "All I'm saying is it would be a damn shame if something was to happen to you—or your sweet granddaughter."

The dwarf leered at Violet, staring at her boobs like he wanted to bury his head between them. Behind him, the giants and other men did the same. Violet's face paled a little more, but she crossed her arms over her chest and lifted up her head. She wasn't backing down any more than her grandfather was.

"By the way, Miss Violet," Tobias drawled in his twangy voice. "You haven't seen my brother Trace around anywhere, have you? Short guy, looks a fair bit like me, has a stick of dynamite tattooed on his arm. Drives a great big ole truck."

My gray eyes narrowed. Dawson had a brother named Trace? With a dynamite tattoo on his arm? That must be the dwarf that Finn had pancaked in the parking lot last night. The one whose body Sophia had disposed of.

"He was going to take care of some business for me in Southtown, over near the community college," Tobias said. "But he didn't come home last night. I thought you might have seen him, seeing as how you take all those classes at the college."

Violet's eyes widened behind the frames of her black glasses. She'd just realized Trace was the dwarf who'd attacked her, and she didn't know how to respond to Tobias Dawson's veiled innuendos, hints, and threats. But Finnegan Lane, being the Southern gentleman he was, stepped forward and intervened.

"Southtown's a dangerous neighborhood," Finn said in a soft tone. "Who knows what could have happened to him in a place like that? Just about anything, I imagine. Rough crowd, down in that part of Ashland. Junkies, vampire hookers, pimps. Not safe for a man to walk those streets by himself."

Tobias fixed Finn with a hard stare. "I wasn't talking to you, son. And what the hell would you know about it anyway?"

Finn smiled. "I grew up down there."

The dwarf stared at Finn with open hostility and suspicion. The two giants and two other men sensed their boss's displeasure. They shifted forward on their feet, as if to storm past him and come up onto the porch. Tobias tensed, ready to give the order. I palmed another knife. This was not going to end well.

But before the dwarf could tell his men to charge and take care of Warren T. Fox once and for all, Donovan Caine stepped down off the porch and pulled open his coat. The noontime sun made the gold badge on his belt glisten next to the dark shadow of his gun.

Tobias took in the badge and weapon. The dwarf's pale blue eyes flicked to the sedan sitting in front of the store. He knew a cop car when he saw one too. "Who are you?"

"Detective Donovan Caine. I'm an old family friend of the Foxes."

Finn flashed another grin and pointed his finger at the detective. "Maybe you've heard of him. He was the one who killed Alexis James, that loopy Air elemental who was stealing from Halo Industries, her own company. Happened about two months ago. It was all over the news. Mayor even gave him a medal for his stellar investigative work."

Donovan grimaced at Finn's sly, mocking praise. The detective knew what had really happened. That I'd been the one who'd killed Alexis James and her flunkies in the Ashland Rock Quarry. And that he'd accepted the credit and accolades for something he didn't even do.

Tobias Dawson knew who the detective was, all right. The knowledge flashed in his icy eyes. But Caine's status as a member of the Ashland police force made the dwarf reconsider his options. Ashland might be a dangerous city, and the cops might be as crooked as the surrounding mountain roads, but folks still stopped to think before they took out a member of the po-po. There were payoffs to consider, bribes, chains of command. Not to mention the fact Donovan Caine was something of a folk hero in the city—an honest cop among a sea of corrupt ones. Caine's death would raise a lot of questions, even for somebody as well connected as Tobias Dawson.

The dwarf's eyes went to Donovan, then Finn, then Warren. He didn't glance at me or Violet. Evidently us mere womenfolk weren't much of a threat. Sexist bastard. Still, Tobias could count as well as the next person. Five of us, five of him and his men. Even odds, even if we were saddled with an old man and two women. But Donovan Caine's badge was the tipping point—for now.

Tobias stared at Warren again. "You have three days to think about my last offer. And it is my *last* offer. I suggest you think real hard on it. Before I have to come back and ask you to reconsider it."

The dwarf spit out another stream of dirty tobacco juice, turned on his snakeskin boot heel, and stalked back to the SUV. He made a circle gesture with his hands. Round up and move out. One by one, his four goons turned and fell in step behind him.

Donovan Caine stayed where he was, face hard, hazel eyes cold and flat, until the vehicle pulled out of the parking lot. The driver took a right at the crossroads and zoomed out of sight. Once it was gone, the detective blew out a breath and rubbed a hand through his black hair.

"Well, that certainly was fun," Finn said in a cheery voice.

The five of us stayed on the porch a few more minutes, but Dawson and his men didn't turn around and come back. When I was sure they were gone, I tucked my silverstone knives back up my sleeves. Then I stepped off the porch and walked over to the spot where Tobias Dawson had stood so I could get a better sense of his magic. The gravel underneath my feet hummed with so much power it made my skin tingle and the spider rune scars on my palms itch. So the dwarf was a Stone elemental then. Someone who could control and manipulate the element. Strong in his magic, just like me.

I wondered if the dwarf had any other magical or special talents I needed to know about—before I killed him. Either way, Tobias Dawson had just morphed from a challenging kill into an exceptionally difficult one. I'd have to take him out hard and fast before he even realized what was happening. Otherwise, I'd be the one who ended up six feet under.

"What are you doing?" Donovan Caine asked, watching me turn around in a circle in the spot where the dwarf had stood.

"Nothing."

The detective knew that I had magic, that I was an Ice elemental, but I'd never told him about my greater, Stone power. My magic wasn't something I advertised, and I still wasn't quite sure what my relationship with Donovan Caine was—or what it would ever be.

Violet Fox hugged her chest with her arms. The brave

front she'd put on for Tobias Dawson's sake had vanished, leaving her round face ashen and sweaty, despite the fall chill. "You didn't do anything, Gin. Why didn't you do something? Why didn't you tell Dawson to back off and leave us alone?"

"Because I didn't want him to notice me," I said. "Not here, not now. That would make getting close to him later more difficult. The dwarf barely looked at me. He won't remember what I look like later, when I approach him again."

"You mean when you kill him," Donovan Caine said in a cold, flat voice.

"Yes," I said. "When I kill him."

Donovan stared at me. His eyes shimmered like liquid gold in his tight face. After a few seconds of scrutiny, he shook his head. "You know I can't let you do that. I can't let you go after Tobias Dawson."

I sighed. Despite the fact the detective and I had worked together before, we were once again right back where we started. With him clinging to his oh-so-high, moralistic ideals and standing in the way of me doing what simply needed to be done.

"I don't see how you have much of a choice, detective," Finn cut in. "Because Tobias Dawson isn't going to stop harassing the Foxes until he gets this land. Which means he's not going to stop until they're both dead. The bastard sent his brother to rape and murder Violet last night. A nineteen-year-old girl who's probably never hurt anyone in her entire life. And here you are trying to protect him, when you should be worried about a young woman and her grandfather. What's wrong with this picture?"

Donovan turned his hot glare to Finn, who stared back at the detective. Both men had their hands clenched into fists. I sighed again. Finn was on my side, of course, just like a brother would be, and his words and logic were dead-on. But there was only one way to get the detective to go along with the assassination of Tobias Dawson—one small step at a time. Which meant it was up to me to tap-dance Donovan Caine in the direction I wanted him to go.

"Finn?" I asked.

"Yeah?"

"Did you bring your laptop with you?"

He sniffed. "Do I ever leave home without it?"

Question asked and answered. Sometimes I wondered how Finn pulled himself away from his computer long enough to chase after anything that had boobs.

"Then get on it. I want you to find out everything you can about Tobias Dawson. Habits, hobbies, business interests, anything that might be useful."

Finn nodded and headed toward his SUV.

"And what are you going to do?" Donovan Caine asked in a low voice.

I gave him a bright smile. "Not me, detective. *We*. We are going to go check out the dwarf's coal mine, and see if we can figure out why Tobias Dawson suddenly has a hard-on for the land Warren's store sits on. What do you say, detective? Up for a little breaking and entering tonight?"

Donovan grimaced and looked away.

"So you're going to help us then?" Violet asked.

I looked at her. "I've been helping you for a while now,

Violet. But yeah, I'm going to take care of Dawson for you."

"Why?" Warren Fox asked. "I knew the kind of fees Fletcher Lane got for his services—and that was years ago. I certainly can't pay you anything close to that."

"Don't worry about the money," I said. "Just give me a couple of jars of honey to take back to Jo-Jo, and we'll call it even."

"You're not even going to charge them?" Donovan Caine asked with suspicion. "Why? So you can take their land for yourself?"

I raised an eyebrow. "And what would I do with a store up here in coal country? I already have a barbecue restaurant to run. That's plenty for me. So no, I don't want their land. Believe it or not, detective, I occasionally lend out my services for free. Pro-fucking-bono, as it were, when the situation warrants it."

"But why?" Caine persisted. "Why do you want to kill Tobias Dawson so badly?"

My gaze flicked to Violet. The image of her ruined face flashed before my eyes, and the sounds of her choked sobs rang in my ears. Despite the fact Jo-Jo Deveraux had healed her, Violet had lost some of her innocence last night. Some small, pure, happy part of her that she wasn't ever going to get back. Just like I had the night my family had been murdered, when everything and everyone I'd loved had been burned to ash in the space of a few hours.

Maybe I wanted to make sure Violet didn't end up like me—hard, cold, distant from all but a very few. Maybe I wanted to get her revenge for her, since I was having so much trouble getting mine. Maybe I just wanted her to be able to sleep a little easier at night, knowing that Tobias Dawson was feeding the worms.

I couldn't pinpoint the exact reason myself, and I couldn't tell the detective all that. I didn't want to reveal that part of myself to him. Besides, he wouldn't have believed me anyway. So I went for my usual flip answer.

"Because Tobias Dawson is nothing more than a rich, spoiled bully who wants to be a cowboy," I said. "Because I'm bored. But mainly, because I'm going to thoroughly enjoy knocking his pompous ass out of that ridiculous hat and ugly boots before I slit his throat."

✶ 17 ✶

There was no further argument about my services or murky intentions, so we got to work.

Finn retrieved his laptop from his SUV and set it up on the counter inside Country Daze. Violet rustled around and found an extension cord so he could save his battery. Finn gave her a saucy wink and a sly, charming grin, working his magic. Violet smiled, ducked her head, and leaned down to get something else for him.

Behind Violet, Warren T. Fox narrowed his dark eyes, crossed his arms over his thin chest, and cast a significant glance at the shotgun on top of the counter. Finn cleared his throat and turned his attention to his laptop. He might be able to charm women, but Finn always had considerably less luck with their male relatives. Especially ones as protective and suspicious as Warren.

Donovan Caine stalked back and forth down the store's aisles, his cell phone stuck to his ear. The detective had begrudgingly offered to help Finn get background info on Tobias Dawson, although he'd made it clear he still wasn't on board with my plan to assassinate the dwarf. Still, it was a baby step in the right direction. Because I was killing the dwarf whether Donovan Caine liked it or not.

While the others worked, I stared out the store's front windows and kept an eye on the crossroads outside. Tobias Dawson might have said he wasn't returning for a couple of days, but I didn't put it past him to double back—with even more men. Which is why I also took the precaution of pulling out my cell phone and calling Sophia Deveraux at the Pork Pit. The phone only rang twice before she picked it up. Despite my instructions to the contrary, the Goth dwarf was still at the barbecue restaurant.

"Hmph?" Sophia answered with her usual, monotone grunt.

"It's Gin. This is going to be a bit more difficult than I'd originally thought. I need you to close the restaurant for the day and come up here. Might as well put a sign on the door saying we're closed the rest of the week, while you're at it."

"Problems?" Sophia rasped.

I glanced at Violet, who was now handing Finn a cold bottle of Dr. Enuf, and Warren, who was still glowering at him. "Not so much a problem as a concern. I need to go do some recon work on Tobias Dawson, and I don't want to leave Violet and her grandfather alone in the store while I go do it. I don't want Dawson and his men coming around behind me and doing something stupid, like burning down the store with the Foxes inside. So you'll be on bodyguard duty, along with Finn. Think you can handle it?"

"Numbers?"

"He brought two giants with him and two other guys who looked like half giants. I don't know exactly how many men Dawson has at his disposal, but I imagine he could strong-arm his whole payroll, if he really wanted to."

Sophia thought about the odds for a few seconds.

"So are you coming?" I asked, although I already knew what the answer would be. Sophia liked a challenge just as much as I did.

"Um-mmm." *Yes,* in not-so-many words.

"Good," I said. "We'll be waiting."

We hung up, and I slipped the phone back in my pocket. The wooden floorboards creaked, and Warren T. Fox came to stand beside me. He too stared out the front windows of the store. Two cars zoomed by, barely slowing long enough to make the left turn at the crossroads before heading toward the interstate.

We didn't speak. Silence was one thing that had never bothered me. Didn't appear to bother Warren much either. But we needed to get on with things. Because the Foxes couldn't hide here in the store forever, and I wanted to make sure they were someplace safe when I left them to go snooping over at the mine.

"Where's your house?" I asked. "Does Violet still live at home with you?"

Warren nodded. "She does. The house sits on the back edge of the lot, behind a stand of trees, next to a small creek. You can't see it from the road."

So not only did Tobias Dawson want the land where Warren's store sat, he also wanted the old man's house. In the South, taking someone's ancestral home was even worse than merely wanting their land. Even more reason for me to kill the dwarf.

"I'll need to see the house in a bit. Make sure it's as secure as it can be."

Not that some wood, nails, and a door would keep out a giant, but every little bit helped. Even a few seconds' delay could mean the difference between the Foxes escaping or not, living or dying.

Warren nodded, and we lapsed into silence again.

"I suppose I should thank you," Warren finally said in a gruff voice. "For wanting to help me."

"You don't have to thank me. Just do what I say, and everything will be fine."

Warren stared at me. "You're a lot like him, you know. Like Fletcher."

I didn't respond. At one time, I would have enjoyed the comparison. Now, I wasn't so sure I wanted to be like Fletcher Lane, with his secrets and hidden agendas. I still couldn't believe he'd known who I really was all these years, that he'd compiled that file about the murder of my family, that he'd known Bria was alive and where she was—and that he hadn't told me about any of it.

Why had Fletcher kept it from me? What had been the point of hiding it? I thought I'd known Fletcher better than anyone. I was his apprentice, after all. The one he'd taught all his secrets to. Now I wondered if I'd really known anything about him—other than what he'd wanted me to know.

"You're hard like he was," Warren continued. "Able to put his feelings aside and do what needed to be done no matter what. I always admired that about him. Fletcher was always stronger than me. Even when Stella left us both, I never saw him break. He never wavered, not once, not even for a second. You would have never known anything was even wrong with him."

Stella, the woman they'd both loved. The one who'd ruined their friendship, then run off with another man.

Warren lapsed into silence again, and his glossy eyes dulled with old memories. After a minute, he shook his head and came back to himself. "Anyway, I know I don't deserve it, but I appreciate your help, especially for Violet's sake. She would have died last night if not for you."

I shrugged. "I would have done the same for anyone else."

Warren shook his head. "No, I don't think you would have. You know there are some people who just deserve killing. Something Donovan hasn't realized yet. Something he won't ever be able to admit to himself. His father was the same way. He tried to help me out with Dawson some years back, but it didn't take."

"So that's how you know Donovan. You knew his father."

Warren nodded. "Daniel Caine, a fine man. Donovan is too. But he's not the one for you."

He was more observant than I'd given him credit for. I raised an eyebrow. "What do you mean?"

Warren glanced over his shoulder, but Donovan Caine was still talking on his cell phone, so he turned back to me. "I mean you and Donovan are on opposite sides. Always have been, always will be. He's not going to change, and he'll never accept what you are, what you've done. It's just not in his nature, no matter how much he might want to."

"And you're telling me this because . . ."

"Because Donovan's a good man, and you're good too, in your own way. At least you should be if Fletcher raised you right," Warren said. "At the very least, you're good at what you do."

"The best. I was the best at what I used to do," I corrected him. "But I'm retired now."

Warren snorted. "Right. Just remember what I said. Don't get too attached to Donovan Caine. Because it's not going to end the way you want it to."

His eyes didn't glow with power, and I didn't sense any magic trickling off him, which meant Warren T. Fox didn't have an Air elemental's sense of precognition. Whether Warren had any magic or not, he was still smart enough to recognize the conflict between me and Donovan Caine.

Finn murmured something, which made Violet giggle. Warren's head snapped around at the sound. He shuffled off to glower at Finn and put an end to the younger man's flirting with his granddaughter. This time, I could have offered him the advice of not bothering. Short of shooting Finn with the shotgun, there was nothing Warren could do. Flirting with the opposite sex was as natural and necessary as breathing to Finn.

I looked past the trio to where Donovan Caine paced back and forth on the floorboards. The detective saw me watching him, frowned, and turned his back to me. Shutting me out once again.

I sighed. Warren T. Fox was definitely sharper than he looked. Even worse, I had a sinking suspicion he was right about me and Donovan. The detective wasn't going to let it work between us, no matter how hot the sex had been, no matter how bright the attraction still flared. My gray eyes traced over the detective's lean body.

A shame, really.

By the time I followed Warren over to his house, made everything as secure as I could, and walked back to the store, it was well into the afternoon. My stomach growled, reminding me that the half of the barbecue sandwich I'd eaten for lunch was long gone. So I perused the coolers in the front of the country store. I picked up a cellophane-wrapped bologna and Swiss cheese sandwich from one of the coolers, along with a bottle of lemonade. Some chips and a candy bar from the display rack near the counter completed my gourmet meal. I took my items to the cash register.

"You don't have to pay for that," Violet Fox protested.

I slapped a ten-spot down on the counter. "Sure I do. Keep the change."

I took my dinner out onto the front porch and settled into a rocking chair. One of the barrels made an excellent table for my food, and I dug in. The lemonade was far too weak and watered down for my taste, and the bread was getting hard and stale, but smothering it with mayo made it palatable enough. Not the best meal I'd ever had, but it would do. I'd hate to go to the trouble of breaking into

Tobias Dawson's office only to have my stomach growl and give me away to whatever guards he might have stationed there.

I'd just unwrapped my candy bar when Donovan Caine stepped out onto the porch. The detective hesitated, then walked over to me.

"Care if I join you?" he asked in a low voice.

"Sure." I sank my teeth into the candy bar. Crunchy, slightly bitter almonds coated with dark chocolate. Definitely the best part of my meal.

The detective stared out at the crossroads. An empty coal truck rumbled by, stopped, and made the turn to go on up to the mine.

"I got some info on Tobias Dawson," Donovan said. "And it's not good. He's a real piece of work, from all reports. He's got almost a complete stranglehold on the mining in the area, so he pays his employees below-average wages. A couple of them tried to form a union a few months back. They all met with mining accidents soon after. Roof collapses, equipment malfunctions, even a cave-in."

"Did you expect anything else? You saw Dawson threatening the Foxes. He's not a nice man."

Donovan ran a hand through his black hair. "But that doesn't mean it's okay for you to just kill him."

"And just because Dawson has money doesn't make it right for him to intimidate people into getting whatever he wants," I pointed out. "So which is worse—me assassinating Dawson for threatening the Foxes or him telling his brother to go rape and murder Violet just to send a message to her grandfather?"

Caine blew out a long breath. "I don't know. I just don't know. But two months ago, I would have taken you in for plotting to kill someone. Slapped my handcuffs on you and dragged you down to the station, no questions asked."

"And now?"

Donovan looked out at the road, although I got the impression he wasn't really seeing it. "Now, I'm thinking about helping you get to him."

"Don't sound so broken up about it, detective. Getting rid of Dawson is the right thing to do."

He shook his head. "No, it's what *you* want to do. I'm just going along with you."

"Why?" I asked. "Why go along with me if it bothers your conscience so much?"

Donovan stared at me. Emotions flickered like candle flames in his eyes. Guilt. Desire. Need. Weariness. Resignation. "I don't know that either."

Tires crunched on the gravel, and a classic convertible pulled into the parking lot. The vehicle was as black as black could be, with a long body and swooping fins. Despite its pristine, gleaming beauty, the convertible always reminded me of a hearse. The top was up, but I didn't need to see inside to know who was driving. Sophia Deveraux had arrived. I got to my feet.

Donovan tensed. "Trouble?"

"Relax, detective. I called a friend to come help Finn watch the Foxes, while you and I sneak off to Dawson's mine."

Sophia opened the driver's door and stepped out.

The detective frowned. "Isn't that your cook from the

Pork Pit? The one who was working when Jake McAllister tried to rob you?"

"Yeah," I replied. "She moonlights as a badass, just like me."

But Sophia wasn't alone. The passenger side door opened, and a mound of bleached, white-blond curls appeared, partially covered with a sheer pink headscarf. Sophia had brought her big sister, Jo-Jo, along with her.

Jo-Jo said something to Sophia that I couldn't hear, and the Goth dwarf grunted back in response. Then the two women shut their car doors and headed toward us. They stopped at the bottom of the stairs. Sophia gave Donovan a flat, uninterested look, but Jo-Jo's eyes lit up at the sight of the rugged detective. In addition to being a social butterfly, the dwarf was also a terrible flirt, just like Finn.

"Well, now," Jo-Jo asked, her pale eyes landing on Donovan. "Who is this?"

I stood and made the introductions. "Jo-Jo Deveraux, this is Donovan Caine with the Ashland Police Department. And vice versa. The Goth chick is Sophia, Jo-Jo's sister."

Jo-Jo held out her hand, as though she wanted Donovan to kiss it. Disappointment flickered across the dwarf's face when he merely shook it instead.

"I asked Sophia to watch Warren and Violet while we check out Dawson's mine," I explained to the detective.

"And I'm here for moral support," Jo-Jo chimed in.

Donovan Caine eyed the dwarf's rose-covered dress, pearls, high-heeled sandals, and manicured nails. No doubt he thought she wouldn't be much good in a fight.

But Jo-Jo was almost as strong as Sophia—and she had her Air elemental magic to supplement her natural strength. Even I didn't know if I could take Jo-Jo in a fight.

"Come on," I said. "Let's go inside where the others are."

* 18 *

Finn was still digging for info on Tobias Dawson, so I left him and the Foxes in Sophia's and Jo-Jo's capable hands. Violet was happy to see the older dwarf again and started peppering her with questions about hot-oil hair treatments.

To my surprise, so was Warren. Jo-Jo must have known him and his parents better than she'd let on because the old man pulled up two rocking chairs, and he and Jo-Jo proceeded to gossip about all the folks they knew up here in Ridgeline Hollow. Then again, Jo-Jo Deveraux was more than two hundred fifty years old. I couldn't imagine how many people she'd met in her lifetime. Hard to keep track of them all, but somehow she managed it. She seemed especially chatty with Warren.

That left Sophia with guard duty. I showed her the various access points to the store and the house out back. Once we finished, the Goth dwarf stuck an iPod in her ears and took up a position on the front porch steps to keep an eye out for Tobias Dawson and his men.

I also made a quick circuit through the store and picked up a few items I thought might be useful. Flashlights, rope, gloves, binoculars. I left a hundred on the counter to cover everything. Then Donovan Caine and I left the others in the store and got into his sedan.

The detective sank into the driver's seat, while I took the passenger's side. Unlike most cop cars I'd been in, this one was clean to the point of being pristine. No fast-food wrappers, no empty soda cups, no trash or debris of any kind littered the inside. The car even smelled like Caine—clean and slightly soapy. Or maybe that was just the air freshener dangling from the rearview mirror. Either way, I breathed in, enjoying the crisp aroma. Mmm.

Donovan started the car and looked at me. "Where to?"

I glanced down at the printouts Finn had given me. Finn hadn't found much on Tobias Dawson yet, but he'd been able to locate several maps of the dwarf's mine—including the building that housed his office.

"Go to the stop sign and hang a left like you're going back to the interstate," I said. "There's an old access road that runs over the top of the ridge and overlooks the mine. We can stop up there and see what's going on below before we make our move."

Donovan nodded and steered the sedan out of the parking lot. He cruised to a stop, then made the appropriate turn. We didn't speak as the vehicle climbed up the twisting, winding road.

As the tourist sign at the crossroads claimed, it was a

scenic stretch of highway, with dense woods that crowded to the edge of the road on both sides. A couple of weeks ago, the fall foliage would have been magnificent. But the elevation was slightly higher here than in the rest of Ashland, which meant the maples, oaks, and poplars had already shed most of their colorful leaves. Still, I found the curving branches of the trees enchanting in their own way, ribbons of wood winding together to make artful shapes.

Through the bare limbs, I spotted the creek Warren Fox had mentioned, the one that curved around the back of his house and flowed past Country Daze. I didn't know that I'd call it a mere creek, though. The rushing water stretched thirty feet wide in some places, tumbling over unusual rock formations. Gravel pull-offs on either side of the road marked popular fishing and wading spots.

I glanced at the map again. "Take the next right."

Donovan nodded and did as I asked.

The smooth concrete fell away to cracked pavement as the car twisted and turned even higher onto the mountain ridge. Gravel replaced the pavement. It ran out into two hard-packed dirt ruts that passed for a road. Despite the terrain, Donovan drove on. We went almost a mile down the ruts before they ended in a small, wooded clearing. The detective stopped the car, and we got out.

The air was even cooler up here than it had been at Country Daze, and it had started to drizzle again. I turned up the collar of my black fleece jacket, hefted the coil of rope over my shoulder, and made sure I had all my other supplies. Donovan reached into the backseat and grabbed a navy rain slicker embossed with the words *Ash-*

land Police Department on the back. He offered the jacket to me, but I shook my head.

"You keep it," I said. "You're the one who brought it, not me."

The detective shrugged into the jacket. I stuffed the maps Finn had given me into my jeans pocket so they wouldn't get too wet.

"This way," I told the detective.

I headed out of the clearing. The drizzling rain had already slicked the assorted weeds and fallen leaves underfoot, so I walked carefully and slowly. I didn't need a sprained or broken ankle tonight. Behind me, Donovan did the same.

A sign at the end of the clearing read *No Trespassing— Dawson Mining Company,* but I ignored it. Trespassing was going to be the least of my crimes this evening. We walked in silence through the wet woods for a few minutes before we reached the lip of the ridge. I crouched behind a tall pine on the edge, and Donovan squatted beside me. Despite the rain, the detective's clean, soapy scent washed over me. Mmm. The smell made me want to turn to him, press my lips to his, and lower us both to the forest floor. Sure, the leaves and earth would be a little damp, but I had no doubt Donovan and I could warm each other up—in a hurry.

Unfortunately, I wasn't here for a quickie with the detective, no matter how pleasurable it might be. So I raised the binoculars I'd brought along up to my eyes. Below me, the ridge sloped downward and then bottomed out, forming a fat U-shape. The ridge we stood on was the base of the U, while the rest of the mountain had been removed to form the open area. Ramps of dirt twisted down either leg of the U, providing access to the topmost portions of the slope.

A variety of machines sat on the basin floor. Backhoes, bulldozers, and other machines designed to move earth—and a lot of it. Others were just big, hulking, complicated brutes of metal with more arms, cranes, and buckets than I'd ever seen. Some of them were bigger than small houses, and I had no idea what their names were or even what they did. There were dump trucks too, with beds and wheels even bigger than the ones on the vehicle Finn had used to run over Trace Dawson.

Across the basin floor was the other end of the operation—the underground mine. A square black hole in the wall of the mountain, held open by concrete support beams. Metal tracks ran into and out of the wide mouth. I supposed at one time the tracks had been used to help move men and equipment down into the earth. Now they looked dull and rusty from lack of use. I could see places where the metal had been torn up and not replaced. I remembered what Violet Fox had said about the coal in the underground mine running out and how it had been idle for some time now. It was easy to tell that the focus had shifted to stripping off the mountain one layer at a time. That's what all the equipment was here for—to cart coal and dirt away, not bring it up out of the ground. Not anymore.

More tracks curved around the far side of the basin and disappeared from sight. According to Finn's map, they led to another area where the coal was stored and processed, among other things. I had a lot of knowledge about a lot of subjects, thanks to all the classes that I'd taken at Ashland Community College, but coal mining wasn't one of them.

But even from my high vantage point, I could hear the stone of the mountain. Growling, snarling, cursing, muttering. The stone was supremely angry at the cruel damage that had been done to it. Once upon a time, this must have been a lovely spot, with steep slopes, trees, and rocky outcroppings as far as the eye could see. But now there was nothing left but stripped, bare earth, rock, and machinery. The stone's vibrations made me want to draw on my magic, to make the whole mine, the whole rest of the mountain, crumble down and bury the men and machines that had been so cruel to her. But I didn't have that kind of power, and it wouldn't help Warren and Violet in any way. So I gritted my teeth and forced the feeling aside.

It was after six now and already growing dark. I passed the binoculars to Donovan Caine, so the detective could watch the workers climb down off their machines and head out of the basin. I kept scanning the area, fixing the overall layout in my mind. It would be easy to lose your sense of direction among the massive machines, especially with the rainy twilight rapidly giving way to full night.

"I don't see anything much. Just machines," Donovan Caine said.

"Look down to the left at the edge of the basin. Down there." I pointed to a small, white building that gleamed like a dull moon. "That's where some of the mine offices are, including Dawson's, according to the information Finn gave me."

"What do you expect to find in there?" Caine asked, peering through the binoculars at the structure. "I doubt Tobias Dawson just leaves incriminating evidence lying around."

I shrugged and got to my feet. I took a moment to swipe the dead, damp leaves from the knees of my jeans. "Maybe, maybe not. Dawson's the big boss around here, remember? This is his mountain. He might be sloppy enough to leave things out in the open."

"And if not?"

I shrugged again and tied one end of the rope around the base of a nearby pine tree. After I made sure it was securely knotted, I tossed the rest of it down the ridge below us. "Then at least we'll have gotten our exercise for the evening."

I reached into my back jeans pocket and held out a pair of gloves to him. They were gardening gloves, white with brown trowels on them, but they'd keep us from getting rope burn on our hands—or leaving fingerprints in Tobias Dawson's office.

"Now, are you coming or not?"

Donovan Caine let out a low curse. But the detective took the gloves from me and started pulling them onto his hands.

For whatever reason, the miners hadn't dug out this side of the mountain yet, which meant the ridge was still covered with rocks and gnarled vegetation. It was a steep, slippery slope, made more so by the drizzle, and we moved with care, using the rope to help us walk our way down the embankment. We moved as quickly as we

could, but it still took us almost fifteen minutes to reach
the bottom.

We crouched behind an outcropping of rock and
peered into the flat area that stretched out before us. The
empty, dug-out feel of the mountain reminded me of the
Ashland Rock Quarry not too far from here. The place
where Alexis James had met her death two months ago.

Donovan looked through the binoculars again. "It
seems like everyone's gone home already," he murmured.
"I don't even think there are any guards around."

"Why would there be?" I asked. "Nobody around
here's going to be dumb enough to steal from Tobias
Dawson. Especially not since he's such good friends with
Mab Monroe. Besides, even if somebody did steal something, he'd look a little conspicuous driving a bulldozer
down into the city, now wouldn't he?"

Caine snorted at the image, but he didn't argue with
my logic.

"Come on," I said. "Let's get this over with."

We eased out from behind the rocks and walked forward. The metal equipment cast out all sorts of dark,
twisted shadows, made even murkier by the drizzle and
thick clouds overhead. A couple of tall, parking lot-style
lights next to the mine entrance burned like skinny yellow
lanterns. The lights made it easy enough to navigate our
way through the equipment maze. But the rain couldn't
quite drown out the smell of exhaust and gasoline that
hung in the air like smog.

The stone's murmurs grew louder and sharper the farther I walked into the basin, until the vibrations rang in
my ears like a never-ending death wail. I gritted my teeth

and blocked out the noise. There was nothing I could do to help the stone. I just didn't have that kind of power. Only time could do that now—if the mountain could ever truly recover from being so viciously brutalized.

It took us about ten minutes of walking before we were within sight of the mine office, a small building made out of sheet metal and fiberglass, covered up with whitewashed wooden boards. A couple of security lights glowed over the front door. I peered into the darkness, but I didn't see any guards patrolling around the building. If Tobias Dawson did have a night shift, they'd probably be farther up around the curve in the basin, stationed at the front entrance to the mined mountain. Not back here in the bottleneck where access was already restricted.

Still, I palmed one of my silverstone knives, just in case.

We crouched behind a bulldozer that was the closest one to the mining office. Nothing moved in the dark night. The drizzle had picked up and turned into a steady rain. A few damp tendrils had come undone from my ponytail. The rain had turned my chocolate locks an even darker brown, and I used the cold moisture to slick them back into place.

"Come on," I whispered to the detective. "Let's do this."

I crept forward. After a moment, I heard Donovan's boots squish in a puddle behind me. I smiled. Just like old times. If a mere two months ago could be considered old times.

I eased over to the front door of the mining office. A sign on the side read *Dawson Mining Company*. Once again, the two *i*'s in *Mining* had been transformed into Tobias Dawson's rune—a lit stick of dynamite.

I wore the same kind of gardening gloves Donovan Caine did, so I had no qualms about reaching forward and trying the doorknob. Locked. Not a problem. I pulled off one of my gloves and reached for my Ice magic. The cold, silver light flickered over my palm, and a few seconds later, I had two long, slender Ice picks. Donovan watched me work with a mixture of curiosity and resignation. Less than a minute later, the lock slid home, and the door opened.

I threw the picks in a nearby puddle so they'd melt, pulled my glove back on, and eased into the building. Donovan followed me and closed the door behind him. I stood still for a moment, letting my eyes adjust to the lack of light. With the darkness and clouds outside, the interior of the building was almost pitch-black, as if it were already midnight instead of creeping up on seven o'clock. Once I was sure no guards were coming to interrupt us, I pulled a small flashlight out of my jacket pocket and flicked it on. Beside me, Donovan did the same.

We stood in a waiting room. Some chairs, a table, out-of-date magazines. A desk in the middle probably belonged to a secretary. Behind it, a corridor led farther back into the building. That's where I headed, with the detective behind me.

The corridor ended at a closed door with a brass nameplate that read Tobias Dawson. Just whom I was looking for. I tried the knob. Locked, so I had to form two more Ice picks to open it. After I'd picked the lock, I turned the knob and held my breath, waiting. But no alarm sounded. Evidently, Dawson just secured his office as a precaution—or to keep his staff from snooping around while he was away. I stepped inside the room. The detective followed me.

I paused for a few seconds, taking in the view. Tobias Dawson's office had just as much personality as the dwarf himself did because everything had a Western motif. The desk consisted of several old-fashioned wooden barrels with a sheet of glass stretched over the top of them. The art on the walls featured bucking broncos and Native American designs, perhaps Navajo, from the looks of them. One of the lamps on Dawson's desk was shaped like a miniature cowboy boot. Another one resembled a curling lasso. I looked up. The dwarf even had a longhorn mounted over the door to the office—its stuffed head and horns at least.

"Somebody really needs to move to Texas," I murmured.

"Forget that," Donovan said. "What are we looking for?"

"Anything that might tell us why Tobias Dawson wants the Foxes' land so badly." I moved off to the right. "So see what you can find in his desk and in the filing cabinets."

Donovan did as I asked. But before he started pulling open drawers, the detective stared at me. "And what are you going to do?"

"See if he has a safe stashed in here somewhere."

Donovan shook his head, but he sat down in Dawson's oversize chair and went to work, methodically opening, scanning, and closing all the files on the glass desk.

I went around the room and checked behind all the

framed photographs, looking for a wall safe. Nothing. I ran my gloved hands over the cheap wood paneling, tapping it in several places. Again, nothing.

I curled and uncurled my hands into loose fists, thinking. Since Tobias Dawson was friends and business partners with Mab Monroe, I imagined there were quite a few documents—legal and otherwise—he wouldn't want his underlings seeing. Locking his office wouldn't be secure enough. He'd need someplace to stash them. There had to be some sort of safe in here. A secret cubbyhole, hell, even a loose floorboard. And I needed to find it—fast. We'd already been inside more than a minute. I wanted to be gone before the five-minute mark rolled around, if not before. Dawson might not have any obvious security here, but it was better not to take any unnecessary chances, especially since I was going to come back later and kill him.

Since I'd crapped out with the walls, I dropped to my hands and knees and scoured the floor, looking for lines cut into the thick rugs. Nothing. Not so much as a single fiber out of place.

"This is weird," Donovan murmured, shining his flashlight across several sheets of paper.

"What?" I asked, still crawling around on the floor.

"It looks like Dawson's hired several gemologists in the last few weeks from a variety of firms," the detective replied. "There are receipts here made out to Jeweltones, Gems, Inc., and Grayson Enterprises, among others."

I frowned. "What would Dawson need with gemologists? He's mining coal, not precious stones."

"I don't know." Donovan pulled out his cell phone and snapped copies of the receipts to examine later.

By this time, I'd made a complete circuit of the office on my hands and knees, and I still hadn't found anything useful. Besides Dawson's obsession with the Old West, the only other thing interesting or noteworthy, at least to me, was the dwarf's rock collection. Such collections weren't uncommon among Stone elementals. Even I'd had one as a kid, before my family had been murdered.

A tall, wide glass case against the back wall of the office housed the collection. Three shelves full of rocks perched above a large block of black granite shot through with silverstone. Some of the stones were worthless. Polished quartz you could find just about anywhere. Odd bits of fool's gold. Others had some serious value. A sapphire almost as big as an egg. A teardrop-shaped ruby. A lovely square-cut emerald. I could hear the stones, of course. The soft, pretty murmur of the quartz. The sly whisper of the fool's gold. The flashy elegance of the gemstones.

My eyes dropped to the bottom shelf, and I focused on the slab of granite. It was nothing compared to the gemstones, but still, I wondered why Dawson would even have it in his collection to start with. The other rocks varied in value, but they were all uniquely shaped or interesting in some way. The granite was just a slab of granite. Black and rather boxlike in its appearance. I knelt down and peered at the stone even closer. Hmm.

There was a lock on the glass case, but I took care of that with a well-crafted Ice pick. Behind me, Donovan kept sorting through papers. I opened the door on the case. The stones' various murmurs washed over me, but I forced the melodies aside and focused on the granite. Its vibration was low and muted in comparison to the other rocks, but I rather suspected that was the point. Still, it only took me a second to attune myself to the stone. And I realized its vibrations sounded . . . hollow. As though the stone was only a thin layer covering something else—like a secret chamber.

"I think I've found Dawson's safe—so to speak," I murmured to Caine.

He looked up from the papers. "Can you open it?"

Picking a door lock was one thing. I had a tougher time getting into a traditional metal safe without Finn's help—or some explosives. But Tobias Dawson didn't have a traditional safe. His was made of stone—my element, my specialty. Still, we'd been inside more than three minutes now. No time to be subtle.

So I pulled off my glove, put my hand on the granite, and listened to its vibrations. Slow, steady, solid, just like the rock itself. There was also a sense it was guarding something, protecting something important, valuable. Tobias Dawson's secrets, whatever they might be.

I drew in a breath and focused my magic on the granite. Peering at the rock, into the rock. And I realized the stone was only a couple inches deep. Any thicker than that, and Dawson wouldn't have been able to put much of anything inside. Also, the silverstone I'd noticed earlier formed a wide, circular shape in the middle of the granite, roughly marking the size of the hollow space inside. The dwarf probably had the metal triggered to his magic, so that no one could open it but him. Since silverstone could absorb magic, anyone who tried to force their way inside like that would probably spin their wheels for quite a while.

But I was a Stone elemental, just like the dwarf. I didn't have to go through the silverstone—only around it. I held my bare index finger in front of the granite and reached for my magic. A silver light sparked on the tip of my finger like it was a tiny blowtorch. I leaned forward and pressed my finger against the granite, forcing my magic into the stone, deeper and deeper until I broke through the rock shell to the hollow space inside. Once I made the initial break, it was easy enough to drag my finger around the perimeter of the block, forming a square shape much bigger than the circle of silverstone at the heart of the granite.

Less than a minute later, I made the last cut in the stone. The rock creaked, and I used my magic to form a small groove in one side so I could hook my finger inside and pull it out. The granite was heavier than I'd expected, and it took me a moment to lug it out of the case and set it on the floor.

Donovan looked up at the sound of my grunts and did a double take. "How the hell did you do that?"

I flashed him a smile. "I have many talents, detective."

I turned my back on him and stared inside the safe. It was an even smaller space than I'd expected, and it was curiously empty, except for a few sheets of paper.

"Here." I plucked out the papers and handing them to Donovan. "Photograph these."

The detective spread the documents on the desk and used his cell phone to snap off some pictures. I reached back into the safe, wondering what other secrets it held. My fingers closed around a small plastic vial, which I pulled out. I played my flashlight over the container.

Black foam filled the inside of the vial, cradling a diamond. The gemstone was small, not much bigger than one of my fingernails, and rough around the edges, but it still sparkled with an inner crimson fire. Definitely a high-quality stone. One that would polish up quite nicely.

But its sound—oh, its *sound*. That's what held my attention. The diamond practically sang with its own purity. The gemstone's inherent vibration was beautiful, breathtaking, enchanting, even. Like a Bach composition played by the master himself. I could have sat there listening to the diamond's clear, pure song for hours.

Too bad an alarm blared out and cut into its lilting melody.

✳ 19 ✳

For a moment I froze, crouched there on the floor, the diamond vial in my hand. The alarm continued to blare like a police siren wailing in my head. Donovan Caine kept sorting through the papers, as if he couldn't hear the unending, violent shrieking. He'd have to be deaf not to hear it.

I frowned and stared at the granite safe. The stone's low murmur had transformed into a sharp, piercing alarm. A rune flashed to life on the front of the safe, on the slab I'd cut out of the rest of the block. A tight, spiral curl burned a cold gray in the middle of the black granite like some sort of all-seeing eye. A spiral curl—the rune for protection. Tobias Dawson had used his Stone magic to ward his safe with a protection rune, one that would alert him if anyone tampered with the granite. I'd done the same thing to protect myself on more than one occasion. Even used the same rune as the dwarf.

Donovan Caine wasn't an elemental, wasn't a Stone, so he couldn't hear the alarm, couldn't see the rune. But I could, and I knew what they both meant—trouble headed this way.

"Fuck," I cursed out loud this time. "Give me the papers. Now."

"What? Why?" Donovan asked in a distracted tone. "There's some interesting stuff here—"

"Because I've tripped some kind of alarm," I interrupted him. "So give me the papers right *now*."

To his credit, the detective didn't ask any questions. Instead, he shoved the documents over to me. I stuffed them back into the hollow space inside the granite, wiped my fingerprints off the diamond vial, then put it inside as well. Although I wanted to, I didn't take the stone. The cowboy dwarf might not pursue us so hard if he still had the diamond. Big, big maybe, but it was the only hope I had.

I hastily wiped down the granite slab and safe with my jacket sleeve, then hefted the stone slab I'd cut out back into its original place. There was no time to be subtle, so I blasted the rock back in place with my magic, sealing it up tight once more. With his Stone magic, Dawson would be able to sense what I'd done immediately, but he shouldn't be able to trace it back to me—or more importantly, the Foxes.

Donovan held out a hand and helped me to my feet.

"We need to get out of here," I said. "Now."

We scurried down the hallway and into the front of the building. I turned my flashlight off and peered through the thin slats in the blinds. Two flashlights bobbed in our direction. Giants, considering the fact the lights were about even with my head. Beside me, Donovan turned off his own flashlight and drew his gun.

"Put that away," I said. "Open the door and head straight toward the back of the basin, where we climbed down. Outrunning them is our best chance. Not engaging in a firefight."

"What are you going to do?"

"Make sure they don't follow us."

Donovan shook his head. "No, Gin. Let me stay and help you—"

"This isn't a fucking discussion," I said. "It won't much matter if they capture me, but you? It'll ruin you, detective. So go. Now. I'm a big girl. I can take care of myself. Been doing it for years."

Donovan stared at me. I could see the gold glint of his eyes even in the darkness and the emotions sparking in their depths. Worry. Concern. Resignation. After a few seconds, the detective reluctantly holstered his gun. He moved toward the door and opened it.

By the time I stepped outside behind him, Donovan had already taken off back the way we'd come in. Twenty steps later, the rain and night and shadows swallowed him, just the way I'd known they would.

I palmed my silverstone knives. But instead of sprinting after the detective, I slid around the side of the building and moved all the way to the back, where Tobias Dawson's office was. Ten . . . twenty . . . thirty . . . I counted off the seconds in my head.

I didn't have long to wait. Despite the rain and mud, their footsteps reverberated through the stone under my feet. Solid, heavy, pounding. Shouts drifted through the rain.

"Do you see anything?"

"No. You?"

"Hey! The front door's wide open!"

I peeked around the side of the building just in time to see two giants run inside. A few seconds later, lights flared in the front room, then spread down the hallway like a wildfire, before erupting in Tobias Dawson's office. I stood off to one side of the windows and watched. It was the same two men Dawson had brought to the Country Daze store earlier this afternoon. The two giants still had on the same grimy work clothes they'd sported then, and they both carried long, heavy flashlights that could easily be used to break bones or crush someone's skull. They had to be the dwarf's top two enforcers.

I watched them sweep into Dawson's office. They didn't bother with anything on the desk, but went straight to the glass case that housed the dwarf's rock collection.

"The lock's been picked," one of the giants rumbled, swinging open the case. "But it doesn't look like anything's been taken."

The second giant came to stand beside him. "Nothing obvious anyway. But somebody was messing with the safe, with the diamond. That's why the alarm went off inside the guardhouse. Because somebody other than Dawson opened the safe."

Well, that confirmed my suspicion the dwarf had used his Stone magic to craft the alarm on his safe. I could do the same thing, although I was usually more interested in keeping people out of whatever building I was sleeping in rather than trapping them inside. That's what would have happened here. If I hadn't been a Stone, hadn't been an elemental, I wouldn't even have heard the alarm. Both Donovan Caine and I would have still been sitting in Dawson's office when the giants came calling. Some definite pain, perhaps even death, would have ensued.

Sneaky dwarf, using an elemental alarm like that. Something to keep in mind next time, when I went in to kill him.

"But it doesn't look like the safe's been opened," the first giant rumbled. "Maybe it's just a false alarm."

"No way," the second guy replied. "The case is open. Somebody touched that safe."

"Maybe. But you know how sensitive that rune alarm Dawson created is. I had to come up here twice last week because the cleaning crew jiggled it while they were dusting. Remember?"

"I remember," the second man said. "But you know how obsessed Dawson is with that diamond and the others he found. We'd still better call him, just to cover our own asses. And get Stan and Donny up here too. They can help us look around."

The first giant sighed and picked up the telephone on the dwarf's desk.

I stood outside, still processing what I'd just learned. Others? There were more diamonds like the one in the safe? I began to get a bad, bad feeling about why Tobias Dawson wanted Warren T. Fox's land so badly. If my suspicion was correct, Dawson wouldn't stop harassing the Foxes until he was dead. Which meant the thought of killing the dwarf just morphed from a pleasant idea into a cold, hard necessity. The sooner the better.

The first giant finished his phone call and turned back to his buddy. "They're on their way. But I still don't see how anyone besides Dawson could even open the safe. All the silverstone in it is keyed to his magic."

"For a rock like that? Somebody would *find* a way," the second guy replied.

As they stood there talking, I crept away from the window and slipped off into the dark, rainy night.

I jogged back to the far end of the basin away from the mine office. I didn't sprint full out, but I didn't dawdle either. I kept my pace just quick enough so I'd still be able to hear the giants behind me when their friends arrived and they decided to investigate the area outside the office. But I didn't worry about them finding anything. The drizzling rain would wash away any trace evidence the detective or I might have left behind, including our footprints.

I reached the back slope of the basin where we'd come down, rounded the rock outcropping—and found myself on the business end of Donovan Caine's gun.

"Nice to see you too," I drawled.

Donovan let out a breath and lowered his weapon. "Sorry. I heard footsteps."

"Don't worry. That's not the first gun I've had pointed at me." Probably wouldn't be the last one, either, but I didn't mention that to the detective.

Donovan holstered his weapon. Then he stepped out from behind the rock and looked toward the mine offices.

By now, more lights burned there, like fireflies that had been grounded by the rain. Faint shouts drifted through the night air.

"Did you kill the guards?" Donovan Caine asked in a low voice.

"No."

Surprise and relief flashed in his golden eyes. "Why not?"

I shrugged. "Because a possible break-in is one thing. Dead guards are another. I don't want Tobias Dawson to realize I'm coming for him. Not until it's too late."

Donovan's relief melted into stubborn consternation, and I half-expected him to start lecturing me about the sanctity of life. To tell me it was just plain *wrong* to go around planning someone's assassination, even if it would save two innocent people in the end. Donovan stared at me like he wanted to do that very thing, give me the good lecture. Then another emotion crept into his golden gaze. The detective almost looked . . . sad.

What did he have to be sad about? It wasn't like I was going to kill him or even one of his friends. I didn't understand Donovan's sudden mood swing, and I didn't care to stand out here in the dark to try to puzzle it out. Not with Tobias Dawson's men lurking around.

"Come on," I said. "Let's get out of here before the guards head this way."

✴ 20 ✴

Even using our rope and gloves, it took twice as long for Donovan and me to climb back up the ridge as it had taken to come down. The drizzle made everything slick, slimy, sloppy. By the time we crested the rim of the ridge, we were both wet to the bone and covered with mud, burrs, briars, dead leaves, and other woodsy debris. It took us several more minutes to reach Donovan's sedan, which was just enough time for the warm exertion from climbing up the ridge to wear off. The rain had picked up and was now a downpour. Despite the Ice magic in my veins, I still shivered with cold. Besides our *squish-squish* footsteps, the only other sound was the *plop-plop-plop* of the rain coming down.

Donovan reached inside the sedan and turned on the interior lights so we could see what we were doing. Then he hit another button, which opened the trunk. "I've got some towels and spare clothes in the back."

I nodded. While the detective dug around in the trunk, I pulled out my cell phone and called Finn. He answered on the third ring.

"Yeah?"

"We're clear of Dawson's office," I said.

A slurping sound came through the phone. Finn drinking another cup of coffee. Sometimes I wondered why his brain didn't explode from all the caffeine. "Find anything interesting?"

"I think so," I said. "We'll talk about it when we get back. Might be awhile, because of the rain. The road we're on isn't exactly the best in the world."

"We've moved over to the house. We'll be waiting for you there," Finn said.

We both hung up.

Donovan closed the trunk and came around the car to me. He opened the front passenger's side door and tossed the dry clothes inside so they wouldn't get wet while we changed. Then he handed me a thick towel. I lifted it to my face and breathed in. It smelled like the detective—clean and soapy. Mmm.

The detective grabbed another towel out of the pile of clothes. He used it to wipe off his face and soak up some of the water in his hair. I did the same with my towel, then opened the back door of the car and slung the towel over the seat. Mud caked my boots an inch thick in places, so I pulled them off and set them on the floorboard, along with my ruined socks. Cold mud squished between my toes, but I'd wipe them off with the towel later. Then I stripped off my fleece jacket and put it on top of my boots. My long-sleeved T-shirt came next. I sighed as I looked at the cotton. I'd bought the pink T-shirt covered with bright green limes when I went to Key West after Fletcher's funeral. It was one of my favorites. I picked a couple of briars off the bottom of the tail, folded it, and put it on top of my jacket.

I was just about to unhook my bra when I realized the detective was staring at me. Donovan Caine's eyes burned like liquid gold in his rugged face.

"What—what are you doing?" he asked in a hoarse voice.

"I thought I'd be nice and not get my wet, muddy shoes and clothes all over your car," I replied. "Is that a problem?"

Donovan didn't answer me. He was too busy devouring me with his eyes. The rain ran down my mostly bare chest in cool, glistening drops. I'd only had my shirt off a few seconds, but the moisture had already soaked into my pale pink lace bra. The cold night air had long ago hardened my nipples. But instead of covering myself up, my own eyes traced over Donovan. The detective had removed his suit jacket and starched shirt. All he wore from the waist up was a white, sleeveless undershirt. The rain had made it transparent too, and I could see the ropy muscles of his chest through the thin fabric. Mmm. Despite the rain flicking against my skin, a low, steady warmth spread through my stomach. This was the closest I'd been to Donovan Caine in two months, and I decided to take advantage of the situation.

"See something you like, detective?" I said in a soft voice. "Because I sure do."

The detective raised his gaze to my face. Emotions

flickered in his golden eyes, like lightning dancing across the sky during a thunderstorm. Guilt. Heat. Desire. But he didn't move toward me. So I decided to up the stakes, so to speak.

I looked at him as I slowly unbuttoned my muddy jeans. It took me a few seconds to slide the stiff, heavy, wet fabric down my legs and over my feet. Not the most graceful striptease, but the golden sparks in Donovan's eyes told me he appreciated the view. By the time I'd tossed my wet jeans into the front seat, the rain had turned my pink panties—also decorated with limes—as transparent as my bra.

Donovan's gaze was even hotter now, and those same three emotions kept flashing in his eyes, one after another, faster and faster, as though his brain were overloaded by the feelings. Guilt. Heat. Desire. Guilt. Heat. Desire.

We stood there, a few feet apart, frozen in the moment, as the cool rain cascaded down on us . . .

Donovan let out a low growl, moved forward, and jerked me toward him. His lips crushed against mine, even as his tongue drove inside my mouth. Mmm. Just what I wanted. I tangled my fingers in his damp, black hair and pulled him closer.

In a moment, the kiss morphed into one of raging heat and raw need. Our lips, our tongues, lashed against each other in punishment and pleasure. We spun around and around in a tight circle in the rain. Mud covered my feet and rocks dug into my heels, but I didn't care. Heat, passion, lust, desire. It all filled me until there was nothing else—and nothing I wouldn't do to slake my need. The mud, the cold, the rain. Everything else vanished, overcome by the fire roaring through my body. A fire I wanted to embrace again and again and again.

Donovan's hand worked at the clasp of my bra. When it popped open, he stepped back long enough to yank the straps off my shoulders and drop the whole thing in the mud. He moved me back, and something cold and metal bumped against my hip. The hood of the sedan.

That would do for now. I leaned back against the metal and pulled the detective down to me. The car hood felt like ice against my back, but I didn't care because I was burning on the inside. Burning for Donovan.

Our tongues crashed together again. Donovan's hands closed over my bare breasts. He squeezed the two mounds—hard—then dug his thumbs into my nipples. I moaned into his mouth. Pressure built between my thighs. My panties were soaked—and it had nothing to do with the rain.

Donovan put his mouth over first one nipple, then the other. Licking, sucking, nipping at them with his teeth until they were so hard they ached. The detective pulled back long enough to catch his breath. I yanked his undershirt up over his head and threw it away. My fingers splayed over his chest, and I marveled at the lean strength of his body. I ran my nails down his chest, and my hands went to his crotch, rubbing his erection through the slick fabric of his pants. Donovan hissed, then raked his teeth down my ear lobe. He leaned forward and sucked on my neck like a vampire, as his fingers continued to work their magic on my breasts. I bit the edge of his jaw, more than ready for him.

I breathed in. Despite the mud, he still smelled clean,

like soap and fresh laundry. Mmm. "You smell so good," I murmured against his jaw.

"Not as good as you feel under me," he growled back.

We kissed again—long and hard enough to make me pant for breath. My fingers found his leather belt, which I loosened. His pants unzipped a second later.

"Take them off," I murmured. "Your shoes too. I want to feel you this time. All of you."

Donovan stepped back. Now, it was my turn to watch as he kicked off his shoes and socks and stepped out of his pants. He wore a pair of black boxers underneath that made his skin glisten like bronze.

"Boxers too," I said in a husky voice. "Take 'em off."

Donovan stepped toward me. "In a minute."

He leaned me back against the car hood and teased my nipples with his mouth and hands again before his fingers dipped inside my panties. He moved his fingers back and forth against me, before slipping two inside and stroking me there, rubbing his fingers faster, harder, ratcheting up my pressure, my need, that much more. My turn to hiss.

My searching fingers skimmed past the open flap in his boxers. I took him in my hand, and Donovan bucked against me. I lightly ran my nails down his length and across the rounded tip of his hard cock. He was as ready for me as I was for him. Donovan growled again, took his fingers out of me, and pulled me up off the car.

"In the backseat. Now."

I was more than happy to comply. He maneuvered me left and back. I ducked my head and sat down on the seat. Donovan used the opportunity to get rid of his boxers. I did the same to my panties. I scooted back into the car.

Waiting. Aching. A moment later, Donovan followed me inside, a foil packet in his fingers, which he laid on the floorboard. I took my little white pills to be on the safe side and avoid any unwanted consequences, but I still appreciated his thoughtfulness.

He leaned forward and kissed me again before moving down my damp body. Donovan lowered his lips to the curls between my thighs. I parted my legs, and he slid his tongue inside me, making quick, thrusting motions, then slow, lazy circles. Teasing me. I moaned and dug my fingers into his scalp, urging him on.

Donovan's tongue flicked over me again, and he eased a finger deep inside.

"So sweet," he whispered against my thigh. "Like hot honey."

Donovan continued his ministrations a few more moments. That's all I could take. I wanted him inside me. Right now.

I grabbed Donovan's shoulders, pulling him up even as I wiggled underneath him and turned him over. Now, he was lying on the seat. There wasn't a lot of room to maneuver in the car, but I was very determined. Now it was my turn to tease.

I trailed my tongue down his chest and put my mouth on him, sucking and licking his straining shaft until it pulsed and quivered with every touch of my hot, heavy tongue. He groaned, and his hands latched onto my arms, yanking me back up toward him. Our lips met again, sucking the breath and life from both of us. Somehow, Donovan maneuvered us once again until he was back on top. He covered himself with the condom. Then

I opened my legs, locked them around his waist, and he thrust into me.

I watched his beautiful hazel eyes dilate as he sank into me, driving deeper and deeper. An ecstasy of gold—for both of us. Donovan rocked back. I dug my fingers into his back and pulled him down hard, so that the full length of him filled me.

Retreat, pull, retreat, pull. We clacked together like two magnets driven crazy by the vibrations the other was giving off. Over and over, Donovan pumped into me, until our hoarse cries of pleasure rang out in time to the gentle rock of the sedan and the tap of rain on the metal roof.

* 21 *

After we finished, Donovan and I lay in the back of the sedan in a loose tangle of bare arms and legs. The imitation leather felt stiff and sticky against my skin. The windows had steamed over, and the smell of sex permeated the car. Beside me, above me, next to me, the detective's breaths came in sharp, raspy puffs. The sounds of a man who'd exerted himself to his full, glorious potential. But Donovan made no move to pull away from me or put some clothes on.

"Well, that wasn't quite what I had in mind as far as warming up goes, but I'll take it," I quipped. "Even if it's going to hurt like hell peeling myself off this seat."

Donovan didn't say anything, but the corners of his lips lifted into a half smile. "You're not the only one. I'm sure my back will be screaming at me tomorrow. Not to mention the burns I have on my knees."

"Worth it?"

He cocked one black eyebrow. "Do you even have to ask?"

No, I didn't. Because I'd been moaning just as loud as he had.

After we caught our breath, Donovan eased up into a sitting position. I followed suit. He reached into the front seat and handed me some clean clothes—a pair of khakis several sizes too big and a T-shirt that hung almost to my knees. The detective was a bit taller than I was. Donovan pulled on a matching set of clothes. When that was done, we turned and faced each other in the back seat.

"So here we are again," I said.

"Yeah," Donovan replied. "Here we are again."

He didn't look happy at the thought. The detective let out a long breath and ran his hands through his black hair—lean, strong hands that had just done marvelous things to my body. I hesitated, then reached over, put my hand on top of his, and gave a gentle squeeze with my fingers. I wasn't sure what prompted the reaction, other than this warmth in my chest I felt for the detective. Or maybe it was the simple fact I didn't want things to end between us like they had the last time we'd slept together. Which had been altogether badly.

Donovan flinched at my touch and slid his hand out from under mine. "We should get back."

I stared at his rugged features. Black hair, bronze skin, golden eyes. But heat and desire no longer brightened his gaze. Instead, the detective looked tired, weary, heartsick. As though all the pleasure he'd just experienced came with a weight that was just too much to bear, even for him.

"All right," I said in a quiet voice, not wanting to push him anymore tonight.

It was after ten by the time we returned to Country Daze. The traffic of the day had long since ceased, and the stop sign at the crossroads looked like a dull red ghost in the drizzling rain. Donovan didn't have an extra pair of shoes in the trunk, so I had to stick my feet back into my muddy boots. First though, I wiped as much of the grime off them as I could with a towel.

Sometime while we'd been gone, Sophia's black convertible had been pulled off to one side of the store so that the classic car rested in the grass. So had Finn's Cadillac. The store itself was dark, the front doors closed and locked.

"Come on," I said. "Finn said they were in the house around back."

The detective and I walked through the gap between Sophia's convertible and the store. Warren T. Fox's house lay about five hundred feet behind the store in back of a copse of maple and oak trees. A creek ribboned around one side of the house. The rain had made it fat and swollen, like a snake that had swallowed more than it could comfortably hold. The rush of water drowned out the sound of the rain slapping against the tin roof.

I'd come back here this afternoon to check out the structure, but I was once again struck by how much the clapboard building resembled Fletcher Lane's house. Both featured the same white boards, the same kind of shutters, the same sloping tin roof. And it wasn't just the house that reminded me of Fletcher—it was everything about Warren T. Fox. The blue work clothes he wore, his grumpy nature, the old-fashioned store he ran. It was almost like Fletcher and Warren were identical twins separated at birth. The kind you read about who built separate, but almost identical, lives for themselves. Once again, I felt that faint softness stir in my chest. Because everything about Warren made me remember Fletcher and the love I'd had for him.

Lights blazed in several of the first-floor windows. I stepped up onto the porch and knocked on the front door.

"Hmph?" Sophia grunted through the heavy wood.

"It's Gin."

A lock clicked, and the Goth dwarf opened the door. Sophia clenched an aluminum baseball bat in one hand. Her black eyes flicked over my oversize clothes, and she stepped back to let us inside. Sophia crooked her finger at us, and we followed her deeper into the house. For a moment, I felt like I was coming home to Fletcher's after a long day at the Pork Pit. Because the inside of Warren T. Fox's house could have been an exact duplicate of Fletcher Lane's. Same sort of well-worn, overstuffed furniture, same clutter of knickknacks, same piles of odds and ends that made a house a home. I blinked, and the illusion vanished.

The others were in a large den. Violet huddled on the sofa, a heavy textbook in her lap, a notepad and pen by her side. Studying. Jo-Jo perched on the other end of the sofa and flipped through a beauty magazine. Several more sat stacked at her bare feet. The dwarf had come prepared.

Warren rocked back and forth in an oversize recliner that made him seem older and more frail than he really was. The television was tuned to the Weather Channel. Warren's brown eyes focused intently on the storm-front graphics on the flickering screen. Finn relaxed in a similar chair, which he'd reclined all the way back. His laptop drowsed on his lap. Finn was doing the same in the chair itself. Soft snores drifted out of his open mouth.

I went over, put my hand into Finn's broad shoulder, and shook him awake.

"What? What?" he mumbled in a sleepy voice. "I didn't touch her, I swear."

"Relax, Casanova," I said.

Finn blinked a few times before his green eyes focused on me. "Oh, Gin, it's you." He frowned. "Why are you wearing a T-shirt that says *Ashland Police Department* on it?"

I sighed. "It's a long story."

Once Finn was more or less awake, I filled the others in on what Donovan Caine and I had found in Tobias Dawson's office. The detective e-mailed the cell phone photos he'd taken to Finn, who started pulling them up on his laptop and going through them.

"Anything happen on this end?" I asked Sophia.

"Quiet," she rasped.

"A couple of folks came in for sodas and cigarettes, but that was it," Jo-Jo agreed.

"Usual customers," Warren cut in. "Even Dawson can't scare off folks when they need their tobacco."

"Those papers you found inside the safe," Jo-Jo said. "What did they say? Anything interesting?"

I shrugged. "Ask Donovan. It was dark. I didn't really see them."

All eyes turned to the detective, who also shrugged. "Like Gin said, it was dark. We only used flashlights inside. They mostly looked like schematics to me. We'll have to wait and see what Finn says."

"You're going to have to give me a few minutes," Finn said, typing on his laptop. "I've got to sort through and read some of this. It doesn't make much sense to me either. Not to mention that the photo quality isn't the best I've ever seen."

"Sorry," Donovan sniped. "I was a little more worried about flashing too much light around and getting caught than taking perfect pictures for you."

We lapsed into silence while we waited for Finn to read and decipher the documents. But I had a pretty good idea of what they'd say. So I leaned against the wall and started thinking about what came next—getting close enough to Tobias Dawson to kill him. Because that was the only way this thing was going to end, if my suspicions were correct. Sophia stood beside me and twirled the baseball bat in her hand like it was a metal baton.

After about ten minutes of reading and clicking, Finn frowned. "That's weird." He looked over at Warren. "Did you know Tobias Dawson has recently started construction on a new, separate mine shaft?"

Warren nodded. "That's the rumor the miners have been spouting. There's been more activity at the mine lately too."

"What kind of activity?" Donovan asked.

Warren shrugged. "More blasting, more drilling.

Sometimes, we can feel the tremors down here. Once they were so strong, they knocked over some sodas in the store. Made a big mess."

"They feel sort of like small earthquakes," Violet added. "They've been going on a couple of months now."

"Well, according to this, Dawson is pouring most of his money and manpower into the new shaft these days," Finn said.

"Why would he do that?" Violet asked.

Finn read some more. His frown deepened. "That can't be right," he muttered. "It's not possible."

"What?" Jo-Jo asked. "What's not possible?"

"What Dawson is drilling for," Finn said. "According to this, it looks like that shaft isn't to get more coal out of the mountain. It's for—"

"Diamonds," I said in a soft voice. "He's found diamonds in the mountain."

Silence. For a moment, everyone looked at me. Then they all started talking at once.

"Diamonds?" Sophia rasped in surprise.

"That's not possible," Violet Fox said.

"Darling, anything's possible," Jo-Jo replied.

"So that's why Dawson wants the land so badly." Donovan shook his head.

"I wonder how big they are," Finn said in a speculative tone.

Warren T. Fox was the only one who didn't say anything. Instead, the old coot stared at me, his eyes dark, pinched, and worried in his brown, wrinkled face. He knew what the diamond find meant as well as I did. Disaster. For him and the mountain.

If the diamond I'd found in the safe was any indication of the size and quality of the others Tobias Dawson had discovered, the dwarf would tear the whole mountain apart to get every last gemstone out of the ground. And it wouldn't end there. Word would eventually leak out about the diamond find, and then, well, it would be worse than the California Gold Rush around here. Everyone would be bulldozing and blasting the area, hoping to find diamonds on their own land and get rich themselves. They'd destroy the whole mountain in their hasty greed—and Warren T. Fox's house and store lay at the epicenter. He'd go under first. The knowledge flashed in his eyes, steady, weary, certain.

Unless I did something to stop it.

I'd never considered myself to be any sort of environmentalist, but these mountains were as much a part of me as they were of Warren Fox. I took the same sort of pride in their beauty that he did. If Tobias Dawson's current mine was any indication of things to come, it would be a public service to stop this now. And there was only one way to do that—by killing Dawson.

Oh, I had no doubt that the dwarf had told a few of his most trusted men what he had found, like those two giants who'd come to the office to investigate the robbery tonight. But without Dawson around, without his mining expertise and know-how, it would be that much harder for his flunkies to do anything about the diamonds. Even if they did make a move later on, I could always take them out too. No, killing Dawson was the key here. Eliminate the dwarf and the rest of the monster would more than likely die along with him.

Besides, the store, the land, the house. They were all that Warren and Violet had ever known. They were simply home. I knew Fletcher Lane would have done whatever he could to help his friend. The old man wasn't here, but I was. And I was going to protect the Foxes—no matter what.

Warren raised his dark eyes to mine, asking a silent question. I nodded. Question asked and answered. Jo-Jo Deveraux saw the exchange. An emotion flickered in her pale gaze. It looked like relief—mixed with a spark of anticipation. About what, I couldn't imagine. But it was there.

After about three minutes, the babble of voices and conversation wound down.

"I just don't see how it's possible," Donovan Caine said. "Diamonds? Here?"

I nodded. "They have them over in Arkansas, why not here in Ashland? Tobias Dawson's found plenty of coal in the mountain. That's all a diamond really is—coal put under pressure long and hard enough to evolve into something else."

"How do you know that?" the detective asked.

"I know a little bit about stones, especially precious ones." I didn't mention the fact I could hear their vibrations, tap into them, and get them to do anything I wanted. I never flaunted my magic, and I wasn't about to do it now.

"But if Dawson's already started drilling this other shaft to get to the diamonds, why is he still threatening us?" Violet asked, confusion flashing in her eyes. "Why even bother? Why not just take the diamonds out on the sly?"

"Because the dwarf doesn't own the mineral rights to

the land," Warren rumbled. "I do. So legally, they aren't his diamonds. They're ours."

"And people might realize that, if he started mining them," Jo-Jo finished. "Word would get around. It always does. And then Warren could cause problems for him. Legal problems."

Warren nodded. "Or try to at least."

We all fell silent. I gave the others a few minutes to think, but my decision had already been made.

"Finn?" I asked in a low voice.

"Yeah?"

"What else did you find out about Dawson today?"

He stared at me with his green eyes. "All the usual info. Finances, business interests, hobbies, homes, social connections."

"Anything we can use?"

Finn stared at me. His gaze cut to Warren. He saw the resolution in the other man's face and realized it matched mine. "Yeah, there are a few angles. Nothing too easy, of course, but I'm sure we can find something. There's always a way in."

That's what Fletcher Lane always used to tell me. I smiled.

The detective stared at me, his gold eyes dark. "Surely there's another way besides killing Dawson."

"And what way would that be, detective? Turn Tobias Dawson into the cops? For what, making threats? It wouldn't take, and you know it. Besides, the police usually require a pesky little thing called proof. And I'm betting there is none. Dawson's too smart for that. Am I right?" I looked at Warren.

Warren shook his head. "It's just my word against his. Dawson's men are the ones who've been harassing my customers, never him directly. But his men would never speak out against him. He pays them too well for that."

"But you own the land, Warren, the mineral rights," Donovan said. "Dawson just can't do whatever he wants with your property. You could take him to court to get him to stop. We have the files from his office. We can prove what he's doing."

Finn snorted. "Yeah, files which you and Gin got by breaking into Dawson's office. No judge would ever allow them in court. And I don't think Dawson would be eager to cough up any more information. Besides, look at it from the money angle. A court case would drag on for years, and Dawson's pockets are a lot deeper than Warren's are."

"Even then," I said, "Dawson could probably buy the verdict he wanted. And while everything was getting settled the wrong way in court, Dawson could continue his reign of terror in the meantime. Make another play for Violet in the meantime. Face it, detective, the dwarf isn't going to walk away from a mountain full of diamonds. Nobody would. There's only one way to get him to stop. My way."

Our eyes met and held, gold on gray. After a moment, Donovan Caine looked away, but not before I caught the weary resignation in his gaze, the sag in his shoulders, the deep lines of defeat in his face. He knew what I said was true. He didn't like it, but the detective was going to let me do it. He knew I was going after Tobias Dawson, and he wasn't going to try to stop me. Not anymore. I hadn't expected the detective to come around so easily. I wondered what had caused the quick turnaround. His friendship with Warren Fox? Me? Something else?

But I didn't feel like celebrating my victory in making the detective agree to my plan. Something was bothering Donovan. Me, most likely, and what had happened between us in the backseat of his sedan. But the detective's anger over my assassinating Cliff Ingles, his corrupt partner, seemed to have faded away, for whatever reason. Donovan hadn't mentioned it once all day. So what had I done now that was so terrible besides give him a couple of orgasms? I couldn't help but wonder.

But now wasn't the time to focus on Donovan Caine and this curious warmth I felt for him. Things needed to be done tonight before I made any kind of move against Tobias Dawson. So I pushed thoughts of the detective away and looked at the others.

"Here's what we're going to do," I said.

* 22 *

"First of all, the two of you"—I jerked my head at the Foxes—"need to disappear for the next few days. Take a vacation somewhere."

Warren shook his head. "No. I'm not running from Tobias Dawson. Never have, never will."

"And what about Violet?" I asked. "She almost got raped and killed last night because Dawson wanted to send you a message. If he even thinks the break-in at the mining office tonight is connected to you, he'll come down here, kill you two, and burn everything to the ground. Is that what you want?"

"Of course not," Warren snapped. "But I'm a Fox, of the Ridgeline Hollow Foxes. My ancestors have lived in these mountains for more than three hundred years. The settlers didn't drive my people out, and I'll be damned if one greedy dwarf is going to make me go anywhere. I've never run from a fight. I'm not about to start now."

A mulish look spread across his wrinkled face, and I knew he wasn't going to budge. Not on this point. Warren might die, but he'd do it in his own store—just like Fletcher had. My heart twisted, and the old man's ruined face swam before my eyes. I shoved the image away. Warren T. Fox wasn't going to end up like Fletcher Lane—not if I could help it.

"Fine. You can stay here in the house."

Warren smiled.

"With Sophia and Jo-Jo as protection," I added. "And you're going to close the store for the rest of the week. That's not a request."

His smile slipped. "Why?"

"Because Tobias Dawson will be sure to be watching. If he sees the store's closed, he might think you're finally softening up. It should buy us a little extra time."

"What about me?" Violet asked. "I can't exactly leave either. I've got classes and exams coming up."

I turned to her. "Do you have a friend you could stay with for the next few days?"

She nodded. "I could stay with Eva Grayson."

I flashed back to that night in the Pork Pit when Owen Grayson had told his little sister she was getting a bodyguard whether she liked it or not. The guy I'd seen Eva with at the community college had looked capable enough. So had Owen, for that matter. Staying with the Graysons was probably the best place for Violet until this thing was over. "All right. Call Eva."

Violet blinked. "Now?"

I nodded. "Now. I want this all squared away tonight. That way, I can focus on getting to Dawson."

I looked at the two dwarves. "You two think you can stand guard duty for a few days?"

"Of course," Jo-Jo said. "Anything you need, Gin. You know that."

"Um-mmm." Sophia grunted her agreement.

"What about me?" Finn asked.

I smiled at him. "Fletcher's gone, so you're my handler now. I want everything you've got on Tobias Dawson. You know what to do with it."

Finn nodded.

And then there was one. I stared at the detective, who still wore a stricken look on his face. "What are you going to do, Donovan?"

He stared at the carpet underneath his muddy shoes. The detective knew what I was asking—if he was going to try to stop me or worse, warn Tobias Dawson that I was coming for him.

"Nothing. I'm not going to do anything. Not a damn thing." Donovan scrubbed his hands through his black hair and let out a bitter laugh. The detective had just sided with an assassin, with the Spider. He'd just condemned another man to death, and he knew it.

"Good," I said. "Then let's get to work."

An hour later we were all set. While Finn slid his laptop into its leather case, Violet gave her grandfather a long, tight hug. Eva Grayson had been thrilled her best friend wanted to crash at her place a few days, and Violet had already packed a bag. Now we stood in the foyer of the house, saying our good-byes.

"You could come with me," Violet told her grandfather.

Warren put a speckled hand on her cheek and shook his head. "You know I can't. That's just not me. The only way I'm leaving this land is when they cart me off in a pine box. Besides, Gin might need me for something. I want to be around if she does."

Violet nodded and tried to smile. Tears filled her dark eyes.

"We need to get you to Eva's," I said in a low voice.

Violet gave her grandfather another hug and picked up her bag. Finn held open the door for her, and the two of them stepped outside.

I went over to Sophia and Jo-Jo. "If anything happens, if Tobias Dawson or his men come back, you kill first and ask questions later, understand?"

The Goth dwarf grunted at me. Jo-Jo nodded her head.

"We know, Gin," Jo-Jo said. "This isn't the first time Sophia and I have done this sort of thing."

I frowned. "It's not?"

The dwarf smiled. "No. We watched out for folks for Fletcher a time or two as well."

Again, there was that mention of Fletcher Lane helping out other people. That secret part of him that I hadn't known about. I don't know why the thought unsettled me, but it did. Or maybe it was just because I was off the edge of the map here. I'd spent seventeen years of my life killing people, and here I was trying to save an old man and his granddaughter from a greedy miner—for free, no less. I wasn't sure what to make of it. Only one thing was certain. It was a hell of a lot more entertaining than my retirement had been so far.

I left the dwarves to watch over Warren and stepped

outside. Violet waited with Finn on the porch. Donovan Caine leaned against the railing, still brooding.

"Take Violet straight to Eva Grayson's house," I told Finn. "No stops."

Finn pouted. "Would I do something like that?"

"Yes."

He stuck out his lip a little more. Violet laughed at his expression. Finn's green eyes swept over her. He grinned.

"Shotgun, Finn," I murmured to him. "Remember Grandpa Fox and his shotgun."

That dulled Finn's smile, but it didn't completely erase it. Few things could ever do that. Finn had pulled his Cadillac over to the house. He opened the passenger's side door for Violet, who gave him another shy smile, then slid inside.

After a moment, Finn tore his gaze away from her long enough to glance at me. "Hope you don't mind sitting in the back," he said in a very unapologetic tone.

"I don't mind at all because Donovan's going to drive me home," I announced.

Finn blinked. "He is?"

"I am?" Donovan chimed in.

"Yeah," I said. "You are."

Donovan's face tightened a little more in the darkness.

Finn and Violet headed back toward Ashland, and Donovan and I did the same in his sedan. We didn't speak, except when I gave him directions to Fletcher Lane's house. We pulled up about thirty minutes later. Donovan Caine peered through the windshield at the rambling, mismatched structure.

"So this is where you live now?" he asked.

"Yeah. It was actually Fletcher's house, the old man who ran the Pork Pit."

"Finn's father, your former handler. The one who was tortured and murdered by Alexis James."

I nodded. Donovan said nothing.

I stared at the detective, my eyes tracing over the rough planes of his face. "You could come in," I suggested. "Spend the night. With me."

Donovan turned his gaze to mine. Heat. Desire. Guilt. All that and more flashed in his eyes, but after a moment, he shook his head. "I don't think that would be a good idea, Gin."

"Why not? A bed would certainly be more comfortable than the backseat of your sedan." I glanced at the mud we'd left everywhere in our frenzy. "Cleaner now, too."

He shook his head again. "I'm not coming inside, Gin."

"Why not? Is it because of what I plan to do to Tobias Dawson?"

Donovan ran his hands through his black hair. "That's part of it. I still can't believe I'm going along with that."

"And the other part?"

He blew out a breath. "Do you remember that night in your apartment, before we went to the rock quarry to rescue Finn and Roslyn Phillips? Do you remember what I said to you about my partner, Cliff Ingles?"

"I remember. You wanted to kill me for assassinating him."

He nodded. "Mainly, though, I wanted to know *why*

you killed him. And since you wouldn't tell me, I did some digging on my own."

I tensed. Damn and double damn the detective and his tenacity.

"A lot more people were willing to do me favors after the Alexis James incident," Donovan continued. He stared out the windshield at the rain instead of looking at me. "One guy who worked vice was particularly helpful. He told me that I should talk to a hooker, one of Roslyn Phillips's girls, strangely enough."

Roslyn Phillips was the vampire madam who ran Northern Aggression, a trendy, upscale nightclub that catered to the rich folks of Ashland and serviced their every need and twisted desire. She was also one of Finn's friends with benefits. I'd killed Roslyn's abusive brother-in-law several months ago, after he'd almost beaten her sister and young niece to death. Roslyn, in turn, had told one of her girls about my services. Loose lips get people dead, and Roslyn's furtive whispers had eventually led to Fletcher Lane's murder. Something I wasn't going to let the vampire forget—ever.

But if Caine had talked to the hooker I had in mind, he knew exactly why I'd killed his partner—and what the bastard had done to the woman's thirteen-year-old daughter.

"I know Cliff raped and beat that girl," Donovan said, confirming my suspicion. "I know that's why you killed him, so he'd never do that to another girl."

No use denying it now. "Yes. That's why I killed him. Because of the girl. When did you find out?"

"Two weeks ago."

Pain deepened the grooves on Donovan's face. The detective reminded me of a mythological character out of one of my literature books, of Atlas, bearing the heavy, heavy burden of others' evil, perverted actions upon his lean shoulders.

"All that time you let me blame you for Cliff's death," Donovan said. "All that time you let me think you were a monster. And you weren't."

I shrugged. "That's debatable. I still killed him. And slicing off a guy's balls isn't exactly the action of a normal person."

Donovan barked out a laugh. "Do you know what the funny thing is? If I'd known about Cliff, about the hookers he was beating, about that girl he raped, I might have killed him myself. But you got there first." His voice dropped to a whisper. "And somehow I feel indebted to you, Gin. Grateful, even. Because you killed him, and I didn't have to."

"So that's what this is still about. Me killing Cliff Ingles. That's why you don't want to come inside. That's why you don't want to be with me." I could have killed the dirty cop all over again for pushing Donovan away from me.

Donovan shook his head. "Not entirely. It's mostly about me. Finding out about Cliff, it's made me think. About a lot of things. And now, this mess with Warren and Violet . . . I'll help Sophia and Jo-Jo watch out for them as best I can."

"But . . ."

"But I'm not going to help you with Tobias Dawson. Not like I did with Alexis James. I can't, Gin. I just can't.

I can't be a part of something like that again. I can barely live with the fact I know you're going after Dawson and the knowledge I'm not going to do a thing to stop you from killing him." His voice dropped again. "And I can't be with you. Not tonight."

"You weren't too concerned with Tobias Dawson and what I was going to do to him when you were fucking me in the backseat a couple of hours ago." My voice was harsher than I would have liked. "Or have you forgotten about that already?"

Donovan flinched. "No, I haven't forgotten about it, none of it."

"But you're not going to do it again. Not going to sleep with me again."

His hands tightened around the steering wheel until the leather creaked. "No, I'm not."

I heard the hard resolution in his voice. Donovan Caine had made himself a promise, and he wasn't going to break it. Oh, I imagined I could get him to forget about his morals, his rules, his vows. All I'd have to do would be to crawl over and start giving him the lap dance of his life. A variation of the striptease I'd performed earlier this evening in the rain.

But I'd made the first move twice now. I wanted the detective to want *me*, Gin Blanco, the good, the bad, and the ugly. Not just succumb to my charms in the heat of the moment, then feel guilty about it afterward.

"It appears we're at an impasse then," I said in a low voice.

"Guess so."

Donovan didn't look at me. *He's not the one for you,*

Warren T. Fox's reedy voice whispered in my head. I didn't want his words to be true, but it looked like they were—at least for tonight. Besides, I had Tobias Dawson to take care of. Fletcher Lane had trained me to put the job first, ahead of my own wishes. Distracted assassins got sloppy, and then they got dead. I especially needed to focus this time, since I had a couple of innocent people to protect. One problem at a time. I'd deal with Donovan and his conflicted feelings about us later.

"All right," I said. "You watch out for Warren and Violet. I'll get Finn to help me with Tobias Dawson."

Donovan nodded. "I think that's for the best."

There was nothing else to say. Not tonight. So I got out of the car. The detective didn't look at me as he threw the vehicle in reverse, turned around, and drove away. I stood there and watched the fog and darkness swallow him up.

For some reason, my heart felt as icy as the rain drizzling down around me.

23

I'd just finished pulling a blackberry cobbler out of the oven around noon the next day when I heard the sound of tires crunching on the gravel outside. I padded into the front living room and peered out a crack in one of the curtains. A silver Aston Martin crouched in the driveway. I unlocked the front door, then went back into the kitchen.

A minute later, Finn stuck his head inside the room. As usual, he wore an impeccable suit, this time in a dark charcoal gray. His cheeks were ruddy from the ever-present drizzle, and water droplets glistened in his walnut hair. He carried his laptop in a black leather waterproof case.

"About time you got here." I dumped a tin pan full of orange-cranberry muffins onto a white plate. "Coffee's on already."

Finn helped himself to a mug of the hot chicory brew.

He took a couple of sips, then moved a basket of sourdough rolls out of the way so he could set his laptop on the kitchen table. "Looks like somebody didn't get any last night."

I glared at him.

Nonplussed, Finn threw his arm out and gestured at the kitchen. "C'mon. I see a cobbler, muffins, rolls, a chocolate cake, and what I assume are strawberry preserves. You always cook more when you're upset."

He had me there. The situation with Donovan Caine hadn't been resolved to my liking, and it had affected me more than I'd realized. Why couldn't the detective just accept me for what I was? Morals. They always ruined everything.

I'd gotten up early with nothing but time to kill until Finn showed up. So I'd started cooking. But the mixing, stirring, and baking hadn't relaxed me nearly enough. Maybe if I made another pound cake or two—

"I take it things didn't end with the good detective in your bed last night?" Finn asked in a sly tone.

In addition to treating me like a sister, Finnegan Lane also had an annoying tendency to analyze my sex life—along with everyone else's.

"No," I snapped. "The detective didn't spend the night, although I invited him to."

Finn shook his head. "Idiot. The man's an idiot. But don't feel bad. I didn't have any luck myself last night."

I raised an eyebrow. "You mean the evening didn't end with you having a threesome with Violet Fox and Eva Grayson?"

"Touché."

Finn took another sip of his coffee. He examined the various treats I'd baked and grabbed two orange-cranberry muffins to start off with.

"I hope you did something last night other than hit on those two girls," I said, dishing up a generous portion of blackberry cobbler into a large bowl.

"If you consider sifting through reams of information on Tobias Dawson, then yes, I did do something useful last night, although it was a thoroughly eye-glazing experience. The man doesn't have nearly enough vices to make things interesting. All he does is mine coal and buy equipment to mine coal and look for more places to mine coal. Did I mention he mines coal?"

"Once or twice." My lips twitched up. No matter how bad I felt, Finn could always make me smile. I loved him for that.

I used my Ice magic to frost a mug, then poured myself a glass of milk and dug into the cobbler. I didn't bother with ice cream this time. I just wanted warm sugar, and a lot of it.

"But you were right about the diamonds," Finn said. "According to the cell phone photos the detective took in Dawson's office, the dwarf is planning a major expansion of his current mining operation. And guess where the new primary shaft leads to?"

I didn't even have to guess. "Warren T. Fox's country store."

Finn nodded. "Actually, our good friend Tobias Dawson has already started shoring up the mine, and he's even crossed over into Warren's land."

"Explains all the rumblings and mini earthquakes

they've heard and felt." I took another bite of cobbler. The oat topping provided a crunchy, chewy contrast to the syrupy sweetness of the blackberry filling. Mmm. Perfect.

"But wait, there's more," Finn said. "Dawson might be mining his brains out, but he's not making a lot of money doing it anymore."

"Why not?"

Finn shrugged. "The usual reasons. Equipment's more expensive, the coal's harder to get to, and there's less of it, which means more man hours and more money invested in getting it out of the ground to start with. Dawson also got sued last year. There was a cave-in at one of his other mines further up in Virginia. Killed almost a dozen men, injured that many more. Despite the dwarf's attempts to keep it quiet, the accident got a lot of press. Dawson had insurance, but he still had to pony up almost thirty million for the families."

I whistled. "That'll put a dent in anyone's wallet."

Finn polished off his muffins and reached for the basket of rolls. I passed him some butter. "It put a bigger dent in Dawson's wallet than most. It wiped out most of his personal fortune. He's barely making ends meet these days and is mortgaged to the top of his ten-gallon hat."

"So he just doesn't want the diamonds, he *needs* them."

"Like a wino needs wine," Finn agreed. "But wait, there's more. Guess who one of his primary lenders is?"

Another easy guess. "Mab Monroe."

Finn pouted. "You ruin all my fun. How did you know?"

I shrugged. "I remembered seeing Dawson's name in the file Fletcher compiled on Mab. Even if I hadn't, it wouldn't be much of a stretch. The woman's got her hands in everything in this city. Including Dawson's pocket, I imagine."

"In a big, big way," Finn said. "Mab's been floating him money for the past few months. She's writing it off as a speculative business venture."

I looked at him. "Speculative venture? So she knows about the diamonds then."

"Probably," Finn said. "Dawson must have told her about them, maybe even given her a couple of samples as a good faith gesture."

"So all Dawson has to do is get rid of the Foxes, and he can tear up the whole mountain mining diamonds."

"Pay off his creditors, become solvent again, and make himself and Mab Monroe a pile of money," Finn added. "You were right, Gin. Tobias Dawson isn't going to stop until Warren Fox's land is his. He can't afford to. Not with Mab Monroe breathing down his neck to come up with something worthwhile."

"Knowing the dwarf's dirty secrets is all well and good, but we knew I was going to have to kill him all along," I said. "What I want to know now is how I can pull it off—and get away clean afterward."

Finn buttered another roll. "I've been working on that too. Like I said before, Dawson is all about his business. Mining is his life."

"So I take him out at his house or the mine office. No big deal."

Finn shook his head. "I did some more digging last night. I wouldn't suggest either one of those options. Dawson has a pretty tight security setup at home. Lots of giant guards, and his house is in a flat, remote area. They'd see you coming. And after your break-in last night, I imagine he's doubled the guards at his office and the mine. Getting in would be tricky, getting out would be a serious problem. Especially if he puts up a fight before you kill him."

I trusted Finn's judgment just as much as I'd trusted Fletcher's. If he said the house and office were out, they were out. "What about going to and from work?"

"Dawson has a driver who's been with him for years. Takes the dwarf everywhere. He drives that big SUV we saw at Country Daze. Bulletproof glass, airbags, reinforced frame, all the usual assorted safety features."

"Which means sniping him through the glass wouldn't work, and the dwarf is probably tough enough to survive a car accident or even a bomb under the hood," I finished.

"You got it."

"So what do you suggest?" I asked. "Because the clock is ticking. Violet can only stay with Eva Grayson, and Sophia and Jo-Jo can only watch Warren at home for so long. Tobias Dawson's going to come back to the store to brace the Foxes again sooner, rather than later. The dwarf needs to get dead, Finn. In a hurry."

Finn grinned. "Ask, and ye shall receive. Dawson doesn't get out much, but he is scheduled to attend a party—tonight, as a matter of fact."

Short notice, but I could make do. I'd done it before. "But . . ."

"But there's only one problem. No, that's not true," Finn said. "There are several problems. But the biggie is this. The party? Guess where it's going to be?"

"I don't know. The Five Oaks country club, maybe?" That's where a lot of upper crust types held their functions.

"Nuh-uh," Finn shook his head. "This shindig is going to be held at Mab Monroe's house—her own personal estate."

"Fuck," I said.

"Fuck, indeed," Finn agreed.

I sat there and ate my blackberry cobbler for several minutes. Mab Monroe's house was the very last place I'd want to do a hit. The Fire elemental wouldn't take too kindly to my stiffing someone within the confines of her own home. Not to mention the fact it would seriously undermine her own security and standing in the Ashland underworld. Killing someone at Mab's mansion was the kind of thing people would talk about for *years*. Mab would do everything in her power to find out who killed the dwarf in her own territory. Who had the audacity to thumb her nose at the Fire elemental like that. She'd have to just to keep the challenges to her power base to a minimum.

But if that's where Tobias Dawson was going to be, then that's where I'd have to do the job—whether I liked it or not. I just hoped I was up to it.

"Tell me the rest of it," I said.

Finn cut himself a piece of the chocolate chip pound cake. "Officially, the party is a business mixer. Mab's invited all her business associates, and everyone else she wants to do deals with in Ashland and beyond. Lots of bigwigs expected to attend. Security to get in is going to be tight."

"So?" I asked. "We've crashed lots of parties before. Surely, Jo-Jo can get us in."

Finn shook his head. "I already called her and asked. You know she can't stand Mab. Jo-Jo declined the invite two weeks ago. You can't use her invitation now and kill Tobias Dawson."

"Because it'll look too suspicious and point Mab in Jo-Jo's direction," I finished his thought. "Okay, so how do we do it? There has to be some way to get into Mab's mansion so I can get close to Dawson."

Finn hesitated. "Well, there's something, but you're probably not going to like it."

"Spill it."

He stared at me. "First of all, you have to realize it's not enough for you to just get into the party. You can't go into Mab Monroe's mansion as you, Gin Blanco. Jonah McAllister's on the guest list. He'd spot you in a minute."

"So I'll wear a disguise. Not like I haven't done it before."

Finn polished off his cake and cut another slice. "True, and I have an idea about that. As part of the evening's festivities, Mab has arranged for a variety of . . . entertainments for her guests."

My gray eyes narrowed. "What kind of *entertainments?*"

Finn cleared his throat. "Hookers. Men and women. Humans, giants, vamps, dwarves. Her guests pick out who they like, do whatever they want, and she foots the bill for the whole thing."

"So you're telling me the best way, the *only* way, to get into this party is for me to pretend to be a hooker, catch

Tobias Dawson's eye, get him alone, and do him before he does me. So to speak."

Finn winced. "More or less. Sorry, Gin. I know it's not ideal, gambling on whether or not you can attract Dawson. But I think this is our best shot at him."

I helped myself to some more blackberry cobbler and thought about things. As an assassin, as the Spider, I'd played a variety of roles over the years. Waitresses, hotel maids, musicians, even a cop a time or two. Dressed up in wigs, makeup, skimpy clothes, and more, all in the name of doing the job. So I wasn't worried whether or not I could pull off being a hooker. What concerned me was the fact I was supposed to do that, lullaby Tobias Dawson, and get away afterward—all on Mab Monroe's home court. Still, Finn was right. This was probably my best, quickest shot at Dawson, and the dwarf needed to die—now.

"All right," I said. "So I'll go in as a hooker."

Finn nodded. "That's actually where it gets a little easier."

"Why?"

He grinned. "Because I happen to be very good friends with the person supplying the evening's entertainment—Roslyn Phillips."

First, Donovan had mentioned her name last night, and now Finn this morning. I hadn't thought about the vampire in weeks, but here she was, popping up all over the place, even if she didn't realize it. Even if I didn't like the fact of how closely we were tied together.

Not only did Roslyn Phillips run Northern Aggression, the most decadent nightclub in Ashland, the vampire used to be a hooker herself. She had worked the Southtown streets for years before she'd saved enough money to move up into management and open her own gin joint. All vampires needed blood to survive, of course, but lots of them also powered up through sex, which is why so many of them worked as prostitutes. Plus, vamps could live a very long time, and hooking, well, it was a skill that would never go out of style or demand. Vamps needed cash just like the rest of us.

Roslyn Phillips was the best of the best. She could do things to men and women I'd never even dreamed of— and she'd taught her staff most of her tricks. But more important than that, the vampire owed me for killing her abusive brother-in-law and for not telling Finn how her loose lips had inadvertently led to Fletcher's death. So Roslyn was going to have to deal with me again, whether she liked it or not.

I scraped up the last of my warm cobbler, then pushed my bowl away. "Well then, I guess it's time to pay Roslyn a friendly visit."

Finn grinned. He and Roslyn had been special friends for years. That is, they often met for dinner, drinks, and a night of hot, sweaty sex when they weren't seeing other people. Sometimes, even if they were.

"Oh, goodie," Finn drawled. "A field trip."

✳ 24 ✳

It was a little after one when we pulled into the parking lot of Northern Aggression, which was located in Northtown, as befitted its name. By eight o'clock tonight, high-end cars of all makes and models would fill the lot, and a long line of eager men and women would be waiting to get inside and satisfy their desperate desires.

But on this cold November afternoon, the nightclub looked like some anonymous warehouse. A big, gray, metal box you'd find in any one of Ashland's industrial parks—except for the enormous rune over the door. A neon light shaped like a heart with an arrow through it perched above the entrance to the nightclub, marking it as something out of the ordinary. The pierced heart was Roslyn Phillips's personal rune and the symbol for her club. From previous visits, I knew the sign would flash red, then yellow, then orange when it was turned on. But right now, it was just a hunk of metal and glass hovering above the door.

"The place looks deserted. You're sure Roslyn's here?" I asked. "I thought she stayed home during the day and watched her niece, Catherine."

Finn shrugged. "Not today. She said she was here looking over the books since it was getting close to the end of the month. She's expecting us."

"Marvelous," I murmured.

We got out of the car and headed toward the entrance. The front door was locked, so Finn rapped on it. His knuckles made a hollow, ringing sound on the reinforced steel door. A few seconds later, something clanged, like a security bar being thrown back, and the door rattled open. Xavier, the nightclub's head bouncer, stuck his head outside. The giant looked even larger, wider, and stronger in the weak afternoon sun than he had at the Pork Pit when he'd arrested Jake McAllister a couple of nights ago. His dark eyes flicked over Finn, then me, then moved back to Finn.

Finn knew exactly what was expected. He smiled and stretched out his hand. Xavier shook it and palmed the offered C-note with surprising grace for someone with hands as big as melons.

The giant grinned. "Always a pleasure to see you, Finn. Come on in."

Finn and I stepped inside, and Xavier shut and locked the door behind us.

"You know I've seen you manning the door here," I said. "But I didn't realize you worked for the police department too until you dropped by the Pork Pit to clear up that little mess the other night. Shouldn't you be out arresting lawbreakers?"

Xavier's grin widened. "Ah, the cop thing's just a part-time gig. Besides, why go out there when they'll all just be coming here later on tonight?"

"Good point."

Xavier grabbed a couple of wooden boxes that had been stacked by the front door, and the *tink-tink* of glass inside caught my ear. Looked like a delivery of liquor of some sort. The giant hefted his burden and headed deeper into the club. Finn and I followed him.

The outside of Northern Aggression might have been a faceless shell, but the inside had a distinct personality, even during the middle of the day. The few overhead lights that were on highlighted the heavy, crushed red velvet drapes that covered the walls. The floor was a wonderful springy bamboo that cushioned our feet, but our steps still echoed in the hollow, empty building.

We crossed the dance floor, and Xavier veered off to the right toward a long bar made entirely of elemental Ice. The structure was almost a hundred feet long and more like an elaborate sculpture than a piece of furniture. Runes had been carved into the slick surface, mostly suns and stars, the symbols for life and joy. Both of which could be found in abundance here late at night, as long as you had enough money to pay for the privileges. The bar, of course, had been created by the Ice elemental who worked as the club's bartender, and he'd used enough of his magic to make sure his creation wouldn't melt before his shift started tonight. I could feel the cool caress of power halfway across the club. My own Ice magic, weak and sluggish though it was, stirred in response.

Xavier put his liquor boxes on the bar and gestured for Finn and me to go on without him. "I've got to get these unloaded. Roslyn's waiting for you guys in her office. You know the way, Finn."

Finn straightened his tie. "Indeed I do."

He headed for the back of the nightclub and pulled open a door discreetly set into the crushed velvet that covered the wall. It opened up into a small hallway that ran in either direction before branching off at both ends. Finn turned left, and we zigzagged through a series of hallways before he stopped at a closed door. Finn knocked on it.

"Come in," a muffled voice said.

Finn opened the door, and we stepped inside an office. Roslyn Phillips sat behind a wide, massive desk that would have made even Xavier look svelte in comparison. A variety of pink and white papers lay scattered on the surface in front of her, along with what looked like an old-fashioned ledger book. A computer drowsed at her elbow, while a red light blinked on her phone. The phone was heart-shaped, with what looked like an arrow forming the handset. The phone matched the runelike shape of the clock on the back wall.

Finn held his hands out wide. A charming smile stretched across his face. "Roslyn, darling, so good of you to see me on such short notice."

An answering smile curved Roslyn's lips, showing her perfect, pearl-white fangs. "You too, Finn."

The vampire got up from behind her desk. To say that Roslyn Phillips was an attractive woman would be like saying Sherman only set a few fires in Atlanta—a complete understatement. Her eyes and perfect skin were a rich toffee, and her cropped, layered black hair highlighted the edge of her strong, square jaw. Silver glasses perched on the end of her button nose and made her eyes seem even larger and more expressive. The vampire had the kind of face that made you do a double-take to wonder if such symmetrical perfection was possible. On her, yes.

Since the nightclub wasn't open for business yet, Roslyn was dressed down in a pair of skinny jeans and a button-up white shirt. But the simple outfit still showed off her body to its full potential. Plump breasts, lush hips, flat stomach, toned thighs, just the right amount of curve to her ass. Roslyn was like a female version of the *David*—only made of firm, warm skin instead of cold stone. The vamp was one of those who used sex to power up, along with blood, and she'd spent years, decades even, learning how to work what she'd been given to her full advantage.

Roslyn came around the desk, and Finn pressed a chaste kiss to her cheek, once again playing the part of the Southern gentleman. The vampire drew back, and her dark eyes landed on me.

"And you brought Gin along with you," she said in a neutral tone.

"Hello, Roslyn," I replied. "Lovely to see you too."

Roslyn's smile turned into more of a grimace. She hadn't forgotten our last meeting at Fletcher Lane's funeral. The one where I'd told the vampire I knew that she'd talked about Fletcher, Finn, and me, about what we did. That her well-intentioned whispers had led Alexis

James to Fletcher and the Pork Pit and had gotten the old man killed.

"What do you need?" she asked in a quiet tone, still staring at me.

Need, not *want*. Roslyn Phillips seemed to be taking our conversation to heart. I'd agreed not to kill the vamp or tell Finn what she'd done—and told her point-blank she would give me and Finn anything we needed for as long as I saw fit. Since I wasn't a forgiving person, that was going to be a good long while. Starting right now.

"Ah, Roslyn, you wound me," Finn said. "What makes you think we need anything? Perhaps I just wanted to stop by and bask in your beauty."

The vampire snorted. "Cut the bullshit, Finn. If you'd come by yourself, I might have pretended to buy that tired old line. But you brought Gin with you. I doubt she's interested in my beauty."

"Sorry, Roslyn," I said. "I don't swing that way."

The vampire shrugged and turned her dark eyes to Finn. "So I ask the question again—what do you need?"

Finn opened his mouth, probably to sweet-talk Roslyn some more, but I cut in. We didn't have a lot of time to waste. We needed to get what we came for from Roslyn and get on with things.

"I need to get into Mab Monroe's party tonight," I said.

Roslyn's eyes widened for half a second before she masked her surprise. "You want to get into Mab's party? Why?"

I stared at the vampire, debating what I should tell

her. The less Roslyn knew, the better. But after our last conversation, I had no doubts the vampire would keep her mouth shut this time. She knew what I'd do to her if she didn't.

"I need to get close to someone."

Roslyn frowned with understanding. "Who?"

"Tobias Dawson."

The vampire blanched with disgust, but she didn't ask why I was interested in the dwarf. Hooking in Southtown for a few decades was a great way to dampen your curiosity. On the mean Southtown streets, you did things without asking the reasons or thinking too much about them afterward. Besides, Roslyn knew the *why* didn't really matter, since the only reason I ever got close to anyone like Dawson was to kill him.

Roslyn crossed her arms over her chest. Her foot turned sideways and tapped on the thick carpet. After a few moments of quiet introspection, comprehension flickered in her dark eyes. "You want to go in as one of my girls. That's why you're here."

I nodded.

Roslyn stared at me, and I let the coldness leech into my gray eyes. I respected the vampire for what she'd accomplished, for being smart and savvy enough to work her way up from a street hooker to a wealthy businesswoman. And I especially admired Roslyn's fierce devotion to her sister and young niece, her determination to provide a better life for them. But that didn't mean I was going to let the vampire renege on our deal. Fletcher Lane was dead, partly because of her. She owed me until I said otherwise.

"All right," Roslyn said in a quiet voice. "I'll help you, Gin."

"Thank you." I might be twisting Roslyn's arm to the breaking point, but there was no need to be ungrateful about it.

The vampire nodded her head. "Follow me."

Roslyn led us out of her office. The maze of corridors snaked all the way around the interior perimeter of Northern Aggression, forming a series of passageways, peepholes, and discreet doors that let Roslyn, her hookers, and the giant bouncers who watched out for them have access to the entire nightclub without having to fight their way through the drinking, smoking, snorting, fucking crowd on the main floor.

After a series of twists and turns, Roslyn opened a door marked *Supplies* and stepped inside. Finn and I followed her.

Finn stopped dead in his tracks, and a wide smile spread across his face. "I think I've died and gone to heaven."

I snorted. "Yeah, hooker heaven."

The room wasn't filled with what I would consider *supplies*, but then again, I wasn't in the nightclub business. Racks and racks of clothes took up a good portion of the room, along with a couple of rows of metal lockers and several vanity tables crammed with makeup, hairspray, and dozens of boxes of condoms, feminine lubricants, and assorted body oils.

Roslyn removed a clipboard and pen from the wall next to a clothes rack. She perched her hip on one of the makeup tables and stabbed the pen at me. "Strip," she ordered.

"Why?"

Roslyn pierced me with a hard stare. "Because if you're going to masquerade as one of my girls, then you're damn sure going to look the part. I'm not sending out shoddy merchandise, especially not to one of Mab Monroe's parties."

I had to applaud Roslyn's dedication to her craft, if nothing else. So I stepped out of my boots and socks, peeled off my jeans, and shrugged out of my fleece jacket. I took a little more care with my long-sleeved T-shirt, making sure Roslyn didn't see the two knives I had tucked up my sleeves or the one I'd hidden against the small of my back. A minute later, I stood there in my bra and panties. The concrete floor felt like ice against my bare feet.

"Underwear too," Roslyn barked. "I need to see everything."

I looked at Finn and made a circle with my finger, suggesting he turn around.

"C'mon, Gin. It's not like I haven't seen it all before," Finn protested.

Roslyn started. "Don't tell me the two of you—"

"Yeah, we did," I said. "When we were kids. Before I knew any better. Now turn around, Finn."

Finn rolled his eyes, but he turned his back and wandered over to the racks of clothes, most of which were either transparent wisps of lace and satin or form-fitting pieces of leather.

Roslyn grabbed a tape measure from one of the tables

and wrapped it around various parts of my body. I stood there and let her work. The vampire regarded me with all the interest a butcher would a cow. Standing there naked wasn't the most comfortable thing I'd ever done, but I knew Roslyn had seen better bodies than mine in her time. Hell, she had one herself. So I decided to focus on more important matters.

"According to info Finn found, some of your girls have had dealings with Tobias Dawson before," I said. "What does he like?"

"Why do you ask?"

I shrugged. "I need to attract his attention tonight. Can't hurt to stack the deck in my favor."

Roslyn wrote down another measurement on her clipboard. "Have you ever seen Tobias Dawson?"

"Once."

"Then you know about his cowboy fetish," Roslyn said.

"You mean the cheesy snakeskin boots and the hat that's almost as tall as he is?"

The vampire nodded. "Dawson not only dresses like a cowboy, but he acts like one too—especially in bed. He likes Texas beauty queens. Big blond hair, big blue eyes, big breasts, tight asses, lots of makeup. Of which the only thing you currently have is a tight ass."

"Thanks," I said in a wry tone.

Roslyn raised her eyebrows. "Just pointing out the facts. You did come here for my professional opinion, after all."

I nodded. "I did."

"Dawson likes to take the lead. In keeping with the

cowboy persona, he likes for a woman to catch his eye, and then he does his best to hog-tie her."

"Literally or figuratively?"

Roslyn stared at me. "Both. One of my girls had rope burns for a week after paying him a visit."

I filed the information away. "What else?"

"He also likes to wear chaps, a cowboy hat, and his boots when he fucks."

"Sounds like a kinky bastard to me," Finn said.

The vampire walked over to a different rack of clothes than the one Finn had been rifling through. "Unfortunately, not as kinky as some I've seen and done."

Roslyn flipped through the clothes for a moment before turning back to me. "I assume you'll want something with a little coverage to it. Where you can stash certain . . . supplies?"

Weapons, in other words. "Yeah. The more coverage the better. I like to be prepared."

Roslyn nodded. "Any particular color you'd prefer?"

"Black."

"Shocking," she muttered.

After a few minutes, Roslyn pulled a black pushup bra and a set of sheer matching panties off the rack. She handed them to me. "Put those on."

I did as she asked. The garments fit perfectly, and the bra pushed my small breasts up to new, gravity-defying heights. Finn let out a whistle of appreciation. I drew my finger across my throat, showing him exactly what would happen if he didn't shut up. Finn just grinned at me.

Roslyn also plucked a black cocktail dress out of the mass of clothes and handed it to me. I slipped into the fabric. The dress was long-sleeved with a sweetheart neckline and bustier-like top. Thanks to the bra, my cleavage swelled on either side of the fabric. The skirt was a mass of black crinoline with tiny sequins sewn into it. The garment stopped just above my knees.

"How's that?" Roslyn asked.

I looked at myself in a mirror over one of the vanity tables. The sleeves were loose enough for me to carry my knives, and I could strap a couple more to my thighs underneath the billowing skirt. "Perfect."

Roslyn nodded, like she'd expected nothing else, and sashayed over to one of the vanity tables. She handed me a box that read *Contacts—Sky Blue*, and a long, curly, blond wig with teased bangs. "With the wig, contacts, and enough makeup, you'll be Dawson's dream girl. I assume you can do your own makeup."

"I think I can manage."

Roslyn ignored my sarcasm. She opened a drawer on one of the vanity tables, drew out an envelope, and handed it to me. A sunburst done in gold foil glittered on the creamy stationery. The rune for fire—Mab Monroe's personal symbol.

"That's one of the invitations for tonight," Roslyn said. "You'll need this too."

She reached back into the drawer and pulled out a black velvet choker. A rune dangled from the middle of the wide band—a silver heart with an arrow through it. The symbol for Northern Aggression. The rune that would mark me as one of Roslyn Phillips's girls and part of the evening's entertainment.

I took the choker from her and rubbed my thumb over

the rune. The metal felt cool under my fingers. "Thank you, Roslyn, for your help."

She stared at me. "No thanks are needed, remember? I owe you. But when the other girls come in to get ready for tonight, we're going to report that invitation, necklace, outfit, and wig as being stolen. Xavier will take down the report. Of course, he'll be busy working the door tonight, so he won't call to tell me about it or even turn it into the cops for a couple hours. That should give you plenty of time to do whatever you're planning to do."

I nodded. I couldn't blame the vampire for covering herself. If things went badly, and they just might, Tobias Dawson and Mab Monroe would probably come knocking on Roslyn's door, demanding to know why I'd been wearing one of the vampire's rune necklaces and how I'd snitched one of the hookers' invitations to the party. This way, Roslyn had an out.

"And do me another favor," the vampire said, her dark eyes serious behind her silver glasses.

"What?"

"Whatever you're going to do to Dawson tonight, don't get caught," Roslyn said. "I don't want to have to deal with the honky-tonk bastard any more than I already have."

I gave her a cold smile. "Don't worry. If I get caught, Tobias Dawson will be having too much fun with me to even think about bothering you."

25

At eight o'clock that evening, my taxi pulled into the long, snaking driveway that led up to Mab Monroe's mansion.

Given her status as the city's richest and deadliest citizen, Mab Monroe lived in the biggest, most impressive home in Ashland. The gray stone structure soared fifteen stories into the air, making it taller than some of the downtown skyscrapers. The mansion's three equal-size wings formed a wide, upside-down W-shape. Tall, skinny windows fronted each floor, along with crenellated balconies. A twelve-foot-tall stone fence ringed the mansion itself, which was set back more than a mile from the main road. From the research Fletcher Lane had done over the years, I knew the expansive, manicured grounds featured several gardens, three greenhouses, an aviary, a golf course, copses, and a small lake. Along with giant patrols, guard dogs, assorted magical trip wires, and some other nasty surprises.

A light illuminated a red banner draped over one of the balconies in the center wing of the mansion. The enormous piece of heavy fabric featured a rune done in shimmering gold—a round circle surrounded by several dozen curled, wavy rays. A sunburst. The symbol for fire. Mab Monroe's personal rune. The same one on the invitation in my purse.

The driver fell into the flow of traffic going through the open wrought-iron gates that designated the entrance to Mab Monroe's estate. The yellow taxi seemed out of place among all the stretch limos crawling up the curving driveway like fat, black beetles. It took twenty minutes for the driver to maneuver all the way up and stop in front of the entrance.

My gray eyes flicked over the security. Five giant guards roamed through the line of limos, opening doors, helping people out of their vehicles, directing traffic, and making sure the waiting drivers weren't getting into too much trouble drinking or smoking on the sly. Two more giant guards stood by the front double doors that led into the mansion, flanking a smaller human holding a large clipboard.

"That'll be twenty bucks," the driver growled.

"Twenty bucks? You only drove me a couple of miles."

Earlier this evening, I'd taken the precaution of parking a car on the side of the road just beyond Mab Monroe's estate. An old, battered burner vehicle with fake registration and fake plates. I'd put a white trash bag in the window, left the hood up, and scattered a few tools by the side of the road. All designed to make it look like the car had broken down and someone was coming right back for it. The car was my insurance policy, in case I needed to make a quicker getaway than the one I had in mind. Once I'd put the car where I wanted it, I'd hiked over to the closest anonymous coffee shop and called the cab to bring me here.

"Twenty bucks," the driver said again.

Since I didn't want him to remember me, I quit arguing, paid him, got out, and walked toward the stairs that led up to the main entrance of the mansion. I could hear it, of course. With fifteen stories of solid, stacked stone looming above me, I'd have to be deaf not to. The stone whispered of power and money, the way I'd always thought it would. But there were other vibrations in it too. Fire, heat, death, destruction. But perhaps most disturbing was a touch of madness that trilled like a whip-poor-will's cry through the solid rock, as though the stone itself had somehow been tortured until it broke. The murmurs grew louder, harsher the closer I got to the mansion, until all I could hear was the stones' wailing cries.

I gritted my teeth and blocked out the noise of the stones' unending pain. My only concern was Tobias Dawson, getting close enough to kill him, and getting away afterward. Not the insanity that permeated the foundation of Mab Monroe's mansion—or why it made me want to seriously hurt the Fire elemental.

I walked up the steps and stopped in front of the double doors.

"Invitation?" the man with the clipboard asked.

I pointed to the black velvet choker around my throat—the one with the heart-and-arrow rune on it. "I believe this is all the invitation I need, sugar. But here's the hard copy too." I gave him a winsome smile and handed over the engraved invitation Roslyn Phillips had slipped me.

The man stared at the heart-and-arrow rune a moment; then his eyes swept over the rest of my body. Behind him, the two giants also leered at me. Looked like Tobias Dawson wasn't the only one here tonight with a thing for busty blondes.

The man with the clipboard pulled his attention away from my boobs and checked the name on the invitation. "I assume you know the rules for tonight, Candy?"

I nodded. "Yeah, sugar, I know how to behave myself. I'm a pro."

Before Finn and I had left the nightclub, Roslyn had given me a list of rules Mab Monroe had sent her for the party guys and girls. Basically, Roslyn's hookers were to make themselves available to anyone at anytime during the course of the evening and do anything—*anything*— Mab's guests wanted. Those guys and girls who went home with one of Mab's guests for the night would be generously compensated after the fact. All outstanding bills, hospital and otherwise, would be paid in full by Mab.

The man with the clipboard jerked his thumb over his shoulder. "Go on in."

One of the giants pinched my ass as I walked past. Although I wanted nothing more than to palm one of my silverstone knives and slit his throat for putting his hand on me, I deepened my smile.

"Now, now." I waggled my finger at him. "I'm here for the guests, sugar. Not the hired help."

His face flushed at my insult. The giant stepped forward, but the other one put a restraining hand on his shoulder.

"She's right," the second man rumbled. "Mab will be pissed if you touch her. Remember what she did to Stevenson last time? Do you want that to be you?"

The giant paled. Evidently, whatever Mab Monroe had done to Stevenson had made an impression on the rest of her guards. The giant shot me a sour look, but he stepped back. I winked at him and headed inside the mansion.

The insane shriek of the stones washed over me again, so loud the spider rune scars on my hands itched from the sound of it. But I gritted my teeth and pushed the noise away, buried it so deep that it was nothing more than a murmur in my head. I needed to concentrate on my mission, not wonder what Mab Monroe had done in her own house to make it sound like that.

A hallway that was at least a hundred feet wide cut through the center of the massive mansion. Despite the relatively early hour, the party was in full swing. The trill of laughter and the murmur of conversation resonated through the house, low and mellow, like hidden cicadas cooing in the tall grass in the summertime. It helped drown out the stones' wails.

During my years as an assassin, I'd gotten close to a lot of wealthy, powerful, influential folks. As a general rule, the richer a person, the stingier he was with his money. Finnegan Lane agreed with my observation. He often regaled me with tales about his billionaire vampire clients who bought cases of off-brand toothpaste at the nearest Sell-Everything so they could save a measly five cents a tube.

But not Mab Monroe.

The Fire elemental hadn't skimped on anything in her mansion. Not a thing. White marble coated the floors like glossy varnish, while gold and bronze leaf glittered on the ornate cathedral ceilings a hundred feet above my head. Genuine Tiffany lamps lined the hallway like soldiers, the hidden bulbs sending out sprays of jewel-tone colors through their stained-glass shades. A few lights glowed in the various rooms that branched off the hallway, illuminating delicate antique furniture from a variety of eras.

Everything in the house was tasteful and expensive, whispering of casual elegance that looked effortless, though it had cost a pretty penny to procure. I might have been momentarily dazzled by it, if the shrieking stone of the mansion hadn't told me exactly how Mab had gotten the money to pay for all this finery—and all the nasty things she'd done in here since.

I walked on, passing dozens of people. Silk, satin, crushed velvet. Everyone sported their Sunday best evening gown or tuxedo. Nothing less would do for one of Mab Monroe's parties. In addition to the stone of the mansion, I could also hear the whispers of the gemstones the men and women wore on their necks, wrists, fingers, and even toes. Beauty, elegance, fire. But even the grandest diamond's vibration paled in comparison to the singing clarity of the one I'd seen in Tobias Dawson's safe. Oh yes, the dwarf could make quite the fortune mining and selling the diamonds on Warren Fox's land to this highfalutin crowd.

I recognized more than a few of the faces I passed. Some, I'd done jobs for assassinating parents, brothers, sisters, or business partners for whatever reason. Some were Mab's sycophants, her loyal subjects. Others would have been happy to spit on her corpse, dance a jig on her grave, and then set about trying to take the Fire elemental's place as Ashland's queen bee.

I didn't speak to anyone, but men and women stared at me as I passed. Their eyes caught on the silver rune around my throat, then slid down my body, as though I were a cut of meat they were thinking about getting from the butcher. According to Finn, I looked like a real, live, fuckable Barbie doll, thanks to Roslyn's clothes and long blond wig. I'd barely recognized myself when I'd looked in the mirror earlier.

But I didn't meet anyone's gaze and walked on as if I hadn't noticed there was anyone else in the mansion at all. I wasn't here to attract their attention. Tobias Dawson was my target, and I had no intention of getting sidetracked or propositioned by anyone else.

The main hallway led out into a grand ballroom. Although *grand* really wasn't the right word for the enormous space, which served as the junction for the three wings of the mansion. It featured a golden parquet floor, tiled here and there with marble, granite, and sheets of hammered bronze. Chandeliers dangled from the ceiling. Some glowed with rubies and diamonds. Others burned with garnets and topaz. A staircase that was a hundred feet wide lay at the opposite end of the ballroom, its pristine scarlet carpet stretching up to the second floor and beyond.

More than three hundred of Mab Monroe's closest business associates talked and laughed and drank on the ballroom floor, their clusters and cliques not even coming close to filling the massive space. They reminded me of dolls that might populate a child's playhouse. Pretty and polished with fake smiles that stretched their painted, plastic faces to the breaking point. But I looked beyond the elegant veneer of the people and furnishings. Despite the rich sophistication on display, I noticed other things, things that weren't as nice as they appeared at first glance.

Like the giants circulating throughout the ballroom. Given the platters of champagne, caviar, and quail's eggs they supported on their enormous hands, you might have thought them nothing more than waiters. But I knew what they were really here for—crowd control, in case folks got stupid and drunk enough to start turning on each other. I imagined Mab Monroe wouldn't cotton to a couple of tipsy elementals deciding to stage a magical duel in her ballroom.

That's how elementals usually fought, by flinging their raw magic at each other, until one person succumbed to the other's power. When two elementals clashed, the inevitable loser could suffer anything from catching Fire, to getting encased in Ice, to having her heart turned to Stone, or even being flayed alive by the very Air she breathed. Depending, of course, on the type of elemental she was fighting. And this wasn't even counting all the other folks who had talents for things like metal, water, and electricity.

Overall, elementals' duels were a quick, nasty, painful way to die, which is why I never engaged in them. Killing the other person first was what mattered to me. Not old-fashioned, outdated, useless concepts like honor and duels. Codes of conduct were for overconfident fools.

Five, ten, twenty . . . I counted almost thirty giants in all, more than enough to control even the unruliest crowd. None of them were carrying weapons, but then again, they didn't need to. One good blow from a giant's fist would break almost anything—especially alcohol-soaked jaws and egos.

I stepped into the swirling crowd, letting the sea of tuxedos and shimmering gowns sweep me along from one clique to the next. A set of glass doors on the left side of the ballroom led out to a terrace. A massive orchestra had been erected on the right side in front of another set of glass doors. I plastered a smile on my face and strolled through the ballroom, flitting from one knot of people to the next, until I reached a quieter space along the underside of the staircase beside a potted bonsai tree with gnarled limbs.

I pulled my cell phone out of my purse and called Finn. He picked up on the third ring.

"I'm here," I said. "Where are you?"

"I see you, Gin. You look smashing, even for a faux hooker."

"Finn," I growled.

"To answer your question, I'm on the second floor, leaning over the railing and surveying the majesty laid out before me."

My eyes flicked up. Sure enough, Finn was exactly where he said he was. Leaning against the marble banister, Scotch in one hand, cell phone in the other. Roslyn Phillips stood beside him, wearing a strapless white evening gown that made her look like a Greek goddess. Mab Monroe had invited the hooker to the party so Roslyn could keep an eye on her guys and girls and make sure they were properly servicing the more important guests. And, as part of our plan, Roslyn had brought Finn along as her date for the evening. Nothing unusual about it, since the two of them were often seen together out on the town.

The grand staircase marched up to the second floor, forming a wide landing, before splitting in two and winding up either side to the upper floors of the mansion. Finn had chosen well. His position gave him a view of the entire ballroom below.

"Let's get started," I said. "Before someone decides to proposition me. Where's Dawson?"

"He's in the center of the ballroom, about a couple hundred feet behind you on the right. Although I wouldn't suggest approaching him now, given his current company."

"Current company? What does that mean?"

"You'll see. Just keep looking in that direction. Dawson's easy to find. He's the only one wearing a cowboy hat tonight."

I peered through the crowd. It took me several seconds to spot Dawson, and Finn was right. He was the only cowboy in attendance. In addition to the giant hat on his head, the dwarf also wore snakeskin boots and another lariat tie topped with turquoise. All of which looked ridiculous with his tuxedo. But Tobias Dawson's fashion sense wasn't what made me frown, then curse. It was the company he was keeping.

Mab Monroe, Jonah McAllister, and Elliot Slater.

* 26 *

"Fuck," I said.

"Fuck is right," Finn replied. "Because no hooker in her right mind would try to get in the middle of that sandwich."

My eyes slipped past Dawson and studied the three people he was standing with. Of course, I'd met Jonah McAllister in person yesterday, when he'd come to the Pork Pit to threaten me into dropping the charges against his son, Jake. The slick-talking lawyer looked distinguished and handsome in his tuxedo, and his thick mane of hair resembled silver that had somehow been swirled around his head.

I hadn't had any dealings with Elliot Slater, the giant enforcer who ran Mab's security detail and took care of any problems the Fire elemental didn't feel like dealing with herself. Slater was one of the tallest giants in attendance, if not the tallest. His seven-foot figure loomed over the crowd. He wasn't quite as wide as he was tall, but his frame was all solid, compact muscle. A cut with one of my knives would have felt like a bee sting to him. Slater's complexion was pale, almost albino, and his tousled thatch of blond hair disappeared into his large skull. His eyes were a light hazel, and the only real color on his chalky face. A large diamond ring flashed on his pinkie. Another inch or two, and I could have worn it as a bracelet.

And then there was Mab Monroe herself. The Fire elemental was a few inches shorter than me, but she radiated raw power, even more so than Elliot Slater did. Her hair was as red as polished copper and curled softly to her shoulders. In contrast, her eyes were a deep, liquid black. Ink would look dull and diluted next to her gaze. Fire and brimstone. That's what Mab Monroe always reminded me of.

The Fire elemental wore a floor-length evening gown done in an emerald green that made her hair seem even redder than it actually was. She wore no jewelry except for a flat gold necklace that ringed her throat. My eyes focused on the centerpiece of the design. A circular ruby a little smaller than my fist surrounded by several dozen wavy rays. The intricate diamond cutting on the gold caught the light and made it seem as though the rays were actually flickering. A sunburst. The symbol for fire. Mab's personal rune, used by her alone. For a moment, I sensed the ruby's vibrations. The gemstone whispered of raw, fiery power. The sound meshed perfectly with the shrieking stone of the mansion. Both made my stomach clench.

As I looked at Mab, I couldn't help but think about the file Fletcher Lane had left me on the murder of my family—and the piece of paper he'd tucked inside with Mab Monroe's name on it. Again, I wondered why Fletcher had written down the Fire elemental's name. Had Fletcher concluded that she'd murdered my family? Had he merely suspected her? Or had he put her name in there for another reason entirely—

"Earth to Gin," Finn murmured in my ear.

I focused on the here and now once more. "How long have they been standing there talking?"

"Not long," Finn said. "I'd say you have another five or ten minutes before Mab and the others drift off."

"All right. Keep an eye on them."

"What are you going to do?"

I stared out at the glittering mass of people. "Find someplace quiet to take care of Tobias Dawson, once I get my hooks into him."

Finn promised to keep watching Tobias Dawson, and we both hung up. I tucked the cell phone back into the purse Roslyn had given me. It was a tiny thing, but I'd managed to stick one of my silverstone knives inside, along with the compact and tube of healing ointment Jo-Jo Deveraux had provided a few days ago. I didn't think Dawson would go down easily, and I wanted to have some healing supplies on hand in case the dwarf got a couple of shots in on me before he died. I couldn't exactly sneak out of Mab Monroe's party unnoticed if I was bruised and bloody from head to toe.

I grabbed a glass of champagne from one of the giant

waiters and headed toward the back of the ballroom. The grand staircase was shaped like a T, and two hallways ran underneath either side of it and connected the ballroom to the other wings of the mansion. I strolled down the left hallway, peering into the rooms I passed. I couldn't very well kill Tobias Dawson on the ballroom floor, so I needed to find a more secluded spot I could lure the dwarf to before I stabbed him to death.

But the hallway wasn't as deserted as I'd hoped. I passed several couples standing against the walls or inside the interior rooms, just out of sight of the ballroom. Some talked softly. Others stared into each other's eyes and sipped champagne. A few necked. But one person in every couple wore a heart-and-arrow rune that marked him or her as a hooker from Northern Aggression.

One man wearing the rune necklace grimaced as his vampire paramour sank her fangs deep into his exposed throat. Her eager, sucking sounds reminded me of a kitten mewling. Another man, a dwarf, stood upright, his head tucked up underneath the dress and his face buried in the crotch of a giant woman wearing the rune necklace. I didn't have to guess what he was doing with his tongue. The giant had a decidedly bored look on her face. She cooed false encouragement to the dwarf, even as she examined her nails as if debating whether or not she needed a fresh manicure. The giant saw me staring. Her brown eyes landed on the rune necklace around my throat, and she shrugged as if to say, *What can you do?* I returned her shrug and walked on.

One thing I didn't see back here were any giant guards. Mab Monroe probably didn't want her more amorous guests to feel like they were being watched. Having a giant loom over you would give just about anyone performance anxiety.

I came to a cross corridor and paused. To my left, a second set of doors led out onto the terrace. Another hallway stretched out in front of me, while another one veered right, snaking back underneath the staircase. I turned right and walked deeper into the mansion. The partygoers hadn't gotten too serious about their sexual gymnastics just yet, so this area was deserted. I passed a couple of rooms, none concealed enough for my liking. It wouldn't do any good for me to kill Tobias Dawson and have someone find his body a minute later. I was going to need longer than that to slip out of the mansion after I'd done the job.

So I strolled through the rooms, sipped my champagne, and pretended to admire Mab Monroe's tasteful furnishings while I looked for a spot to stiff Dawson. One thing actually did catch my interest—a series of rune paintings, not unlike the drawings I had propped up on the mantel in Fletcher Lane's den.

My eyes flicked over the runes mounted on the wall opposite the back of the staircase. A sunburst. A lit match. A teardrop-shaped flame licking at the paper it was on. The framed pieces all had to do with fire or heat in some way, and all were done in burnt siennas, bloody oranges, and fiery yellows. It seemed Mab and I shared the same taste in something besides killing people. Weird. And disturbing.

As I stared at the paintings, an uneasy shiver tickled my spine like a cold finger. Something about the artwork resonated on a primal level with me. *Here,* something old and knowing whispered in the back of my mind. *Here is your enemy.*

Not an unusual thought for a Stone elemental to have while in the house of a Fire, or vice versa. Opposing elements just didn't mesh—and neither did their human counterparts. Air against Ice, Fire against Stone. An old, predictable story. I'd heard that voice, felt this unease, before in other places with other elementals. But never this intense.

Again, I wondered about Mab Monroe's name being in Fletcher's folder. I'd been blindfolded so I hadn't seen the bitch's face back then, only heard her cackling laughter as she tortured me. But it could have been Mab. Rumor put her current age at about forty-five. She would have had enough power, even seventeen years ago, to do all the horrible things that had taken place that night. But why? Why had she murdered my mother, Eira, and my older sister, Annabella? Why had she wanted to kill me? Why had she demanded to know where my baby sister Bria was above all else? I just didn't understand *why*—

Footsteps whispered on the carpet off to my right, and a large, beefy hand clamped onto my ass and squeezed—hard.

"Hello there, sweetness," a male voice said. "If your front looks as tight as your ass, I'm in for a real good time tonight."

He put his other hand on my opposite shoulder and turned me around. I let him and plastered a smile on my face, my lips ready to form an excuse to get rid of the ogling bastard.

I found myself looking up at Jake McAllister. The Fire

elemental had traded in his rock-star jeans and vintage T-shirt for a tuxedo. It didn't improve his looks. His body was still too beefy, his face still puffed out with baby fat. He looked like an oversize kid playing dress-up in his daddy's clothes. But the important thing was that he was here and staring at me.

Of all the people I could have run into here tonight, the possibility one of them would be Jake McAllister had never crossed my mind. So much had been going on lately that I'd relegated Jake and his threat to kill me to the back burner. But luck, that capricious bitch, had decided to fuck me over once again.

Jake frowned, as though he knew me from somewhere but just couldn't place me. Then, recognition dawned on his beefy face.

"You!" he hissed.

Jake McAllister stared at me. A cruel smile spread across his face, making his cheeks puff out that much more. "You shouldn't have come here tonight, bitch. Because we're on my side of town now, and I'm going to kill you." His brown eyes landed on the heart-and-arrow rune around my neck. "After I fuck you a couple of times."

I raised an eyebrow. "You want me? Come and get me, you bastard."

I slammed my fist into his windpipe. Jake's face went beet red, and he struggled for air. While he was gasping for breath, I drove my other fist into his stomach. First one, then the other. *Thwack-thwack*. Like kneading dough. He bent over, and I hurried away, moving deeper into the mansion.

My desire to find a quiet area to kill someone had just turned into a necessity. I had to finish Jake McAllister now. He was right. This was his turf, or at least Mab Monroe's turf, and I had no doubt the Fire elemental would let Jake do whatever he wanted to with me—if I didn't take care of him first before he could sound the alarm. My eyes swept back and forth over the open doors and rooms I passed. There. That would do.

I looked over my shoulder. Jake McAllister had struggled to his feet. I blew him a kiss. His face reddened, and he lumbered down the hallway in my direction. I stepped inside the room, found the spot I wanted, palmed one of my silverstone knives, and waited. Ten . . . twenty . . . thirty . . . I counted off the seconds in my head.

Jake McAllister was quicker than I'd given him credit for—or just more pissed off. Only forty-five seconds passed before he charged into the room.

"Where are you, bitch?" he growled. "I saw you come in here."

I didn't respond. Let McAllister figure it out for himself.

"Hiding from me, huh, bitch?" he laughed. "I knew you'd be running scared of me sooner or later."

I rolled my eyes at his foolish assumption, but still I waited. Heavy footsteps sounded on the tile floor. McAllister's shadow crept closer and closer to my hiding place. I tensed, gathering my strength. If he got away from me, if he screamed, it was over. I had to kill him with the first strike.

Jake McAllister threw back the shower curtain I was standing behind. The Fire elemental had reached for his magic during his lumber down the hall. The power reddened his eyes, and sparks snapped and hissed around his fat fingertips. His gaze met mine, and he smiled.

"There you are, bitch—"

Last words he ever said.

With one hand, I grabbed McAllister's tuxedo jacket and pulled him forward, so that his torso was directly above the bathtub I was standing in. With my other hand, I shoved my silverstone knife up to the hilt in his chest. The blade scraped his ribs before plunging into his heart. Not the best blow I'd ever made, but effective enough.

Jake McAllister's magic snuffed out like a candle in a hurricane. The fiery sparks puffed away, and the red glow vanished from his eyes. His arms jerked and flailed against me, connecting with my chest. I grunted at the heavy, solid blows, but I didn't dare reach for my Stone magic to harden my own skin. Any elemental in close vicinity would sense the power surge. Stones were the rarest of elementals, and any magic user who felt that kind of power would be curious about who was using it and why.

Jake opened his mouth to scream. I left the knife where it was in his heart, clamped my hand over his fat lips, and yanked him forward so the blood gushing out of his chest would fall into the bathtub and not spatter onto the tile floor. And so we stood there, seesawing back and forth over the tub, Jake McAllister trying to jerk away, and me pulling him closer, my hands digging into his face.

After about thirty seconds, Jake's legs wobbled and gave way. His eyes glazed over, and his mouth slackened underneath my hand. I dropped my fingers from his lips. Jake coughed twice. Blood sputtered out of his mouth and flecked the front of my dress. Nothing I could do about that right now. So I put both hands on his suit jacket and dragged him forward. He was heavy, and it took some muscle to flip his legs up and over the side of the tub and then to lower his whole body down the steps and into the bottom without letting him thump down. By the time I was done, Jake McAllister was dead, and I was a sweaty, bloody mess.

First things first. I shut the bathroom door. Then I went back over to Jake McAllister. The bathtub was the fancy marble kind that was more like a small pool than a tub and sat on a raised dais. A couple of steps led up to the rim, and several more led down into the square pool. I got down into the bottom with Jake. The first thing I did was to retrieve my knife from his chest and lay it on the edge of the tub. Then I maneuvered him so his back was facing the rest of the room. I curled his hands under head and splayed out his legs to make it look as though he'd had too much to drink and had crawled into the tub to sleep it off. At least at first glance. If someone turned Jake over, they'd see the blood on his shirt and in the bottom of the tub. But hopefully, I'd be long gone by the time that happened.

Once that was done, I climbed out and assessed the damage. The tub also featured several shower heads which were set into the walls at various angles, hence the curtain that cordoned the area off from the rest of the bathroom. The shower curtain was a rich burgundy flecked with gold—and now blood. But unless you peered closely at it, you wouldn't realize the spatter wasn't part of the intended pattern.

Some of Jake's blood had also sprayed onto the marble tile in front of the tub. I grabbed a burgundy washcloth, wet it, and used it to mop up all the stray flecks and specks. I also cleaned off my knife and tucked it back up the sleeve of my dress. The smell of warm copper filled my nose, but I blocked it out—along with the murmur of the marble under my feet. Instead of the dark tone I'd expected, the stone practically sang with giddiness—as though having fresh blood spilled on it made it *happy*. The noise made my stomach twist.

I worked quickly, quietly. It had taken me less than two minutes to kill Jake McAllister. Nobody should have missed him yet, but I wasn't taking any chances by moving slowly. Once I had the blood wiped up from the floor in front of the tub, I drew the curtain, hiding it and McAllister's body from sight.

In addition to the tub, the bathroom featured two toilets made out of what looked like real gold. They lay opposite two sinks done in a burgundy marble with streaks of white swirled through it. A gilt-edged mirror flanked the wall above the counter. I stared at myself in the glass, assessing the damage Jake McAllister had done to me with his dying struggles. The bastard's coughing had spattered blood all over my chest. I used the wet washcloth to mop up the blood on my exposed skin, then wrung it out, wet it again, and scrubbed the remaining blood out of my wig. It was harder getting the crimson gobs out of the fake blond tresses, but I managed well enough.

Once that was done, I went to work on my dress. I used some liquid soap from a bottle on the counter and rubbed it into the biggest blood splotches. Since the fabric was black, you couldn't tell what the stain was, just that I'd gotten something on me. But I managed to get most of the blood out.

My eyes swept over the bathroom again, but there was no visible sign anything of the ordinary had happened in here tonight. I carefully folded the burgundy washcloth and laid it back in its original spot next to the bathtub.

While I waited for the damp spots on my dress to dry, I rummaged in my purse and pulled out a pressed powder compact I'd brought, along with some lipstick. I'd gotten sweaty during my struggle with Jake McAllister, and I touched up my makeup into its heavy mask once more.

I'd just popped open the lipstick to finish fixing my face when the door to the bathroom opened—and Mab Monroe stepped inside.

✴ 27 ✴

For a moment, we just stared at each other, her black eyes on my faux blue ones. My mind raced as I tried to figure out what the Fire elemental could be doing here—and how I could get away from her.

But since Mab Monroe didn't immediately scream for her giant guards or worse, reach for her Fire elemental magic, I assumed she hadn't heard me kill Jake McAllister—or clean up the mess. Only one way to find out.

Somehow, I plastered a smile on my face. "Oh, hello there," I said in a cheery tone. "How are you?"

Mab frowned. "This is one of my private bathrooms. You're not supposed to be in here."

The Fire elemental's voice was soft, breathy, with just a hint of a rasp, like silk rubbing together. But there was far more power and menace in her light tone than in anyone else's voice I'd ever heard. At the sound, I felt that strange, primal sensation surge through me again. *Enemy*, that little voice muttered in the back of my head. *Enemy, enemy, enemy*.

But I tuned out the voice, widened my eyes, and put on my best oh-no-I-just-totally-fucked-up face. Then I gasped. "Oh, I'm so sorry, sugar. I just didn't know. Nobody told me, you see, and this is my very first time here at one of your parties."

Mab stared at me, her eyes dark and thoughtful. Her gaze went to the fuchsia lipstick in my hand, then moved down my body. Her eyes lingered on the damp spots on the front of my dress. "What are you doing in here?"

"Oh, just freshening up a bit. Lot of competition out there tonight. Girl's got to look her best at one of these things."

The Fire elemental stepped farther into the bathroom. I gave her another smile, leaned forward, and reapplied my lipstick. Mab just stood there, staring at me in the mirror. She might be able to intimidate everyone else in Ashland with her hard stare, but not me. But that didn't mean I was going to do something stupid, like insult the Fire elemental to her face in her own bathroom—with Jake McAllister's cooling body lying ten feet to my right.

Antagonizing Jonah McAllister in my own restaurant was one thing. So was killing his son after he threatened to rape and murder me. But Mab—Mab was different. If only for the simple fact that I didn't know which one of us would come out on top in a fight. But one of us would die, and I didn't want it to be me. I had promises to keep to the Foxes, promises I wouldn't be able to fulfill if I got into a battle with Mab.

So I kept my gaze on my own face and not hers. But in my peripheral vision, I could see the magic glimmering in her eyes. Unlike Jake McAllister, Mab's eyes didn't turn red when she reached for her Fire magic. If anything, they got darker, blacker, until they seemed to suck the light out of the room. Mab was also one of those elementals who leaked power. Well, more like radiated in her case. I could feel her Fire magic pouring off her. It pricked at my skin like a thousand hot, tiny needles.

"What's that on your dress?" Mab asked. "Those spots?"

I capped my lipstick and slid it back into my purse. My fingers brushed the hilt of my silverstone knife, but I didn't reach for it. Killing a punk like Jake McAllister was one thing. He was reckless, stupid, sloppy. But Mab Monroe was the most dangerous woman in Ashland. I had no doubt she could fry me alive with her magic before I even got the weapon out of my purse.

So I closed the tiny bag, turned to face her, and widened my smile. "Well, you see, that's why I came in here in the first place. The gentleman I was with got a little too . . . excited about things. A real early bird, if you know what I mean."

I let out a laugh. Mab didn't join in.

"Anyway, I came in here to mop up some of the damage, before I made the rounds to see if any other guests were interested in my services this evening."

Mab's black eyes never left mine. "And who might this gentleman be? This . . . early bird?"

I forced out another laugh. "Oh, sugar, I didn't ask his name. That was at the top of your list of rules."

She was silent for a few seconds, thinking about my answer. "And what might your name be?"

"Why, Candy, of course, because I'm supersweet."

Disgust flashed across Mab's face. Evidently, she didn't like hookers with cheesy names. But her reaction gave me an idea as to how I could escape this inquisition.

I wet my lips and stepped forward. For a moment, I toyed with the heart-and-arrow rune on my velvet choker, drawing Mab's attention to it. Her eyes flicked to the rune, then back up to mine. I stepped forward and reached for a piece of her hair that had fallen forward over her shoulder. I immediately regretted the move, because holding onto to Mab's hair felt like rubbing a lit match between my fingers. I half-expected my skin to start blistering from the sensation.

Still, I gave no sign I could sense her elemental magic. Instead, I rubbed her lock of hair, curled it around my finger, and pushed it back over her shoulder. I let my fingers linger on her shoulder a moment longer than would be considered polite, then drew my arm back. My fingertips, my whole hand, felt like they were on fire. Somehow, I managed not to look at them.

"You know, I'm here this evening to service the guests any way they'd like," I said in a breathy tone. "And since this is your party, I'd be more than happy to make myself available to you, Miz Monroe. For however long you'd like. Any *way* you'd like."

For the first time, something like amusement sparked in Mab's eyes. "You're very bold, aren't you?"

I gave her a delicate shrug and a lascivious grin, making sure to wet my lips with my tongue again. "You have to be, in this line of work."

Mab's black gaze moved down my body again, this time with more prurient interest. She gave a regretful shake of her head. "As tempting as your offer is, Candy, I'm afraid I don't indulge like that at my own functions. I always keep my business and pleasure separate."

I stuck my lower lip out and pouted. "Too bad. Well, if you change your mind, I'll be around. All night long."

I batted my eyes at her. Mab raised an eyebrow, but the corners of her lips turned up into what I assumed was a smile. I couldn't tell if I'd amused her or if she was just mocking me, but I didn't care to stick around and find out.

"Well, if you'll excuse me, I really do need to get back to work," I said. "Mix and mingle and all that."

"Of course," Mab murmured.

I made a move to step around her. But Mab Monroe shifted ever so slightly, so that my body brushed up against hers on my way to the door. Again, her magic washed over me, so hot it seemed as if my dress had burst into flames. But evidently Mab liked what she felt because her smile widened. I gave her another lascivious wink and kept going, even though my stomach clenched at the feel of her magic pricking my skin, even harder and hotter this time, as if I'd aroused her.

I'd just made it to the door when Mab called out to me again.

"Have we met before, Candy?" she asked. "For some reason, you look familiar."

I turned and shook my head. "I don't think so, and I surely would have remembered meeting *you*, Miz Monroe. You're a legend in this town."

I gave her another smile before I ducked out into the hallway.

Somehow, I forced myself to saunter back the way I'd come instead of running like I really wanted to. I didn't know what bothered me more. The fact Mab Monroe had considered taking me up on my fake offer to fuck her or the fact I'd left the Fire elemental in her own bathroom with a dead body in the tub. Either way, things were starting to get out of hand. I needed to get Tobias Dawson alone—now—or get out. Saving my own skin tonight—and Finn's and Roslyn's—came first. Even before the job I'd promised to do for Warren Fox.

I'd just rounded the corner that led back to the main hallway when someone moved in the shadows off to my left. I palmed one of my knives.

"That was quite a performance you put on back there in the bathroom," a male voice murmured. "Very entertaining."

Owen Grayson stepped out of the shadows. Like every other man on the premises, he wore a tuxedo. Once again, I was struck by how compact, sturdy, and strong his frame was. Almost dwarven, except for his six-foot-one height. His violet eyes glittered in the low light, even as his blue-black hair disappeared into the shadows. The white slash of a scar under his lips offset the crooked quirk of his nose, adding that much more character to his chiseled features.

First Jake McAllister, then Mab Monroe, and now Owen Grayson. Terrific.

"I'm not sure what you mean." I tightened my grip on my knife.

Instead of answering me, Owen Grayson's eyes trailed down my body, one slow inch at a time. Breasts, stomach, thighs, legs. He took it all in. A smile spread across his face.

"You know, *Ms. Blanco*," he said, purposefully using my name. "The dress is lovely, but I think I like the apron and jeans better. Seems more like the real you."

Fuck. Despite the blond wig, Owen Grayson had recognized me. Even worse, he'd somehow heard me proposition Mab Monroe in the bathroom. I wondered if he'd seen me with Jake McAllister as well—and realized the other man had never come out of the room.

"And what would you know about the real me?" I asked in a soft tone.

Owen's smile deepened. "I know you have a silverstone knife in your hand right now."

There was no way he could have seen me palm the knife. So how did he know I even had one? I stared at him closer and realized the reason his violet eyes were so bright was because they were glowing—with magic. A faint trace, barely noticeable, but I felt it. A cool caress, not unlike my own Stone magic. Which could only mean one thing.

"You have an elemental talent for metal."

"Guilty as charged, I'm afraid," Owen said. "It's a small skill."

My eyes narrowed. Because with every word he said, I was thinking more and more about stabbing Owen Grayson and taking the chance I could get out of the mansion before someone found his body. But I decided to play it cool—for now.

"What do you want?"

"I just want to talk." Owen held out his arm to me. "Shall we?"

I stared at his arm, thinking how easy it would be to brush it aside and bury my knife in his heart. He knew what I was thinking. The knowledge flashed in his violet eyes, but his arm never wavered, never lowered. His gaze never left mine. For whatever reason, Owen Grayson wasn't afraid of me. Which piqued my curiosity. At least enough for me to slide my knife back up the sleeve of my dress.

Fucking curiosity. Going to get me killed one night. Maybe even tonight.

I took his arm. "So talk."

Owen tucked me in close to him, and the heat of his body washed over me. He smelled rich and earthy, almost like . . . metal, if metal had any real smell. His arm felt like steel, even through the fabric of his tuxedo jacket. For the first time, I was aware of him as a man, as someone of the opposite sex. Oh, Owen Grayson was decidedly attractive, with his strong body and chiseled features. But what really set him apart was the fact that he radiated confidence the way that Mab Monroe did magic. That hint of power, that confidence, made Grayson even more interesting. And definitely someone worth watching.

Especially since I was still considering killing him.

We walked down the hallway back toward the ballroom. At first, I thought we would go straight there, but Owen Grayson paused and opened one of the doors that led outside. We stepped out onto the stone terrace that lined this side of the mansion, and Grayson shut the door behind us.

The night air was cool, especially since my dress was still damp from where I'd scrubbed away Jake McAllister's blood. Antique-looking iron streetlamps lined the terrace, providing soft, hazy illumination, while wide stone steps led down to a garden beyond. Low moans and sucking sounds drifted up to us, and several dark shapes writhed together in various gazebos in the garden. Other couples stood up against trees or used some of the stone statues for leverage. The party must have livened up a bit, if folks had already come outside to fuck on top of Mab Monroe's prize-winning roses.

Owen Grayson meandered down the terrace, with me at his side.

"I have to confess I was quite surprised when you strolled into the ballroom tonight," Grayson began. "I hadn't expected to see you here, especially not wearing that cheap blond wig."

"Don't care for blondes, do you?" I sniped.

"Sassy brunettes are more my style." He grinned.

I didn't respond.

"Actually, I have a small confession to make. I've been thinking about you a lot these past few days, Ms. Blanco. So much so that I had a friend gather some information on you."

So Owen Grayson had someone dig into my past. No worries. My cover ID as Gin Blanco was rock solid. It had withstood Jonah McAllister's scrutiny, and I had no doubt it had passed muster with Grayson as well. But I didn't understand his curiosity. Sure, I'd saved his sister, Eva, from being burned to death by Jake McAllister that night at the Pork Pit. But most men of Grayson's wealth, position, and standing would have forgotten all about me by now.

"You checked me out? Why?"

"You saved my sister, you saved Eva," Owen said. "She's the most important thing in the world to me. I like to settle my debts. I wanted to find some way to repay you. I wanted to find something you liked, something you wanted or needed, and give it to you. No strings attached."

"I told you that I don't want your money."

Owen waved his hand. "So you've said. But then I got close to you, shook your hand that night in the Pork Pit. And I wondered why someone who runs a barbecue restaurant, even one on the edge of Southtown, would carry five silverstone knives on her person. Seemed like overkill to me."

If he only knew. I had to work very hard not to reach for my knife again. So not only could Owen Grayson sense a metal weapon in my hand, he could also tell exactly how many I had on me. The usual five, at the moment. Two up my sleeves, two more strapped to my thighs, and one in my purse.

"You know about my interest in metal," Grayson continued. "I also have one in weapons as well. Making them is a sort of hobby of mine. So you can understand my curiosity about ones as finely crafted as yours. Silverstone's not easy to shape or purchase."

"The Pork Pit's in a rough neighborhood," I deadpanned. "The knives make me feel secure."

Owen laughed. A hint of sarcasm colored his throaty voice. "I'll just bet they do. But there was one more thing that intrigued me about you, Ms. Blanco."

"And what would that be?"

Owen stopped and disengaged my hand from his arm. Before I realized what he was doing, he turned my hand over and held my palm up. "This."

We stood underneath one of the antique streetlights. The hazy golden glow covered my palm—and made the spider rune scar embedded in my flesh shimmer a faint silver.

"A small circle surrounded by eight thin rays," Owen Grayson murmured. "A spider rune. The symbol for patience. I wondered what the symbol was."

For a moment, I was stunned. Simply stunned. Not only because Grayson knew about my scars, or at least this one, but also because I never showed the marks to anyone. Only Finn and the Deveraux sisters knew what they really looked like besides me, and I wasn't crazy about staring at them myself, for obvious reasons.

Oh, sometimes someone in the restaurant would get a quick, accidental look at them while I was working. But the scars had faded over time, and it was hard to tell they were really runes without studying them up close—or that I had one on each palm. Even then, I just passed them off as burns that I'd gotten from working in the Pork Pit over the years.

Still, despite my surprise, I kept calm, as though Grayson seeing the scar didn't matter to me at all. I shrugged. "So I have a scar. Lots of people do. Hardly worth mentioning."

He shook his head. "Not just any scar. It's silverstone. The metal is in your skin. When I shook your hand that night, I felt it. And now," Grayson cocked his head to one side. "I can hear it."

I stared at him. He must have more than a small talent for metal, if he could do all that. Once again, the thought struck me that Owen Grayson was someone worth watching, someone to be very careful around. Perhaps even someone to get rid of. But my curiosity wouldn't quite vanish enough for me to take that final step. Not yet. Not until I knew exactly what he wanted.

"And what does the metal in my hands sound like?"

He gave me a small smile. "It sounds sad. Hurt. Lonely."

I kept my face blank, even as the emotions and memories raged inside me. The feel of the spider rune medallion burning into my skin, the smell of my own melting flesh filling my nose, my hoarse screams echoing in my ears, the Fire elemental's cackling laughter drowning out everything else. Somehow, I pushed the memories back and focused on Owen Grayson's face, on his violet eyes, which were still glowing ever so slightly.

At that moment, I seriously considered hurting Owen Grayson. Even killing him. Because somehow, Grayson had stripped away part of my defenses, part of my anonymity. He knew too much about me, knew too many things I was so careful to conceal. He could be a threat. To me, to Finn, to the Deveraux sisters. I didn't like threats. So I decided to get down to business.

"My scar sounds sad, hurt, lonely? That sounds like a lame come-on to me," I mocked. "Surely, you can do better than that, Mr. Grayson."

Owen laughed—a loud, hearty laugh. I'd amused him. He was laughing in the face of his own possible death. Despite the stupidity of his action, I had to admire his bravado. It, and this little spark of interest, of curiosity I had about him, was all that was keeping Grayson alive.

"So what do you really want?" I asked once his laughter had died down.

"From you? I haven't quite decided. But the possibilities are interesting." His eyes wandered down my body again in a frank, assessing way that told me he liked what he saw. His gaze settled on the heart-and-arrow rune that hung from my black velvet choker. "Although I never would have taken you for one of Roslyn Phillips's girls."

A hard smile curved my lips. "I'm a woman of many skills."

"I just bet you are," he murmured.

"Let's get down to business," I said. "Because I have other things to do tonight besides stand out here in the dark with you."

Like killing Tobias Dawson. Five minutes had passed since I'd left Mab Monroe in her own bathroom with Jake McAllister. Since I hadn't heard any screams or scurries of activity, she hadn't found his body in the bathtub. Which meant I still had a small window of time left to find, attract, and kill Dawson.

Owen Grayson nodded. "Very well. As I was saying, I was quite surprised to see you here tonight. But once I did, I decided to approach you."

"Why?"

He shrugged. "I thought you might like to dance."

I stared at him. He seemed to be sincere. Owen Grayson attracted to me? My eyes narrowed. Or perhaps he'd just seen the rune around my neck and realized what it meant—that I was supposed to fuck anyone here tonight for free. Either way, I supposed stranger things had happened.

"But I wasn't quite quick enough to catch you before you left the ballroom," Grayson continued. "And then I heard you speaking with Mab in the bathroom. Which interested me that much more, Gin. May I call you Gin?"

"Sure. No need to stand on ceremony at this point. As for what you overheard in the bathroom, I can't *imagine* why two girls talking about getting it on would be of interest to a guy like you." Sarcasm dripped from my voice like hot gravy off a biscuit.

His violet eyes glittered in the semidarkness, and he smiled. "Of course not."

"So you want to fuck me then," I said in a blunt tone. "That's what this little conversation is all about. The talk about my knives, the stroll on the terrace, the handholding and come-on about what my scar sounds like. Interesting technique. Tell me, what was your next move? Maneuvering me up against the wall here? Or me accidentally falling on your dick?"

Grayson laughed again. "Of course I want to fuck you, Gin."

He stared at me. I saw the desire in his violet gaze, but it wasn't as lecherous or prurient as the other looks I'd been getting tonight. Oh, Owen Grayson seemed to be as sexual and fond of the female form as the next man. But genuine interest also shimmered in the businessman's eyes, as though he was enjoying our sparring conversation as much as he would lifting up my skirt.

"But let's slow down, shall we?" Grayson said. "As I said before, I've always had a thing for sassy brunettes. I've decided I rather like you, Gin. You interest me. And no one's done that in a very long time."

"So what are you proposing—exactly? That the two of us go off somewhere quiet to talk before you make your move?" I mocked.

"Hardly." Owen scoffed. "Unlike some of Mab's other guests, I don't need to depend on her generosity for my satisfaction. I thought you might like to go out sometime. Dinner, perhaps a movie, dancing. Whatever you like."

My eyebrows raised. "You want to go out with me? Even though I'm wearing this?" I pointed to the heart-and-arrow rune necklace. "Even though I'm a hooker? Even though you could have me for free tonight?"

He shrugged again. "Call me crazy, but I thought it might be fun."

Fun? I didn't know about that. But there was certainly more to Owen Grayson than met the eye. He thought I was moonlighting as one of Roslyn Phillips's girls, and he was still asking me to go out with him. To be seen in public with him. Which meant he was either genuinely interested in me or working some angle I couldn't puzzle out. Either way, I didn't have time for this tonight.

But there was something Owen Grayson could help me with. And I was ready to cash in on that goodwill he owed me.

"Let's say I believe you, that you really do want to get to know me and not just my breasts," I said. "Do me a favor, and I'll consider your proposal."

Grayson nodded. "All right. What kind of favor?"

"Take me inside and introduce me to Tobias Dawson. I'm sure you know him, since the two of you are so heavily involved in the mining business in Ashland."

His eyes narrowed. "I do know him. But why would you want to meet Dawson? He doesn't strike me as your type."

I gave him a hard smile. "Because I'm here to service Mab's guests tonight, and I hear he's a really big tipper. And that's definitely my type."

Owen studied me in the hazy light. Disappointment sparked in his eyes. His free, easy lay was getting away.

"You said it yourself. You owe me for saving Eva, for saving your sister," I reminded him in a mild tone. "Well, this is how I want to cash in. Now, are you going to introduce me? Or am I going to have to take care of that myself?"

Pretending to be a prostitute. Propositioning Mab Monroe in her own bathroom. Hinting I was going to go fuck another man for the mere promise of money. Owen Grayson had seen and heard me do all those things in the space of five minutes. I resigned myself to the disgusted sneer that was coming my way and the harsh words that were sure to follow. No man liked being cuckolded.

But to my surprise, Owen Grayson just smiled. A familiar emotion shimmered in his eyes, one that had gotten me into trouble on more than one occasion. Curiosity. It burned even brighter than his desire had a moment ago.

"Oh, I'll introduce you to Dawson, just to see what you're up to." Amusement colored Grayson's voice, and he held his arm out to me for a second time. "Shall we, Gin?"

Owen Grayson's curiosity might cause me problems later on, but this was too good an opportunity to pass up. So I placed my hand on his arm. "Let's."

28

Owen Grayson escorted me back into the ballroom. We stood by the terrace door, looking for Dawson. Finally, I spotted the cowboy dwarf, standing near the long, crowded bar. Tobias Dawson drank a shot of what looked like whiskey, chased it with a mug of beer, belched, and wiped his mouth off with the back of his hand. Classy.

"You sure you want to do this?" Grayson murmured.

I paused. Grayson probably thought I was reconsidering approaching Dawson, given the dwarf's obvious disregard for napkins. But really, I was remembering Violet Fox and the way Trace Dawson had bashed her face in. The way Tobias Dawson had spit tobacco juice on the floorboards of the country store. The way that diamond in his office safe had practically sung. The way Warren Fox's shoulders had drooped when I'd told him what Dawson really wanted his land for.

"Yeah, I'm sure."

Owen escorted me through the crowd. We passed Mab Monroe, who was now speaking to an elderly vampire. The Fire elemental saw me on Grayson's arm and raised her champagne glass in a silent toast. I must have made more of an impression on her than I'd realized. Not good, but I smiled and tipped my head to acknowledge her. More importantly, Mab's toast also told me she hadn't found Jake McAllister's body in the bathtub. Which meant I still had enough time left to kill Dawson.

We also swept past Finn and Roslyn. Finn's bright green eyes flicked from Grayson to me, and he raised his eyebrow in a silent question. I shook my head the tiniest bit, telling him that I was okay. Still, Finn's eyes stayed on the two of us, even as he and Roslyn chatted up some giant with legs that seemed to go on forever.

It took us about two minutes to maneuver our way over to the bar. Owen arranged it so I stood between him and Tobias Dawson, whose back was turned to me. Grayson ordered a Scotch.

"And for the lady?" the bartender asked.

"Gin," I said. "With a twist of lime."

Owen's mouth twitched with amusement, but he didn't say anything about my choice of drink. The bartender handed us our orders. I took a sip of the gin. The cold liquid burned down my throat, before spreading a pleasant warmth through my stomach. After we'd put a dent in our drinks, Grayson reached across me to tap Tobias on the shoulder. The dwarf turned. I made sure the first things he saw were my boobs, pushed to new heights by Roslyn's power bra.

Dawson blinked.

"Hello, Tobias," Grayson said. "How are you this evening?"

The dwarf looked around me at the other man. "Oh, hello, Owen. I'm fine. And yourself?"

"Marvelous," Owen replied in a glib tone. "Allow me to introduce my acquaintance. This is . . ."

"Candy," I said in a flirty tone. "Because I'm so sweet."

The dwarf's eyes latched onto my boobs, then flicked up to my blond hair, thick makeup, and blue contacts. He must have liked what he saw, because he smiled. His yellow teeth matched the dirty, sandy color of his hair and mustache. The dwarf tipped his oversize cowboy hat at me. "My pleasure, ma'am."

Given what Roslyn Phillips had told me about Tobias Dawson's cowboy fetish, I decided to play the part of a hooker with a heart of gold. "Aw, aren't you just the perfect gentleman." I lowered my lashes and batted them. "Handsome too."

Dawson's smile grew a little wider, but his pale blue eyes took on a sharp, predatory look. I'd interested the dwarf. Time to reel him in—or at least let him pretend he was the one doing the reeling.

I turned to Owen and put a big, fake pout on my lips. "So when are we going to dance? You promised me a dance."

Again, Grayson's lips twitched with amusement. "Sorry . . . Candy, but I'm not much of a dancer."

"Perhaps I could dance with the lady," Tobias Dawson offered. "If you don't have any objections, Owen."

Grayson waved his hand. "Of course not. I've already

had my fun with Candy this evening. She's all yours, Tobias."

Owen's violet eyes met my narrowed gray ones. More
amusement danced in his light gaze. He was actually enjoying this little charade.

The cowboy dwarf offered his short, stubby arm to
me. "Shall we, Candy?"

I sniffed at Owen, turned my back to him, and beamed
at the dwarf. "Thank you, Mr. Dawson. At least someone
here still knows how to treat a *lady*."

The clichéd patter made me want to gag, but I'd said
worse to get close to targets before. I could drop a few
more groaners if it meant eliminating Tobias Dawson.
My fingers skimmed down the dwarf's arm before settling on his bare, brown hand. For some reason, Dawson
frowned at the contact. Something flickered in his eyes,
but it was gone before I could interpret what it was. But
he suddenly looked at me with far more interest. Perhaps
I'd static-shocked him or something, although if I had, I
should have felt it too.

But I shrugged away my unease and let the dwarf lead
me onto the dance floor. Dawson was barely five feet tall,
which meant his eyes were just level with my boobs. But
his soaring cowboy hat reached up over my teased wig.
The orchestra began a classical waltz, and Tobias Dawson
pulled me close. The only thing that kept him from burying his head between my boobs was the crinoline in my
skirt. It was too stiff and thick for him to maneuver in the
way he wanted to. I'd have to remember to thank Roslyn
Phillips for that small favor.

We danced in silence for a few moments. I kept my

smile steady as we whirled around. Dawson's hand tightened on mine. His palm felt curiously warm against mine, something I'd expect from a Fire elemental, but not a Stone like the dwarf.

"You know, Candy, you're a very attractive woman," Tobias Dawson said. "Then again, I've always been partial to blondes."

I let out a small, girlish giggle. "Aren't you just the sweetest thing? You're a real charmer, if I do say so, Mr. Dawson. I'll have to tell the other girls here tonight to watch out for you."

The dwarf smiled, but his eyes were cold and distant in his face. Again, I got the feeling I'd done something wrong, but I couldn't imagine what it could be. There was no way Dawson could know who I was, that I used to be an assassin called the Spider, that I was working for the Foxes, that I'd come here tonight to kill him. There was no way he could know all that—could he? The dwarf had been smart enough to find a mountain full of diamonds and use a slab of granite as a safe. There was no telling how clever he was.

We lapsed into silence again. The dwarf stared at me. Then his eyes went to the rune necklace around my throat. The dance ended, and we both applauded politely. The orchestra started another tune, something a little jazzier.

I held my hand out to Dawson. "Could I interest you in another dance?"

"Perhaps you'd like to go somewhere more private," Dawson suggested. "I hear Mab's gardens are lovely in the moonlight."

I thought of the secluded gazebos, copses of trees, and thickets of rose bushes I'd spotted outside. I easily could drop Dawson in the garden. With any luck, no one would stumble across him until morning. It was my best option at this point, unless I could somehow maneuver the dwarf back to the bathroom where I'd killed Jake McAllister. Given the way Dawson was staring at my boobs, I doubted he'd wait that long before he forced himself on me.

I smiled at him again. "I'd love to go out to the gardens."

I put my hand on Tobias Dawson's arm, and we left the dance floor. Across the room, I saw Finnegan Lane staring at me. He still stood next to Roslyn, but I saw the relief in his green gaze. Finn knew the longer I stayed the more risk there was of someone trying to proposition me for real—and the slimmer my chances got to take care of Dawson.

Finn wasn't the only one staring at me. So was Owen Grayson. He nodded his head to me as we walked by. I grinned at him in return.

Tobias Dawson opened one of the double doors for me, and we stepped outside. The night air had grown even chillier since I'd been out here with Owen Grayson, and I shivered.

"Cold?" the dwarf asked, closing the door behind us.

"A bit."

He smiled at me. "Don't worry. What I have in mind will warm you right up."

Dawson was saying all the right things, but again, his

smile didn't reach his pale eyes. But I brushed off my unease. All I had to do was get him away from the doors, and the job would be done. Dawson offered me his arm again, and I took it. With my free hand, I palmed one of my silverstone knives.

We walked down the terrace steps and onto a stone pathway that meandered into the dark gardens. A woman cried out softly in a gazebo to our left. A moment later, another woman joined her throaty chorus. Dawson ignored them and moved on. I let him lead me farther into the shadows that cut through the garden like black knives.

The dwarf didn't stop until he reached a gazebo hidden underneath the tendrils of a weeping willow tree. I glanced over my shoulder. We were two hundred feet away from the terrace, well out of sight of anyone looking through the glass doors. I tightened my grip on my knife and got ready. Dawson led me over to a long wooden bench inside the gazebo. I sat down, but the dwarf didn't join me. Instead, he stood before me and rocked back on the heels of his cowboy boots.

"You look like a smart girl, Candy," the dwarf rumbled. "So I think it's pretty safe to say you know who I am and what I do for a living."

I didn't know where he was going with this, but I smiled. "Of course I've heard of you, Mr. Dawson. You're one of the biggest coal miners in all of Ashland. A very respectable businessman. Very smart. Very strong." A little over the top, but flattery never hurt.

He nodded. "I am very strong and very smart. I'm also a Stone elemental, did you know that?"

I shook my head. "No. I'm afraid I don't pay much attention to magic."

Dawson nodded again. "Fair enough. As you said, I'm very powerful. But what few people know is that I have another elemental talent. Something small but very handy at times."

I kept smiling, although by now, my cheeks hurt from the effort. The dwarf needed to step closer so I could come off the bench and stab him, not talk me into a glassy-eyed coma. "And what would that be? A talent for metal perhaps?"

Dawson shook his head. "Oh no, nothing that grand. But I do have the ability to sense others' magic and know exactly what their power is, just by touching their skin. Almost like a magical fingerprint, if you will." His face hardened. "And your sticky palms were all over the safe in my office, bitch."

Uh-oh.

Tobias Dawson had sensed my magic—and worse, he knew I was the one who'd broken into his safe at the mining office.

I immediately came up off the bench, already bringing my hand up, ready to drive my silverstone knife deep into the dwarf's chest. But Dawson was quicker. His fist slammed into my face, and the world went black.

* 29 *

"Are you sure it was her, Tobias?"

A female voice sounded somewhere above my head, although it seemed far away. I couldn't tell exactly where it was coming from. The pounding in my head drowned out just about everything else, although I felt dew-covered grass underneath my back, and the cool kiss of the night wind on my face. Why was I lying down? I couldn't remember anything through the ache in my skull.

"I'm positive," a man muttered. "This is the bitch who broke into my office. She has the stench of that Stone magic all over her. Then there are these."

Something rustled. I wanted to open my eyes to see what it was, but for some reason, my eyelids just wouldn't lift.

"Is that silverstone?" the woman asked again.

Some small part of my mind frowned in thought. I knew that voice, that soft, breathy voice that resonated with so much raw power. I just couldn't remember whom it belonged to.

"Yeah," the man replied. "She had five of them on her."

"And you really think she lured you out here to kill you?" the woman asked. "Perhaps she was just carrying them for protection. Hookers tend to do that, you know."

"I know it was her. I've seen her before. She was at Fox's store yesterday, along with a cop. She must be working for the old man."

Silence. Again, I tried to open my eyes to see what was going on. Once again I failed. The pounding in my head intensified, as though another drum had been added to the band.

"What a pity," the woman said in a mocking tone. "She had such potential."

I sensed someone crouching beside me, and a sweet, slightly noxious smell filled my nose—like jasmine mixed with smoke. A finger trailed down the side of my cheek. Hot needles of pain stabbed my skin, but I couldn't even cry out. No part of me seemed to be working. The burning finger skirted down my cleavage, before sliding off my stomach.

A soft laugh echoed above my head. The sound made me think of fire, smoke, ash. Rough hands holding me down. The spider rune heating up between my palms. Questions. So many questions about Bria. The silverstone searing my skin, melting into my flesh. The Fire elemental laughing as the rune burned me. Laughing. The Fire elemental. *Mab*—

"Very well," the woman said. "Do whatever you want to with her—outside."

Her voice short-circuited my train of thought. I tried to grab hold of the wispy tendrils of memories, but they retreated back into the darkness—a darkness that was slowly swallowing me once more.

"Outside? Why? I want to take care of the bitch right now." The man sounded whiny and petulant.

"Because in case you haven't noticed, Tobias, I'm hosting a function for several hundred people. A dead body in the garden would put a damper on the evening, don't you think? Besides, you claim she came here to kill *you*. So *you* can take care of it. I have no desire to get my hands or any other part of my person dirty tonight. Besides, she's unconscious. No fun to be had there."

"Well, what do you want me to do with her?" the man asked again.

"I don't fucking care," the woman snapped. "Just get her off my lawn. Now."

Rough hands closed around my arms and yanked me up, but by that point, I'd sunk into the blackness once again.

The first thing I was aware of was the soft soil underneath my cheek, interspersed here and there with small pebbles. Tiny little stones that felt like smooth peas muttering against my skin. I concentrated on that sound, that faint muttering, letting it pull me out of the darkness I'd been floating in. After a few moments, I realized I was lying facedown, but I didn't try to move. My head hurt too much for that, the previous pounding now a hot, throbbing ache behind my left eye.

But I focused, and slowly the evening came back to

me. Dressing up and crashing Mab Monroe's party. Killing Jake McAllister. Running into the Fire elemental herself, then Owen Grayson. I also remembered going out into the garden with Tobias Dawson, and the dwarf sucker punching me. And now, well, who knew where the hell I was. But I was still alive, which meant I still had a chance. To run, to fight, to cower in a dark hole until the bad guys went away. Whatever it took to survive. The will to do so no matter what—the very first lesson Fletcher Lane had ever taught me. Something I'd known even before he'd articulated it to me.

So I focused on my body, assessing the damage that had been done. My face felt like it had been hit with a sledgehammer. Given the stiffness and constant throbbing, I was pretty sure my jaw was broken, maybe my left cheekbone too. A couple of my teeth felt loose, and the coppery tang of my own blood filled my mouth. I cracked my eyes open. A bit of light trickled into my vision. Well, at least he hadn't ruptured my optic nerve.

Next I wiggled my fingers and toes. My arms felt sore, as though I'd been manhandled, which I probably had been. My knees were scraped and raw. So were my hands. Minor annoyances. But to my surprise, I didn't seem to have any other injuries. No broken bones, no missing limbs, no trauma between my thighs. Which could only mean one thing. Tobias Dawson wanted to question me before he killed me—or the dwarf just wanted me awake while he tortured me. Neither option was a pleasant one, but I'd faced them both before and come out more or less in one piece. I'd survive this too.

"I think the bitch is awake," a voice said.

The low, deep baritone of a giant. But the most curious thing was the voice echoed like an organ, bouncing off the walls that surrounded us. I listened again, more closely this time, not just to the pea-size pebbles around me but also to the underlying stone beneath my body. And I realized it surrounded me. The ground was soft, but the ceiling and especially the walls were harder, rockier, and all made of stone. Given what I knew of Tobias Dawson, there was only one place I could be—inside the dwarf's coal mine. Dawson Number Three. A place where no one would hear me scream—or ever find my broken body.

Footsteps scuffed on the ground behind me, and I started rocking back and forth and moaning. No need to let the bastards know I had my wits about me just yet. I also opened my eyes and started blinking away the white spots that swam in and out of my vision like lazy catfish. Slowly, I pushed myself up to my hands and knees, then leaned back on my heels. My head and face pounded, but I blocked out the pain, even as I huddled there with my head in my hands.

A pair of boots appeared before me. Cowboy boots. Black snakeskin with red flames and pointed, silverstone tips. I looked up to find Tobias Dawson looming over me. As much as a five-foot-tall dwarf could loom.

"About time you woke up, bitch," he said and hit me again.

I didn't have time to reach for my Stone magic to harden my skin into a rocky shell. Besides, that was a card I didn't want to play just yet. Tobias Dawson might have sensed my magic, might have been able to finger me as the one who broke into his safe, but he probably didn't realize how strong I was. Otherwise, he would have done the smart thing and killed me while I'd been unconscious in Mab Monroe's garden.

But all that knowledge, all that planning, didn't help me with the fist whistling toward my body at warp speed.

I managed to lean back and turn my body enough so that his fist hit my left shoulder instead of slamming into my face. The hard blow bowled me over onto my side, and I felt it reverberate through my whole body. An electric shockwave of pain. A low groan escaped from between my clamped lips, but I forced myself to tense up, to try to defend myself against another sharp blow. But the dwarf didn't come after me again. Instead, he stepped back and regarded me with his cold blue eyes. Since Tobias Dawson wasn't immediately going to beat me to death, my gaze flicked around the area.

I'd been right—I was deep in Dawson's coal mine. Gray and brown rock surrounded me on all sides, and seams of coal ran like black ribbons through the various layers of stone. The passage was wider than I'd expected. Taller too. Concrete beams shored up the roof, and a variety of old, broken equipment lay scattered on the ground. The air smelled of rocks, dust, and metal.

All around me, the stone muttered. Sharp, angry sounds that told of massive explosions and heavy equipment burrowing into the heart of the mountain. The stone didn't like what had been done to it anymore than I had. I listened to that anger, let it clear my aching head. Feeling sorry for myself wouldn't be any help in this situation. But anger—anger was another story. Sure, anger could make you reckless, sloppy, but it could also make you strong. Determined. Both of which were things I was going to need if I had any hopes of getting out of here alive.

"Pick her up," the dwarf ordered. "I want the bitch to see exactly what she's dying for."

Two giants stepped out of the shadows and lumbered over to me. I recognized them as two of Dawson's men, the two that had come with him to Country Daze to brace Warren and Violet Fox. The giants hauled me to my feet. More pain blossomed in my shoulder and jaw, and I let out another low groan. But I didn't offer any resistance to the giants. Not yet.

I was already injured, which meant I needed more of a plan than my usual method of hacking and slashing my way out of trouble. I didn't know how long I'd been unconscious, but Finn had surely realized things had gone to hell at Mab's party. He was probably working his connections, trying to figure out where Tobias Dawson had taken me. Finn might even be on his way to the mine right now, with Sophia and Jo-Jo Deveraux in tow.

But I couldn't count on them to save me. I wouldn't. In the end, the only thing, the only person, you could ever count on was yourself. Another lesson Fletcher Lane had taught me. Something else I'd already figured out for myself long before I'd met the old man.

The giants held me between them and carried me deeper into the mine. They hoisted me up so high my feet didn't even touch the ground. While they carried me, I rubbed my thighs together. But the slots on my garter belt were empty. They'd taken the silverstone knives that had been strapped to my thighs. The ones up my sleeves were gone too. Something bumped against my hip, and I looked down. Dawson or one of his goons had been kind enough to loop my purse around my neck. The top flapped open, and I could see the empty space where my final knife had been. The bastards had been thorough, if nothing else. Too bad for me.

Dawson led the way, carrying a flashlight. The two giants also carried one apiece in their free hands. I eyed the flashlights. Not as weighty as a baseball bat, but a crack across the throat with one of those would be a good way to start cutting my captors down to size. Assuming I had the strength or guile to wrest a flashlight away from one of the three men.

We went down, down, down into the earth. The tunnel grew narrower, tighter. The bits and pieces of equipment on the floor vanished. So did the concrete support beams. Slowly, the violent mutters of the stone gave way to older, calmer vibrations. We walked through a natural tunnel now, instead of a man-made hole in the ground.

I noticed a light up ahead. A soft, white glow, like a beam of sunshine slanting through a cloud. Some sort of industrial spotlight that had been rigged up so folks could see what they were doing in the belly of the mountain. Tobias Dawson rounded a corner and disappeared from sight. A moment later, the giants hauled me around it as well.

And my breath caught in my throat.

Because the narrow tunnel opened up into a circular chamber that was more than two hundred feet wide.

The ceiling was just as tall, with thick stalactites that hung down like elegant stone icicles. That was beautiful enough by itself.

But the diamonds made it truly breathtaking.

The gemstones lay embedded in the rock walls. They were raw, of course, uncut and completely untouched by man. They lacked the polished look of a finished stone, but my Stone magic let me see the pure fire inside them, the beautiful potential they possessed. More seams of coal ran around the diamonds, making the gems seem as though they were resting on a black velvet tray. I could also hear the diamonds. They resonated with the same sort of brilliance the stone in Tobias Dawson's safe had. Often, the more intense a gemstone's vibration, the more beautiful and valuable it was. If the song skipping through my head was any indication, there was several million dollars' worth of uncut diamonds nestled in the heart of this mountain—just waiting for someone to come and claim them.

Tobias Dawson stalked to the center of the cavern. The giants carrying me followed along behind him. The dwarf snapped his fingers, and the two brutes threw me down. I put my hands out to break my fall, but the stone still dug into my palms and scraped my already raw, bloody knees. Even being a Stone couldn't protect me from being injured by my own element like that. I huddled on the ground, once again scanning the area for anything I could use. Any sort of weapon. Hell, I'd even take a bolt hole at this point. Folks who said you were a coward if you ran away from a fight usually didn't live long themselves. I wouldn't care if I was called a coward, as long as I was still breathing in the end.

The top of the cavern was damp, and phosphorescent mold covered most of the jagged stalactites, a strange, pale green contrast to the rest of the gray, brown, and black rock. A drop of water fell down from one of the stones and spattered onto my upturned cheek. I looked up, backtracked the drop, and realized a steady stream of water rushed down one wall of the cavern. Still more water dripped from other stalactites over my head. Hmm. That might be useful.

Tobias Dawson walked in a loose circle around me. His snakeskin cowboy boots clattered on the rough stone. "Do you know where you are?"

I put my hands on the ground and pushed myself up to my feet. Spots swam in front of my eyes again, but I blinked them away. "I have a pretty good idea."

It was hard to talk through my broken, throbbing jaw, and my words came out mushy and mumbled. Just the way my face felt.

The dwarf stared at me. "You broke into my office, into my safe." His floppy mustache bristled with anger.

I shrugged. No use denying it now. If Tobias Dawson's elemental talent for sensing and identifying others' magic was as good as he claimed, no lie of mine would convince him otherwise. Besides, I was already on the hook here. If I played my cards right, maybe things would stop and end with me. I didn't want Dawson to start thinking about who else might have been involved with me—and I didn't want him going after Finn, the Deveraux sisters, the Foxes, or even Donovan Caine.

"Yeah, I broke into your office."

"Why?" the dwarf snapped. "What were you looking

for? Who are you working for? Did Warren Fox hire you to kill me?"

I stared at the dwarf and kept my eyes cold, my face expressionless. I might be on the express bus to dead, but I wasn't going to snitch on the Foxes and take them with me. "I don't know any Warren Fox."

"Bullshit," Tobias snarled. "I saw you at his store the other day."

I raised an eyebrow. "You mean that shack by the side of the crossroads? Yeah, I was there. So what?"

"Why?" Dawson demanded.

"I had to pee," I quipped. "And I didn't feel like getting a briar in my ass by going in the woods."

The dwarf stared at me, considering my words. "I don't believe you."

"Doesn't much matter to me whether you believe me or not."

Tobias spit a stream of tobacco juice out of his mouth. It spattered against my bare, scraped leg. The dwarf was going to pay for that. I might die down here, but before I went, I was going to get at least one good blow in. Just for that.

"Who are you working for? What do you want?" Dawson asked again. "I have ways of making you talk, you know."

My jaw twitched with pain, which kept me from rolling my eyes. Yeah, I'd figured out the dwarf could hurt me the first time he'd slammed his fist into my face. The memory was still fresh in my mind, even if it had apparently slipped his.

"I'm sure you do. As for what I want, well, it's more

about what my employer wants. Maybe we can work out some sort of deal."

The dwarf stopped his circling to stand in front of me. His pale blue eyes narrowed. "I'm listening."

"You let me go, and I tell you who wants you dead. How does that sound?"

The dwarf nodded. "All right. You have a deal."

Lying bastard. He wasn't going to let me go, and we both knew it. But this was how the game was played when you were sloppy enough to get captured. Dragging things out to the bitter end. I'd only get one shot to try to take out Dawson. I knew what I was going to do, but whether I had the strength for it was another matter. Still, it was best to keep him talking as long as possible.

I backed up a few steps from the dwarf so that I was clear of the stalactites and the water dripping down from the ceiling. He didn't follow me. His first mistake. "So you've figured out what I am, what I do."

"You're an assassin," Dawson said. "That's the only explanation for all those silverstone knives you had on you and the way you threw yourself at me at the party."

Well, at least he wasn't stupid enough to think I'd really been attracted to him. That would have been rather sad on his part. I gave him a thin smile. "Actually, I was enjoying my retirement, if you can believe that. But then, as the old story goes, I got one last job offer, and the money, well, it was just too good to pass up."

Another assassin, Brutus, had said those words to me once—right before I'd killed him. Of course, they were a complete fabrication on my part now. But it was just the sort of fairy tale Tobias Dawson wanted to hear, the story he'd already sold himself on. I could see the suspicion in his eyes. All I had to do was fill in the name for him. And even if I didn't make it out of here alive, I still planned on causing as much trouble as I could for one certain individual.

"Who hired you? Why? Tell me right now, or I'll let my boys have some fun with you." Dawson jerked his thumb over his shoulder at his two men.

Behind him, one of the giants rubbed his crotch and rocked his hips forward. His buddy laughed at him and gave me a slow wink. Their casual mockery made my anger ratchet up from a slow simmer to a boil. Those bastards weren't laying another hand on me.

But I still had my part to play for Tobias Dawson, so I took another step back from the jagged stalactites and threw my hands out wide. "Isn't it obvious who I'm working for? Who else knows about this little diamond mine you've stumbled upon? Who else have you told about it? Why don't you think about that for a few seconds and get back to me."

The dwarf frowned and spit out another stream of tobacco juice. His blue eyes turned inward as he reviewed the list of folks he'd shared his underground discovery with. I was willing to bet it was a real short list—with only one woman's name on it.

"Mab," he muttered. "Mab Monroe. That's who you're working for?"

I shot my thumb and forefinger at him. "Give the man a prize."

Dawson frowned. "But why would she hire an assassin to kill me?"

Despite my broken jaw, I managed a laugh. A loud, mocking laugh that echoed off the walls. "Because, you idiot, she wants all this for herself. All these lovely, lovely diamonds, and the money that's going to come along with them."

"No way." Dawson shook his head. "There's no fucking way you're working for Mab. She wouldn't turn on me like that."

I snorted. "Take your head out of your ass. Of course Mab would turn on you like that. It's what she *does*. She's made a career out of it, as a friend of mine would say. You're just the latest casualty in her ever-expanding empire."

Dawson paced back and forth in front of me as he thought about it. I took another small step back. Ten feet now separated me from the dwarf. Not as much as I would have liked, but it was going to have to do. After a few seconds, the dwarf stopped pacing. The doubt in his eyes faded away, replaced by sparking anger. I'd sold him on the lie. Even if I didn't make it out of this cavern alive, Dawson might do something stupid and go after Mab Monroe himself. She'd probably kill him, but at least he'd feel her wrath before he died. And he might inconvenience her slightly. Either way, it was the best I could do, given my current situation.

"Although I am curious about one thing," I said.

"What?" Dawson asked.

"The old man at the store. Why did you brace him like that? Why do you need his land so badly? We're in this cavern right now with all these gorgeous stones. I know you don't own the mineral rights to the diamonds, but why not just quietly take them out of the walls yourself and be done with it?"

Dawson shook his head. "All that Stone magic you have, and you don't really know anything about your own element, do you?"

I shrugged. "Geology isn't my strong suit."

The dwarf pointed to the ceiling, where water dripped off one of the stalactites. "This whole cavern is directly underneath a creek that runs through Fox's property. The ceiling's strong enough as it is, but if I start digging diamonds out of here, there's a good chance the whole thing will collapse in, leaving a giant sinkhole right in the middle of his yard—even bigger than the one that's there right now."

He wasn't telling me anything I hadn't already guessed, but it was nice to have some confirmation.

"And you couldn't risk that," I said in a soft voice. "You couldn't risk him finding out about the diamonds that are on his own land."

"Smart and pretty. A shame you're going to die so young," Dawson mocked.

"I thought we had a deal," I said, although there was no real protest in my voice. I'd expected the double cross.

The dwarf laughed. "Ah, the foolishness of youth. But I'm a sporting man. I'll give you a chance to get out of here."

"Really? And how would I do that?"

Dawson stared at me. "All you have to do is beat me—in an elemental duel."

✦ 30 ✦

"A duel?" I asked.

He nodded. "A duel. That's how I take care of my problems. Haven't lost one yet in more than two hundred years." He looked over his shoulder. "You boys might want to step out of the way for this."

The giants moved off to either side of the cavern, leaving Dawson standing by himself in the middle. The two men looked bored, as though they'd seen their boss do this a dozen times before. They probably had.

The dwarf stood relaxed with his knees slightly bent. He tipped his cowboy hat back on his head to give himself a clearer look at me, and his hands hung down by his sides, fingers flexing and unflexing. He reminded me of some Old West gunfighter who'd just called the town sheriff out into the dusty street for a noon showdown. Yeah, I could see how elemental dueling would fit right in with Dawson's cowboy fetish. Too bad it was going to be the death of him.

"A duel, huh?" I asked again.

"A duel," he repeated. "You and me. Right here, right now. Think about it, how strong your magic is. You might beat me."

But Dawson didn't sound too concerned by the possibility. Bastard was trying to goad me into making the first move. Into doing something sloppy. Oh, I was going to do something all right, but it wasn't going to be what he expected.

Still, I had to play this out to its inevitable conclusion, so I reached for the cool power deep inside me. Gathering it up, letting it fill every part of my being. Although I couldn't see them, I knew my eyes were glowing a bright silver with my elemental power. All around me, the stones' murmurs intensified, sensing my command over them.

But the dwarf wasn't worried. If anything, my reaching for my magic amused him. Tobias Dawson grabbed hold of his own Stone magic. Power poured off him like the water sliding down the cavern wall, and his eyes glowed a dull, slate blue. The dwarf was strong, and his magic felt old and well-worn, like a horse he'd broken in over the years. No wonder he wanted to duel. One burst of magic from him would be enough to take down most elementals. Maybe even me.

The dwarf let out a low laugh. "You have power, bitch, I'll give you that. A lot of raw power. I'm going to enjoy this."

"So why give me this chance, if I'm so strong? If I could beat you?"

"Because I like challenges." Dawson grinned and spit out another stream of tobacco juice. The foul brown mixture landed at my feet.

"Do you know what I like, Tobias?" I asked.

"What?"

"Playing dirty."

I smiled at him and threw my magic at the cavern ceiling.

There was no time for finesse, restraint, or even patience. One shot was all I had, and I took it. I threw everything I had at the cavern ceiling. All my Stone magic and all my Ice power, weak though it was. The water that had been dripping off the formations and sluicing down the cavern wall immediately froze. The resulting crystal droplets glistened like the diamonds embedded in the walls. The sudden surge of Ice caused bits and pieces of the cavern to crack and sheer off from the rest of the walls and ceiling. Dust and dirt puffed up into the air.

Jo-Jo Deveraux had always told me I had more Stone magic than anyone she'd ever seen before. I hoped that meant Tobias Dawson too. But I'd been weakened by Dawson's punches, and I wasn't at full strength. Even if I had been, I was still hammering at stone that had been around long before I'd been born—and would be around long after I was gone. Layers and layers and *layers* of it. But I used my magic, my Stone power, like a hammer, smashing at everything I could feel with raw, brute force.

Across from me, Tobias Dawson frowned, not sure what the hell I was doing, why I wasn't attacking him. I had maybe another two or three seconds before he figured it out and hit me with everything he had.

I drew in a breath and threw another blast of Stone magic at the ceiling, even as I reached for my Ice power, making the frozen droplets and stream of water expand in size. I forced the Ice into the stone like a chisel. Ice, stone. Chisel, hammer.

My vision became a field of silver. Sweat dripped into my eyes, my knees trembled, and my whole body felt weak. It seemed like I'd been toiling away for years, decades, even though only a second, two tops, had passed. I wanted to let go of my magic, wanted to rest. Every part of my aching body screamed at me to just let go and fall into the blackness that was threatening to overwhelm me. But if I did that, if I gave Dawson a second of opportunity, he'd throw his own magic at me, and I didn't have the strength to ward him off. Not now. So I gritted my teeth, pushed the pain away, and kept hammering at the stone. Bringing the ceiling down might be the last thing I'd ever do, but the fucker was going to fall.

Crack! Crack-crack!

It started to work. A large stalactite broke off from the ceiling, plummeted down like a knife, and speared one of the giants in his shoulder. He howled in pain and fell to the cavern floor. Crimson blood splashed everywhere, and the stone underneath my feet took on a darker vibration. Dawson's head snapped around at the giant's screams. Sloppy, sloppy of him to get distracted like that.

I kept working. Ice, stone. Chisel, hammer.

Another second passed. Another piece of the roof broke off, this time above Dawson's head. His Stone magic gave him enough of a warning for him to leap forward to get out of its way. The dwarf hit the ground hard. It didn't even daze him.

"Kill her!" Dawson screamed at the other giant even as he scrambled to his feet. "Kill her before she collapses the whole ceiling—"

Too late.

I felt a weakness in the stone, a little sliver of vulnerability caused by years of water seeping into it. I gathered my strength a final time and forced all the magic I had left into that pocket of air. It wasn't as wide as a needle, but it was big enough.

CRACK!

The bottom of the cavern ceiling blew out with an enormous roar, as though a bucket full of grenades had just exploded next to it. The trickles of water became a rushing torrent that cascaded everywhere, and violent tremors shook the ground under my feet. Dust and dirt and rock zipped through the air like shrapnel. I dived to the ground and rolled back, back, back—away from Dawson, the two giants, and the stalactites that ringed the ceiling over their heads. My eyes latched onto a recess in the cavern wall, and I scrabbled over and into it. The space was just barely big enough to shield my body, but the rock here was harder than that above, which had been weakened by the water.

The stalactites that had been hanging overhead dropped to the ground like pointed guillotine blades. The first wave skewered the giant who'd been injured before, until he resembled some sort of oversize voodoo doll with a mass of rocky pins stuck in it. The second man got half a dozen steps back toward the mine entrance before one of the rock spears split his head open. I saw his blood hit the wall even through the spray of water, dust, and falling rock.

Tobias Dawson was smarter than his minions. Tougher too. Like me, he dived forward, avoiding most of the deadly stalactites. The dwarf bounced up onto his feet. He saw me cowering in the recess, and his blue eyes narrowed in hate.

"I'll kill you for this, bitch!" His roar echoed through the cavern even above the hiss of water and thunder of the splintered stones.

The dwarf ran in my direction, still dodging the falling rocks and cascading water. His blue eyes burned with magic. He stretched out his hands, ready to throw his power at me or to drag me out of the recess and into the falling debris. Probably both. The dwarf might survive the punishment of the ceiling collapse, but I wouldn't. My body wasn't as tough and strong as his. I didn't have my knives, so there was only one thing left I could do to fight him off.

This time, I threw my magic at him.

My Ice magic. It was all I had left. I'd exhausted the Stone to collapse the ceiling. So I focused on the water droplets flicking through the air in front of the charging dwarf, freezing and flinging them at Dawson. I was already weakened from the effort of drawing on so much magic, so instead of the knives I'd imagined, the droplets turned to shards of Ice that did little more than prick the dwarf's thick skin. It didn't slow him down. Another few feet, and he'd be able to reach me. And then I'd get dead.

Determination rose inside me—cold, hard, unflinching. I reached for my Ice magic again. It was harder this time, so fucking *hard*, like trying to scoop up water with wide fingers. Every time I gathered up enough power, it slipped away. So I reached for it again, clenching my hands around the trickle of magic inside me. It tried to slip away, but I held on tight and pulled, yanking it to me, bending it to my will.

And something inside me wrenched.

For a moment, I felt like a raw egg that had been dropped on the floor—broken, messy, oozing. But then magic filled me. More Ice magic than I'd ever felt before. I didn't stop to think about where it had come from or whether this was all some sort of deathbed hallucination on my part. I used the magic to freeze more of the water rushing through the air and threw it at Dawson.

This time, the droplets formed long, slender icicles that zipped through the dusty air like daggers. The dwarf saw them coming. He stopped in his tracks about five feet away from me and brought his own Stone magic to bear, trying to block my attack, trying to use his elemental power to harden his skin against the crude weapons, as I'd done so many times before.

But it didn't work.

Maybe he was too distracted by the chaos around him. Maybe I'd wrecked his concentration with my initial sneak attack. Maybe I'd upset the order of his perfectly arranged duel, and he just didn't know how to recover from the unfairness of it all.

Whatever the reason, my icicles slammed into Dawson's chest with all the force of my silverstone knives. The blue glow of magic snuffed out of the dwarf's bulging eyes, and he opened his mouth to scream. The rest of the ceiling began to collapse, drowning out his hoarse cries.

It should have been dark in the cavern, which was choked by dust, debris, mud, and water. But it wasn't. There was a light on—me. I stared down at my hands. The spider rune scars on my palms, the ones that had been caused by the silverstone metal burning into my flesh all those years ago, were on fire—with icy flames. And I felt the power surge through me again, greater than before. Ice magic that felt almost as strong as my Stone power did.

Not good.

For a moment, my eyes met the dwarf's. Panic, fear, pain, and awe flashed in Tobias Dawson's gaze. And then he was gone, swallowed up by the falling rock, rushing water, and suffocating dust. I curled into a tight ball and huddled in the wall recess as the earth and stone shook around me. The stones' vibrations roared a violent, un-ending scream inside my head. I'd shattered the cavern ceiling with my magic, caused it as much pain as Dawson and his mining equipment ever had. The sound made my stomach clench. But it had been the stone or me, and I'd choose me every single time.

So I closed my eyes and listened to the stone wail as the cavern collapsed on top of me.

* 31 *

I huddled in my usual hiding place, a small crack in the alley wall behind the Pork Pit. The enclosed space always made me feel safe. Secure. Perhaps it was because I knew no one could squeeze in here after me—especially someone as big as the giant I'd just killed.

Half an hour had passed since Douglas had forced his way into the restaurant and attacked Fletcher and Finn. My tears were gone, but blood still coated my hands from where I'd killed the giant. I scratched my fingernail across my skin, leaving a white mark in the rusty brown stains. I'd done it again. Killed again. Just like I had the night the Fire elemental had murdered my family, and I'd collapsed my own house down on top of them all—including Bria, my baby sister. My stomach twisted. Somehow, I forced down the hot bile that rose in my throat.

The back door of the Pork Pit eased open, and Fletcher Lane stepped into the alley. The middle-aged man didn't say a word as he sat down cross-legged a few feet away from me. His green eyes were as bright as a cat's, although his face sagged with weariness and pain from where the giant had hit him.

I stayed in my crack, my little refuge, and wondered if this was the part where Fletcher told me to leave—and never come back. He'd seen what I'd done to the giant, what I was capable of. Who would want someone like that hanging around?

"You've been here a while now," Fletcher said in a quiet voice. "You're a smart kid, Gin. I'm sure you've noticed things. Like me being gone so much."

And coming back with blood all over you, *I thought. I didn't know what Fletcher was getting at, but at least he wasn't telling me to get lost—yet. "Yeah, I have."*

He nodded. "I'm sure you've wondered where I go, what I do. All the trips I take." Fletcher turned his eyes to me, so that I felt the full force of his green gaze. "It's time you knew the truth, especially after tonight. I'm an assassin, Gin. Have been for years."

Maybe I should have been surprised or stunned or even horrified. But I wasn't. After my family's murder and the harsh realities of living on the streets, nothing much shocked me anymore. My childhood and my innocence were gone, replaced by the knowledge people were mean, cold, crazy, and dangerous. So I just nodded my head, as if his revelation made perfect sense to me. In a twisted way, it did.

"Do you know what being an assassin means?" Fletcher asked.

I shrugged. "You kill people for money."

He smiled. "Most of the time. Sometimes though, I get

offered jobs I don't take. Sometimes the people I turn down get angry with me. Sometimes they find me, come after me."

"Like Douglas?"

"Just like Douglas."

Despite the weirdness of the conversation, I found myself curious to learn more about this other life Fletcher led. *"Who did Douglas want you to kill?"*

A shadow passed over Fletcher's face. *"Some little girls."*

"So why didn't you do it?"

Fletcher stared at me. *"Because there are rules, Gin. Things even assassins shouldn't do. Killing innocent kids is one of them."*

I thought of the Fire elemental and all the questions she'd asked me about Bria, my baby sister. I hadn't answered the elemental, not even when she'd burned me with my own spider rune medallion. Because I'd known what would happen. I would die, and then so would Bria.

"What happens when someone breaks the rules?" I asked in a hoarse whisper.

Fletcher stared at me. *"I try to make it so they can't hurt anyone else."*

I knew he meant kill them. I thought of Douglas and the way the giant had looked at me. What he would have done to me if I hadn't done it to him first. I shivered. *"That must be nice. To be able to take care of other people like that. To be that strong."* The last word came out as a raspy whisper.

Fletcher stared at me, a strange look on his lined face, as though he was considering something important. Like telling me to get lost. I decided to make it easy for him. I owed him that much, if only for the last few months of security he'd given me.

"Do you want me to leave?"

Fletcher frowned. "Of course not. Why would you think that?"

I stared at the blood on my hands and didn't say anything.

"Oh, Gin," he said in a soft voice. "You don't really realize what you did tonight, do you? You saved me. Finn too. Douglas would have killed all three of us if you hadn't stabbed him. Don't you dare feel bad about stabbing that sick bastard. You did what you had to do. Nothing else."

The knot in my stomach loosened. Maybe I wasn't such a monster after all. Or maybe I just didn't care anymore.

"I want you to stay, Gin," Fletcher said. "For as long as you want. And, if you'll let me, if you want to, I'd like to train you."

I stared at him, confused. "Train me to do what? You're already teaching me how to cook."

He hesitated. "To be like me. To do what I do. To be an assassin."

Maybe I should have been surprised. Shocked. Horrified. But I wasn't. Instead, I thought of Douglas, the giant. How he'd come at me and how I'd defended myself. I knew my stabbing him had been more dumb luck than anything else. But my family was gone, and I was alone. I was tired of living on the streets and being weak and small and helpless. Tired of hiding from everyone and everything. I looked at Fletcher. It wasn't just that he was an adult, older than me, taller, more muscled. Fletcher Lane had an inner strength that set him apart from other people. I suddenly realized it was a strength I wanted. A strength I needed to survive.

"What about Finn?" I asked. "He's your son. Shouldn't you train him instead?"

Fletcher smiled. "He is my son, and I love him, but he doesn't have the right temperament. He's too reckless, too flashy. You're different. Calmer. You take the time to think things through before you do them."

I didn't know about all that. But I decided to take what Fletcher was offering me. Grab on to it with both hands and never look back. Genevieve Snow was dead. Her family was dead. But Gin Blanco was still alive. And I wanted to stay that way.

"Okay," I said. "You can train me."

Fletcher nodded. "All right then. We start tonight. Come on. Let's go back into the restaurant."

He got to his feet and stretched out his hand to me. I stared at it a minute. I was going to be an assassin. Might as well start acting like one. Which, to me, meant getting to my own feet by myself. Which I did.

Fletcher's green eyes brightened as he smiled—

I gasped in a breath, waking from the dreamy memory. It took me a moment to remember where I was, what had happened—and the fact I was probably buried alive. Panic welled up in me, threatening to break loose. But I pushed down the hot, worrisome emotion, smothering it with cold logic. I was still alive, still breathing. Which meant I still had a chance, however small it might be.

I didn't know how long I'd huddled there under the lip of rock, with the earth shaking below my body and the cavern collapsing in on top of me. Minutes had passed, maybe hours, for all I knew. But it was quiet now. The earth had quit trembling, and the stones had quit falling, which meant it was time to come back to myself.

I opened my eyes to blackness. Again, panic filled me,

and once again, I forced it down. I hadn't been afraid of the dark since I was a child. Besides, Tobias Dawson and his giants were dead. They couldn't hurt me anymore. There was nothing down here but me and the rocks and the water. Nothing I couldn't handle.

So I began to blink, focus, and strain my eyes. The blackness didn't lessen, but that was no surprise since I was underground. So I put my hands out, groping through the darkness. All I could feel around me were rocks, and they partially blocked the entrance to the small recess where I'd taken shelter from the cave-in. I stopped a minute to assess my body. Wiggled my fingers and toes, and went through the whole routine I'd done when I'd first woken up in the cavern. Sore, scraped, raw, aching, bone-weary. Same as before, but everything was more or less in working order.

I reached down, blindly searching for my purse and the healing supplies Jo-Jo Deveraux had given me. But the purse was long gone. So was my blond wig, and I didn't feel the blue contacts in my eyes anymore. They'd popped out somewhere along the way. The only things I had left were my black dress and stilettos, which were no help at all. So I blew out a breath, crawled forward, put my hands out, and shoved.

To my surprise, the rocks moved. Bits and pieces broke off like eggshells where I touched them, and I got to work. I don't know how long I crouched there, half under the recess, scooping rocks out of the way so I could wiggle forward and get to my feet. Slow going given my various aches and pains, but eventually I cleared a space large enough for me to worm my way through. I got up on my knees first, then lurched forward, and used my legs to push myself up and out of the hole. The rocks tore into the thin fabric of my dress and scraped my stomach, but I didn't care.

Slowly, I got to my feet. There was no light, but maybe I could fix that. I uncurled my dirty palms. Even though I couldn't see them, I knew the spider rune scars were still on my hands. I'd always been able to create a little light with my magic, especially with my Ice power. The familiar silver light flickered over my palm anytime I made a simple cube or Ice pick.

But before, when I'd made that final, desperate reach for my Ice magic to stop Tobias Dawson, the spider rune scars on my palms had ignited and burned with cold, silvery flames of Ice magic. Something they'd never done before. I wondered what the silverstone scars would do now that the danger wasn't so imminent. Time to find out.

I reached for my Ice magic. Cautiously, this time, drawing on a small trickle of power. But again, it came to me far easier than it ever had before. It only took a moment of concentration to make the scars on my palms burn with cold silver fire. Better than a fucking flashlight.

"Well, that's something new and different," I murmured.

I held out my glowing palms. The silver light flickered over what remained of the cavern, and I surveyed the damage I'd wrought with my Stone and Ice magic.

Beyond my hole, the stone and earth rose and fell in jagged waves, and dust choked the air like storm clouds of particles. The cavern, which had once been so beautiful and elegant, was now nothing more than a pile of mismatched rubble, like a house that had fallen in on itself. Tons and tons of earth, stone, water, and mud filled the entire stretch of the cavern, blocking the entrance back to the mine shaft. I looked up. There must have been more rock above the ceiling than Tobias Dawson had let on, because the stone had formed a sharp, sloping roof, instead of the natural arch of the original cavern.

I wasn't getting out that way. Because even if I'd been at full strength, instead of beaten, bloody, and exhausted, I doubted even I could have managed to blast my way through so much stone and earth. Elementals had a lot of raw power, but ultimately, we all had our limits. Even me.

So I skirted around the edge of the rubble, slipping, falling, and climbing from one rocky dune of muddy earth to the other. In the distance, I heard the rush of water, like a bowl filling up. I didn't know where the water from the creek had gone when I'd collapsed the ceiling, but it was close by. Another reason for me to get out of here. I hadn't defeated Tobias Dawson to succumb to something as simple as drowning.

I'd just surfed down one particularly large dune when a small sound caught my attention. A tiny, sharp wail in the stone around me. I held out my glowing palms. A flash of light caught my eye, and I peered at the ground. And I realized I was standing on the diamonds.

They littered the ground under my muddy shoes like dull, frozen tears. Most of them had been pulverized to small bits, slivers, and glints that caught the silvery light emanating from my palms. Still beautiful, even in their ruined state. Too bad they were of absolutely no use to me. Definitely not a girl's best friend, in this case.

I walked on until I came to the far side of the cavern, but the earth and stone had fully blocked the exit. Which meant I had to find another way to get out of here—now.

So I surfed back in the direction I'd come from, stopping long enough to take off my ruined stilettos and toss them into the darkness. The broken heels were doing more damage to my feet than going barefoot would. I'd just reached the recess where I'd originally hidden when a spot of white caught my eye against the gray stone. What was that? Another diamond?

I crept closer and realized it was a hand—Tobias Dawson's right hand, sticking out of a mound of earth, fingers stretched wide. I crawled over the earth and stone to get a closer look. But it was just a hand sticking out. Nothing else.

I checked for a pulse, but the dwarf didn't have one. The cold chill of death had already settled into his flesh. Still, I picked up a jagged piece of rock and slashed his wrist just to be sure. I sat there, resting and watching his blood soak into the turned earth and shattered stone.

When his wrist quit oozing, I moved on.

I walked deeper into the back of the cavern to the part I hadn't seen while Tobias Dawson had been challenging me to a duel. The cavern narrowed to a small corridor barely big enough for a person to squeeze through. I stood before it and peered into the darkness, wondering what lay at the end of the midnight rainbow. Only one way to find out. I couldn't go back, and I had to get out.

So I stepped forward into the waiting darkness.

The corridor was as dark as the cavern had been, as black as the coal Tobias Dawson had ripped out of the mountain. There was no light up ahead, nothing to help me see the dangers that waited. And I hadn't escaped the dwarf only to break my leg and end up starving to death down here. So I reached for my Ice magic again. It came to me as easily as before, and I upped the intensity of the flames burning on my spider rune scars until I could see well enough to walk on. Around me, the stone muttered, sharp, angry, and hurt from all the upheaval it had seen today.

"Sorry," I murmured to the rock. "I didn't have a choice."

My voice bounced against the stone and echoed back to me. The sound made me shiver, and I moved on, using my hands to light my way. The passageway grew narrower and narrower, until I had to turn sideways to shimmy through it. But I kept going. It wasn't like I had a lot of other options. There was no going back. Only moving forward.

The passageway opened up again slightly, allowing me to walk through the area square on, instead of twisting from one side to the other. But twenty feet later, it narrowed again. I gritted my teeth and slipped sideways.

And so it went. Sometimes, I could walk through the corridors with ease. Sometimes, I had to turn sideways. Other times, I had to suck in my stomach and force myself through passageways that were little more than a foot wide. But I kept moving. Despite my many injuries, despite my broken jaw and throbbing skull, despite the strange influx of magic coldly burning in my veins, I kept going. To stop would be to rest, to sleep. Who knew if I would ever wake up?

There could be some noxious gas down here already killing me slowly. Some form of carbon monoxide or something equally lethal. No, I didn't dare stop. Not to rest, not to cry, not for anything. If Fletcher Lane had suddenly stepped out of the shadows and offered to tell me all the secrets he'd kept from me, where Bria was and what she was like, I would have walked right on by the old man.

So I trudged along in the blackness, with only the magical silver glow of my palms to light the way. Time ceased to have any sort of meaning. There were only rocks to navigate around, through, over. Sharp rocks pricking my feet. The smell of my own blood. And the murmur of the stones around me.

As I left the destruction of the cavern behind, the stones' murmurs became soft and sweet once more. They talked of water and air and the slow passage of time that had little effect on them. After the screams of the stones and the wail of the shattered diamonds in the cavern, the murmur of the rocks was as soothing as a lullaby. But I pushed the sound to the back of my mind, tuning it out. Because if I listened to it, I would want to stop, just for a few minutes. And then I'd be gone.

I don't know how long I trudged along, just plodding through the dark earth. Minutes, hours, days, the end of time. But I stumbled free of the narrow passageway I was in and entered a larger room, almost as big as the cavern where the diamonds had been. I was halfway across before I realized I was walking directly into a sheer stone wall.

I stopped, blinked, and held out my glowing palms. The passageway branched off into two directions. Left and right. Two more dark holes just like all the others I'd walked and crawled and shimmied through. But this time, I had to make a choice. But which one? And would it even do any good? They both could lead farther into the mountain, turn back on each other, or lead me straight to a dead end. As long as it seemed like I'd been walking, I could be halfway to China by now.

But still, I had to try. Right first. I walked down into the right passageway about a hundred feet and placed my bruised, bloody hand on the stone wall. The usual, low murmurs of water, rock, and time sounded back to me. Same sound I'd heard for hours now.

I sighed, turned around, and trudged down the left passageway. Once again, I placed my hand on the stone and listened to its vibrations. Water, rock, time. Nothing to tell me which way to go.

"Fuck," I snarled in a loud voice.

My curse echoed up to the top of the cavern and bounced back down to me before reverberating through the whole area. I sighed and swiped my hand over my face, smearing blood, dirt, and grime deeper into my skin.

Flutter-flutter. Flutter-flutter.

I froze, wondering if I was imagining the noise. If I was somehow concussed and just didn't know it. If maybe I was already dead, and this was all just a final dream or some sort of purgatory before I got shipped down below.

Flutter-flutter. Flutter-flutter.

Nope, I wasn't imagining it. The noise seemed to be coming from somewhere up above. On an impulse, I raised my hands over my head, palms up. I reached for my magic again, and the cold, silver flames burning in the spider rune scars in my palms intensified. I'd just upped the wattage on my human flashlight.

I frowned and peered into the darkness above my head. There seemed to be some sort of massive figure attached to the roof. What the hell—

Suddenly, a tiny shape detached itself from the ceiling. Then another, then another, then another. It took me a few moments to realize what they were.

Bats.

Hundreds of them.

Evidently my resounding curse had disturbed their peaceful slumber. Because the creatures all abandoned their perches. They hovered in midair for a moment before flapping away. They all headed down the left passageway.

My heart lifted, and I scrambled after them as fast as I could. Bats needed air, light, bugs, water. If they could get out, then I could too. I didn't care if there was only a hole small enough for the winged creatures to flutter through. I'd find a way to get my human-size ass through it too.

Of course, the bats were much faster than me and not hampered by a lack of adequate spelunking footwear. But still, I hurried after them as fast as my aching body would let me. The passageway curved a couple of times before it opened up into a round room. I stopped at the entrance and blinked. Was it my imagination or was it lighter in here? I dropped my hold on my magic. The room went dark, and my heart started to sink again. But I stood there, waiting. And slowly, the area came into focus.

I peered up, and there it was. An opening twenty feet above my head. What looked like early morning sunlight filtered in through a tangle of kudzu vines that dropped down the walls like snakes. I peered at the opening. It looked to be just big enough for me to shove myself through. No time like the present.

I tore a couple of scraps off what remained of my dress and wrapped them around my hands. Then I grabbed hold of the kudzu and yanked on it. The vines seemed sturdy enough to support my weight, so I began to climb.

It was hard. So fucking *hard*. Even harder than reaching for my Ice magic had been to stop Tobias Dawson that final time in the cavern. But inch by inch, foot by foot, I hauled myself up the thick vines. Whenever I found a foothold in the stone, I jammed my bruised, bloody, cold toes into it and rested. The vines under my body smelled faintly of dew. I was about halfway up the wall when I felt a cold breeze whistle down into the hollow room.

The caress of air against my bruised, throbbing cheek made me want to cry.

But I shook off my emotion. Now was not the time to give in to my feelings. I could always slip and fall. And I'd be damned if I was going to die of a broken neck. Not now, when the sweet scent of sunshine was just a few feet away.

I drew in a breath and started climbing again. The walls narrowed to form a sort of circular point where the opening was. I was going to have to let go of the kudzu vines, reach for the edge of the hole, and hope the earth didn't crumble under my weight.

I found a good toehold and rested a moment, gathering my strength once more. For the final time. When I felt strong enough, I bent my knees, kicked up, and reached for the lip of the opening. My hands scrabbled for purchase. At the last second, my fingers clamped around another kudzu vine, this one anchored somewhere above the surface.

I hung there in midair, supported only by my clenching fingertips. At this point, I was weeping openly from the pain in my hands, arms, shoulders. But somehow I hung on.

I slid one hand up the vine. Then the other. Hauling myself upward. Snarls and half screams spewed out of my lips, like I was possessed by some evil spirit. Maybe I was. Because my will to survive was a powerful thing. Alexis James hadn't been able to overcome it. Neither had Tobias Dawson. I wasn't going to let some damp, slippery kudzu vines stop me now.

So I hung there and inched my way up, like a spider climbing up its own web.

Finally, my right hand stretched up into the clear air. I placed it on the edge of the opening, testing the ground. Solid stone, more than steady enough to support me. I scuttled upward and managed to hook my right elbow up and out of the hole. Then the other one. I drew in a breath and strained upward. My head cleared the tangle of vines covering the opening, and the early morning sunlight slanted across my face, blinding me. I closed my eyes and enjoyed its warmth, meager though it was.

And with a final burst of strength, I pulled myself up and out into the dawn.

✷ 32 ✷

I crabbed away from the hole on my hands and knees. I made it twenty feet before the last of my strength gave out, and I did a header into the ground. For a long time, I just lay there on the forest floor breathing in the earthy scent of the leaves that formed a rough, crackling blanket beneath me. There was noise twittering above my head. More bats?

No, I realized after a moment. Birds. The birds were singing. Which meant I'd definitely, finally, escaped from my underground labyrinth.

A smile stretched across my battered face. I let go, and the world faded to black.

Sometime later, I woke up in the same position I'd been in when I'd collapsed. One cheek planted on the ground. Arms and legs splayed out at awkward angles, heavy and numb. I tried to get to my knees and immediately groaned as pain filled every single part of my body.

Fuck. It hurt to be alive.

Somehow I managed to roll over onto my back as tingles of pain shot through my limbs. A maple tree spread its branches over my head, offering a bit of shade. The sun was higher in the sky now. Looked like it was around noon. Once my arms and legs quit burning with pain, I raised my head up and studied my surroundings. I lay in the middle of a thicket of trees. Maples, pines, poplars, and more flanked me like soldiers. Rhododendron bushes and patches of briars snaked through the trees like strings of green and brown Christmas lights.

I sighed. Although I wanted to do nothing more than lie here and sleep for the next three days, I knew I had to move. I didn't know where the hell I was, which meant the others had no chance of finding me. They probably thought I was dead already, trapped beneath the earth with Tobias Dawson and his two giants.

I grinned. I'd enjoy coming back from the grave just to see the look on Finn's face.

It took me awhile, but I propped myself up on my elbows, then sat up. It took me even longer to get up to my knees, then my feet. I looked around the clearing where I'd emerged from the earth and found a piece of fallen wood. Using it as a sort of walking stick, I hobbled forward. Pain pulsed through my body with every step. I'd cut my feet badly on the rocks inside the mountain, and the briars, brambles, and twigs that littered the ground didn't help. But I stumbled forward.

I didn't know how long I walked, an hour, maybe two, but eventually I came to a small stream. Maybe it was the one that had run over the cavern. I didn't know, and I didn't really care. I lowered myself down onto one of the rocks and dipped my feet into the water. Cold as ice, but it felt like heaven on my swollen feet and ankles. I gulped down several mouthfuls of the water and washed off my hands and face as best I could. I was careful to let one part of my body dry before I moved on to the next. I didn't want to get hypothermia from the shock of the cold water.

But the cool wetness helped revive me—and made me realize just how much fucking pain I was in. Every single part of me hurt, but the real problem areas were my broken jaw, aching skull, and scraped, bruised, bloody hands, knees, and feet. Jo-Jo Deveraux was going to have her work cut out for her when she started healing me. The thought made me smile, which turned into a grimace as the muscles in my jaw screamed in pain.

Once I felt strong and dry enough, I used my walking stick to push myself up and plodded on. I'd been walking about thirty minutes when I stumbled across what looked like two ruts in the middle of the forest. I frowned. Did somebody have a house up here? That could be good or bad. Good, if they were gone and had a phone. Bad, if they were home and got a clear look at me.

But I stepped into the smooth track and headed left, climbing upward to whatever might lie at the top of this rise. I got all the way up to the clearing before I realized where I was—on the access road that overlooked Tobias Dawson's coal mine. I could still see the tire tracks in the mud from where Donovan Caine and I had driven up here the night we'd broken into the dwarf's office. Hell, I was probably standing in about the same spot I'd been in when I'd stripped for the detective.

Irony. What a fucking bitch.

I shook my head and trudged on toward the edge of the ridge. Noise drifted up to me from the basin below. Men yelling at each other, along with the grind of heavy machinery. I hobbled closer to the edge of the ridge and stared down. I wasn't particularly surprised by the scurry of activity. Men and women, mostly firefighters, cops, and other rescue officials, stalked back and forth on the rocky floor below me. Some of them had driven their vehicles into the basin, and the red and blue lights spun around and around. The sirens had long ago been turned off, though. The people hung together in small clusters talking among themselves, but mostly what they did was stare at the mine before them.

Or what was left of it.

The right wall of the basin, which had once been just as tall and strong as the others, had crumbled in on itself, like a cheap piece of tinfoil. The entrance to the coal mine and the second, smaller shaft that led to the diamonds had been completely obliterated. Dirt had spilled hundreds of feet outside the original opening, burying the metal tracks that had led inside the mine. The whole side of the basin looked like a sandcastle somebody had kicked over.

Me. I'd been the one who'd done the kicking. I'd used my magic to escape Tobias Dawson, and I'd crumbled half the mountain in the process. I'd always thought Jo-Jo Deveraux had been blowing smoke up my ass when she claimed I had more Stone magic than anyone she'd ever seen. That she'd just been pretending when she said I was even more powerful than she was. But as I stared at the shattered mountain, I really, truly, started to believe her. The thought made my stomach clench.

"Damn," I whispered.

For a moment, another image flashed before my eyes. The ruined, crumbled shell of my own childhood home. I'd used my magic to destroy it as well, to bring all the stones down, to try to save myself and Bria. I shook my head, and the image vanished. But the tightness in my stomach didn't go away.

I looked down and I realized my hands were glowing again. The spider rune scars on my palms burned with cold, silver flames once more—even though I wasn't consciously holding onto my magic. I curled my hands into fists and willed the light, the magic, away. After a moment, the flames died, vanishing back into the scars as though the silverstone in my flesh was somehow the source of their power. I couldn't quit staring at my palms. Was it my imagination or had the spider rune scars become more pronounced? For some reason, they looked like pure silver swimming in my flesh now, instead of the paler scars they'd been before. I rubbed my aching head. Something to worry about later. Much later.

I focused on the basin once more, my eyes flicking over the many figures below. Despite the crowd, it didn't take me long to find him—Donovan Caine. The detective stood near the entrance to the mine, peering at what looked like a map spread over the hood of a truck. Probably a map of the coal mine itself. A white hardhat covered the detective's head and cast his features in shadow, along with those of the man beside him. But I recognized him too. Owen Grayson.

I frowned. Why would Owen Grayson be here? Then I remembered. He was into mining just like Dawson had been. With the dwarf buried underneath the mountain, Grayson was the closest thing to an expert the city of Ashland had been able to call upon. Behind the two men, various bulldozers and backhoes moved earth out of the way. Tobias Dawson was dead. They should have saved their gas.

I stood there on the ridge and stared at Donovan, drinking in the sight of the lean, rugged detective. After this was finished, after I was healed, he and I were going to have a long talk—about us. Because I wanted the detective and he wanted me too—and I was tired of his morals, his guilt about wanting to be with me, getting in the way of what we could have together.

Even though I was thousands of feet away, Donovan Caine somehow sensed my steady gaze, the way people do when you stare at them long and hard enough. His head turned right, then left, trying to find the source of his unease. He said something to Grayson and headed in my direction. Donovan kept looking right and left at everyone he passed. I stepped farther out onto the edge of the ridge, so he could hopefully see me. The detective walked back through the mass of people and machines. After a moment, Owen Grayson followed him. Probably curious as to what the detective was up to.

Donovan Caine was halfway across the basin toward me when he stopped and finally looked up. Our eyes met and held over the distance. Gray on gold. Owen Grayson reached his side and followed the detective's line of sight. He spotted me too. He actually smiled.

At least somebody was glad to see me, because Donovan Caine wasn't. He tipped his hardhat back, and I spotted the frown on his face. The sight, his lack of happiness or even just some relief, cut me more than the rocks that had sliced into my feet.

I focused on Donovan Caine and lifted my bloody hand in greeting. The detective stood there for several seconds—immobile. Then he turned and said something to Grayson, who frowned and nodded his head. Grayson walked a few feet away and pulled out a cell phone. He punched in a number and spoke to someone, still looking at me.

Grayson finished his call and said something to Donovan, who nodded back. Then the detective turned and walked toward the entrance of the collapsed mine. He didn't even glance back at me.

And it fucking *hurt*.

Donovan turning his back on me hurt far worse than anything Tobias Dawson had done to me in the coal mine. Or anything else I'd endured these last few hours. But I didn't have time to dwell on the detective's harsh reaction because of Owen Grayson.

Grayson didn't stay where he was, but he didn't go back either. Instead, he walked closer to me, glancing over his shoulder every once in a while to make sure no one was too interested in his whereabouts. He stopped close to the bottom of the ridge where I stood, close enough now that I could see the grin that stretched across his features.

Too bad the smile was on the face of the wrong man.

But what was even more curious was the fact Grayson started climbing up the ridge. I stepped away from the edge and hobbled back into the clearing. I didn't want anyone seeing me in my current state—or guessing where I'd been. Let them think Owen Grayson wanted a better view of the disaster I'd caused. But there was nothing I could do about Grayson now, so I sat down on the bare earth and leaned against a tree. Waiting.

It didn't take him long to climb up the ridge. He didn't even bother to dust the mud and leaves off his jeans. Instead, he came straight to me and stopped, his violet eyes flicking up and down my body, assessing my injuries.

"You look like you've been to hell and back," he murmured.

I almost managed a smile. "You might say that."

Grayson took off his leather jacket and carefully draped it over my chest. His scent drifted up to me—that rich, earthy aroma that made me think of metal.

"Can I do anything for you?' he asked. "The detective asked me to call your friend Finnegan Lane. I had a rather interesting conversation with him at Mab Monroe's party last night. I don't think Mr. Lane believed me when I told him you were standing on the ridge above the coal mine. He called me a cruel, lying bastard, but he said he was on his way. And that if I was lying, he'd beat me to death with his bare hands."

"Finn was probably just upset. He tends to be emotional in times of crisis."

"And what do you do in times of crisis, Gin?" Grayson asked.

I stared at him. "I survive."

A grin spread across his face, and emotions flashed in

his eyes. Admiration mixed with amusement. A look I'd never seen in Donovan Caine's golden gaze.

"Did Donovan say anything else to you down in the basin? Anything at all?"

Grayson's face shuttered. "Nothing important."

His voice was so kind, so pitying, it made me want to stab him with my walking stick. I hated being pitied.

"Donovan wasn't happy to see me, was he? He thought I'd died in that mine with Tobias Dawson and the others, and he was happy about it. Or at least relieved." My heart twisted as I said the words, but I knew they were true. That was the only way to explain the detective's cold reaction to me. "He didn't want me to be alive. Not really."

Owen Grayson shrugged. "I don't know what Donovan Caine thinks or wants, but I consider him to be an enormous fool."

"Why's that?"

He stared at me. "Because he's down there looking for Dawson, and I'm up here with you."

I didn't say anything. My emotions were too raw, too fresh for that. Owen Grayson opened his mouth again, but the sound of a car engine cut him off. He got to his feet.

"I think your friend Finn is here," he murmured.

Grayson held out his hand to me, but I didn't take it. Instead, I heaved myself to my feet, using my crude walking stick for support.

"You know you can lean on me if you need to."

I shook my head. "No need. I'm fine."

Again that small smile quirked his lips. "I think your definition of the word *fine* needs a serious overhaul."

The sound of the engine grew louder. Whoever it was, they were in a hurry. A few seconds later, Finn's Cadillac Escalade burst through the trees and skidded to a stop in front of us. The tires turned and threw mud all over me and Owen Grayson. I grimaced. A final, messy insult on what had been one hell of a night.

The SUV doors opened. Finnegan Lane stepped out first. His green eyes swept over me, as if he couldn't believe what he was seeing. The other doors popped open, and Jo-Jo Deveraux got out of the car. So did Sophia. The three of them stood there by the vehicle just staring at me.

Finn looked flabbergasted, overjoyed, and stunned at the same time. Jo-Jo had a thoughtful, knowing look in her pale eyes I didn't like. And Sophia, well, the Goth dwarf was actually smiling at me—as much as she ever smiled at anyone.

"Did you guys miss me?" I croaked.

There was a lot of hugging and crying. Finn did most of the hugging, gently putting his arms around me and squeezing as tight as he dared. Jo-Jo did most of the crying. Tears ran down the dwarf's face as though her eyes were the epicenter of a waterfall. They quickly overpowered her waterproof mascara. Sophia remained stoic as always.

"How did you get out of that mountain?" Finn asked. His green eyes kept sweeping over my body as if he still wasn't quite sure that I was alive.

I opened my mouth to answer him when Jo-Jo cut me off.

"Later," the dwarf said. "Look at the poor girl. We need to get her back to Warren's so I can start working on her. Right now. Sophia, if you will, please."

The Goth dwarf came over to me and scooped me up. Her touch was far gentler than I'd imagined it could be, and she held me as though I were some delicate crystal statue she was afraid of breaking.

"I can walk," I protested in a weak voice. "I've been doing it all night and day."

"Which is why you're going to rest now," Jo-Jo said. "You're going to need your strength for when I start healing you. Because it ain't going to feel good, darling. Especially your face."

Sophia strode over to the vehicle. Jo-Jo opened the backdoor for her. Owen Grayson walked over and stopped the Goth dwarf before she could set me inside.

"I'd like to know how you got out of the mountain too," he said. "Maybe you'd like to tell me one night over dinner."

I thought of Donovan Caine and the way he'd turned his back on me. I wasn't sure how I felt about the detective at the moment, much less someone new like Owen Grayson. But I thought of the way Grayson had looked at me—openly, directly, with no hint of judgment in his violet eyes. "Perhaps."

"You have my number," Grayson replied.

I snorted. "Oh yeah, I do."

"I'll be seeing you, Gin. Real soon, if I have my way."

I wondered at the confident promise in his tone—and the strange bit of eagerness it stirred in me. The thought crossed my mind that maybe it would be . . . nice to be chased, to just be . . . wanted, without any guilt or strings or morals attached. Either way, I knew I hadn't seen the last of Owen. Whatever his interest in me was, it wasn't going away anytime soon.

He gave me another grin before Sophia put me into

the back of the Cadillac, and our eyes locked. Gray on violet. Oh yes, I thought, staring through the tinted glass at him.

Owen Grayson was definitely someone worth watching.

Finn drove slowly, but it was still a bumpy ride down the access road. Every jar made my bones rattle together. Now that I was among friends, I could let my guard down, let go of that cold, hard will I'd held on to for so long. And it made everything hurt that much worse. I must have blacked out because the next thing I knew I was lying on top of the square counter in the front of the Country Daze store.

"What are we doing in here?" I murmured, staring up at the ceiling fan spinning above my head.

Jo-Jo's face hovered over mine. "Because when you collapsed the mountain, it created a gigantic sinkhole out back. It's already filled in with water. It hasn't reached the house yet, but it might. So we brought you to the store where it was safer. Now, relax, Gin, as much as you can. Because this is going to hurt."

Jo-Jo's eyes flashed a brilliant white, and her Air power rolled off her like invisible waves. The dwarf put her hand against my forehead. The hot pain of her magic filled me, and I knew nothing more.

The next time I woke up, I was lying in a bed that wasn't my own. I felt better, but bone-tired at the same time, which told me that my body was still recovering from the trauma I'd been through and being blasted with Jo-

Jo's healing Air magic. I shuddered to think how much the dwarf had had to use to put me back together again. But while I'd been unconscious, someone had bathed and dressed me in a pair of oversize black sweatpants, a matching long-sleeved T-shirt, and thick socks.

I threw back the blanket on top of me, got to my feet, and stumbled over to the dresser in the corner. I stared at my reflection in the mirror. I looked the same as always, dark chocolate brown hair, gray eyes, light skin, a few freckles on my nose and cheeks. I wiggled my jaw. Perfect as always, and all my loose teeth felt attached once more. However terrible I'd looked when I'd come out of the mountain, Jo-Jo Deveraux had healed me—all of me. I'd have to get Finn to give the dwarf a bonus for going above and beyond this time.

I opened the door to the bedroom and looked around. I was upstairs in the Foxes' house, from the look of all the pictures of Warren, Violet, and the rest of their family on the walls. I headed right and padded down a set of narrow stairs. I'd just stepped onto the landing when something shimmering outside through the window caught my eye. The small creek that ran by the Foxes' house and country store had turned into a large pond. It stretched out perhaps a quarter of a mile, settled into a new dip in the ground. Probably right over the spot where the cavern with the diamonds had been. The pond was another sign of how my magic had altered the landscape, of how I'd done this thing without even thinking about the consequences.

"Fuck," I whispered.

I shook my head and went down the stairs. Soft voices drifted out from the den, so that's where I headed.

". . . can't believe the amount of power she used, how much magic she was able to tap into."

I stopped where I was in the hallway. Jo-Jo was talking—about me.

"I wouldn't have believed it myself if I hadn't felt it," Warren T. Fox replied in his high, reedy voice. "Felt like the whole mountain was going to tear itself in two. Worse than an earthquake."

"Gin's only just now coming into the full extent of her power," Jo-Jo replied. "She's only going to get stronger."

"I'd hate to get on her bad side," Warren muttered.

I waited in the hallway, but the two of them didn't say anything else. So I padded into the den where they were sitting. Both of them looked at me. Sophia and Finn were nowhere to be found, and Violet was probably still at Eva's. The television flickered in front of Warren and Jo-Jo, showing scenes of the collapsed mine, although the sound was muted.

"Feeling better?" Jo-Jo asked.

I shrugged. "Some. I'm still tired, though."

"You will be," the dwarf replied. "It took me quite a long while to patch you up this time. Whatever you did in that mine shaft, it took its toll on you."

I didn't respond. Instead, I looked at Warren. "I'm sure you've guessed by now, but Tobias Dawson is dead. So are two of his giants. He won't be bothering you anymore."

The old man nodded and rocked back and forth in his recliner. "I figured as much."

"What happened down there, Gin?" Jo-Jo asked. "In the mine."

I sat on the sofa and curled my feet up underneath my

body. "Dawson knocked me out at Mab Monroe's party. He recognized my magic somehow. When I woke up, I was in the mine with the dwarf and two of his giants. We were in this cavern, this beautiful cavern. That's where the diamonds were, hundreds of them set in the stone walls like tiny lamps. Dawson hit me. He wanted to know if Warren had hired me to kill him. All the usual stuff."

"What did you say?" Warren asked.

I smiled. "I told him I was working for Mab Monroe. That she wanted him dead."

Something sparked in Jo-Jo's eyes, but she masked the emotion before I could figure out what it was.

"Then what happened?" Jo-Jo asked.

I shrugged. "I figured I wasn't getting out of there alive and that I might as well take Dawson and his goons with me. So I used my Stone and Ice magic to collapse the ceiling. That's why he needed your land, Warren. The cavern was right under the creek, and the ceiling was too fragile for him to go ahead and mine the diamonds without you knowing about it."

Warren nodded.

"After the dust settled, I was still alive, and they weren't. So I looked for a way out of the cavern, and I found one. End of story."

I didn't tell Jo-Jo about my hands, about the fact I seemed to have more Ice magic now than ever before. That I could feel the cool power rippling through my veins. There would be time enough to do that later. After I'd figured out for myself whether it was just a fluke.

I jerked my head at the television. "What are they saying?"

Warren hit the remote, and the sound came on. "They're saying it was an earthquake. That Dawson and his men were doing a late-night inspection and got trapped inside. They're still digging for them, although everybody knows he's probably dead by now."

I thought of Dawson's pale hand sticking out of the mound of earth and stone—and the way I'd cut the dwarf's wrist just to make sure. "Yeah, Dawson's dead and buried."

"I'm just glad you didn't end up the same way," Warren said.

I stared at the wreckage on the television. The sound of the earth rumbling and the stone shrieking rang in my ears. "Me too."

Jo-Jo went to call Finn and Sophia and tell them that I was finally awake, leaving me alone in the den with Warren. The old coot heaved himself out of his recliner, bones cracking, and disappeared. I watched the news coverage of the mine disaster.

Warren came back a minute later carrying a small picture frame. He stared at it a moment, then shoved it into my hands. "Here. I know I can't pay you for what you did with Dawson and all that you suffered. But I'd like to give you something, and I thought you might want this."

I stared at the picture. A fine layer of dust covered the frame, which I wiped away with the edge of my T-shirt. The picture might have been in color at one time, but it had long ago faded to a dull yellow. Two young men, little more than teenagers, looked up at me. The shorter man was obviously Warren T. Fox. He'd stared into the camera with a serious expression, as though he didn't like having his picture taken. The other man was Fletcher, whose wide grin more than made up for Warren's lack of one. They both wore work shirts and overalls. Fishing rods and tackle boxes lay at their feet, along with a string of fish. Trees ringed the area behind them.

"Is this you and Fletcher?" I asked.

Warren settled into his recliner and started rocking again. "It is. Taken a couple of months before he started up the Pork Pit. Last photo we ever took together."

"Don't you want to keep it then?"

Warren shrugged. "I don't need a photo to remind me of Fletcher. Never have."

He stared at the television, but I still spotted the sheen of moisture in his dark eyes. In that moment, I knew Warren missed Fletcher Lane as much as I did, even if he'd never admit it. And I knew the photo had to be one of his prized possessions. Because it was a symbol of their friendship, of their childhood growing up together, and all the good times and hopes and dreams they'd shared. I had photos of Fletcher, but none like this. None that showed him being so easy and carefree. None that showed him as he really was, without the calm mask he'd presented to so many people, including me, over the years. For the first time, I felt like I was seeing the real Fletcher Lane.

And now Warren was giving the photo to me. His gesture touched me in a way nothing had done in a long time. I might have been an assassin for seventeen years, might have killed a lot of people, but helping Warren and Violet Fox was definitely one of the best things I'd ever done.

"All right," I said. "There's an empty spot on the wall at the Pork Pit. I think this will go nicely there."

Warren nodded. I walked over, leaned down, and kissed his wrinkled cheek. He smelled of Old Spice and peppermint.

"Thank you for this."

He didn't look at me, but a blush crept up the side of his neck. "It's nothing."

"No," I said in a quiet voice, staring at Fletcher's smiling face. "It's everything to me."

Embarrassed, Warren made some excuse about checking on the store, leaving me alone in the den. I sat there staring at the photo of him and Fletcher until Jo-Jo Deveraux came back in.

"What's that?" she asked.

I showed her the picture.

"Nice of him to give it to you," the dwarf replied, sitting on the sofa.

"Yes, it was."

We didn't speak for a few moments. Finally, Jo-Jo broke the silence.

"You want to talk about it?" she asked in a soft voice. "About what happened in the mountain? About your magic? About how you're stronger now?"

My head snapped. "How the hell do you know that?"

Her pale eyes were old and knowing in her made-up face. "I could feel it when I was healing you. Your Ice magic, it's stronger now, isn't it?"

I sighed and told her what had happened in the cavern. About how I'd felt something give inside me and the fact the spider rune scars on my hands glowed brighter than a flashlight. I even gave her a demonstration.

Jo-Jo leaned over and studied my silvery palms. Then she nodded and sat back on the sofa.

"So what happened to me? Is it temporary? Permanent? Did I break my magic or something?"

Jo-Jo chuckled. "Nothing like that, Gin. But yes, I do believe it's permanent." She gave me a steady look. "Have you ever wondered why your Stone magic is so much stronger than your Ice power?"

I shrugged. "Not really. It's rare enough to be able to control two elements. I always assumed my Ice magic was just weaker."

Jo-Jo shook her head. "No, darling, your Ice magic isn't weaker. It's just been contained—until now."

I frowned. "How?"

She jerked her head at my palms. "By that silverstone in your hands. You know as well as I do that silverstone is a magical metal, that it can hold and absorb elemental magic."

"So what?"

"So silverstone can also block magic. In your case, the metal in your hands kept you from fully realizing your Ice potential."

"I don't understand."

Jo-Jo propped her heels up on the coffee table. Her feet were bare, her toes painted pink, just like always. "You know there's a lot of duality in elemental magic. A lot of likes and dislikes between all four of the elements. Now, Stone is more of an internal magic. You don't have to do anything to hear the vibrations of the rocks around you.

Air is the same way. But Fire and Ice are different. Most elementals release those two types of magic through their hands. It's just easier and quicker to form a fireball in your hand than it is to shoot it out of your eyes or your ass."

I smiled at her interesting imagery.

"But you had silverstone melted into your palms So, in a sense, the metal choked your Ice magic every time you tried to release it through your hands. Like a bottleneck. Make sense?"

I thought about all those times I'd formed a cube or a pair of Ice picks. Jo-Jo was right. I almost always used my hands to do those things, but most of the time when I drew on my Stone magic to harden my skin, the power almost always came from within. "I think I get it now. But how was I able to draw on so much Ice magic in the cavern if the silverstone was blocking it?"

Jo-Jo stared at me. "Because you finally brought enough of your Ice magic to bear to overpower the silverstone. You blasted right through that metal, broke down that barrier. Your Ice magic's always been as strong as your Stone magic, Gin. Now, it's finally risen to the surface where you can use it. That's why your spider rune scars look brighter, more of a silver color now. Because your Ice magic is right there waiting for you to tap into it. Because your power is in the silverstone now, instead of being blocked by it."

"You knew, didn't you?" I asked. "You knew the whole time why my Ice magic was weaker. Why didn't you tell me?"

"Because you had to break through the silverstone by yourself," Jo-Jo said. "I couldn't do it for you."

I sat there and stared at the matching scars that decorated my palms. A small circle surrounded by eight thin rays. One on either hand. A spider rune. The symbol for patience.

"You're only going to get stronger now, Gin," Jo-Jo said in a quiet tone. "One day soon, you'll be the strongest elemental in Ashland. Even stronger than Mab Monroe herself."

Stronger than Mab? I didn't know if that was a good thing, seeing as how the Fire elemental only used her power for destruction. All Mab did with her magic was burn, hurt, and kill everyone who stood in her way. I might have been an assassin, but I didn't want to be like her. Not now, not ever.

I curled my hands into fists, hiding the scars from sight, and tried to ignore the shiver that shook my body.

I spent the rest of the night at the Foxes', resting up, and Finn came to get me the next day just before the crack of noon, as was his style. I was sitting on the front porch of Country Daze in some of Violet Fox's borrowed clothes when he pulled up in his Cadillac Escalade. I'd already said my good-byes to Warren T. Fox, who was still inside with Jo-Jo Deveraux. Sophia was coming up later to pick up her older sister, who wanted to spend a few more hours gossiping with Warren.

Finn got out of the car and walked over to me. He slid his designer sunglasses down so he could peer over the top of the lenses. "Nice clothes."

"Lovely to see you too, Finn," I replied in a wry tone.

But I got up and hugged my foster brother anyway. He hugged me back as tight as he could.

"You ready to leave?" Finn asked.

I looked up at the tin sign mounted over the front door. Country Daze. Yeah, *dazed* was one way of putting everything I'd gone through the last few days. I stared at the gleaming sign a moment longer, then turned and smiled at Finn. "Let's blow this gin joint. Take me home. Take me to the Pork Pit."

The incident at the coal mine played out for the next week. Folks worked around the clock for days, digging, moving, and hauling earth and stone out of the way before they finally recovered Tobias Dawson's body, along with those of his two giant workers. The coroner said both the giants and Dawson died of blunt force trauma. He blamed it on the falling debris and resulting cave-in, but I knew the truth. Yeah, the cave-in had taken out the giants, but Dawson had died from those Ice daggers I'd launched into his torso. Too bad the evidence had melted away—just like always. Something I was grateful for.

After the rescue workers recovered the bodies, there wasn't much else to do. So they closed down the mine and went home. A couple of days later, Finn showed me a business article in the *Ashland Trumpet* that said Owen Grayson had bought Tobias Dawson's company for a song—lock, stock, and barrel. No plans had been announced about what would happen to the collapsed mine, and Grayson was quoted as saying he wasn't in a rush to make a decision. Either way, I'd destroyed the diamonds in the cavern, so no one would be sniffing around there anytime soon. Which meant Warren T. Fox, his granddaughter, Violet, and their store, land, and house were safe for now and the foreseeable future.

I was glad I'd been able to help the Foxes, glad I'd been able to do something for someone who had once meant so much to Fletcher Lane. I thought the old man would have approved of me helping Warren, even if the two of them had parted on bad terms all those years ago.

As for me, I lapsed gracefully back into retirement. Auditing classes at Ashland Community College. Reading. Cooking. Running the Pork Pit.

That last one was easier now, since Jake McAllister was out of the picture. The incident at the mine shaft had dominated the news, of course, but there was a small mention about Jake and the fact he'd been found dead at his father's home. The coroner blamed it on natural causes caused by an undetected heart defect—or some such nonsense. There was no mention of Jake being at the party at Mab Monroe's house, and no mention of him being found stabbed to death in one of the bathrooms.

But with Jake dead, his father, Jonah McAllister, had no real reason to squeeze me anymore. At least, not about the robbery and pressing charges against his son. Oh, I imagined Jonah was still angry at me over what had happened the day he had come to the restaurant and that he'd get back around to harassing me sooner or later, if only because he enjoyed that sort of thing. But for now, the Pork Pit was back up to its regular flow of customers. Still, I kept an eye out for trouble. If Jonah McAllister ever connected me with the blond hooker who'd been at Mab's party, he'd get his giants, come to the Pork Pit, and raze the restaurant to the ground—with me inside it.

Which is why I had Finn make some discreet inquiries into the matter. Jonah McAllister was said to be seething with rage over the murder of his son—and the fact the incident had taken place at Mab Monroe's mansion. McAllister had vowed to find his son's killer and take care of her himself—with his bare hands. Mab Monroe was also said to be livid at the fact someone had dared to murder her lawyer's son in her own home.

Mab was also said to be quietly searching for a blond hooker who'd attended her party and had been seen leaving with Tobias Dawson. According to Finn, the Fire elemental had sent Elliot Slater and a couple of his giant goons to question Roslyn Phillips about the mysterious hooker. But Slater had eventually been satisfied that the invitation and rune necklace had been stolen from Northern Aggression without Roslyn's knowledge. Still, I had Finn wire Roslyn a significant amount of money to help make up for what I was sure had been a forceful interview.

And I still wondered about that night at the party and why Mab hadn't just killed me herself when I'd been on the ground in front of her. It would have been easy enough for her to do. Why make Dawson do it? Why make him take me somewhere else? Had Mab known he would take me to the mine? Maybe she'd thought I'd kill Dawson for her, and she could step in and have all the diamonds for herself. It wouldn't have been a bad plan, if I hadn't collapsed the whole mountain in the process.

I didn't know the Fire elemental's reasoning, and I'd never believed much in luck. But I knew that I'd dodged my own death that night. But now she was actively searching for me, and I had no illusions about what would happen if she ever discovered my real identity. The fact was I'd have to be more careful for the foreseeable future—at least until someone else caught Mab Monroe's interest.

Two weeks after the incident at the mine, I perched on my stool at the Pork Pit reading *The Adventures of Huckleberry Finn* by Mark Twain. Fletcher's copy of *Where the Red Fern Grows* adorned the wall beside the cash register, of course, but it had been joined by something new—the picture of him and Warren T. Fox. I think Fletcher would have liked having it in the restaurant.

It was a Monday night again and quiet except for my two customers—Eva Grayson and Violet Fox. The two college girls sat at the counter, slurping down chocolate milkshakes and studying. Their books covered a good portion of the countertop. Eva and Violet had started coming into the Pork Pit at least once a week when they had an hour or two to kill between classes. Sometimes, Cassidy, Eva's other friend, joined them. But more often than not it was just the two girls.

"So when are you going to go out with my big brother?" Eva said, pushing aside her empty milkshake glass.

I looked up from my book. "Why do you ask?"

Eva stared at me. "Because every time I mention I've

been in here, he asks me how you are, Gin. Why don't you give the poor guy a break?"

I raised my eyebrow. "If your big brother wants to ask me out, he can come down here and do it himself, instead of getting his little sister to plead his case to me."

Eva waved her hand. "I'm just filling you in on Owen's good qualities. Not pleading his case."

"What was it you told me you were majoring in again?"

"Marketing," Eva replied with a grin.

"I rest my case."

Violet just laughed and took another swig of her own milkshake.

The front door opened, causing the bell to chime. I looked up, ready to greet a potential customer.

And he walked into the restaurant.

Detective Donovan Caine. Black hair, golden eyes, bronze skin. The detective looked the same as I remembered, except for the lines on his face. For once, they seemed to have smoothed out, as though some great weight had been lifted off his lean shoulders. As though he'd made some decision that had finally brought him a measure of peace. I wondered what it could be, but I had a funny feeling it had something to do with me. Maybe everything to do with me.

The detective came over and rested his hands on the counter. Hands that had done such wonderful things to my body. "Gin."

"Detective."

"Can we talk?" he asked in a low voice.

I hadn't seen the detective since that afternoon I'd waved to him from the ridge, and he hadn't made any effort to contact me. People always talked about the stages of grief you went through when something traumatic happened. Hah. I'd pretty much moved from hurt to just plain pissed, with no stops in between. Still, I was curious as to why Donovan had come, what he wanted to say to me now, two weeks too late. Fucking curiosity. Just wouldn't let me be.

"Sure. Let's chat." I turned my gray eyes to Violet and Eva. "Why don't you girls go in the back for a few minutes and convince Sophia to make you some fresh milkshakes? On the house."

Violet shrugged and walked around the far end of the counter. Eva Grayson studied Donovan Caine with open interest. She sniffed, clearly telling me she didn't think the detective had anything on her big brother. Then she followed Violet.

I waited until the two college girls had disappeared through the swinging doors and were out of earshot before I looked back at the detective. "I saw you on TV at the coal mine. Looked like you had your hands full recovering Tobias Dawson's body."

The detective nodded. "I did. But Owen Grayson was a tremendous help with that. So were all the other emergency and disaster workers."

We could have been talking about the weather for as interesting as the conversation was. But the detective's hands gripped the edge of the counter like he wanted to break it off. He was upset about something. I had no idea what it could be. Because he was the one who'd turned his back on me that day at the mine, not the other way around. So I decided to get to the heart of the matter.

"Why did you come here, Donovan?" I asked. "What do you want?"

The detective stared at me, his golden eyes tracing over my face. "I'm leaving Ashland, Gin. I thought you should know. I thought I should tell you in person."

For a moment I was stunned. Simply stunned. Of all the things he could have said, I wasn't expecting that—and the emotions it stirred up in me. Hurt. Anger. Sadness.

"You're leaving town? Why?"

Donovan ran his hands through his black hair. "A lot of reasons. Too many to get into right now."

"Well, let's get into the only one that matters, the real reason you're here. Me," I snapped. "You're leaving town because of me, aren't you?"

"Guilty as charged." The detective tried to smile. It didn't come off very well.

"Why?" I asked. "You turned your back on me at the mine that day. I got the message. For some reason, you don't want to have anything to do with me. Not anymore. You don't have to leave town to accomplish that, detective. I'm not the sort who runs after a man, begging him not to leave her."

My voice dripped with acid. So did my heart, but I kept my face calm, cold, remote. I wasn't going to let Donovan Caine know how much he'd hurt me that day—how much he was hurting me now. I'd thought we could have something together, a real relationship. That maybe Donovan was someone I could share my heart and life with, dark though they were. But that hope had burned up and crumbled to ash, like so many other things in my life. Hope. A wasted emotion, more often than not.

"I came here to explain," Donovan said in a low voice. "Can you please just let me do that?"

"Fine," I snarled. "Explain."

Donovan drew in a deep breath. "I've thought about you every day, Gin. Ever since that first night we met at the orchestra house. The night Gordon Giles was murdered. I've replayed that scene over and over in my head. And not just that one. That night at Northern Aggression. The time we spent together at the country club. Then, in my car a few weeks ago. That night in the rain. I can't get you out of my head. Your voice, your smell, your laugh, the way you feel against me."

"Why is that a bad thing?" I asked. "We're attracted to each other. That's what people do when they're attracted to each other."

Donovan stared at me. "It's a bad thing because of who you are and what you used to do."

I'd expected the words, but they still stung. I sighed. "If this is still about Cliff Ingles—"

He shook his head. "It's not about Cliff, not anymore. I know why you killed him. Like I told you before, I might have done it myself, if I'd had the chance. No, this is about me."

I just looked at him.

Donovan drew in a breath. "Do you know why I didn't come see about you at the mine?"

"Not really."

"After that night we were together on my car, I felt like maybe there could be something between us," he said in a low voice. "But then you said you were going after To-bias Dawson. To kill him. And I let you. I *let* you. I just stood by in the background while you went after another man—to murder him. I did the very thing I'd always sworn not to do—I looked the other way. Not because Dawson was a bad guy, but because of *you.* I compromised myself because of you, Gin, and what I feel for you."

Guilt, grief, and disappointment flashed in his golden eyes. And I thought back to what Warren T. Fox had told me. *He's not the one for you,* the old man's voice whispered in my head. Somehow I pushed my hurt aside, trying to be calm and rational about this. Trying to get Donovan Caine to change his mind. To stay. To give us a fucking *chance.*

"You know as well as I do that Tobias Dawson was never going to leave the Foxes alone. That he was in deep with Mab Monroe and both of them—*both* of them— would have done everything in their power to get their hands on those diamonds. Dawson dying was the only way to save Warren and Violet."

Donovan shook his head. "I just can't bring myself to believe that, to accept it."

This was the same old argument we'd had so many times now. Too many to count. It wouldn't go anywhere, so I decided to try another tactic. "Why is feeling something for me so terrible? Why can't you just accept the fact I used to be an assassin and that I'm trying to change?"

"Because you'll never change. Not really."

"Oh no?"

"No," he replied in a firm voice. "Think about it. We find out what Tobias Dawson's doing, and what's the first thing out of your mouth? You talking about killing him.

You don't consider any other options, you don't consider anything. You decided you wanted Dawson dead, and you made it happen."

"I did what needed to be done," I said in a cold voice. "Nothing more, nothing less. And there were no other options, detective. Because the police in this town are a joke, and we both know it. The only law, the only justice, in Ashland is what people make for themselves."

Donovan flinched at my harsh words, but he didn't dispute them. "I just—I can't do this anymore. I'm sorry, Gin. But this thing with us, it's over."

"So you're leaving town to get away from me?" I snapped.

Donovan lifted his hands in a helpless gesture. "Yes. No. I don't know. It's not all about you. Part of it is the department. There's so much corruption there. I'm just . . . tired of it all. Of getting up every single fucking morning and knowing that I'm fighting a losing battle. I'm on the edge here, Gin. Close to becoming just like all the other crooked cops in this city. Letting you go after Alexis James was one thing. She came after both of us first. But Tobias Dawson, that was different. If it had been anyone but you, I would have cuffed your ass and dragged you down to headquarters before you got anywhere near Dawson. But I didn't. And I regret it. More than you'll ever know. I'm sorry, Gin. I want you to know that. I really am sorry."

"No," I said. "I'm the one who's sorry. I'm sorry I wasted my time on you. Face it, Donovan. You're not leaving town because I killed Dawson. You're leaving town because you didn't stop me from doing it. Because you didn't have the strength to. Because even now, despite everything, you still want to fuck me. You're running away because your morals are more important to you than anything else, including what you could have with me."

Donovan flinched, but he didn't deny the truth of my words. It was too late for that. Now the detective just looked weary. His resignation only made me angrier. For a moment, the rage surged through me, hard and cold and bitter as bile. I wanted to throw something, break something. I wanted to break *him*. Palm my knife, step forward, and slash his throat with it. Hurt him like he was hurting me.

But I drew in a breath. I might wound Donovan with words, but nothing else. I might be a former assassin, but I was better than that. I'd never killed out of passion, and I wasn't going to start now. The detective wasn't worth it.

"You turned your back on me at the mine because you were glad I was dead," I said. "Because the choice to be with me had been taken out of your hands, and your precious morals were still intact. And then I popped up again, still alive. And you were right back to square one. That's the real truth, isn't it?"

He didn't say anything. And I finally let myself acknowledge something I'd known all along. Donovan Caine wanted me, but he wasn't strong enough to accept me. Not my past, not my strength, not the woman I was. Bitter disappointment filled me, replacing my rage, but I forced myself to ask the final question I wanted an answer to.

"Where are you going?"

He shook his head. "I think it's better if you don't know that, Gin."

I nodded. Maybe it was.

"I also came here to warn you," Donovan said in a soft tone. "Jonah McAllister is out for the blood of whoever killed his son. He won't stop until he finds the person responsible. One of my sources says he's looking into everyone Jake had a problem with—including you. And Mab Monroe doesn't think you died in the mine with Dawson. My captain got a call from her the other day wanting to know if we'd found any more bodies in the rubble. So watch your back."

"Why tell me all this?" I said. "It's not like you care. Not really."

Not enough to stay. That's what I wanted to say, to scream at him. But I didn't.

Donovan shrugged. "I don't know. I guess I felt I owed it to you. The department's already replaced me."

"With who?" I said it more to say something than out of any real curiosity.

He shrugged again. "Some hotshot from Savannah named Coolidge. That's all I know. A woman. Supposed to be a real go-getter. Just like you."

Donovan stared at me again. His gold eyes burned into mine. Emotions flashed in his gaze. Longing. Fear. Regret. Determination. For once, I softened my face and let him see what I really felt for him. Surprise flickered in his eyes, and for a moment, I thought it might be enough to change his mind. But then his face hardened, and I knew I'd lost him. I hoped Donovan Caine's morals kept him warm at night because I never would again. Not now, not ever.

There was nothing left to say. The detective nodded at me a final time, stared into my eyes a moment longer. Then he turned and walked out of the Pork Pit, leaving my gin joint, my heart, cold and empty and aching.

✳ 35 ✳

I gave Violet and Eva their promised milkshakes, then kicked them out and closed down the restaurant for the night. Thirty minutes later, I was just about to leave when the phone rang. On a whim I picked it up, half-hoping that it might be Donovan Caine, calling to apologize or—something. Anything.

"Pork Pit."

"Hello, Gin."

Owen Grayson's deep voice flooded the line. A pleasant sound, but I couldn't hold back my disappointed sigh.

"Owen."

"You don't seem overjoyed about hearing from me," he said.

"What do you want?" Maybe I should have been nicer, maybe I would have been nicer if not for Donovan Caine.

"I just wanted to talk to you, see how you were, since

you haven't returned any of my messages," he said in a mild voice.

My hand tightened around the phone. Since the incident at the mine, Owen Grayson had called the Pork Pit and left me a few messages, none of which I'd returned. Mainly because I hadn't known where things had stood with me and Donovan Caine. Well, now I did. But I didn't need Owen Grayson to swoop in and pick up the pieces. I could do that all by my lonesome. Been doing it for years.

"I've been busy."

"Seeing Donovan Caine?" he said. "Eva called and told me he stopped by the restaurant tonight and that things were tense between the two of you."

My gray eyes narrowed. "Eva's very chatty, isn't she?"

Owen let out a laugh. Somehow the low sound lightened my mood the tiniest bit. "Don't blame her. I asked her to play the part of spy."

"And why is that?"

"Because my offer still stands," he replied. "About wanting to get to know the real Gin Blanco."

I snorted. I didn't think Owen would like the real Gin Blanco and her silverstone knife collection. Then again, he hadn't flinched that night at Mab Monroe's party when I'd been pretending to be a hooker. Which was more consideration than Donovan Caine had ever shown me. Still, I wasn't ready to jump into something new. Not with Owen Grayson, whose real motives were still a mystery to me. Despite the desire I'd seen in his violet eyes.

"Sorry, Owen, but I'm just not in the mood right now," I said in a kinder tone. "I don't think I will be for the foreseeable future."

"No worries," Owen replied in a smooth tone. "I'm nothing if not patient. I just wanted to call and remind you that you had other options, Gin."

"Well, I'll keep those other options in mind," I drawled. "But right now, I've had a long day, and I plan to go home—alone."

"Don't let me keep you then," he murmured.

"Don't worry. I won't."

He let out another laugh, and I found myself smiling back, despite my mood.

"Good night, Gin," he rumbled.

"Good night, Owen."

And just like that, he was gone. But unlike Donovan Caine, I knew that Owen Grayson would be back. For some reason, that thought comforted me, standing in the darkness of the restaurant.

After Owen's call, I drove home to Fletcher's. Checked the gravel in the driveway, then the granite around the door. Once I was satisfied there was no one lurking around, I went inside and headed straight to the kitchen. I poured myself a tall glass of gin, dropped some ice cubes in it, then plopped down on the sofa in the den. I leaned my head back, stared into space, and brooded.

Donovan fucking Caine. He was all I could think about right now. I couldn't believe the detective was actually leaving Ashland. That he was leaving *me*. That we were never going to get the chance to fully explore this sizzling attraction between us. All that promise tossed aside. And for what? So the detective could rest easy at night, his idealistic morals and outdated code of justice still intact? Pointless, all of it.

I took a long pull of my gin, relishing the cold burn of the alcohol. For a moment, I considered retrieving the bottle out of the cabinet and getting sloshed. But it wouldn't do me a damn bit of good. I'd just wake up with a hangover tomorrow. Donovan Caine would still be leaving, if he hadn't already gone. He'd just broken up, more or less, with a former assassin. Not the kind of person you wanted knowing your whereabouts.

I could go after Donovan, of course. Talk to him again, plead my case, ruthlessly seduce him into giving us another chance. Into staying in Ashland. I'd thought about nothing else on the drive home.

But I couldn't do that. Because I still wanted what I'd always wanted—Donovan Caine to desire me, to want to be with *me*, Gin Blanco, the former assassin who called herself the Spider. But he didn't, and he never would. His code of justice wouldn't let him, any more than mine would let me forget about all the bad things I'd done in my life, all the people I'd killed. Or pretend that I wouldn't do it all over again, if it became necessary.

"Warren, you old coot, you were right after all." I raised my glass in a toast, then took another sip of gin.

I plunked my glass down on the battered coffee table, and my eyes landed on the folder—the one that contained the information on my murdered family. That was something else I'd been thinking about a lot these past few weeks. For the first time, I realized why Fletcher Lane had left it for me. He'd regretted his past with Warren T. Fox, for not making amends with his old friend. Fletcher had had more than fifty years to do it, and he'd never gotten around to it. He didn't want me to have those same kinds of regrets, so the old man had given me a choice, given me the information I needed to make a choice. And I knew what I was going to do. I'd known ever since the night of Mab Monroe's party.

Ever since I'd realized she was the Fire elemental who'd murdered my family.

Maybe it had been her smell, jasmine mixed with smoke. Maybe it had been her silky voice. Or even that brief laugh she'd let out while she'd been standing over me, discussing my impending demise with Tobias Dawson. But it had brought all of my memories of that night back to the surface. I hadn't seen the Fire elemental's face when she'd tortured me. But I'd heard her voice, her laugh.

And they were identical to Mab's.

I was sure of it now. Or maybe I'd known all along but just hadn't wanted to admit it to myself. That's why Fletcher had written Mab's name down in the folder to start with. To make me look in her direction and figure it out for myself.

I knew the *who;* now I wanted to know the *why.* Why had Mab killed my mother and older sister? Why had she tortured me? Why had she demanded to know where Bria was? When I found out the *why,* I'd have the final piece of the puzzle.

And then I'd kill the bitch.

Oh, I knew it wasn't going to be easy. That I could die in the process. That I probably *would* die. But Mab Monroe had murdered my family, made me think for seventeen years that I'd killed my baby sister. I'd lived on the streets and eaten garbage because of her. Hidden from junkies and vampire pimps and all the other Southtown trash. Been scared and weak and frightened because of her. But not anymore. And mine wasn't the only family she'd ruined over the years. The Snow family was hardly a footnote compared to all the horrid things Mab Monroe had done.

And then there was Bria. My eyes traced over the picture of my baby sister. Blond hair, cornflower blue eyes, the primrose rune around her neck. She was out there somewhere, waiting for me.

"I'm going to find you, baby sister," I whispered. "One way or another."

My eyes flicked up to the rune drawings propped on the mantel. I stared at the image of the Pork Pit that I'd drawn, of the sign over the front door. Fletcher's rune, as I thought of it. I raised my glass in another toast.

"Here's to you, Fletcher Lane," I said. "I hope I'll make you proud."

Only the ticking of the grandfather clock in the hall broke the silence. I tossed back the gin and set my glass aside. Then I picked up the folder, ready to go through all the information again. And again and again if necessary. Until I found all the answers I was looking for.

Donovan Caine had been right about one thing. Part of me would always be the Spider—and it was time to put my skills to good use. To do the things that needed to be done.

Find Bria.

Figure out why Mab Monroe had murdered my family.

Kill Mab.

"The good ole days are back again," I said.

Then I got to work.

Turn the page for a sneak peek
at the next Elemental Assassin book,

Venom

Jennifer Estep

Coming Soon from Pocket Books

Turn the page for a sneak peek
at the next Paranormal Assassin book.

Verona

Jennifer Bosysp

Coming Soon from Pocket Books

The bastards never would even have gotten close to me if I hadn't had the flu.

Coughing, sneezing, aching, wheezing. That was me. Gin Blanco. Restaurant owner. Stone and Ice elemental. Former assassin. And all-around badass. Laid low by a microbe. Ugh.

It had started as a small, ominous tickle in my throat three days ago. And now, well, it wasn't pretty. Watery eyes. Pale face. And a nose so red and bright even Rudolph would have been jealous. Ugh.

The only reason I'd even crawled out of bed this evening was to come down to Ashland Community College and take the final for the classical literature class I was auditing. I'd finished my essay on symbolism in the *Odyssey* ten minutes ago. Now I plodded across one of the grassy campus quads and feverishly dreamed of sinking back into my bed and not getting out of it for a week.

Just after seven on a cold, clear December night. This was the last day of finals for the semester, and the campus was largely deserted. Only a few lights burned in the windows of the kudzu-covered brick buildings that rose above my head. The stones whispered of formulas and theories and knowledge. An old, sonorous, slightly pretentious sound that was decidedly at odds with the sinister shadows that blackened most of the quad. No one else was within sight. Which is probably why the bastards decided to jump me here. Well, that and the fact that kidnapping me would be such a *bother*.

One second I had my face buried in a tissue blowing my sore, drippy nose for the hundredth time today. The next, I looked up to find myself surrounded by three giants.

Oh, fuck.

I stopped, and they immediately closed ranks, forming a loose triangle of trouble around me. The giants were all around seven feet tall, with oversize, buglike eyes and fists almost as big as my head. One of them grinned at me and cracked his knuckles. Someone was anxious to get down to the business of beating the shit out of me.

My gray eyes flicked to the leader of the group, who had taken up a position in front of me—Elliot Slater. Slater was the tallest of the three giants, his seven-foot figure making even his flunkies seem petite in comparison. He was almost as wide as he was tall, with a solid, muscled frame. Granite would be easier to break than his ribs. Slater's complexion was pale, bordering on albino, and almost seemed to glow in the faint light. His hazel eyes provided a bit of color in his chalky skin, although his thin, tousled thatch of blond hair did little to cover his large skull. A diamond in his pinkie ring sparkled like a star in the dark night.

Up until my retirement a few months ago, I'd moonlighted as an assassin known as the Spider. Over the past seventeen years, I'd had plenty of dealings in the shady side of life, so I knew Slater by sight and reputation. On paper, Elliot Slater was a highly respected security consultant with his own platoon of giant bodyguards. In reality, Slater was the number-one enforcer for Mab Monroe, the Fire elemental who ran the Southern metropolis of Ashland like it was her own personal fiefdom. Slater stepped in and either cut off, took care of, or permanently disposed of any pesky problems Mab didn't feel like dealing with herself.

And tonight, it looked like that problem was me.

Not surprising. A couple of weeks ago, I'd stiffed someone during a party at Mab Monroe's mansion. Needless to say, the Fire elemental hadn't been too thrilled about one of her guests being murdered in her own home when she'd been entertaining several hundred of her closest business associates. I'd gotten away with it so far, but I knew Mab was doing everything in her power to find the killer.

To find *me*.

I sniffled into my tissue. I wondered if Mab had figured out who I really was. If that was why Slater was here tonight—

Elliot Slater looked over his broad shoulder. "Is this her?"

Slater slid to one side so another man, a much shorter human, could join the circle of giants surrounding me. Underneath his classic trench coat, the man wore a perfect black suit, and his polished wingtips gleamed like wet ink in the semidarkness. His thick mane of gunmetal gray hair resembled a heavy mantle of silver that had somehow been swirled and sculpted around his head. Too bad hate made his brown eyes look like congealed lumps of blood in his smooth, tight face.

I recognized him too. Jonah McAllister. On paper, McAllister was the city's top lawyer, a charming, bellicose defense attorney capable of getting the most vicious killer off scot-free—for the right price. In reality, the slick lawyer was another one of Mab Monroe's top goons, just like Elliot Slater. Jonah McAllister was Mab's personal lawyer, responsible for burying her enemies in legal red tape instead of in the ground like Slater did.

McAllister's son, Jake, was the one I'd killed at Mab's party. The beefy frat boy had threatened to rape and murder me, among other things. I'd considered it pest extermination more than anything else.

Elliot Slater and Jonah McAllister tag-teaming me. This night just kept getting better and better. I sniffled again. Really should have stayed home in bed.

Jonah McAllister regarded me with cold eyes. "Oh, yes. That's her. The lovely Ms. Gin Blanco. The bitch who was giving my boy a hard time."

A hard time? I supposed so, if you thought turning

him into the cops for attempted robbery, breaking a plate full of food in his face, and ultimately stabbing Jake McAllister to death was a hard time. But I noticed that Jonah McAllister didn't say anything about me actually *killing* his son. Hmm. Looked like this was some sort of fishing expedition. I decided to play along—for now.

"What is this meeting all about?" My voice came out somewhere between a whiny wheeze and a phlegmy rasp. "Are you taking up Jake's bad habit of assaulting innocent people?"

Jonah McAllister's face hardened at my insult. As much as it could, anyway. Despite his sixty-some years, McAllister's features were as smooth as polished marble, thanks to a vigorous regimen of expensive Air elemental facial treatments. "I would hardly consider you innocent, Ms. Blanco. And you're the one who assaulted my precious boy first."

"Your *precious boy* came into my restaurant, tried to rob me, and almost killed two of my customers with his Fire elemental magic." I spat out the words, along with some phlegm. "All I did was defend myself. What does it matter now anyway? Your boy is dead because of some weird heart condition. At least, that's what was in the newspaper."

Jonah McAllister stared at me, trying to see if I knew more than I was letting on about his son's untimely demise. I used the lull to blow my nose—again. Fucking microbes.

McAllister's mouth twisted with disgust at the sight and sound of my sniffles. Admittedly, it wasn't my most attractive moment. He jerked his head at Elliot Slater, who nodded back.

"Now, Ms. Blanco," Slater drawled. "The reason for this meeting is that Mr. McAllister thought you might have some information about his son's death. Jake did have a bit of a heart condition, but there were also some suspicious circumstances surrounding his death. Happened a couple of weeks ago."

Suspicious circumstances? I assumed that was polite talk for a sucking stab wound to the chest. But I kept my face blank and ignorant.

"Why would I know anything about Jake's death?" I asked. "The last time I saw the little punk was the day he brought his old man there down to the Pork Pit to threaten me into dropping the charges against him."

Lies, of course. I'd run into Jake McAllister one more time after that—at Mab Monroe's party. Even though I'd been gussied up as a hooker, the bastard had still recognized me. Since I'd been there to kill someone else, I'd lured sweet little Jakie into a bathroom, stabbed him to death, left his body in the bathtub, and washed the blood off my dress before going back out to the party. Nothing I hadn't done a hundred times before as the assassin the Spider. I certainly hadn't lost any sleep over it.

But right now, it looked like I might lose a whole lot more.

"See, that's the problem. My good friend Jonah doesn't believe you. So he asked me and some of my boys to come down here and see if perhaps we could jog something free from your memory." Slater smiled. His lips drew back, giving me a glimpse of his pale pink gums. The giant's grin reminded me of a jack-o'-lantern's gaping maw—completely hollow. "We're going to pay these sorts of visits to anyone Jake might have had a problem with. And your name was at the top of the list."

Of course it was. I was probably the only person in Ashland who'd ever dared to stand up to Jake McAllister. Now his daddy was going to make me pay for it—and there wasn't a damn thing I could do about it.

Slater took off his suit jacket, handed it to Jonah McAllister, and started rolling up his shirtsleeves.

I sniffled, blew my nose again, and considered the situation. Four-on-one odds were never terrific, especially since three of the four men were giants. The oversize goons were hard to bring down, even for a former assassin like me. None of the giants showed any obvious elemental abilities, like letting flames flicker on their clenched fists or forming Ice daggers with their bare hands. But that didn't mean that they didn't have magic. Which would make them doubly hard to get rid of.

Still, if I hadn't had the flu, I might have considered killing them—or at least cutting down a couple so I could run away. Although I'd dragged myself out of bed this evening, I'd grabbed my silverstone knives on the way out the door. Five of them. Two tucked up my sleeves. One nestled against the small of my back. Two more in the sides of my boots. Never left home without them.

Of course, being an elemental myself I didn't really need my knives to kill. I could just use my magic to take down the bastards. My Stone power was so strong that I could do practically anything I wanted to with the element. Like make bricks fly out of the wall of one of the surrounding buildings and use them to brain the giants in their watermelon-size heads. *Splat, splat, splat*. It'd be easier than using an Uzi. Hell, if I really wanted to show off, I could just crumble all four of the buildings that ringed the quad down on top of them.

I was also one of the rare elementals who could control more than one element. Stone and Ice, in my case. Until recently, my Ice magic had been far weaker than my Stone power. But thanks to a series of traumatic events, I could do a little more with it now. Like create a wall of Ice knives to fling at the men. I'd sliced through a dwarf's skin doing just that. Giants weren't quite as tough as dwarves, at least when it came to cutting into them. Even if they did have more blood to spare than their shorter compatriots.

But the odds or how to go about killing the giants wasn't what was holding me back. Not really. It was the consequences; what would happen afterward when their boss, Mab Monroe, got involved.

Seventeen years ago, Mab Monroe had used her Fire elemental magic to kill my mother and older sister, a fact I'd only recently learned. She'd also tortured me, using her magic to superheat and burn a spider rune into my palms. I was planning to deal with Mab myself after I figured out a few things, like why she'd murdered my family in the first place and where my long-lost baby sister, Bria, was now.

Taking care of Jonah McAllister and the rest of his hired help tonight would definitely tip my hand and draw even more of Mab's attention my way. I didn't want

Mab and her minions to realize that I had any elemental magic. To suspect that I was anything more than the simple restaurant owner Jonah McAllister wanted dead for tattling on his son to the cops. At least, not before I killed the bitch for what she'd done to me.

All that left me with only one option tonight—I was going to have to let the bastards hurt me, beat me. That was the only way I could keep my cover identity as Gin Blanco safe, along with who I really was, Genevieve Snow.

Fuck. This was going to hurt.

Elliot Slater finished rolling up his sleeves. "Are you sure you don't have anything to tell us, Ms. Blanco?"

I sighed and shook my head. "I told you before. I don't know anything about Jake McAllister's death except what I read in the newspaper."

"I'm sorry to hear that," Slater murmured.

The giant stepped forward and flexed his fingers, ready to get on with things. Time for me to put on a little show. I widened my eyes, as though it had just sunk into my flu-addled brain what Elliot Slater was planning to do to me. I let out a phlegmy scream and turned to run, as though I'd forgotten all about the two giants standing behind me. I ran right into them, of course, and they reached for me. Even though I had no real intention of trying to break free, I still struggled to keep up appearances. Yelling, flailing, kicking out with my legs.

While I fought with the bigger, heavier men, I managed to discreetly slip the two silverstone knives that I had up my sleeves into the pockets of my jacket. I didn't want the giants to feel the weapons when they finally latched onto me. Most innocent women didn't go around wearing five knives on them, and being so heavily armed would be the final nail in my coffin as far as Jonah McAllister was concerned about my involvement in his son's death.

The two giants laughed at me and my weak, exaggerated blows. After a minute of struggling, they seized my upper arms and turned me around to face Elliot Slater once more.

And that's when the fun really started.

Elliot Slater snapped his hand up and slammed his fist into my face. Bastard was quick, I'd give him that. I hadn't braced myself for the blow, and I jerked back in the giants' arms. The force almost tore me out of their grasp. Pain exploded like dynamite in my jaw.

But Slater didn't stop there. He spent the next two minutes beating me. One punch broke my drippy nose. Another cracked two of my ribs. And I didn't even want to think about the internal bleeding or what my face looked like at this point. *Thud, thud, thud.* I might as well have been a piece of meat the giant was tenderizing for dinner. Every part of me hurt and burned and throbbed and pulsed with pain.

And the giant laughed the whole time. Low, soft, chuckling laughs that made my skin crawl. Elliot Slater enjoyed hurting people. Really enjoyed it. The bastard's hard-on bulged against the zipper on his black pants.

Slater hit me again and stepped back. By this point, I hung limp between the two giants, all pretense of being tough and strong long gone. I just wanted this to be over with.

A hand grabbed my chin and forced my face up. I

stared into Elliot Slater's hazel eyes. At least, I tried to. White starbursts kept exploding over and over in my field of vision, making it hard to focus. The light show was better than fireworks on the Fourth of July.

"Now," Elliot rumbled. "Do you want to reconsider what you know about Jake McAllister's death? Maybe you have something new to add?"

"I don't know anything about Jake's death," I mumbled through a mouthful of loose teeth. Blood spewed out of my split lips and cascaded down my navy fleece jacket. "I swear." I made my voice as low, weak, and whipped as I could.

Jonah McAllister stepped forward and peered at me. Malicious glee shimmered in his brown gaze. "Keep hitting her. I want the bitch to suffer."

Elliot Slater nodded and stepped back.

The giant spent another two minutes hitting me. More pain, more blood, more cracked ribs. As I coughed up another mouthful of coppery blood, it dawned on me that Slater just might beat me to death, right here in the middle of the campus quad. Jonah McAllister certainly wouldn't have any objections to that. Damn. Looked like I was going to have to go for my knives, blast them with my elemental magic, and blow my cover after all, if I still had the strength to do that—

"Enough."

A low voice floated out from somewhere deeper in the shadows. A soft, breathy sound that reminded me of silk wisping together. I knew that tone, that sultry cadence, knew exactly whom it belonged to. So did my inner psyche. *Enemy, enemy, enemy,* a little voice muttered in the back of my head. A strange, primal, elemental urge flooded my body, the desire to use my Stone and Ice magic to lash out and kill whatever was within striking distance.

Elliot Slater ignored the command and hit me again, adding to the pain that racked my body.

"I said *enough*." The voice dropped to a low hiss that crackled with power, menace, and the promise of death.

Elliot froze, his hand pulled halfway back to hit me again.

"Let her go. Now."

The two giants who'd had their hands clamped around my upper arms dropped me like I had the plague. I lay on the ground, my blood soaking into the frosty grass. Despite the pain, I curled my beaten body into a small, defensive ball. I also palmed one of my silverstone knives. The weapon felt cold and comforting against the thick scar embedded in my palm.

Something rustled, and Mab Monroe stepped out of the shadows to my left.

The Fire elemental wore a long wool coat done in a dark forest green. Her red hair gleamed like polished copper, but her eyes were even blacker than the night sky. A bit of gold flashed around her pale throat in between the folds of her expensive coat.

I couldn't see that well, given the starbursts still exploding in my vision, but I knew what the gold flash was. Mab Monroe never went anywhere without wearing her signature rune necklace. A large, circular ruby surrounded by several dozen wavy rays. From previous sightings, I knew the intricate diamond cutting on the gold would catch the meager light and make it seem as though the rays were actually flickering. Or perhaps my vision was just that messed up at the moment.

Still, I knew what the rune was. A sunburst. The symbol for fire. Mab Monroe's personal rune, used by her alone.

At the sight, the silverstone scars on my own palms started to itch and burn. Mab wasn't the only one here with a rune. I had one too. A small circle surrounded by eight thin rays. A spider rune. The symbol for patience. The rune had once been a medallion I'd worn on a chain around my neck, until Mab had used her Fire elemental magic to superheat and burn the silverstone metal into my palms like it was a cattle brand. That's how she'd tortured me the night she'd murdered my family. I was looking forward to returning the favor—someday soon.

Enemy, enemy, enemy; the little voice in the back of my head kept up its muttered chorus.

Mab Monroe walked over and stood beside Elliot Slater and Jonah McAllister. She glanced down at me with all the interest she would give a cockroach before she crushed it under the toe of her boot. Her dark eyes swallowed up the available light, the way a black hole might. I lay very, very still and tried to look like I was a mere inch away from death. Not much of a stretch tonight.

"I said enough, Jonah," Mab said. "Or have you forgotten that you and Elliot work for me?"

After a moment, Elliot Slater stepped back and bowed his head in deference. The other two giants did the same. But Jonah McAllister was too angry to heed the hard edge in Mab's breathy tone.

"This bitch made problems for my son, and I think she knows something about his death," McAllister barked. "I want her to pay for that. I want her to *die* for that."

Mab stared down at me again. "You're letting your emotions cloud your judgment, Jonah. Ignoring the facts. It's most unbecoming."

"And what would those *facts* be?" McAllister demanded.

"That Ms. Blanco is just a woman, a mere, weak woman with no elemental magic or other notable strength or skills. Otherwise, I'm sure she would have used everything at her disposal to keep from being so viciously beaten tonight. She's not the person you're looking for, Jonah. More importantly, she's not the woman *I'm* looking for."

McAllister's brown eyes glittered. "You and your obsession with that blond whore. Why can't you accept the fact that she's dead? Buried somewhere in that coal mine, just like Tobias Dawson and his two men were?"

Mab's eyes grew even blacker. She reached for her Fire elemental magic, holding the power close to her like she might a lover. As an elemental myself, I could feel her magic, especially since she was consciously embracing it. Just the way Mab might have been able to sense my Stone and Ice magic, if I'd been stupid enough to actually reach for any of it.

Of course, I would have felt Mab's magic anyway, since she was one of those elementals who constantly gave off waves of power. The Fire elemental literally leaked magic, the way water would drip from a faucet. Unlike me. As long as I didn't draw upon my own elemental strength, didn't use it in any offensive way, others couldn't sense my power. A trait that had save me more than once over the years.

But Mab's power pricked at my skin like hot, invisible needles, adding to my misery, but I stayed still, giving no indication I could sense it—or that I knew what they were talking about.

"I doubt that hooker was a real hooker, and they never found her body in the rubble of the collapsed mine," Mab replied in a cold voice. "Until I see her body, she's not dead. I'm going to find her, Jonah, and then we can both have our revenge. She killed Dawson, and she's the one who killed your son. Not Ms. Blanco."

They were talking about the night of Mab's party, when I'd dressed up as a hooker to get close to Tobias Dawson, a greedy mine owner who was threatening some innocent people. Dawson was the one I was supposed to kill that night, but Jake McAllister had spotted me before I'd had a chance to do the hit. Mab had caught me in the bathroom a few minutes after I'd stabbed Jake McAllister to death. Evidently, the Fire elemental had put two and two together and realized that I'd stiffed Jake, then done the same to Tobias Dawson later on in his own mine. Not good.

"I agreed to this little test with the understanding that Ms. Blanco would live through it, should she prove herself to be innocent of your son's murder," Mab continued. "She's done so, at least to my satisfaction. Nobody would willingly let themselves be beaten the way she has."

So Mab Monroe didn't understand the concept of self-sacrifice. Not surprising. I might have laughed, if it wouldn't have hurt so damn much. At the moment, I would have endured a whole new beating just to get them to leave me alone in the darkness. Still, I was doubly glad that I'd let Elliot Slater hit me. Otherwise, I would have been dead by now, ambushed from the sidelines by Mab Monroe and her Fire elemental magic.

"Who cares if the bitch lives or dies?" Jonah McAllister scoffed. "She's nobody."

"That might be true, but unfortunately, Ms. Blanco is not without friends," Mab replied. "Most notably the Deveraux sisters."

"I don't care about those two dwarven bitches," Jonah snapped. "You could easily kill both of them."

Mab gave a delicate shrug of her shoulders. "Perhaps. But Jo-Jo Deveraux is quite popular. It might be entertaining, but killing her wouldn't win me any favors. Besides, I have other concerns at the moment, most notably Coolidge."

My dazed mind latched onto the odd name. Coolidge? Who the hell was Coolidge? And what had he done to piss off Mab Monroe?

"You've had your fun, Jonah. Face it, Ms. Blanco isn't the one who killed Jake. And she's suffered plenty tonight for whatever insults she laid on him previously. Now, are you going to come quietly so we can talk business? Or should I start looking for a new attorney?" Malice dripped from Mab's voice like acid rain.

Jonah McAllister finally realized he wasn't going to win this one. And that if he kept arguing with his boss, she was likely to use her Fire elemental magic to fry him where he stood. So the lawyer clamped his lips together and nodded his head, acquiescing to his boss's wishes. At least for tonight.

Then the silver-haired bastard turned and kicked me in the stomach as hard as he could.

The blow wasn't entirely unexpected, but it still made me retch up even more blood. Something hot and hard twisted in my stomach. I needed to get to Jo-Jo Deveraux soon so the dwarven Air elemental could heal me. Otherwise, I wouldn't be breathing much longer.

"Fine. We'll move on to the next person, then." Jonah McAllister leaned down and grabbed my brown ponytail, pulling my face up to his. "You talk to the cops about this, bitch, and you will die. Understand me?"

Cops? Oh, I had no intention of going to the cops. No siree. I was going to handle this matter all by my lonesome. But to keep up the act, I let out a low groan and nodded my head. Satisfied that I was suitably cowed this time, McAllister let go. I flopped back onto the ground.

"Let's get out of here," the lawyer growled. "The bitch dripped blood all over my coat."

Jonah McAllister stepped over my prone body and disappeared into the darkness. Elliot Slater and the other two giants followed him. But Mab Monroe stayed where she was and studied me with her dark gaze. Her power washed over me again, the invisible, fiery needles pricking my bloody skin. I bit back another groan.

"I do hope you've learned your lesson this time, Ms. Blanco," Mab said in a pleasant voice. "Because Jonah's right. Next time you cross one of us—any of us—you will die. And I promise you that it will be far more excruciating than what you've experienced here tonight."

A bit of black fire flashed in her eyes, backing up her deadly promise. Mab Monroe smiled at me a moment longer, then turned on her boot heel and vanished into the cold night.

Bestselling Urban Fantasy
from Pocket Books

BENEATH THE SKIN
BOOK THREE OF THE MAKER'S SONG
Adrian Phoenix
Chaos controls his future.
One mortal woman could be his
salvation. The countdown to
annihilation will begin with his choice.

THE BETTER PART OF DARKNESS
Kelly Gay
The city is alive tonight... and it's her job
to keep it that way.

BITTER NIGHT
A HORNGATE WITCHES BOOK
Diana Pharaoh Francis
In the fight to save humanity, she's the
weapon of choice.

DARKER ANGELS
BOOK TWO OF THE BLACK SUN'S DAUGHTER
M.L.N. Hanover
In the battle between good and evil
there's no such thing as a fair fight.

Butt-kicking Urban Fantasy
from Pocket Books
and Juno Books

Hallowed Circle
LINDA ROBERTSON
Magic can be murder...

Vampire Sunrise
CAROLE NELSON DOUGLAS
When the stakes are life and
undeath—turn to Delilah
Street, paranormal
investigator.

New in the bestselling series from Maria Lima!

Blood Bargain
Book Two of the
Blood Lines Series

Blood Kin
Book Three of the
Blood Lines Series

"Full of more interesting
surprises than a candy
store! —Charlaine Harris

Available wherever books are sold or at www.simonandschuster.com

22186